It's A DATE

THE DATE SERIES BOOK ONE

J. Epps & S. Brümmer

It's A Date
Published by Jessica Epps and Sasha-Lee Brümmer
2015 Edition
ISBN: 978-0-9863049-0-3
Copyright © 2014 Jessica Epps and Sasha-Lee Brümmer
Editor: Lisa Aurello
Cover Designer: Judi Perkins
Interior formatting by Cassy Roop of Pink Ink Designs

PINK INK
DESIGNS

This book is dedicated to her best friend, and my best friend—to each other.

Soundtrack

Addicted to You – Avicii

Always In My Head – Coldplay

Am I Wrong – Nico & Vinz

Broken – Seether ft. Amy Lee

Bright Lights and Cityscapes – Sara Bareilles

Cellophane – Sara Jackson-Holman

Chocolate – The 1975

Delirious (Boneless) – Steve Aoki, Christ Lake, Tujamo, Ft. Kid Ink

Drunk in Love – Beyoncé ft. Jay Z

Freight Train – Sara Jackson-Holman

Gods & Monsters – Lana Del Rey

Hideaway – Kiesza

Love, Save the Empty – Erin McCarley

Once Upon a Dream – Lana Del Rey

She Is Love (Acoustic) – Parachute

Stateless – Bloodstream

Titanium – Madilyn Bailey

Yours – Ella Henderson

Christmas:

Christmas – Mariah Carey

Have Yourself a Merry Little Christmas – Frank Sinatra

Silver Bells – Michael Bublé

CHAPTER
One

Heather Lane

EVERYTHING IS DARK: it's as if his dark malevolence has overtaken the room. I shudder as he steps forward. "Heather…" he croons sardonically.

The look on his smug face terrifies me. I take a step backward and then another. And another still. Soon I start sprinting to get away from him, but he's right behind me—I can feel him there. My heart is racing and I can't run away fast enough. Why won't my feet take me farther?

My scream is earsplitting, "Help! Someone!" but nobody seems to hear my cries. I can't tell if it's the sound of my heart slamming into my chest that drowns out the sounds escaping from my lips, but I can't hear myself. I'm choked up with fear as I run. I look behind me to see how far I've gotten when I see him reach for me. My heart crashes into my chest and I try to yell again, but I hit something with such force my body is almost ricocheted off of it, but I sink instead.

First, a warm sense of calm overcomes my entire body as my

motor movements are slowed down. As the damp feeling increases, immersing me, I realize I'm trapped—trapped in a cramped space with small windows looking out. I'm not the only one here: there are three other bodies in this aircraft cabin. I start to panic as I try to get up, but there's a harness holding me down, holding me in. I can't breathe. The dense weight of the water pushes against my chest, trying to force out my last breath of air as I struggle…futilely.

I'm stuck, and I lose my last breath, watching as the bubbles float up above me and then vanish. My body forces me to try to breathe, so I do, inhaling the liquid burn.

My body jolts: my automatic reflex is to thrash upward. I force my eyes open as I sputter for breath. I'm hyperventilating: for God's sake, I can't get enough oxygen into my lungs. Blinking, my eyes dart around the room, seeing my bathroom.

The tub's water has cooled drastically and I'm shivering as I wipe my face and look at myself in the mirror. Holy crap.

Bracing my hands on the edge of my oversized tub, I stand, my legs trembling from either the cold or my terrifying nightmares. Both probably. Ugh, if these dreams don't stop, I'll need to seek professional help. What in the heck did I ever see in him? I reach for my white towel and wrap it around my body, trying to warm myself as I step out of the cool water, once again taking charge of myself.

I saunter into my bedroom and turn on the fireplace, sitting on the bench at the end of my bed to warm up, when my phone starts buzzing. I reach back and grab it off of my bed, "Hello?" I can hear the despondent tone in my voice though I try my best to mask it, knowing without a doubt that it's either my sister, Danielle, or my best friend, Dillen—my double D's.

"Heather! It's me. You better be packing your things, sister."

Groaning quietly so she can't hear me, I say, "Of course I am, Dani. I'm not the procrastinator—that would be you." Stretching my legs out, I point my toes toward the fire, trying to warm my feet.

"Oh hush, you." she spits out. "Wait, are you okay?"

"Not really…" I say under my breath, "…I had another nightmare. Well, two formed into one this time."

"Oh sweetie, it's okay. I shouldn't have left when these things still haunt you, day in and day out. I'm just glad you're not with Nik anymore. He wasn't good for you," she says in her motherly tone.

My sister chose to follow her long-term boyfriend, Brannon Henley, to Los Angeles. I currently live in West Chelsea, in Lower Manhattan, having opted to move into a one-bedroom apartment at the Eleventh Avenue Condominiums. The building overlooks the Hudson River and is undeniably beautiful.

"I'll be all right." I get up, making my way downstairs to my kitchen. Lazily, I stride past my pink L-shaped sectional, headed for my fridge to make myself something hot to drink. I love my apartment. My living room is surrounded by double-story floor-to-ceiling windows, covered by long, sheer white drapes, keeping the outside world at bay, but allowing the perfect amount of light in too.

"Heather? You're going to be okay, right? I can always move back."

"Oh no, please don't. I know how happy Brannon makes you," I say as I fill a mug with milk to make hot chocolate.

"Are you excited about the tour?"

I shrug even though she can't see me. "Yes and no," I answer, pausing briefly when the microwave beeps. "I'm happy to be traveling again, but you-know-who is being a disgusting, spine-chilling jerk as usual and I'm just over it."

"Well, you should have listened to your knowledgeable sister before dating the creep."

Huffing into the phone, I answer, giggling, "I guess I should have listened to the sex-pert."

It's easy to hear the smile in her voice when she responds, "Oh yes! Even Brannon can vouch for me. I cannot begin to tell you how yummy he is in bed. All we did today was fuck."

I cringe when I hear her language. "Dani! Why do you have to curse so much? You've got the filthiest mouth."

She laughs on the other side of the line. "Heather Adalyn Lane. You dated the most vile man for two months—I'm sure you can deal with me saying fuck."

Exhaling noisily, I know she's right on this one. "Honestly, Danielle Torin Lane, I know I raised you better." A small laugh escapes me as I try to use a maternal tone on my older sister.

"You love my filthy mouth, and without it you'd be utterly lost. I've been meaning to ask you: what are you going to do for Christmas, since you're going to be on tour with the company?"

"Oh, umm...I hadn't really thought about it." My thoughts go back to previous holidays spent alone and I'm amused at how lame my life is. "I'll probably end up making hot chocolate in my hotel room and curling up by the fire...pretending it's snowing outside."

She doesn't say anything for the longest time, and I can tell that I've upset her. My sister practically raised me from the age of twelve onward yet she's barely six years older than I am. Apart from the three months I spent in foster care, I've always been under her protective eye. She's my lifeline. Our parents died on their annual anniversary getaway to Clayoquot Wilderness Resort in British Columbia, Canada. The beautiful island is accessible only by boat or floatplane, and their plane crashed just off the shore of their destination. Officials said it was the sudden and direct impact that killed both of our parents instantaneously. To this day, they are unsure why the plane went down. I still have nightmares about losing them.

I'm brought back from the memory when I hear Dani's voice again.

"Heather, no. I won't tolerate that. Where is your last stop before Christmas? I'm telling Brannon that you're staying with us over the holidays." She's insistent, and I know I don't stand a chance at this argument, but I try regardless.

"Oh no, Dani, I'm not going to ruin your Christmas." Trying to deflect the conversation I ask, "Did you buy him anything yet?"

"Yup, I bought him a bunch of sex toys to use on me. Now back to our conversation...you will be coming to visit for Christmas. I will not take no for an answer." When Dani has her mind set on something, it's impossible to deter her from her goal.

I try whining instead, drawing out the last syllable of her name, "Daneeee...I'll feel like the third wheel. Plus, I want to get back to the snow if I can. It doesn't feel like Christmas without snow." Looking out the windows, I watch as the snow flurries turn into fluffy snowflakes.

"My answer is no. You're not changing my mind. I just Googled where your last show is going to be and I may have just booked you a first-class ticket from Phoenix to LA." I can hear her smug smile over the phone.

Suddenly I freeze and look down at my feet. Distant memories flood my mind again and a sick feeling settles in the pit of my stomach. I try to calm my voice before I answer her, but knowing my sister, she'll know what's wrong.

"Um...Dani." I start to chew on my cheek nervously. "I'm driving on my own throughout the tour."

The line goes silent for a long while. She sniffles before she is able to bring herself to reply, "I'm so sorry. I…" She pauses to blow her nose before continuing, "I didn't even think about your fear of flying. I'm canceling the ticket. Will you be able to drive to us on Christmas Eve? We could come to you, too."

I'm so thankful that she doesn't need any more of an explanation and I know she loves me like no other. I find myself wanting to comfort her and tell her how important she is to me too. Exhaling softly into the phone, I whisper, "Okay, I'll come."

Her squeal is deafening and a small smile forms across my face.

"I'm so beyond excited right now! I cannot wait to see you and squeeze you. Okay, I have to run because someone has opened his Christmas presents early…" She pauses for me to answer and I hear an odd vibrating sound in the background.

I gasp into the phone when I realize what's going on. "Oh. My. Eww, Dani! You sicko." Screeching into the phone and shaking my head, I try to erase that nauseating image from my mind. She always knows how to brighten my day, even in the most bizarre ways.

"Tell Brannon I said hi and behave. I love you, sister."

I hear hurried footsteps as she screams away from the phone "BRANNON! THOSE WERE YOUR CHRISTMAS GIFTS!" I scrunch my nose, not wanting to hear any of this.

"Bye, I love you," she yells out then hangs up quickly.

I place my phone on the kitchen counter, wanting it out of my hands as a disturbing shiver runs down my body. I head back upstairs to my bedroom, where clothes are strewn everywhere in my failed attempt at packing.

Perching on the edge of my bed, I try to decide on which pairs of panties to bring with me. Thinking about my conversation with Dani, I'm quickly reminded of how different we are. She's clearly the more sexually adventurous one, whereas I'm more...reserved. I'm not inexperienced when it comes to sex, it's just...I don't know, my few experiences were nothing spectacular, just your average garden-variety sex. So I put boyfriends on the back burner and dove head first into my dancing career and the decision has proven to work to my advantage.

Until I met Nikolai Demski.

IT'S THE DAY BEFORE I get on the road by myself while the rest of the cast and crew from the First Position Ballet Company take a private plane to embark on our Christmas tour. I'm incredibly anxious. There's a package waiting for me at my door when I get back from the store to stock up on candy. I swiftly glance over the shipping label and see that it's from Dillen Ascher. I squeal loudly and race inside, setting it on the kitchen island, and grabbing a pair of scissors to open it. Burrowing through the packing pillows, I pull out a very pink, very fluffy fleece throw blanket and hug it to myself excitedly. It's the softest, most impeccable blanket I have ever felt. Dillen sure knows my weakness is pink and blanket related—have to remember to pack it for my trip.

I will get to see Dillen, my best friend, in early February for a charity showcase here in the city. She's flying in with the Royal Ballet to dance with me in one of New York City's most prestigious theatres. God, I can't wait to watch her and her company amaze thousands of people, and raise money for a noble cause. Plus, she always knows exactly how to make me smile. I quickly text her.

Hi, you butt. I just got the blanket. It's so perfect. I absolutely

love it! Thank you so, so much.

It's late there so I'm not surprised that I don't get a response back from her before I head to bed for the night.

December 17th

EIGHT DAYS UNTIL the final Christmas show. We've been performing and traveling nonstop for the past three weeks. I've driven down the East Coast from Boston, Massachusetts, to Tampa, Florida, as the rest of the company flies from city to city. We've stopped in multiple cities on the way down, putting on an unforgettable performance of The Nutcracker in each theatre. Our last show, however, is in Phoenix, Arizona. I don't understand why we're going out of our way for one city, but the owner of the ballet company is insistent.

I've managed to drive from Tampa to Houston, Texas, in the last thirty-two hours and I'm irrefutably exhausted. I have another sixteen hours to drive until I get to Phoenix. I'm hoping to make it there before the company arrives on December 19th.

The only thing that is keeping me going is my small candy stash sitting in the passenger seat. That, and my Starbucks. You might say that I have an obsession with sweets—any kind of sweets. I think it all started when Dani took over raising me. She didn't really complain about my sugar intake like Mom or Dad would have. So I'm totally blaming her for my addiction. Luckily, my metabolism hasn't slowed any, so my body hasn't reaped the effects yet.

I don't think I can drive another mile. I pull up to the Four Seasons in Houston and park next to the valet stand while the two men ogle my sleek black Buick Verano convertible with burgundy leather interior. I love my new baby. "Be careful with her, boys," I say as a warning when I climb out and grab my candy stash. The bellman brings in my suitcase while I check in for the night. I'm desperately in need of a good night's sleep.

CHAPTER
Two

Noah Ryan

THESE FUCKING GIRLS won't get off of me. They're lingering at the hotel room door like it's the first time they've ever had an orgasm. They're begging me to let them spend another night. Shit. I'm already hung over as fuck; I just need them out of my line of sight. My jaw aches and my tongue hurts from the assault on their bodies. The two of them kiss in front of me, in an attempt to entice me, but I shake my head, mumbling, "Have a good evening, ladies." I close the door and lean back against it. I've had enough of needy hookups that get nowhere fast.

I'm not even hard anymore. What a shame. It's been another waste of an evening trying to work these girls over in preparation for a fucking of a lifetime that never took place. The hotel room smells of overpowering perfume and cigarettes, and I'm suffocating. I can't even crack a window open to get a breath of fresh air in. I decide to hightail it out of here and get a different hotel room before passing out for the rest of the night and into the next day.

WHEN I WAKE up, I haul ass to my truck, dropping everything in the bed before getting in and starting her up. My pickup is my only girl. I sit in traffic for a good forty-five minutes before arriving back home. Once I've cured my hangover and gotten my shit together, I sit in my apartment in Tempe, Arizona, and review everything that I believe will be on the bar exam. For the past three years I've been studying to become an attorney. I'm a recent graduate of Sandra Day O'Connor College of Law at Arizona State University. People always ask me how I find the time to do all of this shit. I don't know the answer to that, but what I do know is that busy people will always make time.

My phone goes off too loudly as a text from Mae comes in. My eyes shift away from my notes as I glance at my Galaxy's screen.

How are your studies coming along, Noah?

Mae, my mother for a lack of a better word, has always been involved in my life. Hell, I'd be dead if it weren't for this kind woman's open arms and earnest heart. If my fate were left up to my parents, I'd be six feet under. I'm grateful that I have no recollection of my parents, nor the dumpster in New York City where I was abandoned as a week-old infant. Mae found me on my deathbed and took me in as her own. Once the adoption went through, I was legally hers, and for that I will forever be in her debt.

A smile forms on my face as I read the text message. I type out a quick response to inform her that I am, indeed, keeping my nose stuck in these damn law books. I hit send and moments later my phone starts vibrating on the wooden desk. I answer without having to look at the caller ID.

"Mae, how are you?" I ask, distracted by my notes.

"Oh Noah! You are so wonderful. I am so very proud of you. Look at everything you have accomplished." She sniffles and I know she's on the verge of tears from my accomplishments alone. Pushing my notes aside, I remove my reading glasses and give her my undivided attention.

"I would be nothing without you, Mae. I'll be back this weekend, and I don't plan on leaving Scottsdale for the remainder of the year. I'm taking you to see The Nutcracker on Christmas Eve at the Phoenix theatre."

Mae loves the ballet. I grew up accompanying her to performances whether they were a local high school show or a world-renowned traveling company. Hell, we went to every ballet performance in town that she knew about.

I can hear the joy in her voice when she replies, "I would love that. It will be just in time for Christmas. Tell me you will be home for Christmas, son?" Realizing she is asking a question I just answered, I frown. This old age shit must be hard on her.

"I'll be there Mae, and I'm looking up ballet tickets as we speak." I move to my laptop and pull up the Phoenix theatre's website where I purchase two tickets, choosing seats as close to the orchestra pit as possible. "I'll see you on Friday, Mae. Call me if you need anything."

"I simply cannot wait to hug you. Goodbye, my dear Noah," she says enthusiastically.

"Goodbye, Mae," I add before hanging up. I purchase the tickets before shutting my laptop down to get back to the never-ending process of studying.

Thursday, December 18th

I HAVE BEEN studying for the past twelve hours and I doubt I could cram any more information into my head. Now I have to endure the grueling process of waiting for my exam date and studying my fucking ass off some more.

I know without a doubt that I'll pass the character and fitness test, which isn't really a test at all. It just involves an FBI background check with all the damn bells and whistles. It'd be a waste of three years if I don't pass the simplest step in the process of acquiring my license. Hell, I need to pass this check in order to even take the exam. I pack up my shit and nod to the librarian as I walk past her on my way out. She knows me by name now.

Once I get back to my apartment, I quickly shove shit in a duffel bag and call it packed. I've decided to surprise Mae and arrive a day early. I grab my duffel and toss it onto the passenger seat of my truck.

After the short drive from Tempe to Scottsdale, I park outside of Mae's house and kill the engine. Leaping out of my pickup, I go to the door and knock repeatedly. Given her age, it takes her longer to get to the door, but I know she's coming because she calls out in her singsong voice, "Who is it?" She slowly swings the door open and before I know it I'm entangled in a Mae hug.

She holds onto me as she says, "You are early, Noah! How is your studying going? Oh my...you always have your head stuck in your books."

I walk inside with her while she questions me and I hug her again before replying, "Why don't we sit down and we'll talk about everything?"

"Oh I would love that," she says eagerly.

Mae makes herself a cup of tea and a large steaming cup of black coffee for me. We sit down at the kitchen table and I tell her about all the boring shit that comes along with studying. While Mae sips her tea, my gaze moves to the clock above the kitchen door, noticing that it's getting late.

"Mae, you should get some rest. I'm here until December 31st, and we'll have plenty of time to talk."

She squeezes my hand before getting up. "Let me know if you need anything. Your room is ready for you as always."

"Thanks, Mae. Goodnight."

In a loving voice she murmurs, "Goodnight, my son."

Once I hear her bedroom door screech shut, I get up and head to my childhood room. Nothing much has changed since I left. Mae and I didn't have much when I was growing up, but she always made sure we got by. She was constantly working two or even three jobs at a time to pay the bills and put food on our table. Since then times have changed, and we're fairly well off. I haven't had to worry about money for the past six years, and it's a weight lifted off of my shoulders.

It all turned around when her boss, the owner of Vento Diner, unfortunately passed away seven years ago. His will stated that Mae Ryan would be the sole owner of the diner. She's been working at Vento's since she was eighteen and has been the diner's utmost loyal employee. She's put her heart's work into the place, which is now thriving.

Damn, we've come a long way.

After reminiscing, I pull my shirt up and off of my torso then unbuckle my belt and step out of my jeans. Kicking off my boxer briefs, I fold up my clothes before getting into bed. There is no other way to sleep than stark naked. Ah. I stretch out and take up most of the available space on the bed, unlike many other nights when I've had to share my mattress with a very naked female…or females.

Christmas Eve

DRESSED IN A tux, I'm holding Mae's gift in my hand as I wait for her in the foyer. Mae and I have always exchanged gifts on Christmas Eve.

I glance up when she walks in. She's wearing an iridescent rosy dress this evening. "Well don't you look like Christmas itself? Merry Christmas Eve, Mom." I wrap her in a hug. She's beaming and I know it's because she loves it when I call her that, but somewhere deep down inside, it's fucking painful as hell for me. I can't stand to think of her as a parent. When anyone asks me about my parents, I cringe. Mae is my guardian angel.

I have to remind myself to breathe before I pull away from her.

I feign a smile and hand her a gift box. "I got you something."

She looks at the small white box wrapped in a red ribbon, "Oh Noah, you shouldn't have."

An exasperated laugh spills out of me and I hold my hands up in disagreement. "You deserve more than I could ever give you."

Despite her admonishment, she excitedly reaches for the box and pulls off the ribbon. She gasps when she sees the golden heart brooch.

"Oh it is gorgeous, but I can't accept this. It's too much," she says quietly, but I know there's no way in hell she'd give it up now.

"Don't worry about it and just accept it."

Her smile brightens as she hugs me again, "Thank you, Noah. Merry Christmas Eve, my handsome son."

"You're welcome, Mae. Are you ready to head out?"

"Yes, I am. Oh Noah, I almost forgot about this." She opens her purse and pulls out a box wrapped in childish Christmas paper. "This is your gift." She smiles and places the box in my hand. I rip open the paper and box, pulling out a black stainless-steel watch.

Tilting my head to the side, I admire it. "You have truly outdone yourself. Thank you," I say sincerely as I slide the watch onto my wrist and fasten it: it's the perfect fit. I glance at myself in the hallway mirror as I hold up my wrist, turning it so I am able to see her gift reflecting back at me. I smooth my lapels before turning back to her. "This is great, Mae. Now let's get you to the ballet."

CHAPTER
Three
the ballerina

Heather

THE NUTCRACKER IN Phoenix is the last show on the tour this year. Although ballet has been a passion of mine since I was a little girl, I have no problem admitting that I will be pleased when this tour comes to an end. It's Christmas Eve and I'd rather be tucked into bed, reading a good book.

The cast is currently stretching backstage as the lights flicker on and off as a five-minute warning. Each and every one of us is completely done up. Our faces are masked with foundation and glitter that take mere minutes to apply, but hours to remove. I dab a tissue against my lips to blot off some of the caked-on lipstick. The makeup artist refuses to change the brand because it looks remarkable on stage, but it feels like little grains of sand on my now rosy lips. Apart from loathing the lipstick, I don't mind the glitter. It adds a little special something on stage.

The lights dim as the curtain opens across the stage. As my fellow ballerinas begin the scene, I watch from the dark wings, hidden from view as I peer out at this evening's crowd. The show is completely sold out and all eyes are trained on the Christmas tree as it grows and mice invade the stage. My eyes move from face to face in the crowd as they light up when The Nutcracker reappears. Observing children's expressions change as they watch an all-consuming show is like watching the groom as his bride walks down the aisle—no one ever notices the look of pure love in his eyes or the dazzling smile on his face because the guests are preoccupied with the spectacle of the bride.

The children are on the edge of their seats, watching the white dress as I study their little expressions. The cast and crew are well aware of where I'll always be when it's my time to shine. As Nikolai approaches me from behind, my eye catches an elderly woman in the crowd. She's sitting on the edge of her seat, engrossed in the performance.

I look to her left and see a woman with her daughter, pointing to the stage as the gingerbread man defeats the army of mice. I glance to the right of her and see her companion is a younger gentleman. He's not watching the show. Instead, he watches the elder woman as she falls in love with every single character on stage. I've never seen anyone watching another person enjoy the show for as long as I can remember. He's watching the groom instead of the bride and I can't help but stare at him. Sitting there, he oozes sex. His jaw is strong and angled and I find myself wanting to bite it. Oh my, where did that come from?

A tap on my shoulder brings me back to the stage. I nod to Nik so he understands that I'm ready to go on. Nik has been dancing all of his life, just as I have. He moved to New York City from St. Petersburg, Russia, nine years ago and has been a hit with the ladies ever since, including myself. I recently broke up with him because he's too domineering. All he wanted was sex.

He's beyond in love with himself; it's become a huge turnoff. There's cocky and then there's Nik. In addition to his good looks and rock-hard thighs, there's his aggressive sexual drive. In the beginning I found him charming. He said he was fine with waiting for a sexual relationship with me—and that couldn't have been further from the truth. He uses his looks and accent as a weapon to get all the sex he wants. When he realized I wasn't going to sleep with him the second I said, "I'll go out with you," I became a challenge to him, and he's been trying to conquer that challenge ever since.

Before we leave the confines of the wing, I adopt my stance and Nik lifts me up with ease. The smoke machine fills the stage with an eerie blue fog as he carries me into the spotlight, which strikingly catches the crystal beading on my bodice. A snowflake-shaped, classical pancake tutu, embroidered with thousands of crystals that sparkle under the stage lights, comprise my costume skirt. With his hands on my hips, Nik lifts me higher as he follows our practiced choreography then proceeds to walk in a small circle, showcasing my hand-stitched, one-of-a-kind, custom-made costume. The stage is all encompassed in a winter wonderland as I perform my role as the Snow Queen.

Even though Nik looks utterly professional at the moment, I know that look on his face—it's deceptive. Those cold cobalt-blue eyes haunt me and I know he's enjoying having his hands all over me. The way he grips my thighs as he hoists me high above his head and his fingers linger over the bodice of my costume at every pass makes my stomach churn. Careful not to make eye contact with Nik, I try to keep focused on the crowd before us, as they watch our graceful dance. Thoughts of why I ever fell for this Russian jerk fill my mind as we dance Tchaikovsky's Snow Pas de Deux.

Act I ends when Nik and I are standing side by side as we watch Clara, the main character, exit the stage. I suddenly feel Nik's arm snake around my waist and I try to stay in character, but this is not part of the choreography. He digs his fingers into my side and my smile falters. His dominance frightens me.

As the curtain falls and we are freed from the audience's view, I try to escape his painful grip, but I can't move: he's too strong. Scowling up at him, I clench my jaw. "Let go of me, Nik Demski!"

He smiles through beautifully whitened teeth yet I find his smile appalling. Undeterred, he tightens his grip on my waist and leads me offstage before the stage gets crowded with crew members rearranging props for the second act. He manages to keep up the appearance of a perfect gentleman, all the while acting like a true asshole. We're not needed back on stage for the next act, so he knows he has time to spare. The dark of the wings covers us as he presses my back against the wall.

"What are you doing?" I cry, knowing no one will be able to hear me over the rupture of applause.

"Heather, you shouldn't have ended what we had going on."

I can feel his warm breath on my cheek as I try and pull away, but his grip once again tightens on my hips.

"Going on? I wasn't going to give up anything to you that easily, Nik. Let go of me!" He grabs my wrists as I try to pull away, his grip becoming painfully tight, and I look up into those lifeless eyes. I wince when I see him sneering down at me.

"I don't like to be told no, Heather." He leans in closer and I turn my cheek, trying to keep as much distance from him as I can, struggling to free myself from his grip.

"You teased me...You knew what you were doing the whole time," he adds in a voice all too familiar. He wants me to bow down to him and let him have his way with me. I feel the bile rise in my throat as he pushes his knee up between my legs.

"I've missed that sweet-tasting pussy of yours, Lanie. Let me have another taste." His thick accent is low and it brings the darkest of memories back. My nightmare is holding me captive once again.

"Stop it, Nik," I growl, struggling more as panic sets in.

"Mmm...You know I'll never stop, Lanie. I always get what I want. You know this," he moves his hand between my legs and touches me there.

Just as I'm about to scream, a backstage crew member calls out, "Intermission! I need everyone off the stage." Nik's grip falters and I pull free of him. Making my escape, I flee the stage and duck into my dressing room, bolting the lock on the door behind me.

I'm grateful for my little sanctuary as I'm on the verge of tears, but I know I can't cry. The makeup artist will be livid if I mess up my makeup before the final curtain. She has multiple faces to mask and re-mask during our intermission and adding mine to the mix will not be acceptable or professional.

I plop down on my pink sofa chair, which I'm glad I requested on my rider, and stare up at the ceiling, reliving what just happened with Nik. What does he not understand about 'no' and 'we're over'? Groaning internally I mumble, "Men…"

I'm so glad I dumped his butt. I cannot deal with such a malevolent man like him. I'm going to put good in and get good out of my life.

When my breathing has returned to normal, I get up and grab a bottle of water, downing the icy-cold liquid. The lights flash in my dressing room as Act II of The Nutcracker is about to begin. Thankful for the reprieve, I grab my book from my duffel and lose myself in Aleatha Romig's captivating story of Consequences.

Noah

THE LIGHTS OF the Phoenix theatre's lobby flash off and on, essentially telling us to get our asses back into our seats so the next act can begin.

"What did you think of the first act, Mae? Was it as good as last year's?" She's flipping through the show's program and barely paying attention to a word I'm saying.

"Mae?"

She smiles and points to the program. "Oh look! I found her. Isn't she just beautiful, Noah?"

Rubbing my jaw, I look down at the page and she's pointing to one of the performers, a ballerina, and a fucking gorgeous one at that. "She is. Who is that?"

Her head jolts up as she gazes at me with an expression of disbelief on her face. "Noah. That is Heather Lane. She was just dancing on the stage as the Snow Queen. I believe this is her first tour and wow. I can see what all the buzz about her in the ballet world is about now. She's magnificent."

Surprised that she keeps up with ballet so wholeheartedly, I nod in agreement, but I just have no idea what she is talking about. Hell, she was never a dancer, at least not to my knowledge. "I guess. Let's get you back to your seat so you can see more of this Lane girl," I say dryly.

"HEATHER Lane! Don't be dismissive of such a talented ballerina; she is not a football player," she snaps as her eyes burn into me.

"Yes, ma'am."

Shit. What the fuck was that about? My adoptive mother is a sympathetic and loving woman, but there are times when she completely loses who she is. It happens when she gets pissed, and there's nothing I can do about it.

Mae places her arm in mine. "I need to get to my seat. Now," she demands. I'm shocked into silence as I lead her back into the theatre and to our seats, which are in the center of the third row. Hell, we are so close to the stage, I can see the scuffs on their bizarre-ass shoes.

I applaud the dudes who do ballet because I would not be able wear nut-hugging tights and those damn toe-crushing shoes. I flinch as I think about what their feet look like. I recall my one and only up-close-and-personal interaction with a psychotic ballerina. That's one mistake I'll never forget. Note to self: don't ever let your mother set you up with somebody.

Act II starts with the angels and then the Sugar Plum Fairy. Being a twenty-nine-year-old man, I highly doubt I should know the names of all of these characters, but I do. I can list them off, starting from Drosselmeyer to Mother Ginger. I seriously need to stop coming to these things.

Mae nudges me as people stand and applaud; confused, I look around and realize that I must have fallen asleep. Ah well, I'm sure the Sugar Plum Fairy's Cavalier put on a flawless performance. Straightening my slacks, I stand up next to Mae as she reaches for my hand and squeezes.

In a barely audible voice I hear Mae say, "Oh, there she is."

I look up at the stage as the Snow Queen takes her bow with her partner then straightens her lithe body. Staring into the audience, her eyes scan the faces before pausing, looking straight at me. I don't notice Mae yelping with excitement at my side as I take in the pure beauty of the woman in front of me. Her eyes don't leave mine as she steps back then forward again, raising her arms into the air. Her fingers are laced with her dance partner's, and jealous anticipation smashes into me like a boulder falling onto a highway.

Her beauty enthralls me and I find myself captivated, incapable of looking anywhere else. She's like a siren, drawing me in with her splendor. I have to stop myself from jumping over the two rows in front of us to reach her and claim her as mine. The pull I feel toward this stunning woman is magnetic in nature and growing by the second, along with the intense need to touch and connect with her.

I need her. It's primal.

I want to claim her as my own. Her expression tells me there is something wrong, and my gut tells me it's him. That bastard needs to let go of her hand before I do something drastic to a complete stranger.

My world comes to an abrupt halt and starts revolving on a different magnetic axis. Fuck the north and south magnetic poles: I'm spinning on Heather Lane.

The curtains close and the houselights are brought back up so the audience can exit without tripping over each other. I'm still gazing at the stage. The red curtain has taken place of what I want to see.

Get your shit together, Ryan.

Mae is already at the end of our row when she calls out, "Noah? Is everything okay?"

I pick up the program on the armrest before walking over to her. "All good. Are you ready to head home?"

She scowls at me and shit, what have I done to bring out this aggressive side of her?

"No! I want a few autographs from the performers," she demands. My eyes widen and I nod—I'm pussy-whipped by a woman I know nothing about.

We head out to the lobby where a crowd has gathered in hopes of meeting a distinguished ballerina. The lobby is alive with the spirit of Christmas as Silver Bells by Michael Bublé serenades one and all. I stand behind Mae and watch as the dancers pour out of the door labeled 'Backstage' and begin signing programs for people of all ages. As Mae strolls into the crowd, I signal to her that I'll be standing in the corner, away from the hordes of ballet fans. I have no doubt in my mind that she hopes to meet Heather Lane. Hell, I'm hoping my world doesn't combust when I get a second glimpse of her.

Heather

I MANAGE TO fake a smile as I walk out into the lobby, feeling Nik's hand at the small of my back. All I want to do is leave and go to my hotel. There is nothing I desire more than to be done with him and this tour. Stepping away from his hand, I bend down and sign a program for a little girl in a bright pink tutu. Smiling brightly as I sign my name in a neon-pink permanent marker, I tell her, "I love your tutu. Did you know that pink happens to be my favorite color?" She giggles and hugs me quickly before returning to her mother.

I step forward into the throng of people, hoping to lose Nik, but he manages to stay close to me each and every time I move. After a few more autographs in my signature pink marker, I look up into the eyes of the elderly woman I saw while on stage. I'd say she's in her late sixties, with gray hair that is pinned back and wearing a rather outdated red dress.

Her smile is infectious as she says "Oh Heather! It's such an honor to meet you. I have been keeping up with you ever since you joined the First Position Ballet Company."

I'm a little taken by surprise as I accept the program from her trembling hands. Signing my name with a practiced flourish before handing it back to her, I murmur, "I'm so happy you enjoyed the show this evening."

"I have been going to the ballet every Christmas Eve for the past thirty-two years, and darling, your impersonation of the Snow Queen was the best I have ever seen," she blurts out quickly and before I realize what's happening, she's taken my wrist in her fragile, petite hand. I'm unable to hold in the laugh that escapes me as she pulls me to the other side of the room.

Her excitement is contagious. She comes to an abrupt stop and I'm breathless. She's fumbling in her purse for something and eventually fishes out a disposable camera. Suddenly her voice rings out, "Son. Quickly! Take a picture."

With a goofy smile plastered on my face and Christmas music filling my ears, I turn and glance in the direction of the camera. It seems like the room stills and the music pauses as I am now face to face with him, the stud who was watching the groom as the bride walked down the aisle (of course I mean the ballet). I'm frozen. The way his eyes roamed up and down my body during the final curtain made me feel as if he were making love to me in front of every single person in the theatre. I welcomed it. He looks up from his watch in that second when everything feels like it's happening in slow motion. His eyes find the elderly woman, but quickly flash up to me.

The harsh comment of, "What are you waiting for, son?" quickly fills my ears. I try to speak before she continues, but I've lost all of my words. I have nothing to say.

Nothing.

"I'm sure Miss Lane has a lot more to do than wait to have a photograph taken," she adds to her question. I suddenly feel extremely shy as if I'm not used to being in front of thousands of people. I can't drag my eyes off of him, yet I feel like I should turn away and run—run from this man whose eyes bore into me.

I've never really felt unattractive...well, there are those times when I feel bloated and disgusting and nothing fits right. But in this very moment, with his eyes locked on mine, I'm suddenly self-conscious. Even with my hair and makeup professionally done, I feel like I'm the furthest thing from appealing. Standing here in front of this gorgeous man, I feel like I've just rolled out of bed with my hair disheveled and my makeup smeared across my face.

His eyes never leave mine as he steps toward this elderly woman and me, taking the disposable camera from her.

She stands next to me, completely invading my personal space, as he holds the camera up. It covers his face and I suddenly detest the object, until he speaks.

"Smile for me."

His low, slightly raspy baritone voice resonates through my being. My mouth gapes open.

Gapes.

He peers over the camera at me as if he's waiting for me to smile for him. I do what he asks, but instead of my normal smile, he gets a crooked one and the flash goes off.

The woman squeals and is about to hug me when I feel a large hand circle around my bicep. I break eye contact with the Greek god and focus straight into the eyes of a malicious man...Nik. I follow his gaze and I can quickly tell he's sizing up this hunky man in front of me. He straightens up as he pulls me to his chest.

"It's time to go, Heather," he whispers sharply into my ear. I manage the most insincere smile I can and step out of his grip. Turning back to the elderly woman, I reach out and hug her, grasping onto the motherly feel that radiates from her pores.

Before I can let go of the sweet, fragile woman, Nik grabs me and hauls me against his chest even harder, hissing under his breath, "I said, we're done here." His fingers dig into my skin and I'm afraid his nails will draw blood soon if he doesn't let go. Tears threaten my eyes, but then I feel him. I feel him approaching with such force that I almost want to cower into Nik's hold. He's unbelievably close to me and my body is high on him. His cologne surrounds me and...holy crap! I want to bathe in it. He smells amazing. I've never smelled a scent like that before, a scent that totally fits a man perfectly. I don't know this man, but it's him...mouthwatering, crisp, powerful...flawless.

Unexpectedly, Nik wheezes and struggles for air as a muscular hand circles around his throat. My eyes move from the large, tanned hand, to the cuffs of his suit, to his chiseled jawline. He moves so fast that I can't even take in his irate expression: he pulls Nik away from me and slams the slimeball up against a concrete pillar adjacent to where we are standing.

This time, the room really does go silent. All you can hear is Nik dragging air into his lungs. It all happens so fast. One minute I'm stuck in Nik's grip and the next this Greek god has freed me. I hear heavy footsteps approaching fast as two security guards make a pathway up to the two men. I watch as they pull this man off of Nik and yank him back a couple of feet. Nik grabs his throat as if in pain and the Greek god takes a few more steps backward with his hands raised in the air as if in surrender.

"I'll see myself out, gentlemen." His deep, raspy voice echoes in the silent lobby as he turns to the elderly woman and offers his arm to her.

"Damn right you will!" the first security guard snaps as the other stands between the two men.

Right then, with everyone watching, he looks up at me as if to get one last glimpse. Once again, I'm iced up. The Snow Queen can't move.

I'm utterly embarrassed by the turn of events and I turn away from the stranger who saved me. I know I should stay and thank him for what he did, but I simply can't face a soul right now. Too afraid to turn around, my legs finally decide to start working as I make a beeline for my dressing room.

CHAPTER
Four
irrefutable attraction

Noah

MAE AND I get back to the house, and I haven't said a word since we left the Phoenix theatre, since I lost sight of her. What is there left to say when your world feels as if it is spinning backward? I've come to the realization that my life up to this point has been rotating on a false axis.

A false motherfucking axis. Shit.

Once we're inside, I hug Mae briefly before heading to my bedroom. I shut the door and sit on the end of the bed as I loosen my tie, staring across the room at a bleak pale-gray wall. Methodically I remove my new watch, placing it on the bed as I replay the last hour of my evening. The second she turned and went in a different direction than me the floor felt like it fell out from underneath me. I'm enamored with her.

Heather Lane.

Who the hell is she?

Abruptly, I realize that it's the twenty-first century; I get off the bed, the mattress whining in protest. It takes all of three steps to get to the other side of the room where my tablet is charging on a small oak desk—I'm determined to find out more about this mystery woman who has set my world spiraling out of control. After unplugging the tablet, I slide my finger across the screen to bring it to life before I type in "Heather Lane" into Google Images. A plethora of pictures fills my screen. She is in every one of them.

There are pictures of her dancing, signing autographs with fans, kissing the same fucking douche I pulled off of her tonight, and then there's one of her alone.

She's not looking directly at the camera, but her smile nonetheless sets me on fire. Clicking on the image to enlarge it on my tablet, I can tell that she was at a white sandy beach when this photograph was taken. On the bottom right-hand corner, this past summer's date is digitally printed on it. In the photograph, Heather's rich dark-chocolate hair falls in waves alongside her porcelain skin, as her jade green eyes are fixed on someone or something beyond the camera's view. Such a pure beauty—I doubt she's wearing any makeup in this picture. My eyes move to her full roseate lips, which are parted in the most alluring smile.

Without thinking, I save the image so I'm able to remember her exceptional smile. I need to see her again.

After further research, I find that she's rather significant in the ballet world. Thousands of fans flock to her social media pages asking her questions about something called a grand allegro...shit, I don't know what the hell that is. I look that up too.

I watch some of her dance videos online, which practically have a million views. It's apparent that she's a world-renowned ballerina. No wonder Mae was so absorbed in her. This clarifies why throngs of people were clamoring to get her attention tonight.

A few hours later I find myself lying in bed as the ceiling grows in on me in this damn small room. It's almost three in the morning and I need to fucking do something. I can't lie here and think about her smile. I know nothing about this woman, other than she's prominent in everything ballet.

Let it go, Ryan.

I can't.

In another five minutes, I'm in sweatpants and a lightweight workout shirt, walking out the door. I hit play on my Galaxy before strapping the workout band on my arm. Avicii's song *Addicted to You* starts playing. For fuck's sake.

After stretching, I take off sprinting out of the neighborhood. I'm running fiercely and putting all of my pent-up energy into my body's movements. There is not a soul in sight on this Christmas night as I hit a main street.

The stoplights flash from red to green, as the roadways lie empty. I move from the sidewalk into the street, thinking that this is probably the only time I'd get to run without restrictions in Scottsdale. Along the double yellow lines I run as Avicii sings.

Addicted?

Fuck. All I know is her name. Let it go, Ryan, I tell myself repeatedly.

I run for what feels like five minutes, but when I look at my watch an hour and a half has passed. I've been so stuck in my own head that I've completely lost track of time and where the fuck I am. I stop in the middle of an enormous intersection to get my bearings; the street signs pinpoint my location at East McDowell and North Central. I look down at my feet and notice the Phoenix Metro Light Rail tracks. I know for a fact without having to look up that the Phoenix theatre is on my right—I've run 10.8 miles from Scottsdale to Phoenix.

To her.

My shirt is soaked and plastered to my body. There is not a dry patch anywhere. I pull the shirt up over my abs, peeling it off as I walk to a trash can on the corner of the street. I toss it into the trash, not wanting the extra weight of a sweat-drenched shirt.

Bending forward, I try to catch my breath before stretching. How in the hell did I get here? I don't remember seeing any street signs or thinking about running in a certain direction.

My fingers run through my short dark hair, now very damp, as I try to process this. She's truly fucked with my head and she didn't say a single word to me.

I'm pacing in small circles with my hands on my torso trying to remind myself to breathe when the sky abruptly lights up in an electric blue. My eyes flicker up to the darkening skies that are rapidly approaching. Oh come the fuck on!

There's no taxi in sight and the Light Rail ends its services at two in the morning. My phone reads 4:23 in the morning. Groaning as I start running, I know I won't make it back to Scottsdale before this fucking storm hits. My phone is blaring with weather alerts in an attempt to inform me of the approaching storm. What it's really doing though, is advising me that I'm in for one hell of a 10.8 mile run.

I take off, deciding I'd rather run through this monstrous storm than quake on the sidewalk. I can't sit around—I've always been proactive. As I'm running, I realize that this might be one of Arizona's notorious dust storms. If it is, I'll need to get inside somewhere. What a night to go for a run. Just as that thought crosses my mind, the floodgates open and massive raindrops start falling from the darkened sky.

I find myself exhaling in relief until three bolts of lightning strike simultaneously, approximately two miles in front of me. Grunting, I push myself harder, racing through the thrashing downpour. I'm vastly regretting my decision to lose my shirt as the rain starts to sting my warm chest.

The run seems ten times longer since I'm aware of how long I have to run this time. When I finally get to Mae's house in Scottsdale, it is 5:52 a.m. I know Mae doesn't wake up until 6:30, as she does every morning, so I drop my sweats and boxers at the front door then walk down the hallway to the bathroom attached to my room. I'm fucking freezing cold and scorching hot at the same time. I decide that taking a shower would be the smartest thing to do in my muddled condition.

The bathroom fills with steam as I step into the shower. I force myself to stand under the burning water in order to rein in my body temperature. After washing and getting warmed up, I grab a towel to dry off before wiping my hand along the mirror to see myself enough to shave. Mae will be up in half an hour so I don't see any reason to force myself to sleep.

Half an hour passes when I hear Mae call out, "Noah? Son? Are you awake?" Her knuckles rap against my old, hollow wooden door. It's got the word fuck carved into it. Although it's been painted numerous times, I can still see the evidence of my rebellious teenage years.

I've gotten dressed in a black V-neck shirt and jeans. "Yeah, I'm up. Come on in." The door creaks open as she enters. I get up and walk over to her, pulling her into a hug, "Merry Christmas, Mae" I say fondly.

"Oh! Merry Christmas, my son," she says as she pats my back. "I'm going to make us a full Christmas morning breakfast. Is there anything in particular that you would like to eat?"

"Yeah…bacon," I say, smiling. "Are we expecting anyone to stop by today?"

"No, not that I am aware of. We both know that we are all that each other have. I wish I had a family to bring you up in, but I had to make do with what I had."

I squeeze her shoulder to comfort her. "I know, Mae. I couldn't have asked for more. Let's go get breakfast going. I'm starving." She steps back and walks back down the hallway to the kitchen to start a Christmas breakfast for two.

It's been just the two of us for as long as I can remember. I've never known any of Mae's family members and she detests speaking of them. I try not to bring them up, but not having family around during the holidays has proven to be fairly lonesome throughout the years. Ridding the conversation from my mind, I sit down at the kitchen island as Mae moves around the room preparing breakfast.

"Mae?" I ask as I pull my phone out to play Christmas music—an attempt to drown out the thunder outside. Sinatra's *Have Yourself a Merry Little Christmas* starts playing as she gestures for me to continue. "What was your favorite part of the ballet?" I query. I already know the answer but I want Mae to talk about her, to tell me more about Heather Lane.

CHAPTER
Five

unaccompanied

Heather

A FTER MANAGING TO escape my dressing room unnoticed, I make my way out the back and onto the busy street, blending in with people exiting the theatre. I hate the fact that I'm constantly looking over my shoulder as I walk, but I can't help it. I just know that any second, Nik is going to come out of nowhere and this time I'll be on my own.

Two blocks later, I arrive at my hotel and slide my keycard into the slot to open the double doors of my suite. I set my ballet bag onto the plush couch and grab my phone off of the charger. Thirteen missed calls, three voicemails, and seven text messages from Dani. In each text she's demanding that I call her as soon as I'm done with the show. I don't bother listening to the voicemails, but instead I hit call and I'm taken straight to her voicemail. Thinking it's rather odd for Dani to not have her phone on, I listen to the voicemails she's left me.

She sounds excited and disappointed at the same time in the first voicemail as she asks that I call her ASAP. In the second one she tells me that Brannon surprised her with a trip to the Greek Islands. Oh my. The third and final message is her apologizing profusely as she tells me she's at the airport and about to board the plane. I hear a flight announcement in the background and hang up; I'm not interested in hearing the rest of the voicemail.

"Looks like it's fake snow and hot chocolate for me this Christmas," I mumble as I cross the living room to the bedroom, fishing out my makeup remover to scrub my face with.

After an hour of trying to remove all of the makeup, I collapse onto my bed, groaning in relief when I'm off of my feet. A giant weight seems to be lifted off my shoulders now that the tour has officially come to an end. I'm safe and alone in my room, and able to think about whatever I want. Of course, I'm thinking of him. I don't even know his name and yet…just thinking about the sound of his voice has my body buzzing.

I shut my eyes, hoping to see him. His ocean green eyes consume me, just as they had when I was standing a few feet in front of him. Willingly, I replay his words in my head, "Smile for me." I squirm on the bed and grab a pillow, covering my head so the next suite over can't hear me scream.

What in the F, Heather?

My mind is running on overdrive while I think about him and the way he wore that suit… and his cologne…he smelled so good. Suddenly I feel like I'm wearing too many clothes and I sit up and toss the pillow aside. I grasp the hem of my tank and pull it up. A small, shy smile plays at my lips as I wonder what it'd be like to undress in front of him.

Get a grip, Heather!

I peel off my tights and lie on the king-sized bed in my favorite pair of white lace panties. Before I know it, I'm thinking about the Greek god again. Even though he wore a suit, I could tell he has a broad chest and trim waist. If he had only taken off the suit jacket, I would have been able to see how his white button-down hugged his body in ways I can only dream of. Oh my, I bet he has the sexiest feet.

Stop it, Heather!

This stranger consumes my thoughts and I'm struggling to sleep. Tossing and turning under the white duvet, I decide it's time to let this fantasy man go. Looking over at the clock, I see that it's seventeen minutes after midnight. Reaching up, I turn off the side lamp and lie back down.

"Merry Christmas, mystery man."

I'M SPIRITED AWAY from the plush hotel bed in Phoenix and into a surreal world where he's waiting for me. The nameless Greek god is standing before me.

He's naked. Gloriously naked.

I swallow back a moan when he steps toward me and I want to touch his tanned, toned skin. His muscles flex as he approaches and he ducks his head to kiss my neck, but instead he teases me. He won't touch me. I can feel his warm breath on my skin. I look down at my body and I'm naked too. I don't remember getting undressed, but I decide not to fight against it. My body moves toward him, but I can never reach this gorgeous man. He says something, but I don't catch it. In order to get his attention, I move my hand down to my sex and start touching myself. I've never touched myself in front of anyone before, but this man has me so hot and needy.

He opens his mouth to speak again and mouths something. Why can't I hear him? I want to hear the voice that made my head spin. I take an appreciative glance at his naked body again. My eyes move up from those sexy feet to his…oh, his manhood and then up to a coy, sensual smile that's leisurely spread across his face.

His smile tells me he's pleased and that for some reason he finds my tight, ballet-trained body attractive. Oh, I'm sure I'm something he'll chase after if given a chance. That sultry grin he's giving me is his tell-all. I'm ready to scale up his body and shove my tongue into his mouth violently, then beg for him to do me…take me like he's never taken anyone else before. My toes curl as I move my fingers faster across my wet, sensitive skin and my mouth drops open as the pleasure is almost too much to take. I find his eyes again and he's looking straight into me—straight into my soul. He hasn't once glanced down to where my hand explores my folds, but I'm about to lose myself from my own touch when the whole lot vanishes.

I'm jolted awake.

The room is pitch black and I'm heaving, trying to fill my lungs with as much air as I possibly can. As my eyes adjust in the darkness, I look at the bedside clock. I blink a few times until my eyes fully focus. The blue numbers on the digital clock read 4:23 a.m.

I can only imagine how incredible he is in bed. The way his body would move over me... A girl can dream—literally.

I move my hand down to touch my panties and they are completely soaked, but I'm still so pent up with sexual tension. I know I was dreaming. I've had half a dozen wet dreams on this tour, but for some reason I don't feel satisfied. I don't think I...I don't believe I had an orgasm this time.

My nipples are peaked and the sheets underneath me are damp with what can only be my perspiration. My overwhelming need to have a body-writhing orgasm is surfacing. I need one. I need an orgasm that is going to start in my toes and run up to my wet folds then penetrate into my core.

Swinging my legs off of the bed, I decide that a cold shower would be a better option than playing with myself when an eruption of electric light fills the room for a second. This bottled-up sexual need is going to have to be just that. Bottled up.

I sag back down onto the bed, deciding not to drive through the storms today and just spend this Christmas in Phoenix…heck, even smaller, in my hotel room. I don't think anything will be open today.

I get up and walk to the windows when the thunder sounds again. Peeking through the curtains, I gasp at the downpour where a man is running in the middle of the street. In this weather? What an idiot. My phone buzzes a few times with severe thunderstorm warnings and flash flooding. I watch the rain descend over the city of Phoenix before returning to bed for the night.

SUNLIGHT POURS THROUGH the window and onto my face. I open my eyes and check the digital clock. It reads 11:38 a.m. I make my way to the window and see that the storm has subsided and left a beautiful blue-skied day in its wake.

A grumbling stomach makes me realize I haven't eaten since before the show. I grab a candy bar from my depleting collection, but put it back, deciding to order breakfast and hot chocolate instead. After a few hours of flipping through TV channels, I know I need to get out of this room. I simply cannot watch *A Christmas Story* anymore. No matter how hard I try, two hours of watching Ralphie seems to be all I can handle. After showering and making myself presentable, I go down to the lobby where only a few guests are meandering around.

Heading over to the concierge desk where a young blonde woman is seated, I politely wish her a Merry Christmas before asking if there is anything that's open today. I'm expecting to hear a no, but when she answers me, I'm taken by surprise.

"Oh yes, Miss Lane. There are a few local diners open if you'd rather not eat in our dining room."

"I ordered room service earlier. Is there anything else that is open? Perhaps something other than a restaurant?" I ask.

Her fingers dance across the keyboard as she looks for an answer, "Um. Mainly just restaurants and movie theatres, Miss Lane. Here's one: it's a small movie theatre about twenty minutes northwest of the city." In the neatest handwriting, she jots down the address of the theatre on a pink sticky-note.

Taking the note from her outstretched hand, I say, "Great. Thank you." Smiling, I walk to the valet men at the lobby doors. I hand them my ticket and minutes later I'm in my convertible with the top down…in December. I end up exploring the mostly abandoned city for the day.

The twenty-minute drive to the theatre flies by as I take in the warm air and gorgeous sunset. I ease down on the brake as my GPS informs me I have arrived at my destination. I look around with a scowl on my face. I don't see any sign of a movie theatre. I've pulled up behind a line of cars and I sit up to see what is causing the holdup. Then I see it: a huge movie screen out in the open. Oh my God, how cute is this? It's a drive-in theatre. The line moves agonizingly slowly as I wait to find out what movie I'll be watching.

When it's my turn to purchase a ticket, I'm told that the theatre's annual Christmas Day show is the 1953 black-and-white movie *Roman Holiday*. The ticket salesman tells me that I will be parked in spot number thirty-one, then hands me a flyer with information on what radio station to tune my radio to. I nod and pay, then follow the signs until I find my parking bay.

Looking at my watch, I decide I still have time to go visit the concession stand that I passed when I entered so I get out of the car and walk back to the guy behind the window.

"Hi. Uhm…I'd like some Milk Duds and some Twizzlers, please. Oh…and a bag of Swedish Fish." I try to hold back a giggle when the guy's eyes go wide. "Oh, and a Coke, please." Giving him the sweetest smile I can muster up before paying, I head back to my car.

Settling into my seat, I open the bag of Twizzlers first. I still can't believe I'm sitting in my convertible on Christmas Day, about to watch a movie in a drive-in theatre. Maybe I can survive without snow on Christmas after all. The screen comes alive and I turn on my radio to the designated station. Glancing over to my left, I see a couple that looks like they're very much in love. She cuddles into his side and he wraps an arm around her shoulder. I almost melt.

"Awww," I say to myself.

With a heavy sigh, I turn back to the screen and watch the opening scene.

CHAPTER
Six
enthralled

Noah

HOURS AFTER I'VE first laid eyes on her, I am still unable to get her out of my mind. Mae and I have had Christmas dinner and she has fallen asleep, just like every other Christmas. Ever since I got my driver's license, I've been going to the theatre on Christmas Day. It has been my reprieve for as long as I can remember. I love Mae, but I need my time alone, time away from her ongoing questions.

Every year the privately owned drive-in theatre has shown *Roman Holiday* at seven in the evening. It is pretty much the only thing that is open on Christmas Day in a fifty-mile radius of Scottsdale. I'd say it has become a part of who I am. I could recite the damn film to anyone who asks. Deciding it's time to leave, I grab some healthy snacks and a liter of water before heading out to my truck and driving the thirty-two miles to get to this theatre. Once I pay, I'm given my spot, number forty. I'm usually about ten spots closer, but fuck it. I'm here and I can kick back and enjoy something that is not all about Christmas.

Growing up with Mae has made me rely on my peers for my entire social life, as well as to get by and get the hell away from the house. I've got one close friend, but the motherfucker is a damned manwhore. He'd rather be banging chicks on Christmas than watching these old films. He would kick my ass for coming to these damned black-and-white romance movies once a year.

Okay, more than once a year, but it's my escape. I don't have to worry about shit when I'm out here. I'm away from everyone and everything I know. I need this place the same way it needs patrons to survive.

I pull into my spot and tune my radio to the AM station. The film starts playing when I reach over and start chewing on my carrots and ranch, chugging my water when I get thirsty— healthy snacks after all the damn stuffing and slices of pie I ate tonight. I move my seat back to get comfortable, accidentally laying my hand on the horn. It releases a long, drawn-out beep.

Fuck.

All the couples and their mothers must be looking in my direction. I raise my hand to the couple parked in front of me as an apology.

"Sorry, man, I didn't mean to shut down your piece of ass." Chuckling to myself, I add to my comment when he looks away, "Lucky asshole."

I've been so consumed with studying for the bar exam that I haven't had time for myself. Shit, I used to play football in high school and college. I knew my shit; it's why I got a full scholarship to Arizona State. With the amount of scholarship money left over as well as my living-expense loan, I've been able to live a very comfortable lifestyle. I know I'll be paying it off once I graduate, but fuck it. They forbid me to work the first year in law school, and I've got to live somehow. I'm grateful that I haven't had to worry about working throughout my undergrad and grad career as it would have taken away from my study time.

Mae has always said that I would be surrounded by true friends and I found that friendship in Coen Reed. Coen and I played for

Arizona for the four years of our college career. He's the one asshole who I have kept in touch with in the almost three years since we graduated college. He went on to be a skydiving instructor while I headed to grad school to get my law degree. All he does is fucking play. I decide to text the motherfucker while the movie plays.

I type out a quick message: **Hey ass-hat. What are you doing for New Year's?**

His reply comes almost instantly. **Dipshit. I'll be with your ass at a bar somewhere in Phoenix.**

Chuckling, I respond: **I'll see you at Trione at 10 pm for NYE.**

Thirty minutes into the movie, I need to piss. I climb out of my truck and head to the lavatories. There's a long-ass line for the women's bathroom and I laugh. Shit, sucks to have a vagina, I guess. As the thought enters my head, I pause to watch a woman who looks just like Heather Lane walk into the women's bathroom. I freeze. There's no way in hell that's her. She's probably long gone by now. Regardless, I decide to wait. I watch as woman after woman walks out of the bathroom while I wait to see if I'm hallucinating or not.

Finally, Heather Lane emerges from the bathroom and I can't help but stare at her. She's beautiful…possibly the most beautiful woman I have ever seen. She looks completely different from last night, with her hair down. I want her even more. My body automatically moves toward her.

Step by step.

She's walking away so I have to quicken my pace in order to catch up to her. I'm attracted to her like a polar opposite. I need to say something—I can't let her get away this time. I hear myself call out, "Excuse me, Miss Lane?"

She turns on her toes and I still when her eyes focus on mine.

I'm the man who tore the fucking asshole off of her last night. I'm the man she ran from.

What the hell are you doing, Ryan?

When she sees who is calling out her name, she stops walking away. I can't tell if she's delighted, scared, or pissed that it's me. Hell, does she even recognize me?

I feel my world tilt again. I've been fighting all day to get it back on its normal axis but seeing her just fucked up every ounce of effort I put into it. I am taking a shot in the dark with this woman. I stand there like the fool I am for her as I wait for her to say something… anything.

Heather

AS I'M WALKING back to my car I'm watching the screen ahead of me, hoping I haven't missed too much of the movie, and out of nowhere, I hear my name being called. Out of reflex, I turn around to the sound of a deep, raspy voice. In the process of pivoting on my toes, I realize that nobody knows me around here. Who the heck could…? As soon as my eyes focus in the dark, my heart does its own pirouette. Oh…it's him…the Greek god.

I can't move.

Not an inch.

I'm stuck.

He takes a step toward me and then another. How…how did he see me? I stand there and do nothing but take him in. Every movement he makes. Every time his lips crook up in the corner. Every single inch he moves toward me. My body becomes so much more aware of him. I tingle in places I didn't know I could tingle just from a man's eyes on me.

I'm not sure what to say to him. I'm embarrassed. I'm excited. I'm enthralled. As he walks toward me, my eyes roam his body. Holy F! The suit he wore at the show looked amazing on him, but it hid every single thing from me.

Every. Single. Thing.

From what I can see in the dim lighting, he's wearing jeans that ride low on his hips. His black V-neck shows off his arms, and I think I'm going to pass out at how much man he is, how toned and tanned he is. He closes in on me and stops what seems like a hundred miles away when I want him less than an inch away from me.

"Heather," I say softly.

He smiles at me and I'm butter in this heat. He holds out his hand to me in an effort to shake mine as he says, "Good evening, Heather."

I'm shaking inside. The way my name rolled off of his tongue...I want to hear him say it again. I'm selfish. I extend my hand and reach for his. His large hand closes around mine gently, yet I can feel how strong he is. I pray that he can't feel me trembling. I've totally forgotten about the movie and apparently forgotten how to speak. I stutter out a few words that I hope make sense, "I...I'm sorry...and you are?" I want so badly to finally know this mystery man's name.

He's still holding onto my hand when he replies "Shit. Yeah. Noah. Noah Ryan." His eyes move from mine to our hands and he loosens his grip when he realizes his fingers are still wrapped around my hand. My hand feels cold and wanting when he lets go. It's bad that I want this man to touch me again...even if it's just another handshake.

I smile and I'm sure I'm smiling like an idiot. I finally know his name.

Noah.

Could that be any more perfect for him? Congratulations, Noah's mom, you nailed it. I try to keep my voice calm as I respond, "It's nice to meet you, Noah. Merry Christmas."

The smile that forms on his face when I respond nearly knocks me off of my feet. "Merry Christmas, Heather. I saw you and wanted to apologize for last night. I didn't mean to scare you."

I'm too busy watching his mouth move to realize he actually said something. Shaking my head to clear my thoughts, I realize I'm still on my toes, a habit of a lifetime. I lower myself onto my heels and look up at him. "Oh...uhm...no. I'm sorry I didn't get a chance to thank you." My cheeks must be the fiery color of my toenails. I quickly steal a glance at my manicured feet to see my

"Sexy Silhouette" color.

"You have nothing to be sorry about. I'm just glad I didn't scare the shit out of you. I don't know what I was thinking. The way you..." He pauses in the middle of his sentence as if he's realized he's going to say something he'd rather not.

Ah! Please don't stop talking. Oh my, I want to hear his low, raspy voice again. I want to feel his vocal vibrations move through my skin, and I want to touch the slight bump of his Adam's apple. I'm finding it so difficult to concentrate, let alone breathe around this man.

I look down at my painted toenails again to try and get myself to focus. Dammit, Heather. Every interaction I've had with this sexy man has had to do with Nik and without someone else present, I'm flustered and blushing and I don't know what to say to him.

When I look up at him, his smile has fallen and he speaks before I can. "I...uh...you were amazing last night. I'll let you get back to the movie. I'm sorry for interrupting."

I grin and reply, "Thank you, that's always nice to hear." I find myself wanting to catch a hint of his smile again. "And you're not interrupting."

I watch as his eyes move down from my black chiffon cami to my linen white shorts and further down my bare legs. He pauses when his eyes reach my Jimmy Choo sandals. He almost laughs to himself before he looks up into my eyes again, like he's got a little inside joke with my feet. I feel like he just memorized every single inch of my body, like he just undressed me and made love to me with his eyes.

"I was about to head back to my truck. Would you mind if I walked you back to your car? That's if you're not with anyone else?"

I want to bounce up and down with joy, but I keep my feet planted. Oh crap, I'm acting like an idiot. "Sure. I'm just over here." Pointing with my thumb as I turn around, I begin to walk toward my car. My years of training to be graceful all vanish. I'm so self-conscious that I feel like I'm tripping over my own feet.

Maybe he'll catch me? Oh my. I want those hands on me again. Maybe I should trip and see what he does?

I look over my shoulder at him as he takes a few quick steps to catch up to me. In my peripherals, I'm watching his body move. He shoves a hand into his front pocket, and all of my thoughts about tripping are gone as I imagine him without those faded blue jeans on.

"Have you seen this film before?" he asks as I walk up to my convertible "Damn. Nice ride, Heather," he adds and my body wants to scream to get rid of all of this sexual tension that is buzzing in the air between us.

I spot my pile of candy lying on my driver's seat and I quickly turn to block his view. Leaning against the door and looking up at him, I answer, "No, I've never seen it. Have you?"

"Yeah, about once a year actually. Since I was sixteen."

The wind blows and a strand of my hair gets caught in my lip gloss. He raises his hand as if he's going to tuck the strand behind my ear but then he drops his hand.

No! No! Oh hell. Please just touch me once more.

It's like he can read my thoughts. He raises his hand again and moves the strand of hair from my lips and tucks it neatly behind my ear. I feel shy and wild and oh so needy. I inhale deeply when I catch the scent of his cologne as he brings his hand back. Oh. He smells of pure, clean, floral woodiness. His cologne leaves a crisp, fresh scent on him, making him smell so sweetly intriguing and uniquely masculine.

And Holy F! I want to lick him. *Crap, Heather. You sound like your sister.* The power of his cologne, his scent, his yumminess, is dramatic. I've forgotten my words again.

"Heather?" His raspy voice brings me back from myself. "I'm glad I was able to meet you."

God, I love the way his voice sounds. I beam up at him. "It was great meeting you, Noah." Saying his name a bit too slowly, I quickly glance down at my feet then back up at him. "And thank you for last night."

"I'd do it all over again. Enjoy the weather here in Phoenix and have a safe trip to wherever you're going." His hunky smile lights up his face as he turns and walks away from me. He gets into his truck a row behind me.

When I watch him walk away, I literally moan. My ovaries might be crying out to me. I open the door and sag down in my seat, feeling like I've just run a full marathon. My legs are so wobbly and I'm so warm. Plus, my hands feel clammy and wet. Right then, the movie ends and the screen goes dark. I'm sitting there staring at my phone, wanting to call my sister...but why? I've got nothing to tell her other than I've just spoken to the most gorgeous man I've ever laid eyes on, a man I'll never see again.

I hear a truck start and I turn around to watch him, watch this Greek god, Noah, drive away from me. I want to jump out of my car and in front of his, begging him not to go. I don't beg for anything, but for this man, I will.

My libido is in overdrive as the parking lot empties out and all I can do is sit there, my flushed complexion staring back at me in the rearview mirror.

Noah Ryan.

Makes me so unbelievably flustered.

CHAPTER
Seven
fervor

Noah
December 31st
New Year's Eve

IT HAS BEEN six long days since I last saw her. Six days and I'm still trying to right what she did to my world. I've sworn to myself that I won't take this obsession with her into the New Year: I'm leaving her behind and she'll be part of a Christmas I'll never forget.

She'll be the one that got away.

After spending the rest of the week with Mae, I'm finally at my apartment and alone. Family over the holidays can be stressful, I'm told, but Mae...I'm pretty sure she can be worse than having an entire family. I love her dearly, but I'm glad I can finally escape. Everything in my one-bedroom apartment is just as I left it. It's one big-ass man cave. I am a bachelor after all. There is rustic wood and steel everywhere; the leasing agent called it modern and edgy.

As long as there are no trinkets and paintings of fruit on my walls, I couldn't care less.

My phone goes off with a text and I pull it out of my pocket. It's Coen.

You still up for drinks tonight, man?

Damn right I am. I punch in, smirking as I hit send.

Nice. I'll see you there in a few hours.

Feeling good about tonight, I grab my duffel and head out to the gym, deciding to hit it hard today. I need to get rid of this sexual frustration.

THREE HOURS LATER I leave the gym and drive home for a quick shower before heading out to Phoenix for the night. I'm pleased I booked a hotel room because I'm not driving drunk back to Tempe after this New Year's Eve celebration. And there's a more than slight chance I'll be bringing someone back to the room with me. There's no way in hell I'm bringing a woman back to my place—never let them know where you live. I don't need a crazy-ass stalker.

There's a line outside of the club door, which wraps around the building, stretching all the way down the street. Trione is Phoenix's most popular club and people come here from all walks of life. I manage to get in without having to stand in that long-ass line— being friends with the bouncer has its perks.

The music is blaring and the booze is already flowing when I arrive at 10:00 p.m. Searching the bar for Coen, I spot him chatting up some blondes before the three of them down a double shot of amber liquor. Shit. He's going hard tonight.

I walk up and smack him on the back. "Coen, you motherfucker! Getting the ladies going already?"

He looks over his shoulder at me and grins. "There's the lady killer now!" he says to the two blondes. The alcohol has obviously affected him: the goofy-ass grin on his face gives him away. Looking over his head at the bartender, I order a round of shots. If he's going hard, I have some catching up to do. I hand my card over to the bartender and start a tab before I hold up my shot glass. Bending down to the obviously augmented blonde, I shout over the music. "Don't believe anything he tells you. He's a fucking liar."

The girls laugh as if it's the funniest fucking thing they have ever heard. "Here's to the last two hours of the year. And to two hot blondes!" I throw the shot back and breathe through my teeth as the three of them drunkenly yell something incoherent before taking theirs.

It's been about forty-five minutes since I got here and these girls are toasted. Coen usually picks the ones without inhibitions and these girls are no different—easy lays. This one with the large tits has been hanging all over me since I've arrived. Don't get me wrong: she's good looking and I'm sure a decent fuck, but I highly doubt she could handle it. None of them have been able to—my blessing and a curse. No point in wasting my time.

I'm tipsy as shit and these girls—Brandy and Sophie...Sofia?— are getting annoying. I spin my bar stool around and check my watch: it now reads 11:01 p.m. I lean my elbows back against the bar and look out at the dance floor. Big-tits asks me to dance, but I decline with a shake of my head. I tilt the bottle of beer back and take a long drink as I eye a woman on the dance floor, a hot little brunette moving to the music so sensually. She knows how to move her body. Now that's the kind of woman I'd get off my ass for.

She's facing the other direction as she moves her tight ass to the music. I take the last swig of my beer when the brunette turns around, her hands in her dark-chocolate hair as she shakes her tits. I choke on my fucking beer. I'm coughing like a dumbass when the blonde pats my back. My body takes it as a sign to go get her, and my alcohol-induced mind agrees. Slamming the empty bottle down, I move off the bar stool and make my way across the dance floor to Heather Lane as Coen yells, "Yo, dipshit. Which one are you tongue fucking for New Year's?"

I turn around and flip him the middle finger when I walk straight into something. "Oh shit!" I grab hold of an arm and a hand, unsure of what I'm holding onto while pulling up so I don't knock whomever it is over. When I'm able to look down at the person I just ran over, Heather Lane's jade green eyes peer up at me. Just my motherfucking luck.

She looks up at me with the cutest dazed smile. I can tell she's about to say something when I see the recognition flash in her eyes—what a rush when the girl you lust after recognizes you. Her eyes light up for me, and I can't explain the way that makes me feel. "Noah!" she screams excitedly.

I'm drinking her in, in all of her beauty. Once again, she's flawless. She starts moving to the music again and I chuckle, "Hey, my fault," I say while getting sidetracked by her swaying hips. "I didn't know a graceful ballerina could move like you do, Heather."

My eyes catch on her tight black sequined dress as a strap falls off of her shoulder. Fuck. Me. The sexiest drunken giggle escapes her lips and my eyes flicker back to her face.

"I'm a dancer, Noah. Trust me...I can move."

Damn right you can! My eyes wander over her body again and even though I'm having a damn good time watching her wiggle that tight ass in front of me, I want to get her alone. I can't get her out of my head. Taking a chance, I lean down as I gently touch her elbow. "Can I buy you a drink?"

The sides of her lips curl up as she nods. "I'd like that, Noah."

Shit. If she says my name one more time my balls will implode. I hold out my hand to signal to her where to go and she walks in front of me. Smirking to myself, I get another look at her ass.

She gets up onto a bar stool and I stand behind her. "What would you like?"

She swivels to the side and looks up at me. My eyes are fixated on her lips when she speaks.

"A French martini, please."

I have to smile at her drink order. Don't ask me why, but I happen to know that fucking drink is pink. I get the bartender's attention and ask for a top-shelf French martini and a bourbon on the rocks. "Make it a double," I yell out as the bartender turns away. A few moments later we have our drinks and I reach for her hand.

She doesn't fight me on it, so I lead her away from the bar and into the VIP section.

"I know the owner of the club. He'll hook us up with a private spot. I'd like to get to know you a bit before you leave Phoenix."

I look behind me and down at her when I don't hear a reply. Her eyes are glazed over; she's nibbling on that lip of hers while her eyes are locked onto my ass. Not gonna lie, I fucking dig it.

"Heather?" I probe as Nate, the owner, starts walking us toward an available booth. Her eyes flicker up to mine as a bright rosy blush replaces her pale complexion.

"Right…sorry, I, uhm, got distracted." she says as we walk up to the booth. The music isn't blaring in my ears and I can actually hear her when she says, "So I'm guessing you come here quite often."

I can't tell if she's throwing me a line or asking me why I received preferential treatment just now, but I laugh. "Damn. I'm going to pretend that wasn't a horrible pickup line."

When we slide into the booth, her dress hikes up her thighs and I want my hands on her smooth skin. Yesterday. I check my watch when I slide in next to her and we have all of forty-five minutes until we ring in the New Year. Letting go of her small hand, I move my arm to rest on the table. She sips on her martini as I watch her lips move on the rim of the thin glass. They should be moving on the head of my cock.

She speaks before I can this time. "I'm glad I get to see you again before I head back to New York."

New York? Well fuck. "Oh yeah? I thought I'd never get to see you again, actually. I'm surprised that you are here…and alone." My eyes move down from her eyes and to the black dress that shows off too much cleavage. I'm immediately envious of every motherfucking asshole that has laid eyes on her tonight. I want to take my shirt off and cover her up. I want to be the only man who gets to see her like this, who gets to watch those cheeks pinken as her breasts move with every solitary breath she takes. I realize I'm still staring at her breasts when a waitress comes by and asks us if we'd like another round of drinks. I nod curtly, pissed that she took two seconds of my attention away from this gorgeous woman in front of me.

When I turn back to her, she's eyeing the waitress as if she wants to smack her. I'm glad I'm not the only one who feels so abnormally possessive. Hell, if she were mine, I'd be in so much shit. I'd fuck up any dickwad who looked at her. I clench my fists to rein in my sudden anger. I need to cool it on the alcohol.

"Noah?" she asks softly.

"Yeah?" I answer as I set my glass down on the table.

"This is going to sound horribly silly, but what is in this drink? I feel even drunker now than I did five minutes ago."

I can't hold in a laugh when my first thought is that she's drunk on me. "I know the feeling, but the combination of vodka and champagne is going to give one hell of a hangover." Her giggle sends a chill down my body, all the way to the head of my cock. She has this unspoken grip on me and it's so damn tight. I know, without question, that this woman is going to be the end of me. She's fucked up my entire world. I've been so entirely consumed by the mere thought of her that I haven't studied for my exam since I laid my eyes on her.

She's in her own little world as her body moves to the beat; she's watching the crowd on the dance floor. I don't recognize the song playing, but it's got something to do with bodies grinding and a surfboard? She's almost grinding on the booth.

I want to be the damn booth.

She has my balls knotted up.

I slide out of the seat as the waitress walks by to deliver our drinks. Offering Heather my hand I say, "Come dance with me..."

Thankfully she slips her hand into mine and takes one more sip of her martini before getting up. Keeping hold of her hand, I let her lead the way as I watch her sexy, tight body start to move before we even get to the dance floor. If she continues at this rate, I'll be hard in seconds.

She moves closer to me on the dance floor. I place one of my hands on her hip so every one of these assholes with a hard-on for her understands she's with me. I start moving with her and before I know it, she's turned around and dancing with her back up against me. She's trying to damn well kill me. I move my hips in a circular motion to keep up with her and I know I'm grinning like an idiot.

I'm not sure if she knows what she's doing to me, but hell, it's sexual.

I watch her grind her ass into me and I'm done. She's got me as hard as I've ever been. My fingers dig into her hip and I pull her against me. I know I'm drunk, but I decide that I have to touch more of her. My hand slips from her hip, to her flat stomach. She doesn't break for a beat as the song comes to an end. The DJ announces that we have thirty minutes to go until the New Year.

She throws her head back and leans against my chest as I run my hand over her dress. I can feel the amount of strength she has in her core from dancing all of her life, but hell, I know she can feel how much I have in my slacks.

Her tight ass is pressed against my dick and I swear she knows what she's doing. She's attracted to me or else she wouldn't be playing this game. I'm wanting my lips on her skin. She keeps rolling her head back against my chest, exposing her damp neck. If I have to watch her pull that strap up onto her shoulder again, I'm going to rip it off with my teeth. I don't want it on her. We're dancing without an inch between us and I watch as she's about to touch that damned strap again. I halt her hand and put it around my neck. Fuck it. I lean down and grab that strap with my teeth, tugging on it and pulling it down…exposing her bare shoulder, tasting it with my tongue.

I lean in and speak closely to her ear so she can hear me, "You're suggestive as hell, Miss Lane."

Her hand moves up into my hair; damn, it feels good. Inhaling her scent, I pull her even closer to me. I need to get her back to that booth. I want her alone, but I can't stand the thought of not touching her.

I look up and see Coen giving me the thumbs up. Man, fuck off. Not now. I move my attention back to her as my hands are roving down her body's natural curves, over her ass to the place where her dress ends. She hasn't stopped my advances yet. In fact, I know she's been throwing out signals. Unexpectedly, she stops dancing and turns around. Sliding my hands up around her waist, I splay one against her lower back, ensuring I'm not intruding. If I just had the balls to lower my hand to her ass again.

"Can we get another drink?" she asks me with this sexy little grin.

"Yeah, let's head back to the booth. If I remember correctly and it's not the alcohol, I believe we ordered another round," I say as I keep my hand at the small of her back while we walk through the throng of people.

Once we get back to our table, she reaches for her drink and I hone in on her lips again. She drinks about half of it before putting it down. I take a swig of my bourbon as my eyes roam her body. Before I know it, she's moving closer to me—so close that her bare thigh is pressed against mine. I look down and watch her cross one of her legs over the other, my fingers itching to touch her pale skin.

"I like the way you dance," she says provocatively.

A growl escapes me when she moves her hair over to one shoulder, exposing her neck to me. "I'm glad I could keep up with a professional." I take a chance of a lifetime and place my hand on her knee, impatiently running my thumb up and down her soft skin.

She scoots closer still and I can feel her leaning into me. Maybe it's her perfume, but damn, I'm unbelievably horny right now—I need to connect with this woman. I watch her bring her hand up and start playing with the buttons on my shirt and I almost groan out loud. I'm a wreck with her around.

I want her to know that I want her. Even though I'm drunk—and I'm sure she is too—she needs to know before she leaves town. As painful as it is, I pull my eyes from hers and graze her jaw with my teeth. My left hand tips her chin up so I have full access to her neck. Her sharp intake of breath spurs me forward and my tongue darts out to taste her soft skin.

Christ, she smells so damn good. My dick is painfully hard and I want nothing more than for her to feel it, to feel what she does to me. As I lick up her neck, I can feel her pulse race and flutter against my tongue. She's trembling and her skin is too hot—a telltale sign of arousal. I'm pretty sure she's wet between those sexy thighs. I want those same thighs on either side of my head while I eat her out. I groan against her neck at the thought and suck briefly. Her chest is heaving and her hand moves to my thigh, digging her nails in. I want those nails scratching down my back. I'm mere moments away from slipping my hand under her dress and moving her panties aside. I want to know if I'm correct. I want to feel her pussy clench around my fingers. I want her to come on my hand...right here in front of everyone.

The speaker blares as an announcement is made. We have two minutes until midnight. Shit, where the hell has the past hour gone? I'm looking down at her fingers as the waitresses, in their tight little outfits, start passing out glasses of inexpensive champagne around the club.

One minute.

One minute, and I know that I can't leave her in this year. I know that I'll be holding onto every second I've ever spent with this woman. The big flat-screens in the VIP area light up with numbers, which are rapidly counting down to zero.

Her eyes follow the line of buttons up my dark shirt to my eyes. As the crowd starts to get rowdy, screaming and whooping envelop the room. The sound of champagne bottles opening one after the other fills my ears as people start shouting the countdown.

Ten.

I can't keep my eyes off of her.

Nine.

She's fucked with my head.

Eight.

I take her hand from my shirt.

Seven.

I lace my fingers with hers.

Six.

No words in the damn dictionary could fill the space between us.

Five.

My mind is racing.

Four.

I have no idea what is happening between us, but I don't want this countdown to end it.

Three.

This feels right.

Two.

She's my New Year's resolution.

One.

Everything in the room goes quiet. All I can hear is white noise as balloons and shiny shit start falling from the ceiling. My world has come to a standstill and the spinning has stopped. I hesitate, unsure of her reaction.

Fuck it.

Impatiently, I slide my hand up her neck then behind her ear. I tangle my fingers in the loose strands of hair that fall to her shoulders. I'm ultra-aware of my heart pounding in my chest. There's a thudding at the back of my ears, which I'm certain is not from the alcohol.

There is no order to my movement, but there is an exciting mix of improvisational chaos and want that I need to fill, as we both move in. I press my lips against hers gradually. I tease the seam of her lips with my tongue and once her lips part for me, I'm tenderly biting, sucking on her, as our tongues intertwine and move sensuously against each other's. Her tongue expertly strokes mine while our heads dance from left to right, over and over, both of us trying to get closer, deeper. Wanting to taste more of each other. My cock jerks in my slacks as she presses her chest against mine. Her nipples are perked up and pushing against me.

Hell, she tastes like pineapples, raspberries, and champagne. I fucking want her.

I'm keeping her.

CHAPTER
Eight
we all start as strangers

Heather

I'M TRYING TO think back to what paved the way to this kiss. My lips are locked with the sexiest man in this club, and the music is booming around us as our lips move to our own rhythm. I've seen how all the women look at him and chase him around the club—some have literally been following him. I've looked past the fact that I know nothing about him—just his name, and now his lips.

I have nothing to lose. He kisses me gently, like I'm something to be treasured. I can't seem to get close enough to him as I lose myself in his fervent kiss. I whimper against his lips as he tugs on my hair. I'm gasping for breath, but I don't want to stop this kiss. He's been laying small touches on me all evening, but this is by far the best.

My body is reacting to him so fiercely. I want him to get this form-fitting dress off of me. I whimper against his lips when someone slams a hand on the table. I pull away and stare up at this stranger who just ruined this most perfect moment.

"Nice fucking catch, dipshit!" an intoxicated man in a bright blue button-down says.

Noah actually growls at his blonde-haired acquaintance. "Get lost, Coen. I'm busy."

"You're really not going to introduce me to this fine piece of ass?" He gestures toward me.

Noah straightens up as if he's ready to kick this guy's ass, and I can't help but giggle in my semi-drunken state. "She's much more than a fine piece of ass. Apologize, you fucker."

Coen raises his eyebrows and takes a step back. "You chode. Shit. My fucking apologies...?"

He looks at me with a questioning look. Oh. He's waiting for me to tell him my name.

"Heather. It's nice to meet you, Coen," I say as I hold out my hand to shake his.

His eyes fall to my breasts and I feel like covering up. I don't want him to look at me like that when Noah is right here. He smirks and says, "You know, you're the first chick I've seen this dipshit kissing while we're out. I've known him going on seven years now. There's got to be some big catch about you, Heather."

"Coen, go get those damn blondes and get your dick wet. I'll text you later."

Oh my...he's bossy, too. "Bye, Coen," I croon.

"Fuck you too, man. See ya, sweet cheeks," he says with a wink.

Noah shakes his head and chuckles. "Sorry about that. What do you say we get out of here?"

"I'd like that. A lot. Probably too much," I say, as Coen walks away trying to give Noah the blow job signal with his hand and tongue prodding his cheek.

He looks down at me to ask, "Are you with that guy from the show? I wouldn't want to be stepping on any toes, so to speak."

I quickly shake my head no, letting him know that there's no one else.

"Good. Let's get some food in you. Is breakfast all right with you?" he inquires.

I nod, probably a little more enthusiastically than necessary.

I'm jumping up and down inside; I don't want this night to end at midnight. This Cinderella needs more time with her Prince. Watching him stand up to his full height, I give him my hand when he reaches for it and I'm more than eager to touch him again. But also immediately I try talking myself out of this.

Simmer down, Heather...this is just a fling for him. You really can't believe what Coen said. You weren't born yesterday. That was his wingman. He's simply following the Guy Code Rules.

But I'm drunk and hungry and he's...oh so yummy. I think I might break all of my rules tonight. So I say, "Good idea. Is there anywhere open around here this late?" I almost fall as I step out from the booth, but even in his drunken state, Noah catches me. When he touches me, my skin almost burns. I'm so hot for this Greek god.

"Careful now, beautiful," he says as I hold onto his biceps to stabilize myself.

I may have just taken my last breath. His term of endearment throws me for a loop and I'm seriously thinking of letting this man do whatever he wants with me. I giggle and squeeze his tanned, muscular arm, sizing him up. "I'm blaming you for getting me drunk," I joke.

He takes my hand and laces his fingers through mine as he leads me out of the club. "I'll take the blame for it. Now I've got to right my wrong, and get your little ass sobered up." He hails a cab and we get in. He tells the driver to go to Vento Diner in Scottsdale.

"We're going to Scottsdale? Why don't we stop somewhere in the city center?" I ask.

"I think you'll like this place. I've been going to it ever since I can remember."

Pursing my lips, I eye him playfully and deviously ask, "Noah? Are you taking me to Chuck E Cheese?" Suddenly realizing that he hasn't seen any side of me other than drunk or quiet, I burst out into a fit of drunken giggles and lean into his shoulder while I laugh.

His chest vibrates as he laughs with me.

Would he mind if I bit him? I just want to sink my teeth into him...anywhere. Lick him, bite him, suck on him—anything that involves my mouth on that darkly tanned skin of his.

"No, that would be the complete opposite actually; I've never been there. And when the hell did you become so talkative? I thought your vocabulary consisted of yes, no, maybe, and ballet terms."

"Ah! I have a wider vocabulary than you know," I say as I lean back against the taxi's door and move my feet onto his lap.

"We'll see about that, won't we?"

He looks down at my feet and raises his eyebrow in question. "Pink, huh?" I notice his voice sounds deeper...thicker. I wiggle my pink toes as they peek through my glittered heel. "I love pink!" I watch him slowly lift my foot using the tip of his finger, cocking his head to the side as he eyes my 'Sammy Red Bottoms.' I let out a laugh because I can't take it anymore. "Shoe fetish, Noah?"

I put my foot back down on his hard thigh, wanting to get rid of my shoes and run my toes all the way up to the prominent bulge in his pants.

"Not that I'm aware of, but I'm open to many things."

Oh my.

"Pink drink, pink toes, and pink lips? I think I'm noticing a theme here, ballerina."

I smile sweetly. "You've figured me out already. Am I that obvious?" Feeling the cab come to a stop, I gracefully slide my feet off his thigh and sit up. Quickly grabbing my clutch, I throw a twenty-dollar bill at the driver before hopping out with a giggle. Drunk and mischievous Heather has come out to play. I laugh when I hear his protests from the car.

He grumbles and says, "You're seriously not going to let me pay for the damn cab? Shit," he says as he gets out. "Breakfast's on me. I'm sure you can't scarf down one of their breakfast plates here. You're too damn little."

"Don't let my size fool you, Noah." Oh he does not know what he's in for. I can put down some food. We walk into the diner and he just goes and sits down at a booth like he owns the place. "The sign says 'please wait to be seated,'" I call out after him.

He looks at me with the most sex-stimulating grin on his face and replies with a wink, "Don't you worry, little ballerina. I've been here a time or two."

Oh my God, I want to do something naughty to this man.

I quickly join him at the booth and take a seat across from him. The waitress walks up to us with the biggest smile on her makeup-plastered face.

"Noah!" she sings, and he gets up to hug her.

Oh no you don't. I call dibs on this Greek god. Let go, hussy.

He sits down and orders two 'Ryan's Breakfast Feast' plates for us. I haven't even glanced at the menu, but I think it's kind of sweet that he ordered for me. "I'll have orange juice too, please," I add quickly.

I'm still drunk and my brain is fuzzy, so my judgment is impaired, and I tend to say what is on my mind, whether it's a good idea or not. I lean forward after the waitress leaves and I whisper playfully, "Noah?"

He rests his elbows on the table and looks at me, "What is it, ballerina?" He takes a drink of his water while his eyes move down to my breasts.

It excites me that he's looking at me like that, and I smile when he calls me that again. It sounds so good coming from his lips. His lips...Mmm. My eyes flicker to his lips and I get distracted, thinking about our kiss. God, his lips are immaculate.

"Heather?" I hear him urge. Busted. I quickly regain my focus on his eyes. Oh crap, was I staring?

"Huh? Oh. Did you order bacon?"

"Bacon? Hell, is that even a question? Breakfast isn't breakfast without bacon, woman. Wait. Are you a vegetarian?" He looks alarmed.

I decide to take a little risk. I get up and move to his side of the booth, making him scoot over on the seat so I can sit closely next to him.

I choke out a laugh. "A vegetarian? Uhm, no," I answer with a grin. "I'm just making sure you ordered enough because I plan on eating mine as well as yours."

"Oh yeah? We'll see who wins this bacon battle."

"Mmhmm"

"How about I make a deal with you?"

A deal? Oh this better be good. "That depends on what's at stake." I move my hair to one side of my shoulders.

"Those lips. Give me those lips again and I'll give you my bacon."

My jaw drops.

I think I might be hearing things, but he's waiting for an answer. Screw butterflies: my stomach is doing somersaults.

YES! I shriek internally. Our eyes meet. "Right here?" I ask, because I don't trust myself with just an innocent kiss. After feeling his lips on mine earlier, what I want to do to him right now is rather illegal in public.

He tilts my chin up with one finger. My body shudders and my sex clenches, "Right here. I don't see anything wrong with kissing you."

Then his lips are on mine, taking his part of the deal. Taking all of my thoughts and jumbling them up. I nip his lip with my teeth and he groans then pushes his tongue into my mouth. He's so sure of himself. He's running his tongue over my teeth, making me wet... Oh my! That was so hot! Our tongues tangle together again as he occasionally sucks, which sends me reeling.

I am wet. *Dripping.* These panties won't last long if he keeps this up. I can't get close enough to him. Somehow, my hand blindly finds his button-up shirt and I grip it, holding onto him for dear life. If anyone tries to ruin this kiss for me, I won't be held responsible for my actions.

He tastes so delectable. I inhale deeply, trying to get a sufficient amount of air into my lungs, not wanting to pull away for anything. My tongue is twirling against his when I whimper into his mouth and feel his hand slide up my neck.

The pad of his thumb runs over my neck as we stroke our tongues against each other's. I'm certain he can feel my pulse drumming eagerly. His smile breaks our kiss and he pulls away. "That...was well worth losing my bacon over." He's so close I can feel his warm breath wash over my face as he speaks.

I'm ravenous, blinking up at him with a dazed expression. My voice is merely a whisper as I say, "I'm not hungry anymore."

"I am…but not for any actual food sustenance."

I bite the inside of my cheek when he admits he wants more of me. He's so alluring. His raspy voice alone is enough to give me an orgasm. I want to lead him to the back of this diner and have my filthy little way with him.

The waitress brings our breakfast over and sets it down on the white tabletop. She asks Noah if he wants anything else, but completely ignores me. I'm shooting invisible daggers at her with my eyes. Back off, pigtails.

"Do you need anything else, Heather?"

I shake my head no. When the waitress scurries her flirty-ass away from us, he moves his bacon over to my plate before he starts to eat. How the heck does he making chewing look erotic? His chiseled jaw moves lazily and I find myself wanting to bite him again.

As I sit there and eat quietly beside him, I feel my buzz slipping away. Oh no! Come back. I'm so much bolder when I'm drunk. I'm wondering if I should try to make small talk with him right now or just let the man eat.

Half an hour later, I'm stuffed. That was the best breakfast I have ever eaten. We get up and leave the diner, but as we're getting into the cab I realize we didn't pay.

"Am I still too drunk not to remember you paying?"

Noah shrugs it off. "Nah, I don't tend to pay at places my mother owns." Then it clicks: the 'Ryan's breakfast.' Ha. Noah Ryan.

We're in the cab on the way to my hotel in Phoenix when he turns to face me. "I've enjoyed spending time with you, Heather. I understand that you have to leave soon, but I was hoping I'd get to see you again before you go?"

I smile softly, completely sober now. Crap…where is my courage? Willing myself to be more than just shy, I say, "I'd like that."

"How about you come over to my place tomorrow? I'll make you dinner and we can put a movie on?"

He cooks too? I nod and take my iPhone out of my clutch, and hand it to him. "I might need your number then, Noah."

"Touché. That was smooth as hell." He moves his fingers over the screen as he inputs his number; he calls himself and I can hear his phone vibrate against his pocket. "Now I've got yours too. I'll give you a time and address when I get up in the morning. It all depends on how hung over I am." The laugh that vibrates throughout the interior of the cab is so spicy and sexy. I want his lips against mine again.

The cab pulls up to my hotel and parks at the entrance. Swinging the door open, I look back at him after I get out and he looks as if he's ready to pounce on me from the backseat.

He does.

He grabs my waist and pulls me flush up against his hard body. I can feel every dip and roll of his muscles when I run my hand down his chest.

He presses his lips to mine briefly, which leaves me wanting more before his smile sideswipes me, and my heart is about to beat out of my chest.

"Goodnight, little ballerina."

My body won't budge.

He gets back into the cab just as effortlessly as he got out. I manage to wave my fingers, "Until tomorrow…"

He's pulling the door shut, but right before it closes he states, "It's a date."

I anxiously fumble to get my phone out of my clutch, hurriedly typing out a text.

Happy New Year.

It takes a few minutes, but I get a reply when I walk into my hotel room. **Happy New Year indeed, ballerina.**

CHAPTER
Nine
date night

Noah
New Year's Day

IWAKE UP with one massive motherfucking hangover. I didn't think I drank that much; however, my body detests me this morning.

I'm pacing the length of the hotel room trying to figure out what to do for this date, impatient as all hell to see Heather again. Come hell or high water, I need to make this work.

I've never cooked a meal for anyone beside myself. All I know I'm good at cooking is pizza. She'll assume that I ordered that shit in, or that it was frozen.

Screw it. Pizza it is.

After a long steam shower to freshen up after last night, I dry off and check out of the hotel before heading down to my truck. I make a stop at the grocery store and the local farmers' market on the way back to my place in Tempe.

I want to make such an impression on her that she doesn't want to head back to New York. I don't want her 2,500 miles away. Could she live any farther from me? This shit is too stressful.

Deciding that my shit job of cleaning won't cut it, I call a professional cleaning company and tell them it's urgent. Within the next hour, the cleaners are at my place and scrubbing every fucking surface while I get the pizza together.

Somehow this woman has managed to come into the New Year with me after I fought hard to keep her out, but I've decided not to fight it anymore. Grabbing my phone I shoot her a quick text.

Are we still on for tonight?

The agonizing twelve minutes it takes for her to text me back was the longest twelve minutes of my life.

Oh definitely! When and where?

Good. How does 7 p.m. sound?

Sure! That's perfect.

I look forward to our date, Heather.

Shit. 6 p.m. The cleaning company finishes up then leaves after I pay them. Another five minutes pass before a text message comes in.

How about 7:01? ;)

Laughing at her witty side, I respond. **Damn. Screw 7 p.m. Get your ass here now.**

I'd love to, Noah, but I have one slight problem.

And what would that be?

You haven't given me your address.

Shit. I quickly type out the address and hit send as I step into a pair of jeans, deciding to go without socks or shoes this evening. Once I've got my shirt on, I grab my Eau de Lacoste Blanc cologne, spraying it onto my chest and forearms.

About twenty-five minutes later, there's a knock on my door. Knowing I'm roughly twenty minutes from her hotel, I look at my watch and smirk. She must have left almost immediately. I walk to the entrance hall, scanning the place before opening the door.

She's looking down at her feet and fidgeting nervously. She's in the sexiest pair of body-hugging leather leggings, which have these little brass zippers that run from her ankle and, halfway up her calf. Her deep turquoise blue shirt hangs past her flawless little ass, and I hate it. However, the V-neck running down her cleavage makes up for it. I have a clear view of her perfect tits.

"Fuck, you're adorable, you know that?" I say as I move aside. She looks up quickly and I love the blush that's forming on her cheeks. She steps through the threshold of my apartment and lightly places her hand on my chest.

"I'm going to make a swear jar for you," she says cheekily, as she walks farther into my apartment, her jade green eyes taking in my life.

"Hi, by the way," I say, as I lean against the wall in the entryway.

She's looking everywhere, but then her eyes find mine again and her genuine smile knocks the air out of my lungs, leaving me gasping.

"Hi to you too, stranger."

"You look beautiful, little ballerina. What can I get you to drink?" I ask gruffly, tugging at her hand to pull her into the kitchen with me, as she laughs at my sobriquet.

"Do you have any iced tea?"

"Yeah, I do." I swiftly push her back against the cold refrigerator, trapping her between my arms. "But first I'm going to take what I've wanted since the cab drove away last night."

She looks up at me through those long fucking lashes and her lips are parted. "What have you wanted, Noah?"

"This…" I bury my hand into her now straight dark-chocolate hair before taking her mouth, kissing her heatedly. Her body moves away from the fridge and closer to mine. I slip my hand down her blouse, to the small of her back, holding her against me. Her lips are soft and demanding as she lets out a soft cry then takes a quick intake of breath as if she wasn't expecting a kiss.

Damn, she tastes so good. I feel her petite hand slide up my chest and all my senses are heightened by her touch. I'm going to devour her tonight. The apartment is quiet; the only sounds that fill the space are the ones coming from our mouths.

My lips automatically move from hers down to her throat as a guttural growl escapes from my chest. Biting and sucking on her silk-like skin before I pull away, I attempt to bring myself back from her sexual allure.

"Do you still want that tea, ballerina?" My voice is raspier, thicker with want.

"What tea?" she asks breathlessly, blinking up at me with those striking green eyes, and smiles, pushing against my chest. "Ugh, you are so going to get it, Ryan." She moves out of my grip and walks over to where her purse sits.

"Get what?" I ask.

"You'll just have to wait and see."

"It better be worth the wait."

The oven goes off and I move to take the pizza out. "I made a Margherita pizza with fresh tomatoes from the farmers' market. Will you eat this?" I ask anxiously.

"You made that?" She sounds genuinely surprised.

"Hell yes, I made it. Not all men are lost in the kitchen." I turn and wink at her. "Why don't you pick out a movie and I'll bring the pizza over."

She nods enthusiastically and walks over to the couch in heels that any other woman would break their ankles in, but Heather pulls them off faultlessly. She bends forward to pick up the remote, giving me a good look at her ass.

I'm going to make her mine.

I can't stand the thought of any other man having her. Thinking of another man's hands on her makes my blood boil.

Heather

I PLOP DOWN on his larger-than-life couch, grabbing the remote, and turning on the TV. I decide on the movie and hit play as Noah brings the pizza and drinks over. This Greek god really can cook. My mouth is watering from the aroma—well, not only the aroma.

I move my hand to my neck where his lips were; a quick carnal shiver runs down my body. I take a deep breath to try and steady myself but my tender sex is throbbing. I'm in need of much more than a kiss.

"Go ahead and dig in," he says as he sits down next to me. He's close and I can smell his cologne. Oh my, he makes my head twirl.

Trying not to be so nervous, I move to the edge of the couch to grab a slice. "Mmm, I love fresh tomatoes." I feel his eyes move down the back of my body and to my ass. I think he has a thing for asses.

"Well? I'm waiting for your critique," he probes as I take a bite and groan in delight.

"Mmm, this is so delicious." Not only is this pizza good, but also the cook himself is mouthwatering. I look over at him and he's so stinking relaxed, sitting back against his couch, smirking. "What?" I ask, because he's just watching me.

Shaking his head as he picks up a slice of pizza, he says, "I'm still trying to grasp that you're here. In my apartment. I've wanted to have you alone and to myself since I saw you on stage."

I smile and tuck my hair behind my ears. "Oh really? You have a thing for tutus?" I take another bite then boldly reach over and steal a tomato off of his slice.

"First my bacon and now my tomatoes? Damn woman, you are risking your fingers. And, yeah, I was fond of your tutu, but I liked…like…you more. The rest could have been litany for all I know."

Pausing mid-chew to look at him, my heart is now in my throat. He was paying that much attention to me? Crap. I hope I didn't look like a fool on stage. Setting my unfinished slice on my plate, I ask, "Do you care if I take my shoes off?"

"Is this a harbinger of you nesting in my apartment?" He adds cockily, "I'm not going to stop you."

I laugh and slip off my heels, curling my feet up on the couch. "No," I reply, looking down and noticing his bare feet. I bite the inside of my cheek. I want to...*Heather, stop!*

"I wouldn't mind," he says quietly.

I stay quiet, not wanting to tell him that I wouldn't mind either. The movie continues in the background when I turn to face him. "I'd like to know more about you. What do you do?"

"And so the interrogations begin." He chuckles lightly then finishes his pizza before continuing. "I'm currently studying for the bar exam."

I'm sure my eyebrows shoot up to my hairline because I'm beyond surprised. An attorney? Then what would explain all of the muscles? In a split second, my mind wonders what Noah would look like shirtless. I squirm uncomfortably because the ache between my legs just intensified. I take a much needed breath and reply, "I wasn't expecting that."

He takes a drink and leans back, stretching his arm out behind me on the couch. "Most people don't," he says with a shrug. "I'll be sitting for the bar exam in February. I recently graduated from law school, and I'm ready to have all this shit over and done with."

My toes wiggle against the couch. "What kind of law do you want to practice?"

"I'm hoping to practice family law—marriages, adoptions, divorce, and all that shit." He's gazing at me with those ocean green eyes and neither one of us is watching the movie anymore—it's just background noise. Thank goodness because I'm sure he could hear my heart beating loudly if it were quiet in here.

"So that woman you were with at the show...is she your mom?" I ask with sincere curiosity.

"You could technically call her that. She adopted me as an infant. She took me in as her own when the adoption went through. Her name's Mae."

I think my heart just broke for this man. I'm not sure I want to dig any further. I feel horrible for asking, yet he doesn't seem upset by my question. "Well, she seems lovely."

"She is. She has her feisty moments, but what woman doesn't?" he adds jokingly.

I gasp at his obvious dig. "Hey!" Shoving my feet over and

pinching at his thigh with my toes.

"Shit, woman, calm yourself." He grabs hold of my ankle, wrapping his fingers around my leather leggings.

I bite the inside of my cheek when his warm fingers brush the arch of my foot. My, his hands are hot! Those fingers send sparks into my body. He's so strong; I just know he could manhandle me in bed. I internally fan myself because I'm evidently flushed.

"I'm not sure if I can calm myself right now." *HEATHER! Did that really just come out of your mouth?*

"I don't blame you." His fingers move to the little brass zipper on my leggings; he pulls up on it and toys with it, teasing me.

I try for nonchalant. "Undressing me already?" Geez, I so wish he would.

His eyes shoot up to mine. I think he's shocked at first, but then a slow, cocky grin forms on his face as he starts pulling the zipper up my leg. "You'd like that, wouldn't you?"

I smile a very sexy one of my own. "Maybe. Maybe not." He's caressing my ankle with his thumb now, and I'm screaming inside.

"I'd say you're well on your way to enjoying it. You keep squirming. Hell, and I'm well on my way to this foot fetish if this is the only part of your body I get to touch."

I...holy crap! My body is buzzed with anticipation when a moan fills the room. A sex scene is unfolding on his large flat-screen TV.

My eyes flicker to the screen for a moment. Do I do this? Do I make this leap? This isn't going to turn into anything—we live too far apart. *It's just for tonight, Heather: let go and do what you want to do for a change.* Looking back over at him, I see his eyes are fixed on me. "Who said you couldn't touch more?" His eyes dance down my body and I'm sweltering.

"That was all the invitation I needed." With his free hand he reaches up and turns the lamp off. My eyes take a second to adjust to the darkness, and when they do, he's running his big tanned hand up my calf and to my thigh. I go weak.

For the love of the color pink, he's taking his time as his hand works slowly up my thigh. Is he toying with me on purpose? It's working—oh, it is so working. I'm practically panting. He parts my legs and moves up my body, his hand still resting on my thigh. My breasts are heaving drastically as I lose control of my breath.

"Tell me when to stop," he says in a low voice.

I can only nod. I'd sound completely desperate if I used my voice. I am desperate. I want him so badly. It's been so long for me and he's pushing every hot button I have. My stomach is tight with anticipation and we're still fully clothed. He lowers his body to mine and I feel some of his weight. I can hear myself breathing. I want him. I want this. Possibly more than I've ever wanted a connection with somebody before.

The hand that was on my thigh is now roaming north to my butt. He pushes his hand between the couch and me, finally cupping my ass. His touches are drowning my panties. My legs are trembling. I'm so nervous, but so turned on. He definitely knows what foreplay is. And holy hell, does he take his sweet time.

He's face to face with me when I run my hands into his soft dark hair as he brings his mouth down to mine. He's inching his hand up under my thin blouse and the skin-to-skin contact has me arching my back off of the couch. When he reaches my black lace bra, his fingers find the clasp, undoing it effortlessly.

Oh my, a man who knows what he's doing. I cannot believe how turned on I am.

He's going straight for what he wants. Maybe he's not an ass man...maybe he likes...oh, who cares. His tongue skillfully strokes mine and I'm loving how soft his touches are, but for some reason I feel like there's something behind his touches. Something he's hiding.

The moans coming from the TV only intensify what's happening between us. He licks my teeth then pulls back to trace his tongue across my lower lip. I almost come. He hasn't even touched me there yet and I'm about to erupt! I can sense that he has a smug grin on his gorgeous face: he knows exactly what he's doing to me. He moves his lips to my ear and whispers, "I want to see you, little ballerina."

That's when I notice it.

The hard, pulsing shaft constrained in his jeans. His lengthy penis presses against me as he lowers his hips to mine. He's so incredibly hard for me. Just for me. I did this to him.

My breath comes out in a rush. I want him to touch me so badly. I want him everywhere. He starts kissing down my neck and I can't take it. His descent is slow, but I know where he wants to go. "Where do you want my tongue, Heather?"

The couch dips when he moves lower, playing with the hem of my leggings, which are too high up my stomach. His fingers run under the hem and my body jolts violently. "Please..." I hear myself say almost in a moan. He ducks his head down as his hands push my blouse up. I'm about to hyperventilate as his lips drop to my stomach. He's reveling in playing with me. My hips rock as I push his hand up under my shirt. I almost don't recognize my own voice: it's so erotic. "Touch me, Noah," I plead.

"Tell me where."

Without looking, he moves my blouse up and off of my body, not waiting for my answer. I pull on it and anxiously get my hands out of the sleeves before throwing it onto the floor. He's kissing my hips while he looks up at me. I'm fumbling to get my bra off: my nipples are painfully hard and tender, waiting for his touch. His eyes travel up to my breasts when I finally rid them of my bra.

I'm winded again when his tongue darts out and licks around my navel. My stomach clenches. Agonizingly slowly, he traces his tongue all the way up to my breasts, to my tender nipple and... oh! His hot breath surrounds my left nipple as he takes it into his mouth. He's deftly sucking and nipping and I'm gasping. He moves to my right nipple and pays as much attention to it as he did my left, before kissing back down to my hips. He growls in approval as his fingers edge my leggings down, revealing my black lace cheeksters. I'm so frenzied I just want to push them down for him.

I'm suddenly grateful that I treated myself to a Brazilian strip wax for Christmas.

I've never wanted someone like I want him to enrapture me right now. There's another moan. How long is this sex scene? Surprised, I realize it came from me, not the television.

Once he manages to get my leggings off, he lifts his body to study me. I'm lying on my back and eyeing him. I tense up when I feel his fingertips graze my stomach with the lightest of touches. Licking my lips, I watch this beautiful man lean down and angle his head. My eyes flicker from his parted lips and back to his eyes in the dim light. My heart is about to beat out of my chest and I wish he'd just put me out of my misery, kiss me like he does—like it's the first time, every time. He's gliding the backs of his knuckles over the bare skin around my navel and I'm writhing with anticipation.

My breath catches when I feel him slip his fingers under my panties, teasing my hips with the tip of his finger. What is he doing to me? I'll beg if he wants me to. I'll do anything he asks. Chewing on my cheek nervously, I'm startled when his deep, raspy voice invades my dirty thoughts.

"Are you okay?" He breathes into my ear.

I nod anxiously and he starts kissing down my stomach toward my sex. He feels like a thunderstorm rolling over my body, electrifying every inch of me. Luscious lips glide across my skin, leaving thunderous quakes behind as he moves to kiss his next desired spot.

I'm trembling with need as he works my body over with only his lips, bringing me to the verge of pleasure again and again. How is he not affected by this? I'm a trembling mess and he's so composed. Suddenly, he stops and kneels up. It seems to happen in slow motion, the way he grabs his shirt and pulls it over his head. I try not to stare as he lays it over the back of the couch. My eyes roam across his perfectly sculpted chest and my mouth goes dry.

He's got the sexiest nipples I have ever seen on a man...and he is all man. Before he's able to move back down to me, I look farther down. Oh. My. God. The front of his jeans are tented, and I'm staring in amazement. I have no way to describe what I'm seeing other than...massive.

Oh yes...he's very much affected.

As he leans down to place his lips against mine, I hear and feel the rumble at the back of his throat. The storm continues to brew as he teases me. He isn't touching me there, but he's oh so close.

He kneels up and pulls my cheeksters down my legs. He removes one of my legs from my lace panties, but not the other, leaving them at my ankle like an ankle bracelet. His mouth is on me, sucking and nipping on my toes, moving to the arch of my foot. He takes a deep breath, breathing in the scent from my panties before kissing and licking back up my calf to my thigh where he sinks his teeth in. I gasp at the much welcomed intrusion, when his voice fills the room.

"I can smell how turned on you are and it makes my cock throb, Heather." He settles himself between my legs, spreading them wider apart. Then he's there, touching my now wet folds, caressing me in ways that make my body break out in goose bumps.

His raspy voice rips through the silence as his index finger runs down the only strip of hair on me. "I like this."

I writhe underneath him, wanting him to give me some sort of relief. He seems to read my mind as he gradually pushes his middle finger up and into me. He pulls it out then repeats the action, moving even slower the second time around.

I'm about to catch fire. Ignite under his electrifying touch.

He's watching his finger disappear inside of me when his warm tongue brushes against my clitoris, paralyzing me. An almost inaudible whimper escapes me as my eyes flitter shut. I can't stand to watch him relish me. His tongue works my clitoris, flicking, circling, and then he sucks on me. I'm unable to hold it in anymore when he growls and snaps his tongue back and forth as he adds a second finger inside of me.

Pointing my toes as my body stiffens, an outpouring of pure, raw ardor takes over my body.

A soul-shattering orgasm rips through my being.

Pure ecstasy courses through my veins.

He's making me come like a freight train.

My body thrashes underneath him, but his mouth stays on me as if he wants everything I have and more. He's running his tongue over my folds again before I even have time to recover.

"Noah..." I whimper. My breasts feel heavy and full.

He cockily flicks his tongue against my folds before answering, "Yes, ballerina?"

"I..." Words fail me.

"That good, huh?" he questions in a low, sexy voice.

Looking down my body at him, I can see his lips glistening with my arousal and suddenly I'm ready again. I can't believe he's still half dressed. Does he not want me? I'm starting to feel self-conscious. My voice is soft but I still sound needy. "Say something."

"You're fucking beautiful, ballerina." He kisses his way up my body, kissing each of my breasts on his way up to my lips. He locks his lips with mine so I can taste myself, only pulling away after our tongues desperately sought and found each other. "You taste unbelievable."

All of a sudden the TV goes black from being stagnant for too long; I can barely see the outline of his jaw anymore so I move my hand up and cup his cheek. Feeling a little braver in the dark, I tell him, "I've never experienced an orgasm like that before."

He takes my mouth again and groans. "Would you like another?" he asks, biting my lip seductively and his right hand moves to cup my breast.

Smiling against his lips, I shake my head. "It's your turn, Greek god." I reach out and caress his chest with my fingers, touching his bare skin for the first time. I slide my hands down his abs to the sexy V that leads down to his hard bulge.

"I'm not sure you can handle this."

He's so cocky and I love it. My fingers run along his waistband and he sits up quickly. I can barely see his arms moving, yet I can't mistake the sound of a zipper being pulled down. I can't wait to have him in my mouth.

I hear his jeans drop to the floor; I'm not sure if he's naked or not, but I move toward him. He cups my face and kisses me hard before letting go.

"Enjoy yourself, ballerina. I know I will, with that beautiful mouth of yours."

His tongue flashes across my bottom lip and I'm dying to know what he tastes like. Biting the inside of my cheek, I kneel between his legs. His calves are toned, muscular, and covered in a light dusting of hair. I don't hesitate to lean forward, kissing down his jaw, my hands caressing his tight pecs and down his well-defined abs. Dropping lower, my breasts brush against his erection and I can't take it anymore. I kneel down on the plush rug, positioning my body between his hard thighs as I reach up for his cock and…oh.

Oh… he's…

Enormous. Heavy. Thick.

I can feel the veins that run to the head of his cock. He's already pulsing. My mouth is watering. From just my touch, I can tell that he's impeccably manscaped.

I slowly move my hand down his extensive shaft to his balls, cupping them with one hand while I grasp his shaft with the other. I graze my lips against it as I move my hand up and down exceptionally slowly. I flick the frenulum with the tip of my tongue and he grunts noisily. I'm getting wet from the sounds he's making and I love how sensitive he is there. I circle the head of his penis with my lips, and my jaw feels strained…but I want more of him. I start taking his heavy shaft into my mouth, one inch at a time.

I start pumping my fist up and down as my lips meet my fist, setting a steady rhythm for my mouth and hand. He's getting so worked up, I get a taste of his sea-salty pre-come and I moan against his shaft, sending vibrations all the way down to his balls, knowing the sensation will bring him to his knees.

I can't take him all the way into my mouth—I don't know what woman could. He's more than three of my hands fisted in length but his thickness is what I can't get over. I've never seen or felt anything like it before. Suddenly I'm caught daydreaming about how much come he'll give me and I'm so wet right now. Pulling him from my mouth, I start kissing and sucking on the base of his shaft…running my tongue all the way up to the tip, following his thick veins…gently, I graze my teeth against the head.

This time when I take him into my mouth, I circle my lips around his head and gently bite down as I lightly scrape my nails down his thick thighs.

"OH SHIT!" he cries out.

I hum as I take what I can of his shaft into my mouth again; his entire penis is wet from my mouth and his pre-come. Inspired by my lust for him, I want to give him an experience he'll never forget.

Situating myself so I'm able to take him a little deeper, my lips move up and down his length. Our body temperatures are rapidly rising as I tighten the grip of my mouth around him, attempting to hollow out my cheeks, but he's just so big!

The erotic sounds of arousal that are coming from his lips make me moan in return. We share his pleasure—he wants me to enjoy this too. I let go of his balls and search for his hand; he tries to lace his fingers with mine, but I decide on something I know will make him go wild.

I stop sucking and pumping him long enough to say, "Show me how fast you want it." Taking him back into my mouth, I place his hand on the back of my head.

His fingers tangle with my hair, gripping onto strands as he grunts and starts to show me how he likes it. He gently pushes on the top of my head until I'm following his rhythm. I'm giving him a devilish look, not caring if he can see me or not. The sensual connection between us tells me that he knows exactly what I want.

I can hear him gritting his teeth as he hisses out, "I'm going to come in your dirty little mouth…stop now…if you don't want it."

The moan that escapes me is his final undoing. Circling my hand around his heavy balls, I lightly tug at this highly sensitive part of his body.

I want him…all of him…and he gives it to me. His fingers clench in my hair and his hips jerk. He starts coming violently and his thighs clench. I'm swallowing everything I can, yet I feel his come seep from my lips. His cock twitches again and it sends another surge of heat down my throat.

The pure satisfaction I get from pleasuring him gives me such a high. I swallow everything, licking my lips as I kneel back.

"Damn, Heather." He's breathless. "That…might have been the best head I have ever had."

A blush makes my cheeks rosy, but I can't help it. This Greek god is so much man…I want him again. He pulls me up and kisses me softly—as if he's saying thank you without muttering the words.

CHAPTER
Ten
libidinous excellence

Heather

H IS STRONG, ATHLETIC body lies sated on the couch as I put
my bra back on. We've completely worn each other out and I
don't think we could manage another world-shattering orgasm. I
hear him get up and pull on an article of clothing and find myself
hoping that it's not anything below the waist. I want to see the
monster I was sucking on.

I hear a click and the lamp bathes the living room in a soft light.
He's wearing black boxer briefs that sit low on his hips, and all I can
see is that immense bulge.

"Come here," he utters.

I get up and take my panties off of my ankle then walk over to
where he's standing. He cups my face with one hand, and I lean into
his touch as he inspects me.

"Are you okay?" he asks with genuine concern.

All I can do is nod because I'm more than okay. "I need to go
clean up," I say in a whisper.

His smile makes my stomach clench. He leans down and kisses me briefly. "The bathroom is through my bedroom." He's pointing to one of the few doors in the apartment. I move away from him and start walking over, but stop when he pats my ass.

"So you are an ass man," I say coyly.

"Possibly. I've never been one before, but with your perfect little ass...how can I not be?"

I shrug innocently and walk into his bedroom. I shut my eyes and inhale his scent. He always smells so good. There's not much in the room other than a king-sized bed, the two lamps, one on each nightstand, which light up the room, and a huge black and white painting of the scales of justice hung above his bed. It looks like an extension of his headboard. It must be one of a kind, and unquestionably impressive. The scales are an afterthought in the painting. They are so faded in the background that someone who doesn't appreciate art wouldn't notice them.

Across the bedroom from me is his dark wooden desk, piled high with law books and notebooks. I must say, I'm liking how studious he is. I walk into his bathroom and shut the door.

After I clean up and feel refreshed, I put my panties on and wash my hands. I'm eyeing the cologne bottle he's left on the countertop. I make a mental note of the name, which I know I'm going to forget. Crap!

Cracking the bathroom door open, I call out, "Noah? Would you mind bringing me my purse, please?" Moments later there's a knock on the bathroom door. I open it just enough to get my purse in then shut it. "Thank you."

"No problem. I'm opening a beer—do you want one?"

"Oh yes, please."

I'm digging in my purse for something...anything...when I come across an old perfume strip from the Phoenix mall. I squeal excitedly as I grab a pen from the bottom of my Burberry tote. I think this perfume test strip is from something I sampled when I was buying this very outfit.

I quickly write down the name on his cologne bottle on the thin white strip then spray the cologne on it a few times before putting the test strip in a safe pocket in my purse. I want to remember him, to remember how he smells. There's an ache in my chest, and I'm not entirely sure why, but no man has ever made me feel so alive before.

After composing myself, I walk out in just my lace bra and cheeksters to the living room, where he's waiting for me on the couch in just those sexy, tight boxer briefs.

"Thanks for letting me use your bathroom."

He winks and holds up a beer bottle. "Not a problem." Taking the beer from him, I look around for my leggings and blouse, but I don't see them. "Where..?"

"Yeah, you won't find them. We're staying just like this. Exposed."

Biting the inside of my cheek, I nod and sit down next to him. "Fine by me. Did you enjoy yourself?" I ask quickly before taking a sip of my beer, trying to block the blush that appears. My libido is in overdrive.

He nods and adjusts his hefty, substantial, abundant, pulsing cock.

"You're okay with just oral?" Oh my. My questions are getting rather particular.

"I am. Are you?" he questions with a cocked eyebrow.

I shrug. "I am...for now."

"Are we going back to the interrogation room?"

"Why not? Is it bad that I want to know how many women have been lucky enough to have you?"

He takes a long drink from his beer, like he's purposely postponing his answer, or completely avoiding the question.

"That many, huh?"

When he doesn't respond beyond shaking his head as he carefully puts the empty beer bottle down, I try again. "Noah? You have before? You know...right?"

The sexiest smile forms on his face and I even want to lick his teeth. He leisurely shakes his head no. There's something there, behind that confident smile...embarrassment maybe? I can't even believe what he's saying to me. I pick my jaw up off the floor and attempt to talk.

"Shut up!" I say disbelievingly. "N-Never?" I stutter.

He says nothing.

"Why not?" I blurt out before my filter catches it.

He cocks his head to the side with that panty-dropping smile and I can tell he doesn't want to say why. Quickly, I add, "I mean... that's..." And my words fall off there.

What in hell do you say when the most gorgeous man you've ever laid eyes on tells you that he's never slept with anyone? I'm suddenly the one embarrassed and I feel my cheeks flush. If he calls me out on it, I'm blaming all the alcohol.

"I'd rather not force myself onto..." He pauses, "...into a woman. I'd need to warm her up first and every woman I've tried with can't take much more than the foreplay, never mind my cock. I'd give you more details, but I doubt you'd want to hear them."

I take another drink and it's well needed. I peek back up at him through my lashes and he's already staring at me.

CHAPTER
Eleven
quid pro quo

Noah

I HAVEN'T BEEN able to sleep since she left. It's become another sleepless night. Her question is playing on repeat in my head: "Noah? You have before? You know…right?"

FUCK!

My gift to women and fucking personal curse—an equal substitution. She hasn't contacted me in the last three days. I don't blame her. Who the hell wants to be with a man who is so well-endowed that it completely strips his sex life from him? Not her. Not Heather Lane.

I should be studying, but instead I've been a moping son of a bitch. My phone vibrates on my nightstand and I grab it, hoping it will be her. When it's not, I groan and want to fling the damn phone across the room.

Hi, my son. I hope you are doing well. I have not heard from you since you went back to your apartment. Alisha at the diner said she saw you with a very pretty, young brunette on New

Year's Eve. You know, you should really be taking Alisha on a date, not some strange girl.

I text back. **Hi. I'm fine. I've been busy studying and it wasn't a date. And I'm certainly not interested in Alisha. I have to go. I'll stop by soon.**

I don't want to know how long it took her to type all of that out, but right now I'd rather wallow in my self-pity than anyone else's.

An hour passes and I'm finally showered and dressed. After trying to sit down and study, I decide to go to the local library. On my way out, I grab the mail and start opening it in my truck as it starts to rain.

I eye a large bubbled envelope and put the rest of the mail down. Running my car key through the top to open it, I pull out a large stack of papers. Flipping through it, I can tell it's my application for the character and fitness test I submitted to the Committee on Examinations, and Committee on Character and Fitness at the Supreme Court of Arizona. The examining authorities seek extensive and in-depth information on all applicants. They check things like personal history all the way to academic dishonesty.

I turn the pack of paper around in my hands and read the opening letter.

THE SUPREME COURT OF ARIZONA

Committee on Character and Fitness

IN THE MATTER OF BAR APPLICANT NBR-9141-011

Submitted: November 15th

Opinion Issued: December 27th

Applicant NBR-9141-011;

Noah Bradley Ryan, of Tempe, Arizona, for the Committee on Character and Fitness.

A per curiam decision. The applicant seeks admission to the Arizona Bar. The standing committee on character and fitness of the Arizona Supreme Court filed a report recommending the applicant be denied admission to the Arizona Bar exam. Attached is an order instructing the applicant a cause why his application is being denied. Due to acts involving dishonesty and misrepresentation, applicant NBR-9141-011 is flagged and denied the Character and Fitness certificate...

I stop reading then read it over a few more times before slamming my fist into the middle console of my truck. How the fuck am I denied? THIS IS BULLSHIT! Everything I submitted was true, every last damn dated document.

I get out of my truck and storm into my apartment, forcefully slamming the door shut. I grab a beer from the fridge before sitting down at the kitchen island to read the rest of this nineteen-page document. The document states that I have to meet with a character and fitness examiner this week to discuss my denial.

Four beers and one denial document later, I'm lying on the floor looking up at the fan rotating on the ceiling. My birth certificate is fake? It was state-issued when the adoption went through. My hand forms a fist around the copy of my birth certificate they sent back to me, crumpling up the piece of shit and hauling it across the room.

I know I shouldn't do this since I've been drinking, but I grab my phone to shoot a text to Coen: **Hey fuckface. Do you still have that FBI contact?**

His reply is immediate. **Yeah man. His name is Joel Aldrich. Everything good? You plan on tracking down that hot piece of ass from NYE?**

No. My character and fitness test for the bar was denied. I need to figure out what the hell is going on.

Oh fuck, man.

He gives me Joel's contact details. I save them before calling the New York City adoption agency. I'm put on hold for forty minutes and transferred from person to person. An endless tirade on my part ensues as they search for my adoption documents, which will have my assigned birth certificate attached. I have the entire fucking agency in a panic looking for my fucking adoption records. I know they aren't closed because my birth parents left me to die.

The director of the agency is now on the phone with me telling me that there are no records of my adoption at all. They have checked the records for the state of Arizona as well, and they have come up with nothing. I thank the guy and hang up.

Where the hell do I go from here?

I'M PACING MY bedroom, waiting for a phone call from Joel, Coen's FBI contact. My Galaxy vibrates in my hand and I answer, overcome with anger.

"About fucking time!" I spit out harshly.

"Noah?" I hear Heather's soothing voice say.

"Shit…I'm sorry, ballerina. I've been waiting on a phone call."

"Swear jar." Her giggle fills my ear and I can't fight a smile. "Wait, is everything okay?" she asks, sensing that there's something off in my voice.

"I've just had a rough day. What about you? I haven't heard from you."

She groans. "I'm sorry. When I was leaving Arizona, I stopped to get Starbucks. I ended up burning my tongue on my latte, so I took off the lid while driving to cool it down. Then, my dumb butt dropped my phone in the drink."

I start laughing at how dramatically she's telling me her little tale.

"I'm serious! I didn't want to stop at a phone store on the way because I was afraid I'd lose your number. I had to get home to my technology-buff neighbor who helped me get all of my contacts onto my new iPhone." She takes a deep breath and sighs.

"I'm sorry about your phone, but I'm glad you made it home. I was getting concerned."

I think I can hear her smile, making my mood worse because I want to fucking see it. My smile. Made for me.

"Concerned about me, Noah?" She giggles. "I made that good of an impression?"

She jokes, but I'm serious. "Yeah, you did. I'm pissed that I can't just show up on your doorstep and kiss the hell out of you," I say, as I pick up her gold ring that she left in my bathroom.

She's quiet for a long second; I want her to speak.

"I wish you could too," she finally says.

I growl into the receiver as I form a fist around her ring. "I know. You left a gold ring at my place. No one else but you and I have been in here, so it has to be yours. It's got a minute pink pearl in the center."

I hear her breathe a sigh of relief on the other end. "Oh thank God! I thought I'd lost it."

"I could mail it to you, but it obviously means something to you. I wouldn't want it getting lost in the mail. So I can hold onto it until I see you again…if you'd like." I'm sitting down on the end of my bed, turning the ring around in my fingers, wondering if it's from that prick at the ballet.

"No, don't mail it. I'd like a personal delivery."

"I can arrange that since I won't be sitting for the bar in February after all. Are you going on tour soon, or staying in New York?"

"Wait, what? Why aren't you taking it?" She sounds concerned.

"I received a letter a few hours ago telling me I've been denied my character and fitness test due to dishonesty and misrepresentation. It's got something to do with my birth certificate and adoption documentation. Apparently, there is none."

There's a genuine concern in her reply and it makes me want to drop every fucking thing I'm doing and go to her. "Oh Noah, I'm so sorry. There has to be something you can do, right?"

"I'm going to try. I'm waiting for someone from the FBI to call. Coen, the douche you met at the club, knows someone. Once I figure out what the hell is going on, I'll have to appeal their decision." Damn, this is going to take forever.

"Do you want to talk about it?" she asks me in the softest voice.

"No, not right now anyway. I appreciate it though. Tell me about this ring. Why's it so important to you?" I ask, wanting to talk about anything, but this damn bar exam.

I wait for her to say something. I pull my phone back to make sure she's still on the line. "Uhm…it was my mother's."

"Was your mother's? I'm sorry, Heather."

She sighs heavily into the phone. "Ah, it's okay. It happened a long time ago."

I find myself hoping her father was able to be there for her growing up, since her mother couldn't. "How old were you? Shit, we don't have to talk about this."

"I was twelve. It's okay. I don't mind."

Twelve? Damn. "Do you mind if I ask what happened?" I hope I'm not pushing her too far, but I'm glad we're talking.

"Uhm...give me a second?" She asks and I wait. Suddenly I hear a cork being pulled from a bottle. Shit. Have I caused her to drink?

"Okay, I'm back. I need a little liquid courage. When I was twelve, my parents went on their annual anniversary getaway to a small island just off of the coast of British Columbia. The only convenient way to get there is to fly in on a floatplane." She pauses to take a drink, I think.

"I'm listening."

"The plane crashed just off of the coast. Both my mother and father died instantly."

Holy fuck. I scrub my hand down my face. "Shit, Heather, I'm sorry." A million and one questions pop into my head.

"It's okay."

"What were their names?" I ask.

"Ayla and Mark," she replies softly. "That ring was her engagement ring."

I look down at it in my palm. "I won't let anything happen to it."

"Thank you. I must have left it there when I used your bathroom."

"That's where I found it. I'd like to kiss your pain away, ballerina." Fuck. No matter the shit that happened to me today, she's all I'm worried about right now.

I hear her demeanor change almost instantly. "I wish you could too. You're very talented with that mouth of yours."

Smirking, I reply, "The feeling is mutual. When can our lips meet again?"

She's laughing and I find myself smiling. "Are you saying you want to see me again, Noah?"

Fuck, I want her. "I'm informing you that I'm coming to see you. I'm asking when you have time for me." I hear a gasp on her end then a lot of noise.

"Oh sh-shoot. Really?!"

"Heather? What happened?" Staying very quiet, I'm trying to hear what's going on.

She's mumbling into the phone. "Oh, I spilled my wine. Are you really coming?"

"Careful now, ballerina. Give me a day or two and I'll let you know when I can come up. But yes, if you'd like." I close my eyes as I speak. "I want you, Heather."

"YES! I'd like." She all but shouts into the phone and I have to chuckle.

"Damn, you're adorable."

"Swear jar!" she yells out.

"It's a good thing I don't have one, or I'd be broke." My phone beeps: I have an incoming call from Joel. "Ballerina, I have to go. I'll text you later."

"Okay. Bye, Noah."

"Goodbye, beautiful."

I end the phone call with Heather and answer Joel's. After I introduce myself, I inform him of my issue. He asks for my details, anything and everything I know about my adoption. He tells me he'll get back to me when he finds something, which won't be long, he assures me.

CHAPTER
Twelve
burning desire

Heather

A S SOON AS I hang up with Noah, I bust out in a happy dance, squealing excitedly and throwing myself onto the bed. I'm so freaking excited! He said he's coming to see me. I'm so addicted to him already. This is not good, but I can't help it.

I want him.

I've completely forgotten about the *Gevrey-Chambertin* pinot noir that I spilled on my carpet, and scroll through my phone contacts to call Dani.

She answers on the first ring. "Heather! I was just about to call you."

"Sister! How was your Christmas and New Year's?"

"It was so good, but I missed you oh so much. We got back to LA about an hour ago and I had to speak to you," she blurts out excitedly.

I can't help but giggle. Even though Dani and I are complete opposites on most things, we still have our enthusiasm in common.

"So..? Tell me, what did he get you for Christmas?"

"Brannon got me the most gorgeous Prada bag. Did you get my package yet?"

I pause. Crap. "Uhmm...no. I still haven't picked up my mail. I had it held for a little while longer."

"Why haven't you picked it up yet? You've been home for over a week."

Squeezing my eyes shut and biting the inside of my cheek, I answer, "Well, actually I just got back. I stayed in Phoenix longer than I anticipated."

"HEATHER LANE, you hate hot weather over Christmas. Who is he?"

Busted. Crap, she knows me too well. "WHAT? What makes you think it's a guy?"

"The fact that I can hear you smiling and dancing around from here. Tell me who he is!" she demands.

I can't lie to her, so I fess up. "Okay, fine. He's so F'ing hot, Dani. I can't even begin to describe how gorgeous this man is. And ugh...cocky! But in a good way. Not like Nik." I make a gagging sound.

"Oh shit! Did you sleep with him? How big is he? Did he make you come? Tell me!"

Clapping my hand over my eyes as I lay on my bed. "Ugh, Dani, seriously? No, I didn't sleep with him."

"BUT HE MADE YOU COME? Heather! I need a picture of this hunky man. Wait...he's in Arizona?"

"Did I say that? And yes. He lives too far away for any type of anything. But that's why I was in Phoenix."

"You didn't say I was wrong. Awww...so you want something with him? My little sister has a mad crush on someone."

I roll my eyes and sit up, looking out my bedroom windows. "Oh stop. I do not. I was just having fun for once."

"Then why are you so happy? Are you ever going to see him again? Did you get his number?"

Sighing into the phone, I flop back down and rest against my pillows. "I don't know. Maybe, and yes. He says he wants to come and see me but...you know how guys are. Chances are I won't hear from him again."

"Oh sister. I can tell you're really into him. If he's just another frog we'll find you someone else. Brannon's coworker here in LA is pretty hot. He's from London and he has the sexiest English accent."

Scrunching my nose up, I say, "Oh please, no more accents. I'm pretty much ruined because of Nik. Oh and by the way, he went into full-on jerk mode at the last show on Christmas Eve. It was so humiliating."

"I'm sorry. You deserve so much better. Someone Mom and Dad would have been proud to call their son-in-law. I love you. Come visit me soon?"

I look down at my hand where my mother's ring used to be and hope like hell that I at least get my ring back, if nothing else. "I love you too. Maybe I'll visit in a couple months. Tell Brannon I said hi."

"I will. Call me soon. I have to come...I mean run. What?" She giggles and hangs up.

I laugh because she's so ridiculous. Putting my phone down, I'm talking to myself, "Ah, Dani, what am I going to do with you?"

I rush downstairs and out to the front desk in my building's lobby to pick up my mail. There's a package from Dani and some other bills. When I get back upstairs, I open the small bubbled envelope to find a little box inside with a Christmas card. I quickly read over it, squealing. I open the box, which reveals a pink pouch. Inside of the pink pouch is a gorgeous, delicate necklace with an elegant letter H dangling from the side.

My sister knows me well.

THE NEXT WEEK crawls by. I'm back in the dance studio, rehearsing for an audition I have in two weeks. I'm distracted and my ballet mistress can tell. I haven't heard from him since that night on the phone and I'm cranky because of it.

I'm in the middle of a pirouette when I fall flat on my butt. I bring my hand down and slap the wooden floor before getting up and moving to the barre. I position myself on the barre to stretch, first for my left leg then again to my other leg as thoughts of Noah's lips on my skin fill my mind.

I step back from the barre and place my hands on top of my head. My reflection is staring me down. I hate that I let this Greek god get to me; I hate that I let him in.

"Heather, I don't know what is bothering you, but you need to get your head into your routine!" my ballet mistress, Flora Lindsay, yells out.

"I'm going home, Ms. Lindsay—I can't do this today. My heart is not in it." My heart hasn't been present since Arizona. He has it and I doubt he even cares. Asshole.

I walk over to my bag that sits in the corner of the room. Sitting down next to it, I look over at Mistress Lindsay apologetically while taking off my pointe shoes and slipping on my Sorel snow boots. Suddenly I wish I were in warmer weather—somewhere like Phoenix. No, Heather. Don't do that to yourself again.

On my way out of the studio, I put on my pink peacoat and head out in the snow to my car. My drive home is miserable and I plan on spending the rest of my day at home in front of my huge fireplace. I pull up to my apartment building and drive into the car-sized elevator that whisks me up to the nineteenth floor. The doors slide open, allowing me to pull forward into one of my parking spots.

I look over at my phone and it's like an annoying reminder that he hasn't called. I've decided that I'm done waiting and chalk up our New Year's Day to a silly fling. Feeling so crappy about myself, I get out of my car and go inside.

Pouring myself a larger than necessary glass of wine before sitting down in front of the fireplace, I put on Dear John to try and lose myself and forget him.

Reaching over and grabbing my bag of gummy bears, I pick out the white ones and eat them first. My eyes keep flickering to my phone. So I just do it.

I pick it up and send him a text: **Hey. Just mail me the ring**

please. I attach my address to the text.

Tossing my phone off to the side, I'm feeling a little better now that I've gotten that off my chest.

CHAPTER
Thirteen
his misfortune

Noah

A LL HELL HAS broken loose. My world has crumbled and gone to shit. How the hell can any of this be true? I'm racking my brain for any signs that I should have noticed throughout the years. Anything. However, I can't remember anything that I should have detected. She always valued kindness and harmony, even honesty.

She was my protector. She saved me. She stole me.

The endless parade of questions swamps me. She's my mother, my guardian angel.

My hands form into hard, unbreakable fists just as my cell comes to life with a phone call from Joel.

"Joel, tell me this shit is not true," I demand.

"I'm going to need you to calm down, Noah. This situation has gotten out of control. I've had to open up five other kidnapping files under the name of Mae Ryan."

"Five? Are you fucking with me? Is this some sort of sick joke?"

"I'm afraid not. Have you spoken to her since I told you what

I've dug up?" he asks in a concerned voice.

"No, I haven't spoken to anyone."

"Good. I've just emailed you a picture of her mug shot from thirty-two years ago. Check it now and tell me if you recognize her."

I open my laptop and wait for it to turn on then open up the email. A black-and-white picture with the word 'WANTED' scrolled underneath it fills my screen. I'm staring at a woman who has a psychotic look in her eyes. I know without having to inspect the picture any further that this woman staring back at me is Mae.

Mae. My mother.

Joel's voice breaks the silence, "Noah? Are you still on the line?"

"Yeah. I'm here. That's her," I say curtly.

"I was hoping I was wrong about this shit. She's been on the run for thirty-two years. Thirty-two-motherfucking years."

"How is that even possible? How the hell has no one noticed?" I'm getting pissed as I look at the photo. I know that look in her eyes. She gets it when I piss her off or shit doesn't go her way. It's her damned wild side—the side of her I never understood.

"The records say that the trail went cold. The five cases before yours were all newborns—infants taken straight from the maternity ward at a hospital. All five of them were Caucasian girls. The infants were said to be found in and around dumpsters along the FDR on the Upper East Side in Manhattan."

I run my hand over my jaw and take a seat on my couch, feeling like my legs are going to give out.

"The only child she kept was you. It must have had something to do with the babies' gender. That's the only difference I am able to find between you and the other infants. Her first victim was a four-hour-old female." He pauses to read more of the records. "All of them were just hours old. The FBI has footage of her posing as a nurse in the baby nurseries and NICU's."

"I don't want to hear any more. Who am I, really? Can you answer that? Where do I come from?"

"I'm going to have to do a lot more digging to get you that answer. Hundreds of kidnappings are reported each year."

"Well, figure this shit out."

"Noah, I will, but I need to hand over what I've found to someone who can deal with this in more detail. I'll find your birth parents, but when it comes to Mae, I'm afraid I won't have any say in it."

"What do you mean, you won't have any say? What if I choose not to press charges?"

Hell. Press charges? Everything Mae has ever done and said to me has been a lie. She didn't find me in a dumpster. She was the sick bitch who put week-old infants into dumpsters. I was never in a dumpster. I was taken from my parents.

All these years I've loathed the thought of my birth parents, when they were, in actuality, the innocent party. I was ripped from my mother's arms into this…fuck. I can't.

Joel interrupts my racing thoughts. "The federal government will be pressing charges whether you do, or not. Due to the age of the case, New York State cannot prosecute, and Arizona State is unable to press charges because the crime was not committed in Arizona, only in New York. Once I hand these files over, she will be arrested and later sentenced…"

In the past week, I've found out that my birth certificate was fake, my appeal was denied, and I am a victim of a serial kidnapper. I've been living with a serial kidnapper my entire life. Everything about my life is lie.

My name is not Noah Ryan.

I was not adopted.

I was kidnapped as an infant from my mother's arms…by the woman I've called my guardian angel for twenty-nine years.

Joel's voice breaks through again. "The moment I hand this over they will come for her. The next time you will get to see her will be in a jail cell or an interrogation room."

"Give me an hour. I need one hour."

"I can do that. Listen, I apologize for having to deliver this news to you," he says.

"I asked for it. Thank you."

"I'll be in touch," Joel says before the line goes dead.

What other choice do I have but to go see her, to face the woman I loved and now loathe. I have to hear what she has to say.

Moments later I'm in my truck and headed to Vento Diner where I know she will be, the place she loves more than she loves anything else in this world. Possibly more than she loved kidnapping innocent infants.

Fifteen minutes pass slowly, but before I know it I'm parked in front of Vento's. After a few minutes of reining in my temper, I walk through the front door of the diner and am quickly greeted by Alisha and Mae. Both women are all smiles, laughing at some stupid joke they have between them about some patron.

"Mae, I need to speak to you privately. Now," I insist.

She furrows her brow as if she does not approve of the tone of voice I am using. "Of course, son. Let's go back to my office."

I lead the way. I don't want to follow this woman for another minute of my life. I don't know who she is. She takes a seat at her desk and I seat myself at one of the chairs in front of it.

"Tell me what my birth name is."

"Sweet boy, you know I don't know the answer to that. The only thing you had on you when I found you was your blue blanket," she says innocently.

"That's bullshit." I cock my head to the side as I continue, "My character and fitness test came back over a week ago. I was denied to sit for the bar exam due to dishonesty and misrepresentation. Apparently I sent in a fake birth certificate." She tries to speak, but I hold my hand up to stop her. "So I had an FBI agent dig into it."

Her smile falls.

"Why did you take me?" I ask.

"Noah Ryan…what are you talking about?"

From my pocket I pull out the wanted picture I printed off and hand it to her.

"Noah…this is…ridiculous."

"Why? Tell me why you took me."

She's shaking her head. "I did no such thing. I saved my son!"

"Bullshit. You are a serial kidnapper. Did you get pleasure out of taking me from my family? Did you enjoy watching me grow up with nothing?" I probe.

She stands up suddenly and smacks her hands on the desk. "THEY DID NOT DESERVE YOU!"

I'm thrown. What the fuck…

"So you took me? You took me when I was hours old?"

"You are my son!"

"The fuck I am! This is so screwed up!"

Right then, Alisha bursts into the room. "Ms. Ryan, I am so sorry to come into your office like this, but the police and FBI are here. They said they needed to talk to the owner," Alisha rambles on quickly.

Mae's eyes don't leave mine as three FBI agents and five police officers walk into the cramped little office.

Five.

How appropriate.

The officers cuff her while reading off her Miranda rights…

"Noah…" she pleads "I love you, son…"

Alisha stumbles out of the office, confused as all hell.

"Go to hell, Mae. I will never forgive you." I don't know if I mean what I say, but in this moment, I want nothing to do with such a twisted bitch.

I can't watch her be taken into custody. I can't watch her as she screams and puts up a fight against the officers.

I'm walking out to my truck when I get a text from Heather, asking me to send her mother's ring to her. I want her. I don't want this life—this life that's not mine. A name that's not mine. I have nothing keeping me here anymore, and everything drawing me to New York.

MY STORY HAS made national news. It will be airing on the eight o'clock news tonight. I've asked them to keep my name out of it, but anyone who knows Mae knows me. Yesterday, I watched my life disintegrate. Today, I'm getting the hell out. I have to do this for myself. I have no attachments, and one addiction. Avicii couldn't have said it better. Zipping up my duffel, I dial Coen's number.

"Hey dipshit," he answers.

"Hey dickwad."

"What's going on? Did you get a chick pregnant?"

I snort. "No, you fucker, I'm leaving town."

"Excuse me? Where the hell are you going?"

"I'm not sure how to put any of this into coherent words, so I'll explain everything later."

"Are you sure about this, Ryan?" he asks.

"I am. I have no doubt about it."

"Let me know if you need anything."

"I will. I'll talk to you later, dickwad."

I hang up and turn off my phone and every other electronic device I have. I don't want to be witness to the news when it comes on. I'd rather not hear my story being told from a stranger's mouth.

Two hours later feels like a lifetime, but the mere minutes won't go by fast enough. I'm waiting at the airport. My plane leaves in two hours, and I've got her mother's engagement ring.

CHAPTER
Fourteen
pink blanket

Heather

I'M DEEP IN a dream...or another nightmare. I can't be sure. But there's a consistent knocking coming from behind me. I'm so confused, and it gets louder. The noise pulls me from my sleep and I realize it's coming from down the hall. I sit up, looking around my room, half asleep. The only light on is coming from the low glow of my fireplace and my holiday-scented candle. Oh crap! I never blew that out. I hear the knocking again and I sleepily get out of bed, padding down the hall in my pajamas. I open my door without looking, expecting to see my night-owl neighbor.

What? I squeeze my eyes shut and then open them again. My whole body goes still. It's...

"I'm sorry I woke you, ballerina. I should have called first," Noah says, as he stands at my front door with a black duffel in his hand. I breathe in, smelling his cologne.

"What time is it?"

"It's after one in the morning." His reply is so sexy and I'm pretty sure I'm still dreaming.

"You're here?"

"I'm here. I'm sorry it took me so long."

I should be so mad right now but... He's standing on my doorstep looking so yummy in dark navy sweatpants and an Arizona State University sweatshirt, but he looks utterly exhausted too.

Shaking my head, I'm still so confused. "How'd you get by the doorman?"

He grins. "I think he mistook me for a resident and just let me go up. Maybe I should come back in the morning."

I back up and open the door, letting him in. "Don't be silly... come in."

He walks in and drops his duffel on the bench. "I wanted to see you before I got a hotel room. I wanted to return this to its owner." He takes his wallet out of his pocket then removes my mother's engagement ring from it. It looks so small in the palm of his hand. I reach out and take it from him, sliding it back onto my middle finger.

My heart is pounding in my chest. He's here. He's so close. He brought my ring to me. All the way to New York. "Noah, I...thank you. You didn't have to do this." Looking him up and down, I notice that he's wearing a frown just beneath the surface. "Do you want something to drink?"

"I don't want to keep you up...I just...had to see you. You do something to me. You make me forget about everything that's going on."

He snakes his arm around my waist, and I suddenly realize what I'm wearing when his hand touches the skin at the small of my back. I'm stunned by his admission and I love that he has to touch me.

"You look beautiful, even in the middle of the night." He slowly pulls me closer to him until I'm merely an inch away. With his one hand at the small of my back, he knots his other in the back of my hair. And with just the right amount of confidence and gentleness, he presses his lips against mine.

I'm melting into his touch. His lips are so talented. He's holding my petite frame to his large muscular one yet I still can't believe he's here in my place. Please don't let this be a dream.

Without warning, he tears his mouth away and starts kissing my neck. I'm completely turned on by the urgency behind his kiss, but I can't tell why he's feeling this way.

His fingers are raking over my open back as I feel his growl against my neck. He darts his tongue out then sinks his teeth into my neck.

I've never been so wet before in all of my life—not even with him on New Year's. I've never been bitten before, but holy crap, he makes it so hot! I want it again. My hands run up his chest and I'm about to shatter in his arms. "Noah…"

I can feel his breath on my throat. "Heather…I missed the way you feel, how good you smell, the sound of your voice. Tell me no other man has touched you." He kisses up my jaw and then down to the other side of my neck where he does the same thing, and this time I whimper when the sharp twinge sends chills through my body.

I move my hands around his neck and up into the back of his hair. I gasp when he bites me again. Not because of any pain but because the ache between my legs just became unbearable. "No…nobody."

"Good. You're mine. Understand? I'm an only child, ballerina; I don't share well." His hand on the small of my back moves down, sliding underneath my satin shorts to cup my ass. I think I'm going to come the second he moves his hand lower.

I'm pressing my body against his and I know my voice sounds needy. "Yes."

He yanks my hair back and kisses me hard as he grabs me and lifts me up. I automatically wrap my legs around his torso as he carries me to the couch in my living room. "Are you on some sort of birth control or do I have to run out and get condoms?" he asks and I surprisingly want us in my room, in my bed. I've never let a man come into my bedroom before, but him…oh, I'd let him in.

Before I can answer him, he's laying me on my back on the couch and leaning over me with his hand gliding up my thigh. I'm going to come—I want him so badly. "Yes, I'm on it."

A slow, sexy smile forms across his face.

"Wait...take me upstairs to my bedroom."

The rumble in the back of his throat is so yummy that I want to bite him. He scoops me up again and carries me up two flights of stairs without losing his breath.

"If you make me wait another minute, your body is going to regret it later...but I have to warm you up first, baby."

I whimper because that sounds so hot...yet he has no idea how warmed up I already am. He's so strong. And the way he croons baby, I decide that I'll let him do whatever he wants to me. He ever so gently lays me down on the bed. My eyes flicker down to his huge erection in his sweatpants as he takes his sweatshirt and tee off. The dim light from my candle and fireplace is all the light we have to go by, but it's more than enough. This time I'll get to see him. He kicks off his sneakers and socks, and then drops his sweats and steps out of them. My bedroom just became an inferno.

I'm still lying there in my satin shorts and cami just watching him stand there and devour my body with his eyes. I want him there. Inside of me. I crook my finger at him, begging him to come to me.

I slide farther up the bed and he follows, moving up my body. His hand traces up my stomach and beneath my satin cami to tug on my nipples. My back arches in response, as my fingers deftly work to undo these damned three buttons.

His strong, corded arms are tight. He angles his head to the side and takes my mouth again. Oh my God...are we really doing this?

He whispers softly, "Are you sure?"

I've never been so sure of anything in my entire life—this man owns me. "Yes," I gasp as we get my cami off and his hand moves down under the lightweight fabric of my shorts to cup my aching sex.

"Are *you* sure?" I repeat his question, hopeful.

"Am I sure? Baby, there was a reason no one else could handle me. This has always been destined for you."

I'm literally squirming with need. His fingers tease my entrance with the lightest of touches while his lips work their way down my stomach. "Noah, please..."

I can feel the electricity from the storm moving over me. He gets my little satin shorts off, and then he slides a finger into my wet sex. He doesn't wait for me to get used to his finger before adding a second. I whimper as he pushes my knees up with his free hand and puts his mouth on me. There.

"Ohhh." My hips rock against his lips. My thighs fall open wider and I can feel his appreciation rumble through my sex.

"You taste so damn good, little ballerina," he says quickly, before he darts his tongue out to circle my clitoris again.

He's so F'ing good at foreplay, but I want more…I want him inside of me. I can't imagine how he feels. I want to make him come, make him lose his mind. My body jerks when his teeth graze my folds and my whole body tightens.

"Do you think you're ready for me, Heather?" I hear him ask, as he takes his boxer briefs off.

Oh. I'm so ready and I want to see him. To feel him sink into me. I know he's going to stretch me, and I want it. Now.

I'm writhing on the bed and my mouth waters when I finally get a good look at his massive erection. Oh. My. God. "Yes. I'm ready." *I hope I'm ready.*

He climbs my body again and grabs his thick shaft. He teases me with the head of his cock. I can't stand it. The thunderous storm that he is intensifies and I'm about to beg him for it.

Looking up at him, I can see his eyes are dark, filled with lust. I can tell he's just as affected as I am yet he's holding back and I don't want him to.

"Please, Noah."

The wide head of his cock is wet from my arousal and I think he's enjoying the way it looks—he obviously likes seeing the way his cock slides between my folds.

"You have to tell me if this is too much for you," he says in the heaviest, sexiest, throatiest voice I have ever heard. He tries to ease the head of his cock into me, already stretching me out. I gasp and immediately edge back from him.

He stops moving the instant I move back. He looks up at me pained and I don't know what to do. He's so, so big. "I'm sorry…try again? Please? I want you more than I want to breathe."

I can see his jaw working. He's determined, yet he's still holding back.

"Please?"

A growl comes from deep in his throat as he grabs hold of my hips. He pushes his cock against my opening again. I can't help the scream that escapes my lips. He's stretching me beyond my limits... so far out of my limits.

He stops moving and his fingers grip my hips. I can't believe this is happening. He's barely inside of me.

"Talk to me. It's too much, isn't it?"

I don't want him to be right. I don't.

"No, no, please. Don't stop. I want this, Noah." I try and do anything that I can think of. I take his hand and move it to my clit. "Touch me."

His thumb starts massaging my clit as he leans forward to take my mouth again. "If I can't have you, then I want you to come. I want to watch you come again."

I kiss him like it's going to save my life. Passionately, full of lust and want. My breath is coming out in a rush. "Please. Try again. I want you."

"I want you too, baby." He grabs my hips and starts to push in again. I grit my teeth in pain, not wanting him to see that it hurts.

This is so not what I dreamed our first time would be like. It hurts so badly! I should be able to do this. Stretch! It's what I do. *I'm a ballerina*, I'm screaming at myself.

He gently presses his lips against mine and pulls out what he's managed to squeeze into me. "I'm sorry," he says with a voice that is full of emotion. "I won't hurt you."

I look up at him, completely deflated. Now I know why he's never been able to sleep with anyone.

He pulls back and gets off of my bed, pulling on his boxer briefs. My heart does a double beat; I feel like I just stopped breathing. He's going? I sit up and pull a pillow across my chest. "Are you leaving?"

"I can't hurt you," he says as he picks up his shirt.

"Wait! Just try again." I don't want him to leave. He came all this way and I can't even do this for him. Biting on my nails nervously, watching him dress, I try not to show the hurt in my voice.

"Please don't go."

He stops and looks up at me. "You want me to stay?"

"Yes." I move the pillow from my chest and try to entice him to stay. Then I get off of the bed and walk up to him slowly.

The massive erection in his briefs gives him away. I know he wants to stay. I'm standing naked in front of him, just like in my dream.

He's not saying anything to me, barely even looking at me. I stand up on my toes and brush my breasts against him, pressing my lips to his softly. "Stay with me?"

"Are you sure?" he says in return as his hand slides down my back and cups my ass, his other hand moving into the back of my hair. He likes to hold me like this.

"Yes, I'm sure." I move my lips up his jaw, kissing him softly. He seems to like it. "Come back to bed?" I love the way he smells and I run my nose along his thick neck and down to his shoulder, biting down on his muscle.

I hear him smile as he wraps his arms around my body to carry me to bed. I crawl up to the headboard and move my comforter so each of us can get underneath it. Once we're both underneath the white comforter, he pulls on my pink blanket that I usually use on my couch, to cover the comforter.

"I'm sorry," I say because I truly am. I can't stand to see this look on his face.

He moves closer to me and pulls me against his warm, toned body. "You have nothing to be sorry about. I've had a week from hell and having you in my arms right now is all I could ask for."

I'm unsure how to respond so I nuzzle his chest and breathe him in one last time before my dreams take me away.

CHAPTER
Fifteen
taking what's mine

Noah

I'M IN NEW York City. I'm in her bed and she's fast asleep in my arms. It's the first time I've slept since I found out about Mae Ryan. Heather has me by the balls, whether she thinks so or not. I'm glad I'm here, but today is the day she's going to ask questions— questions I'm not sure I can answer with a cool head. The last thing I want to do is scare her. I lightly run my fingers up and down her small yet strong arms, causing her to stir and move closer to me.

I'm glad I'm not the only one who's affected by the magnetic pull between us. She's my polar opposite and now that I have her in my arms, I'm not letting her pull away.

Shit. I'd say I'm in balls deep, but that's not the truth, especially after last night. I can't even fuck the woman who drives me wild. I'm going to have to work her body over multiple times before I'll be able to get into her snug little pussy to take what's mine.

I'm not giving up on her.

Not this woman. Not this time.

She exhales and opens her eyes, blinking up at me. I get hard knowing she's naked under the comforter and blanket, which I've noticed is pink. Her little outfit last night did me in. She was in black satin shorts that cut high up her thigh with ivory lace edging… and a matching thin-strapped top with three small satin buttons that barely closed up the front, riding high above her navel.

My cock throbs when I think about her wearing it again. I think she feels my cock grow because with a cheeky smile on her gorgeous pale face, she reaches down and grabs my shaft in my boxer briefs.

"Well, good morning, handsome."

I smirk and place my hand on her ass, pulling her naked, warm body as close to mine as possible. "I'm having a hard time not touching you right now. I want that swollen cunt pressed up against my lips."

She abruptly moves to straddle me, utterly naked, making me forget about what the day will undoubtedly bring. "Is this your subtle way of asking me to try again?" I ask, grabbing her hips.

"I want those lips on me as much as you do."

"I'll take you however I can get you, ballerina."

She grabs my hands, moving them to cover her breasts. Her tits are the perfect size. They are just about a handful, and I fucking love them. I start stimulating her nipples with soft tender touches, not entirely sure if she wants it to be rough, so I don't chance it. Moving my hands to cup her, I trace my fingers along the outer edges of her breasts, running my thumb along the fold where they fall against her. Her breasts are heavy with hard nipples that peak as my fingers move up to tease her gently. I place kisses around each breast, ignoring those peaked nipples. Her breath escapes her lips in a rush, wanting more.

I don't place my lips onto her nipples until her body is trembling with desire.

"Do you like that?" I ask her with a warm look of amusement on my face.

The sensual grind of her waist against my manhood gives me her answer. "Touch yourself and show me what you like," I say, wanting to satisfy her.

She shakes her head. "I like exactly what you're doing."

Her skin looks flushed and her breathing is labored as I run my tongue around her areolas. I'm watching her react under my touch and it's turning me on. My cock throbs beneath her. She must feel it because she teases me by grinding her wet folds over the fabric of my boxer briefs. She wants me, a fierce, white-hot, searing hunger.

I want her to feel so incredibly comfortable in her skin while I make her mine. "You have the most beautiful tits, baby."

She reacts by moaning my name. The sexual responses I'm getting out of her are wild and damned hot.

"I've wanted you inside of me all night long," she whimpers as I tug on her left nipple, wanting to see how rough she'll let me be.

"It's going to take a while for me to get you ready. Do you think you'll be able to handle me?" I ask.

She doesn't vocally answer my question again, but she reaches out her hand and tosses the pink blanket that's covering us off of the bed. Her damned pink glitter is stealing into my dark, brooding storm. It's the only hint of color I see in my now black-and-white world.

She thumbs at my boxer briefs to get them off, and when my cock springs free she all but jumps on it. She's panting heavily as I reach up and brush the hair off of her cheek. I want her. I'm going to take what's mine. I think she's ready to feel the wrath of my storm, to feel me like nobody else has.

Grinning as I roll her onto her stomach, I push her perfect little ass up, leaning over as I kiss her spine, all the way down to her ass. God, I hope she's yearning to feel me inside of her. Heated desire burns through my veins when she kneels up. I quickly lie flat on my back, pulling her over my mouth until I'm underneath her wet little cunt. She's wet and ready for me in any way I want to give it to her. I'm kissing, licking, touching, and tasting her folds trying to get her tense body to relax. I reach up and run my finger through her folds, touching her lightly, teasingly.

I run my tongue over her clit slowly, so she feels every centimeter of my tongue against her. She moans her appreciation as I circle my tongue around her pink, wet, swollen clitoris. I've never really enjoyed eating a woman out until now. I always did it just to get them off and get the hell out, but she's so damned gorgeous no matter how I look at her. I love making her come; I want to make her beg for more until I've worked her body over so vastly that she's speechless. I want her to be pleasured in ways she's never been pleasured before. I'm possessive over this woman, and I'm going to take her. I cup her ass as the tip of my tongue teases her wet lips.

I start moving my tongue in different directions in quick darting motions until she shrieks out. Her needy sex spasms and I know I've found her spot. Her legs start intermittently shaking.

"Damn Heather, you are so wet."

"You make me so hot," she responds breathlessly.

Her hands move down to the top of my head to hold me in place. I'm running my hand over her smooth ass as I lick her slowly, sensually. She's soaked with arousal as I lap up all I can of her. It happens gradually, but I can feel her entire body stiffening. I grab hold of her hips to steady her as she loses control and comes. She's shaking in my hands and she's lost all control over her body. I lick her until she's stopped trembling and is able to steady herself on her knees.

"Noah...I...Oh...Can you do that again?"

Kissing her pink pussy, I grin, "I'll make you come like that as many times as you want."

"The things you do to my body, Noah..."

"I know, baby, just relax and enjoy yourself. Don't fight it."

I get her onto her back and start my assault on her pussy all over again, this time lying between her legs, adding my fingers inside of her to increase the pressure, and to stretch her out. When she comes, her eyes roll back from the sheer pleasure of her body-curling orgasm. Her sweet, wet walls clench around my fingers as I push against her spot. I don't remove my fingers from her cunt until she's sated. Her body wants to lull her to sleep, but that will not be happening on my clock.

She relaxes and moans softly, begging me for more, and I take her to the edge again and again, giving her all the earth-shattering orgasms she wants. I need her ready to go all day because I'm not stopping until my cock jerks violently inside of her.

After she's come five consecutive times, I move back up her body, kissing her highly sensitized skin. Her nerve endings are screaming, but I know she can handle more than what I've given her.

"I think you're ready for me," I whisper in her ear as I kiss her damp throat.

"Mmm, show me," she says quietly.

"I think it'd be easier if you got on top—that way you can control it. I won't hurt you," I say as I move onto my back. Her room smells like sex; the temperature has risen dramatically, and we're just getting started. My cock is lying heavily against my stomach, when her tight body moves over mine. She's suspended over me, and I want to feel her cunt squeeze my cock more than I want to breathe.

Heather

I CAN'T COUNT the number of times this Greek god has made me come. He moves so expertly over my body that if he didn't admit to being a virgin, I would never have known. I still can't believe that no woman has lasted long enough during foreplay for him to bury that huge heavy cock inside of her but I'm almost glad. He's completely at my will now as he lies naked on my bed. I'm almost weak from all of the explosive orgasms he's given me, but I want more. I have his hefty shaft in my hand as he prepares to impale me.

I take the libidinous lead with all the suggestive confidence I can muster up, and run his head between my lips.

"Take me how you want me," he says in a smoky, cool voice.

I'm moving slowly as his head pushes between my folds, stretching me already. I whimper in delight. It doesn't hurt because he stretched me and warmed me up so much—all I feel is body-trembling pleasure. He's gritting his teeth as I push my sex down on his almost convulsing cock.

"FUCK!" I yell, as he stretches me even more. If I don't go slowly enough, I'll come just by the sheer size of him.

He's watching me take his ragged virginity. He's not innocent or pure, but I'm taking what no one else has ever ventured to take before.

His erection is made of steel as I sink down farther until I'm sitting on him. He's balls deep inside of me and he feels so incredibly good. I can feel every thick vein on his dense cock.

"Holy hell, baby! Are you okay?" he asks in shock.

I only nod because I can't speak. I'll scream if I do. I'm not in pain—I'm just so...so...full! I've never been so full in my life before. Not with the three men I've had before Noah. Never.

I decide to try moving by rotating my hips in a circular motion, conjuring a grunt from his lips. It makes me whimper. I have full control over him and it feels empowering.

I lean back, wanting him deeper. I love how he feels inside of me. I'm resting my hands on his shins, and he has a full view of his solid cock buried deep, deep, deep inside of me as I slowly move up and down.

"Noah..." I moan out.

His hand moves down from my heavy breasts to my very swollen clit. His thumb starts rubbing me. He's worried about getting me off? I've never had a vaginal orgasm, but I know with his size, thickness, and sexy, raspy voice, he'll make me come. It feels all too good.

I move his hand away and bring it up to my mouth, biting on the pad of his finger then sliding it between my lips and sucking on it.

"Don't worry about me, Noah...just enjoy this."

His growl seems to make my windows tremble. "Heather," he chokes out, "I'm not coming without you."

He's so bossy and so determined, and he's stealing all things sane about me. My back is arched as I move up and down his shaft when he starts taking control, quickening our pace.

"Hold on," he hisses with tortured desire.

My core tightens.

His fingers are digging into my side as he lifts me up so he can fully pull out of me then drive back into me with immense force. My breasts bounce violently as he pounds into me.

"Ohhh...!" My head falls back; I can't catch my breath.

"You like that? Tell me how fucking good I make you feel!" he demands. I can't look down at him for the pleasure boiling through my body is immobilizing.

"If….if you do that again I will come!" I screech breathlessly.

The sexy bastard rotates his hips as he starts going hard, hammering my wet, sensitive sex. I lose it. I'm coming uncontrollably for this man. He holds me up as he continues to pump into my pulsing walls. I've gotten tighter while coming and he's grunting with each and every thrust up into me. I can barely comprehend the electrified orgasm that is spiraling through my body.

My fingers are digging into his muscular calves as I hold on for dear life. I want to feel him come inside of me so badly. I want him to lose himself. I love that I've taken this from him—I feel so powerful.

His chest heaves with heavy breaths as he slams up hard, burying his head deep inside of me, and then stilling. He's so completely motionless. He groans through his teeth as his cock jerks wildly inside of me. Then I feel him. He's warm and I feel every single time his cock jolts and empties another warm load into me. He continuously groans and it's the sexiest thing I've ever heard. I've done it. I've given him this. This is mine.

After a few moments, he opens his eyes and looks up into mine. His eyes are wild and satisfied. Neither of us says anything, but he moves. He wraps his arms around my waist and holds me so I'm able to sit up. I feel warm and extremely wet. When I look down, his sultry sea-salt come is leaking out of me. He follows my eyes down and smirks. He moves my hand south and slowly drags my index finger against us. Placing my finger against my lips, he implores, "Suck." He wants me to taste his salty goodness and my sweetness combined.

I'll do anything this man asks me to do, so without hesitating I open my mouth and suck on his finger. Moaning in appreciation, I hold his hand with both of mine while I lick and swallow our juices then look up at him through my thick lashes.

"How do we taste, ballerina?"

My sex is aching again. What is he doing to me? I smile sweetly and run my hands into the back of his now damp hair.

"You tell me..." I say right before I press my lips to his, pushing my tongue into his mouth. He kisses me back passionately, and slowly. His chest is still heaving as he thrusts his tongue into my mouth. We taste so good together.

My breathing finally slows and I pull back to look at him. Do I ask if he's okay? I've never taken anyone's virginity. Was he really? Technically, I mean? No...maybe? I don't care.

He's mine.

Before he helps me off of his cock, he pulls out and pushes himself back in, watching our orgasms move in and out of me. When he helps me off of his lengthy shaft I tiptoe over to the bathroom to clean up. A few minutes later he walks in, butt naked and hard. After he cleans himself up, he kisses the back of my head and goes back into my bedroom. It's dark outside; I can tell through my bathroom windows. We've been at this all day. I've missed ballet rehearsal and Ms. Lindsay is going to be furious, but I don't care. Today was picture-perfect.

I wash my hands and walk back out into my bedroom. He's lying on my bed, face down, with my favorite, fluffy pink blanket strewn across his fine tush.

I can't help but giggle at him. "Noah?"

"Mmm?" he groans into the pillow, muffling his voice.

I walk over timidly, pulling on my pink satin robe. Getting up on the bed, I lean down and kiss a small freckle on his back. God, it's the sexiest freckle. I find myself wanting to lick him everywhere. "Are you okay?" I ask quietly.

He rolls over onto his back and pulls me down to him by the tie-string on my robe. "I'm great."

He wraps me in his arms and pulls me on top of his chest,

moving my hair out of my face.

His good mood is infectious. I don't really know where this is going...us. But at the moment, this is all I want. I look up at him and smile while my chin rests on his chest. "Are you sure you've never done that before?"

"I'm sure. Shit, I didn't even ask if you wanted me to stay. Shit, I'm not good at this."

I feel my eyelids fall heavily. Fighting it as hard as I can, I speak softly, "Of course I want you to stay."

He hums and I feel his chest vibrate against my cheek.

I think he's tired too. He reaches his arm out and pulls the pink blanket over the two of us before wrapping his arms around me, holding me on top of him.

I'm completely comfortable lying chest to chest with him, my legs in between his, with his hands at my back and butt. I hope he's comfortable too because I'm not moving.

This is my spot.

His breathing shallows out and I know he's asleep.

I smile sleepily because...Fuck! He's so cute. So sexy and so, so...perfect. I allow myself to close my eyes and take a quick nap before I wake him again.

CHAPTER
Sixteen
breathtaking fantasy

Noah

I THINK I'VE been inside her three times since she took something from me that no one has ever ventured to take. I remember falling asleep with her on top of me then waking up to her lips rimmed around the head of my cock. I fucked her then we passed out in a tangled mess of limbs. My cock woke me up a few hours later, so I rolled her over and kissed her soft skin until she woke up so I could take her again. Then there was that point in the night where she showed me just how flexible she was. And yeah...I fucked her good.

Her body is a fantasyland, the one that I've fantasized over many times. She's got the tightest little cunt I've ever tried to fuck, yet she's the only one who's been able to take me. I can't keep my lips off of her...or my hands for that matter.

The feeling of being ensconced inside of her gorgeous, warm pussy was overwhelming. Every solitary stroke of my cock inside of her tight, wet, beautiful channel was significant. She never once made me feel inadequate… The entire evening has been incredible.

She lost complete control with me; I think she might have forgotten her own name as an ocean of ecstasy flooded her repeatedly.

I've made women come by any means necessary, but the way Heather looks at me when she comes is breathtaking.

We're in the shower right now and I'm about to take her again.

I have her pressed against the glass, kissing her neck as the hot water hits my back. She's a horny, wet, slippery mess with little drops of water on her peaked nipples. Grabbing one of her legs, I haul it up and place her ankle behind my back and above my naked ass. She's looking at me, pleading.

"Noah, I have to get to the ballet studio."

I growl against her neck as I sink my teeth into her. "I'll make this fast, baby."

Her body is overtaken with goose bumps as I line myself up to her tight cunt and push my ridged cock into her, stretching her out again. I don't need to stretch her out every time because my cock has been inside multiple times since I've arrived. The sex over the last twenty-four hours has been entrancing.

The sounds that come out of that mouth of hers fill the glass-enclosed shower, her moans surrounding me. I could come just listening to her orgasm. She's fucked my world upside down, and now I'm fucking her inside out. I'll be damned if I let her leave me for ballet rehearsal right now.

We're all mouths and teeth, kissing desperately, wanting to feel each other in every way possible. Her hands grip my hair as our lips are smashed together.

I'm pounding her hard and she's beyond sensitive. She comes almost instantaneously. I join her as she pulses against my cock. My lips move down from her lips to her neck where I sink my teeth into her wet skin. Damn, I love biting her.

We're still for a few minutes as we try to catch our breath. I slowly slide out of her and kiss her until her heart's content.

She's completely wrung out, and I can't say that I'm sorry about it. It makes my cock hard just knowing that I can wear her out like that. Hell, I'm surprised she can even walk right now.

"You are going to get me in so much trouble!" she squeals as I grasp her ass.

"Should I go to your studio with you? I'll make sure no one messes with my girl."

She stops rinsing the soap off of her body and looks up at me. "Your girl?" she questions.

"I mean, yeah." I say, washing my hair. Does she not want that?

She leans up and kisses me swiftly while I have both hands in my hair. "Your girl."

I catch a shy smile before she turns around and finishes showering, wringing out her hair. My eyes roam down her body and linger on her ass. That ass. Damn. I'm like a horny teenager again, one who's recently discovered free porn on the Internet.

She gets out of the shower while I'm rinsing off and disappears into her bedroom. I decide to turn the water onto cold to finish up my shower, so I can say goodbye to her before I bend her over and take her from behind.

A few minutes later I walk out into her bedroom then downstairs to her kitchen with a white towel around my lower waist to make her coffee. Does she drink coffee? She had dropped her phone in her coffee…so she must drink it?

I'm looking around her kitchen for a coffee maker, and I come up empty-handed. She comes down two flights of stairs from her bedroom to where I'm standing. She's wearing what looks like a pink one-piece swimsuit and some tight fucking leggings.

"You don't have a coffee maker? I was going to brew some for you."

"Uhm, no. I have a thing for Starbucks drinks."

I chuckle and shake my head.

She winces as she takes a step in my direction and I frown, fear spilling into my gut. "Are you okay?" I walk toward her, unsure of what I should do.

"I…uh…I'm just really, really sore," she replies then turns away from me and rummages through her purse.

I grin. Damn right you are.

I walk up behind her and cup her ass. "I've got to get some shit done today then I'll get a hotel room. I don't plan on leaving New

York anytime soon."

She quickly turns around on her toes. I'm surprised when I see her reaction: she's ecstatic. "Really? You're staying in town? For how long?"

Her smile is contagious. She keeps showing me glimpses of her personality, whether she realizes it or not. Up to this point she's been guarded and reserved, but I can see it; she can't hide shit from me.

"I'm thinking about getting an apartment. There's not one single reason for me to be in Arizona anymore, and one damn gorgeous reason to be here." Damn…I've literally just made a decision to move across the country to be with her.

I can feel her eyes on me. She's quiet for a few moments before she speaks, "But…what about your mom? And the bar?"

"She's not my mother and I've decided not to take the bar in Arizona since I was denied. I'll try again here."

She looks at me with those gorgeous jade green eyes, and I think I've confused her.

"I'll tell you about it later. Would you like to go to dinner with me tonight?"

She nods and her cheeks turn a pale pink color. "I'd like that, Noah."

I fit my hand to the small of her back, pulling her against my body. "Have a good day, ballerina." I kiss her like she's never been kissed a day in her life before she leaves for practice.

CHAPTER
Seventeen
heartrending

Noah

MY TWO HEADS are now solely concentrated on her and that sweet ass upon walking into her bedroom. When I make my way back up to Heather's room, it's like the first time I've seen it. The huge windows are the first things anyone would notice, completely taking up the far wall in her room. On the right-hand wall, her large king-sized bed with white leather headboard sits. At the end of the bed she has a white leather bench…I fucked her on that too. A few good feet from the foot of her bed on the adjacent wall, is a gas fireplace. It was on and glowing when I arrived and carried her into the room. There is a large crystal chandelier hanging above her bed. The colors are neutral and white, but warm. The only color in here comes from that pink blanket of hers. She likes soft things. The white rug under my feet is soft as hell.

I'm pretty sure that I've never slept so well in all my life. Who knew that a down topper could lull you to sleep like that? It also muffles any sound. We've fucked all night on this bed and not once did I hear a squeak. The only noise was from the sheets rubbing against our naked bodies, and her ball-gripping moans.

Without snooping around, I glance around the room to gather information about this woman who has my head and balls in a vise-grip. She's so damn perfect it's ridiculous.

I smile to myself as I pick up my clothes from the floor. Taking my phone out of my sweatpants pocket it buzzes and comes to life. An Arizona number that I don't recognize is calling. Ignoring it, I check all of the missed calls and voicemails.

I've been gone for all of one damn day. Shit!

Every single one of the voicemails and missed calls is from Mae. She's asking for forgiveness, asking that I come and see her so we can talk, and telling me how much I mean to her…how much she loves me. If she loved me she would have never taken me.

My Galaxy starts buzzing as Joel's name appears on the screen.

"Joel," I say as a greeting.

"Noah, I'm glad you answered. Listen, this shit has blown up and I need you to get back to Arizona."

"I'm not going back—that I can assure you about my life. The rest of it is up in the fucking air somewhere."

"I understand that you must be going through a lot right now, but I need your head in it," he says.

"You have no motherfucking idea what I'm going through." I take a seat on the white leather bench and run my hand through my wet hair. She's my only damn reprieve. She's the only thing that will numb the pain and I'm not leaving. I need her like my body needs water.

I can hear him exhale loudly. "Listen. According to the federal code 18 U.S.C. § 1201, Mae is facing a Class B felony offense and is looking at one to eight years in a federal prison."

"That's it? Eight years max for kidnapping?"

"Unfortunately yes. It wasn't considered a Class A-1 aggravated felony because you weren't physically abused or molested. You weren't, were you? We cannot charge her with the other kidnappings. She hasn't admitted to them yet, and she never crossed state lines with the others."

"No, I wasn't. Why are you telling me all of this?"

"She raised you, Noah. She's part of who you are today."

That is none of his fucking business! "I don't give a shit," I say, knowing that I don't mean it. Mae has always been my one constant in life, and now…she's gone. Everything was a lie.

"My sincere apologies. I don't mean to intrude. I just thought you should know. She is being charged with kidnapping. And now we wait for a trial date. I believe there are media crews surrounding your apartment in Tempe, Mae's house, and the diner, as well."

"All right. You should know that I'll be breaking the lease on my apartment. I've decided to move to New York. I'll get a moving crew in as soon as I can. As for the house and diner, both of those are in her name…if that's even her name."

"It is. Mae Ryan."

"Speaking of names, have you figured out who the hell I am, or do I need to hire a private investigator?" I ask impatiently.

"Noah, I need you to calm down. This shit is insane, and stupid, and all kinds of fucked up. There are so many damn records to go through."

"Yeah. I realize that. Twenty-nine years of records. Just keep me updated on the trial. I've decided not to press charges against her on top of the federal charges. I won't add to her hurt."

"You're a good man. You need to talk to her at some point…"

I interrupt him, "Hell no, I don't. I won't. I'm not the least bit interested."

"I understand. During an interrogation yesterday, Mae decided that she would plead guilty. She didn't want you to be ashamed of her."

"It's a little too late for that, man. I need to go. Call me when you find anything else, please."

"Will do. Get some rest." He hangs up.

With a few strokes of my finger, I get to my voicemail and hit play on one of Mae's messages.

"Oh my Noah. It's me, sweet boy. It's your Mae. I understand that you are extremely upset with me right now, but son…I love you. I always have and I always will. You'll always be my boy, Noah.

Please come and see me. I can't say much over the phone, but I will answer any questions you have for me. Please, sweet boy. I love you. I'll call you again when they let me use the phone. Goodbye."

I hang up and start pacing the length of Heather's room while I call a moving company in Tempe, Arizona. Once I get the move scheduled, I call Coen.

"You've reached dipshit," he answers with a laugh.

"Hey man…"

The line goes silent for too long before he finally speaks again.

"I saw the news. I can't believe what she did; that's completely messed up, bro. Where are you?"

"I'm in New York City. I needed to get away, far away from her."

"That makes sense," he says and I can tell he's thinking about the situation at hand.

"I need to ask you for a favor."

"Shoot."

"I'm going to mail you the keys to my truck and apartment. Can you run the apartment keys to the leasing agent and sell my truck? The papers are in my safe under my desk."

"Fuck, dude, you really aren't coming back, are you?"

"Not a chance in hell."

"Well, shit. I'll take care of that mess for you. Is there anything else you need?"

"No," I say. "Thanks, man, I owe you one."

"Nah, you don't owe me shit, Ryan. I'll let you know when it's done."

"Thank you, fuckface. I'll talk to you later."

"Live it up, asshole."

He hangs up and I put my phone down on her bed. I need to sleep.

I pull on a clean pair of sweatpants before grabbing my headphones. I hit play on my playlist then get back into her bed. I know I told her I'd get a hotel room, but I like the way her bed smells. Lying face down, breathing in her scent and closing my eyes, I pass the hell out while listening to "Titanium" by Madilyn Bailey.

Heather

CRAP. CRAP. CRAP. I was so late to ballet today. Mistress Lindsay is going to kill me. I can't tell which hurts worse, stretching when I'm sore or being stagnant. I'm going over my very precise choreography, but I keep messing up. He's stuck in my head. I shut my eyes and inhale deeply. Oh, those lips of his. He knows exactly how he makes me feel and I love it. I've never had so much sex in a twenty-four-hour period.

I've caught myself checking my phone over ten times today. He hasn't told me where he's staying at yet or for how long. What he said today threw me for a loop. I'm so confused.

Wait. He said I was his girl. What does that even mean? His fuck buddy? That he's claimed me? That…he's my man? I wouldn't be opposed to the latter. I quickly grab my phone and text him and then Dani.

I hope you're finding your way around New York.

I hit send and then type out the text to Dani. **He's here! He's in New York.**

I'm biting on my nails nervously waiting for Noah's reply when I hear Nik walk into the studio. You can't mistake his Russian accent and his voice makes me cringe internally. I thought he was going to miss practice, but he's later than me. Ugh, I hope my practice time is over soon. I don't have the energy to deal with him.

A text comes in from Dani: **WHAT! He came to see you? Heather! He must have a thing for you too. What man flies across the country for someone he doesn't like?**

Nik walks up behind me then, when I'm all giddy about Dani's text. I can feel him breathing against my neck. I whip around on my toes. "Leave me alone, Nik!"

"Well, Heather, you must have missed me. You weren't here yesterday. We had a rehearsal together."

I roll my eyes and brush past him. "I was busy."

"Busy? Mistress Lindsay is pissed that you missed it. So am I." He's following after me now. "I wanted to get my hands all over you again. Have you changed your mind about my cock?"

I stop abruptly and turn around, pointing at his chest. "You are so disgusting! I will never sleep with you."

He puts his hands up in the air, acting like I'm the crazy bitch when everyone in the studio turns to watch us. I already feel raw from Noah working me over: I'm emotional and I need to get out of here.

"Whatever you say, small tits."

I'm completely frozen in place. Embarrassed. Humiliated. I can't even form a retort. I'm startled and jump when my phone vibrates in my hand. On the verge of tears, I hastily turn around to grab my bag. I can hear whispers and murmurs behind me. I swear, I am this close to quitting.

I quickly take my pointe shoes off and slip on my snow boots before walking briskly across the studio and out into the subzero weather. There's only one place I want to be right now, and that's in his arms, holding me. I get into my Buick and pull out of the parking deck and into traffic, wanting to get home. My eyes tear up and I can't help but feel so down on myself. I hate that I dated that jerk. I detest him.

I wipe under my eyes with the back of my hand as the tears fall. How can I go from being on cloud nine to feeling like crap? And I still haven't heard from him. Maybe this was just sex to him? Figures.

I officially hate today, and I'm grumpin' hard. I'm done with it. I pull into my building and I'm whisked up to my floor in the car elevator. I don't bother taking my things out of the car. I want a shower, my bed, ice cream, and Channing Tatum.

I unlock my door and walk inside, dropping my purse on my foyer table. I don't have the heart to text my sister back, not with the way I feel. The place is dark and quiet and...lonely.

I walk through the darkness, and head up to my room, flipping on the lights. I freeze when I see a broad-shouldered Greek god in my bed. He's here? He's lying on his stomach without a shirt on, my pink blanket lying at his feet.

My heart flutters and there's a pinch of excitement in my stomach. Should I wake him? He shifts slightly, and I can see all of his muscles move as he raises his arm above his head, elongating his torso. He's gorgeous and so...scratched all to hell. I cover my mouth with my hand. Oh crap! I did that?

He sleeps so silently. I quickly walk on my toes to my closet, getting changed into something a little sexier than what I would usually wear. After brushing my teeth and running a brush through my hair, I crawl into bed after turning the lights off. I know I just met this man only two weeks ago, but I feel so safe with him.

I lie down next to him and he takes a deep breath before opening his eyes, and blinking a few times. I've moved his phone and earphones to the nightstand, and silenced them.

"What time is it?" he asks in the sexiest sleepy voice.

I answer him quietly. "It's after ten. Go back to sleep."

He groans and nuzzles my pillow before turning onto his back, "I'm sorry. I didn't mean to sleep this long. I can go," he offers and I shake my head.

"I don't want you to go. Did you sleep all day?"

He's still half asleep and his responses are slow and groggy. "Mmm, yeah. I think. I haven't slept all week."

I frown even though he can't see me in the dark. "Is everything okay?"

"No," he says quietly. A few seconds later his breath shallows out as he reaches for me, moving me on top of himself, just as we slept last night. His arms surround me and hold me as I rest my cheek against his chest. This is where he wants me.

I feel him kiss the top of my head then he says, "I missed you... even in my sleep."

I'm blushing in the dark, replying softly, "I think I missed you too." Suddenly my good mood evaporates when Nik seeps into my thoughts.

"You're my girl, right? Do you remember saying that?" he queries nonchalantly.

I'm unsure of what to say. For the second time tonight, I'm speechless. Does he really mean that? I...what are we? This was supposed to be a New Year's Eve fling. Do I want it to be more? Yes. I can't help it, with this man, "Yes..."

"Yes, you remember, or yes, you're my girl?" He tilts my chin up and presses his lips to mine gently. My entire body comes alive as electricity surges through my veins. As I exhale in a rush...I brush my lips softly against his.

"Yes, I'm yours." He's kissing me so tenderly. I can't help but feel the way I do about him.

He growls against my lips playfully. "My little ballerina."

I STIR AWAKE when there's a loud banging. Noah kisses me softly before he moves me off of his warm chest and I'm instantly cold. He groans and sleepily drags his legs off of the bed to pull on a pair of jeans. In my heavy-eyed state I watch his muscular rear walk out of my room and I yawn. I hear him mess with the latches and deadbolt on my door before I drift off for a few seconds, the warmth of the spot he was just lying in lulls me to sleep.

My eyes shoot open when I hear Noah raise his voice. "What in the ever-loving fuck are you doing here?"

I sit up quickly and pull on my white satin robe, and I tie the sash hastily before rushing out of the room. I question to myself as I hurry down the stairs, who in the world could be here that would make him so angry? I freeze when I hear that unmistakable accent and my heart drops into my stomach. Oh no.

I don't hear Nik's reply, but I know it can't be good because Noah lets the door shut behind him as he steps into the hallway.

"Who the fuck do you think you are coming around here at three in the morning?"

I cringe because he sounds irate. I'm actually frightened for Nik at the moment.

Nik ignores his question and asks, "Where is Heather?"

"She's not here, asshole. Get lost before I fucking do something about it."

My hand is on the doorknob and I'm about to open the door when Nik speaks. "I know she's here."

"Fuck off." Noah's voice is deep and curt.

"How about you fuck off while I fuck Lanie, huh?"

I gasp and cover my mouth with my hand. I can't believe how bold Nik is. He clearly has a death wish. Suddenly without warning, the door vibrates and the unmistakable sound of a body being thrown into it startles me. "I'll fucking ruin you if you go near her. Understand?"

I stagger back and Nik's eerie laugh penetrates through the door. "Try me, pretty boy."

The door rattles again before I hear a crashing bang on what sounds like the opposite wall before the door handle turns.

I step away quickly to avoid getting hit by it. I'm unsure of who's coming in.

Noah steps back into my apartment and I get a glimpse of Nik rubbing his throat as he sits on the floor, leaning against the opposite wall before the door shuts.

I look up at him, taking in his furious expression and flushed chest. I don't even know what to say. He looks down at me and we stay silent for the longest moment. Is he mad at me?

"Does he usually stop by at this hour?" he's speaking in a hushed tone. He wants to know if I'm into Nik?

I shake my head adamantly and my eyes are wide with fear. I'm afraid of losing him just when I finally got him. "No. No, he's never been here this late," I whisper.

"How did he get past the doorman, I wonder?"

I shrug slightly. "I guess the doorman knew him from… previous visits."

His body doesn't relax, but he walks up to me and lifts me into his arms to carry me to my room.

I find his protective side incredibly sexy. He's still as tense as ever so I nuzzle into him to try and get him to relax.

He gets me back into bed before he takes his jeans off then gets under the comforter with me. I pull my robe off before he lifts me onto his chest.

"What did he want?" I ask timidly, knowing exactly what he wanted but I want to see if he'll tell me the truth.

"You...but you belong to me now."

I peek up at him and see his rigid expression. His arm is propped behind his head and he's staring up at the ceiling.

"I know," I say with a smile. I can't argue with him because he's right. He visibly relaxes with my words and I lean up and kiss him softly. "Now go back to sleep." I hum before lying back down in my spot.

His arms automatically move around me. I feel safe and oh so wanted by this man. I close my eyes and allow myself to once again fall asleep with this Greek god.

CHAPTER
Eighteen
breaking her walls

Heather

IDESPERATELY NEED to talk to Dani. I'm lying awake on
Noah's chest, listening to him breathe, contemplating what's
going on between us. He's been asleep since the brief interruption
of Nik's visit last night. I think our light rainstorm just turned into a
dust storm of impressive proportions.

I feel elated, yet so terrified. I'm so hooked on him already. I've
slept with him for the past two nights, and I can tell he's so tense.
The only time he was utterly relaxed was when I was on top of him,
willingly taking his virtue.

He moves and I look up at his face as his hands come alive on
my body, moving down my back to my ass…naturally. He's such an
ass man, but I don't mind it. I actually find it adorable.

"Good morning," I say sweetly. His body automatically relaxes
at the sound of my voice, and it surprises me.

"Good morning, beautiful."

Oh I so could get used to this. I slowly move off of him and sit up cross-legged on the bed.

"Can we talk?"

He pushes himself up with those sexy, muscular, tanned arms and rubs his hands over his face. He's way past a five o'clock shadow today.

"We can talk. If you think I'm intruding, don't worry about it. I'll be looking for an apartment today."

"Oh no. That's not it at all. I really like having you here." I'm blushing: I know I'm as pink as my blanket right now.

"What did you want to talk about? The asshole who visited last night?"

"No, I don't care about him, and you shouldn't either. I actually want to talk about you," I say nervously.

"Ah. Well, I've been through some shit these last few days. Do you remember I told you I was denied to take the bar exam in Arizona?"

"Yes, I remember."

"I found out the reason why I was denied. It had to do with my birth certificate. Apparently I submitted a fake one with my application. One of my buddies has a friend who's an FBI agent, so I called him and told him what was going on. He put in a favor for me and started digging around."

I'm so invested in what he's saying I don't even realize that he's taken my hand into his. He easily laces our fingers together and I squeeze his hand softly in an attempt to reassure him. I think he likes touching me whenever I'm around, as if it grounds him in some way.

"I got a phone call from him a week later, and to put this easily, Mae is not my mother. She told me she found me in a New York City dumpster and took me in as her own when the adoption went through. Well, the FBI agent, Joel, found out there are no records on my adoption, anywhere. After that revelation, he proceeded to tell me that Mae Ryan is a wanted criminal—a serial kidnapper. I was the only infant she held onto."

"WHAT?" I blurt out. "I mean...she kidnapped you when you were younger?"

"Yeah."

Holy crap! "Noah...I'm so sorry. How many other children were there?"

"A total of five others that they know of. All of the kidnappings happened hours after the child's birth, as did mine."

I move closer to him and he pulls me onto his lap, wrapping his strong arms around me. I want to be there for him.

"Do they know where you came from? Or who your parents are?" I inquire as I run my fingers over his pectoral muscles.

"No. They're currently looking into all the kidnappings from 1985 in New York State." He moves my hair to one side of my shoulder and nuzzles my neck, breathing me in.

He looks completely exhausted and now I know why. "Do you have any other family members back in Arizona?"

He shakes his head from side to side. "No, Mae has always been my only family. For twenty-nine years this woman essentially held me against my will. It's been difficult to comprehend."

Twenty-nine? That's how old he is? An older man by five years—I love it.

Heather! Snap out of it! This man is confiding in you...

"I'm sorry," I say as I cradle his strong jaw with both of my hands before kissing him passionately.

He sucks gently on my bottom lip before moving back.

"It's your turn now: tell me something about yourself." He doesn't want to talk about Mae or his situation anymore. I think it's too painful for him.

I inevitably squirm on his lap. "What do you want to know?"

"Let's start with siblings: do you have any?" He's running the pad of his thumb along my collarbone and I'm having a hard time concentrating.

"Hmm? Oh. Yes. Her name is Dani and she's thirty. She recently moved to LA with her boyfriend, Brannon. We used to live together in Tribeca."

"Are you enjoying living on your own then?"

"I am, probably a bit too much though."

"There's nothing wrong with that, ballerina."

I love that nickname he uses for me. It's so unique and special, and just for me. "I know. Can I ask why you've decided to move to New York?"

"I think the honest answer might frighten you away, but the one person I wanted to be with when my life came crashing down around me was you." His hand moves across the back of my satin nightie, sending a hot shiver through me.

"Me? Why me? What about that guy you were with on New Year's Eve?"

"Coen? He's a good friend, but for once in my life I decided to do something for myself rather than putting everyone else first."

I nod because I completely understand. I get him. "I've done that with my ballet career for years now. It's only brought good things into my life." Good things like him, I want to tell him.

"What else would you like to know about me?" he asks.

"What about your apartment?"

"I've arranged for my apartment to be packed and moved up here. I just have to find a new place soon."

"Oh wow. You seriously know what you're doing."

His smile almost makes me pass out. "I know what I want."

Does he mean me? Surely not.

He chooses right now to press his lips against my neck. I moan in appreciation and move a strand of hair out of the way so he can do it again. He ducks his head down again and this time bites me hard, his teeth sinking into my skin, and I yelp. Not because it hurts, but because I'm taken by surprise. His lips are still against my skin when he chuckles and I can feel the tremor from deep down inside of him.

He moves me easily so I'm straddling him and takes my hand again. I love the way he holds my hand, as if he truly cares about me. He kisses me, but it's not just a kiss. It's a blissful moment of trust, heaven, and adoration. Kissing him is different.

Storms brew beneath my skin with every solitary kiss he places on my lips.

"I crave you," he murmurs against my lips.

"Kiss the hell out of me," I insist.

He eagerly obliges.

HE TAKES ME again.
     And again.
     And again.

My body aches in places that it's never ached before. I consider myself to be in great shape and I'm normally able to keep up with anyone, but him? He can't get enough, and honestly, neither can I.

We're both lying on my bed naked and quiet as we watch a snowstorm hit the heart of New York City.

"So much for looking at apartments today," I tease him. It's already midafternoon.

"I've enjoyed far better things today," he says as he kisses the back of my shoulder, gently dragging his lips over my skin.

I look over my shoulder at him and he touches his smile to mine.

"Tell me more about yourself. If I'm yours, I want to know you," I say innocently.

He traces his finger along the line of my bottom lip. "I never thought I'd chase after a girl, especially to the other side of the country."

My tongue darts out and I lick him playfully. "I'm not just any girl, Noah."

"No, you're not. You're my girl. There's a huge fucking difference, and you better hold onto that tongue, baby."

A smile lights up my face, "Okay then...first things first. I need to know...Chinese or Mexican food?

"Chinese. Hands down, every time. Pork dumplings are the best damn things ever made. What about you?" He runs his hand down my naked curves as he speaks.

"Gross, Noah! Dumplings? Aren't they mushy?" I cringe.

"Mushy? No. Don't bash it before you try it, ballerina" He pats my ass as if he forgives me.

Shoving him playfully, I say, "Uh-uh, I will never eat that. I'll only eat shrimp dishes. And lo mein. Oh, and crab rangoon."

"Not even if I beg?" he says in a horrible attempt at a pout.

Laughing and shaking my head, I respond, "No. I'll puke."

"At least we agree on the Chinese part. Right?" He pulls me closer and I can feel him getting hard again. This man can go on for hours. "Next question, who is your favorite actor or actress?"

"Hmmm, that's a difficult one." My finger starts outlining his pecs while I think it over. I can feel his eyes on me. I feel like he's undressing me all over again, but I'm already naked. Plus, I'd rather he undressed me with his teeth.

"Well?" he asks.

Blinking up at him, I smile. "Well...I think Johnny Depp is my favorite actor. But...I think Channing Tatum is sexy!"

"How the hell am I supposed to compete with Tatum?"

I start laughing because he sounds completely serious, "You are so much sexier than him."

He growls and pulls me closer to him yet again; my breasts are heavy and my nipples ache.

"Good. I'll fight for my girl's attention," he says, as I lie against him. He's always so warm, and I'm always so cold. I giggle to myself because we're polar opposites, but fit perfectly together.

Lying there, my body leaning against his chest, we're quiet for what seems like forever. I've got a million and one questions for him but I don't know where to start. I hardly know him. Well... biblically I know him. Really, well. I know he likes for me to lick the vein that runs along his inner bicep. He likes it when I bite his rock-hard shoulder. I can't help myself: I usually bite him there when I'm horny, which is all the freaking time now. I know for a fact he loves it when I hold one of my legs over my head. He goes so deep when I do that. And the way his teeth graze my inner thigh right before he's about to sink his teeth into me does something wild to me.

But I don't know much else about him. Emotionally. Personally. But that's what dating is, right? Getting to know someone? Their likes and dislikes. Things that annoy them, frighten them. I want to know more but at the same time, do I? I don't want to fall in love. I don't want to get too close.

Okay, so it's settled then, Heather. Keep it simple. Keep it fun. That's what guys want anyway.

Breaking the silence, I ask him "Favorite ice cream?"

He's running his hand down the inside of my thigh when he answers, "I like raspberry sorbet. What's your favorite wine?"

Smiling as I run my fingertip along that vein on his bicep, I reply softly, "Toad Hollow's Risqué. French fries or tater tots?" I peek up at him. "And think about your answer carefully, Ryan: this is a deal breaker."

He takes my hand and moves it to his lips, kissing my fingers and then playing with them with his own, "I enjoy both. However, I only like skinny fries."

I groan dramatically. "Skinny fries? Nope...that's it. We can't be friends."

His laugh is so deep-throated and sexy. "What's wrong with skinny fries? Don't tell me you eat those bullshit steak fries or crinkle fries. Fucking nasty."

"Hey! I love my crinkle fries. You have to eat, like, a hundred skinny fries just to be satisfied."

"I don't see the problem there. Do you do anything outside of ballet?"

"Uhm, not recently. Ballet has been my life. What about you? Are you too consumed in your studies to do anything fun?" I ask.

"Yes and no. I was a volunteer firefighter for two years in law school, but my workload became too much and I had to stop volunteering."

Now that explains all of the muscles. "I see...What is your favorite holiday?"

He raises his eyebrow at me because he knows I'm stealing his question and asking two in a row. "It was Christmas, but New Year's just took its place. What do you say I take you out to dinner...and what would be your ideal date?"

"You mean like an official dinner date?" I ask sweetly as I move and sit on my knees...exposing my breasts to him.

"Yes, like an official date. If you're not doing anything else tonight, go get dressed into something tight and sexy, ballerina."

"Okay, deal, but I'm not telling you my ideal date. You'll laugh at me."

"I won't. Tell me," he demands.

"Fine. My ideal date would be camping underneath the stars, away from the city and its lights."

The smile he gives me is making my knees weak underneath me. "Good answer. Now go get dressed for our date. We'll make it an early dinner."

Suddenly remembering that I have unavoidable plans, I reach for a pillow and pull it to my chest. "Uhm…I have this thing that I need to go to this afternoon. Very soon actually."

He raises his eyebrows in question. "A thing?"

"I have a photo shoot near Times Square. You're welcome to come with me. It'll be me and a few other company members."

"You'd want me to come with you? Is he going to be there?"

Leaning forward I bite his shoulder then look up at him when he smirks down at me. "I think so."

His body stiffens as he runs a hand into my insane sex hair. "I'll be going with you then, ballerina. I'll kill him if he even tries to touch you."

I freeze. *Don't panic, Heather. Breathe.*

"Why don't you go get ready?" He taps my ass and I get up to go shower. I can feel his eyes on my bare ass as I walk into the bathroom.

A COUPLE OF hours later we walk into the photographer's studio. There are a few dancers hanging about as Nik is having his photos taken. He's only wearing his dance tights and I want to gag. All the girls are watching him, all so infatuated with him.

I'm beyond tense. I can't stand being in the same room as Nik, and from previous experiences with this photographer, I know he's a sleaze too. I set my bag down next to me as the makeup artist comes over. Noah's still standing next to me—he's taking in the entire room. I'm watching him in the mirror as his now icy gaze turns to Nik. His jaw tenses when he looks back down at me.

"Are you okay?" he asks.

Feigning a smile, I nod. "I'm okay. You?"

He runs his hand over his jaw and nods toward Nik. "Is that ass-hat always around?"

My eyes flicker over in Nik's direction as the makeup artist applies some blush to my cheeks. "Generally, yes."

"Do you have to be in these photos with him?" He's still watching Nik as if he wants to physically hurt him, especially after last night.

"No. These are just individual shots for the magazine article." My heart is beating rapidly. Ugh! I don't want a scene.

"Good. I don't want him touching what belongs to me." Noah leans down and moves my hair behind one of my ears before pressing his lips to mine while the makeup artist is trying to apply my mascara.

I smile against his lips. I'm actually turned on by his possessiveness. I find myself wanting to reassure him. "It's going to be okay. Promise. It'll be quick."

"Do I have to leave? Or would you like me to stay and watch?" He moves back so the makeup artist, who is clearly checking out his ass, can start applying my mascara again.

"Please stay?" I ask because I don't want him more than five feet from me. And if this makeup artist doesn't stop checking Noah out, I'm going to have a diva moment.

"I'm not going anywhere, little ballerina. Especially not when that fucker is around."

When the blonde makeup artist finishes, I get off of the chair and the photographer calls my name out, but before I can take a step toward him, Noah grabs me, wrapping his sexy, muscular arms around my waist and kissing me greedily. I swear the entire room is watching us, but I don't care. He's what I want. Circling my arms around his neck, I kiss him back with equal, if not more, fervor.

I'm getting lost in our kiss when I hear someone cough behind me. "Miss Lane? We're ready for you."

His hand is resting on my ass and I know without a doubt that it's him telling me he'd much rather be buried inside of me than here. He wants me naked and underneath him. Our eyes lock as he squeezes my ass cheekily. I follow the assistant leading me away from my Greek god.

He belongs to me.

I'm taken behind a large set of screens so no one can watch me change into the outfit they have picked out.

I groan when I look at my reflection in the mirror. Well, this should go well. The black sheer lace tights I'm wearing go well with the pink pointe shoes that lace around my ankles. But the black bustier...

"Dear God, help me," I mutter on an exhale. Okay, so my boobs are pushed up and almost popping out of this thing. Who chose these outfits again? Sighing because I know this isn't going to turn out great, I step out from behind the partition and lock eyes with Noah.

Noah

HOLY FUCK.

Is she trying to get me hard in public? That outfit is showing off everything she has.

She's looking at me as if she's asking for approval though. I sure as hell don't approve with all of these men around here, but if it were just the two of us I wouldn't mind.

Shit.

I'd fuck her in that for hours, just like we have been. Neither one of us has gotten much sleep these last few nights, but she still manages to look gorgeous.

I wink at my girl as she sits down on the large white bed. A bed? They want Heather on a bed in lingerie for all these assholes to see? And then on the cover of a magazine? No. There's no fucking way. I look at her again and she looks beyond uncomfortable. I loathe these assholes for making her feel this way.

My body automatically starts moving toward hers until I'm crouched down next to her while she sits on the bed. "Are you okay with this?" I ask quietly so others can't hear me.

The photographer pipes in before she can answer me. "Yo, dude, you can't be in here unless you're her agent or related somehow."

I ignore him and turn back to Heather. "Are you okay?" I insist she answer me this time. She shrugs and looks up at the photographer and someone standing behind me. I look over my shoulder at the fucker who I pinned against Heather's door last night. The douche bag is standing mere feet away, with an evil grin on his smug, cocky face.

I know they are messing with her mood right now. I want her to enjoy herself, and as much as I hate others seeing her in this outfit, I want to see that smile of hers again. Turning back to her, I try and give her the best smirk I can manage. "You look beautiful, ballerina. Enjoy yourself," I say before cupping her face and kissing her hard, pushing my tongue between her plump lips and tasting her.

Raspberries. Pineapples. My girl.

I want all of these dickwads to understand that she belongs to me and me alone.

I hear one of the fuckers groan then yell, "Come the fuck on!"

I chuckle against her lips and she's smiling again. "Put on a show for me, Heather."

She's blushing and I can't stand how turned on I get when that pink color invades her soft complexion. She looks up at the photographer and smiles cheekily. "He's my boyfriend."

Boyfriend?

Fuuuck.

It's been a long-ass time since I've been called that. I don't mind that word coming from her rosy lips though. It belongs there, just as she belongs in my arms, and on my cock.

I'd do just about anything for this woman. I'd kick both of these perverts' asses for even looking at her the wrong way. She deserves to be treated with the utmost respect and nothing less. I take care of what's mine—I don't want her frowning around me.

I get up and wink at her before stepping away, purposely positioning myself in front of the male ballerina's view of my girl as the photographer starts snapping pictures. "Beautiful, darling. Don't move. That's perfect!"

My girlfriend.

As the lights flash, she's smiling at me like she did when I first kissed her. The asshole behind me clears his throat, but I decide not to give him the time of day.

"Excuse me, jerk," I hear the guy say in a Russian accent. I turn to look at him as he continues to speak. "You're blocking my view."

I almost laugh at the dick. "Nah, man, I've got a perfect view of my girl right here. Thanks for asking though." I say confidentially before turning back to Heather.

"Are you fucking with me?"

He almost yells it, but I decide to ignore him for Heather's sake. She looks gorgeous with her hair fanned around her on the bed. I want some of these pictures. Shit, I want all of them. She belongs to me.

"You're doing great, baby," I encourage her while I watch the photos pop up on the screen to the right of me and I'm having the hardest time not ravaging her right here and now. Her smile turns my world on its head.

"Thank you, my Noah."

That's right, baby, yours. "Are you wearing that out to dinner?"

Her blush creeps up on her this time like it's trying to hide in her complexion. "Maybe I'll wear it underneath my coat so you can take it off later," she teases.

"You won't hear me complaining," I say, but I'm quickly interrupted by the rude asshole.

"You fucked this prick, Heather? And not me? What the fuck?"

I'm about to reply for her when she speaks from the bed. "That's none of your business, Nik. Would you please leave?"

"You heard the lady," I say without looking back. I want to be inside of her.

He scoffs and mutters something in Russian before walking away. And fuck if it wasn't a smart idea because I'm about to lose it.

"Watch your mouth around my girl," I call out after him.

I keep focused on her because if I don't, I'll follow that dick right outside. I'm about half a foot taller than him and I have a good twenty pounds more in muscle. I don't know what in the hell this guy is thinking.

"All right, gorgeous, you're good. We've got what we need," the photographer chimes in.

Heather gets up quicker than I've ever seen her move and she scurries behind the partition. I keep back and make sure nobody goes back there.

While she gets changed, or covers up, I speak to the photographer. "Hey man, nice job. Where can I get a copy of these?"

He hands me his business card and I slide it into my jeans' back pocket. "Email me and I'll charge you."

"No problem. I'll be in contact."

Heather walks out from behind the partition. "Are you ready, ballerina?" She nods and pulls her coat tighter around herself before we walk out of the photographer's studio and I hail a cab.

After sitting in the stop-and-go traffic for a good twenty minutes we pull up to an Italian restaurant, on the Upper East Side. Once we get out of the cold and into the restaurant we are seated immediately. I take the seat next to her instead of across from her. I want her close—close enough for me to touch her. She's looking over the menu as I run my hand down the inside of her thigh; the urge I have to bite her there again is intense.

"Are you still wearing that outfit?"

Her blush returns as she looks up at me from her menu. "You'll just have to wait and see."

"Well, either way, it's good to know that we won't be having dessert here, but rather in a hotel room close by."

"Oh? A hotel room?"

"Why not?" I ask. "It's closer and I get to have my hands all over you much sooner than I would if we were to drive back downtown in New York City traffic to go to your place." I inch my hand up some more. The waitress comes up to take our order at the very moment I cup her between her thighs. I think she whimpers as she asks for the Campanelle Carbonara.

"We'll have a bottle of Chardonnay, please. And I'll have the Shrimp Pasta Fra Diavolo."

Heather gasps and I swear I haven't moved my finger an inch over her cunt.

"I was going to order that," she says excitedly.

"Yeah? Maybe I'll let you share a bite or two. It's supposed to taste good, so good." I crook my finger against her cunt so it pushes against her clitoris. "But my dessert is going to taste even better."

"Noah Ryan! We are supposed to be on a date." Her legs naturally open for me as I circle my finger against her. I love how she says no but her body says otherwise.

"We are, but I know you a little better than any guy taking you on a first date, wouldn't you agree?"

"Obviously, but we're in public. Someone is going to see..."

"No one is going to see, baby." I lean toward her and kiss her neck. "You have no idea how much you turned me on during that photo shoot."

She looks down at my lap and giggles softly. "Oh I think I know."

I kiss her sweet lips—her body language is practically begging me for it.

"I don't think you should have your dessert before dinner," she barely whispers against my lips.

"It's a good thing that we can get this to go then. I'd like to play with my dessert, and I want you to watch." I'm hard as hell under the table and there's no way in hell I'm getting up right now.

"We can't take our wine to go." She giggles the cutest fucking sound and pats my cheek then pulls away to take a sip of her water. The waitress comes back and I move my hand from her pussy to her knee as our food is placed in front of us. She's damn cheeky enough to fork up one of my shrimp before the waitress finishes filling our wine glasses. Well, I'll be damned.

"A ballerina who loves to eat. I like it."

She's doing a little dance in her seat while she chews and it's fucking adorable. "Ah! I love to eat."

"Yeah, you love to eat my food," I joke with her before taking a bite. She's sipping on her wine and I notice that we're watching everything the other is doing. Every small movement. I know I don't want to miss a thing that she does, or her little quirks, and surprisingly, I don't think she wants to miss mine either.

"Thank you for coming with me today. I'm sure it wasn't all that fun," she says, as she takes another piece of my shrimp without a care.

I fork up some of her pasta and groan in appreciation of the chef. "No problem. Your boyfriend isn't very keen on other men watching you in lingerie, so I'm glad I was there. Did you enjoy yourself?"

She shrugs and I'm secretly glad she didn't say yes. "Yes and no. I don't like it when Nik is there. But I did enjoy the photo shoot itself."

"Nik…what an ass-fuck," I say as she steals another shrimp. Squeezing her knee, I switch our plates around so she can have my shrimp pasta.

I watch her nod. "Yep." She stares down at her plate in silence and I wonder if she's thinking about him. And I can't stand it.

In an effort to distract her, I pick up my glass of wine and hold it up to her. "To my beautiful girlfriend."

Thankfully she smiles and her beautiful jade green eyes find mine. "Stop it."

"Make me," I dare her as I lean in to kiss her tenderly. She's giggling as I kiss her. "What is it?"

She shrugs and bites my lip.

"Fuck. Someone is a little feisty."

"Swear jar, Ryan."

"I'd comply, but I still don't have my swear jar, Miss Lane."

"You're lucky I like you," she utters before biting my shoulder.

I know exactly what she needs. What she wants.

Me.

I have no doubt that this beautiful woman is ready for me again. How the hell did I get this fortunate? I chuckle and take another bite. "You like me, huh?"

She eyes me as she chews. "Don't push it," she says after she swallows.

No, this isn't a normal date, because I've already been inside of her. But I still don't know much about this stunning woman sitting next to me. What I do know is she's afraid as fuck to let me in. Not physically...but emotionally. I think she still thinks this is short term. I chuckle to myself because she couldn't be more wrong.

"What are you thinking about?" she asks as I finish her pasta with chicken.

"Honestly? You."

"Me? Why?" She's seriously interested.

"Because you belong to me now, baby." I squeeze her knee and she beams up at me.

"I really like it when you say that. It's sweet."

"When I say what? Baby?"

She blushes before I can finish my question, and sips her wine so she doesn't have to answer me.

"Why are you so shy with me out in public, but when the lights are off in your bedroom you're a sex fiend?"

Her eyes flicker around to the tables next to us and I know she's making sure nobody heard me. She clears her throat and replies, "I'm not shy. Why do you think that?"

"You're rather quiet when we're out. Am I the reason you're nervous?" I think she's biting the inside of her cheek again when the waitress walks up. "I hope you've enjoyed your dinner. Would either of you be interested in dessert this evening?"

"I would, but that's nothing you can help me with. Just the bill will be fine. Thank you."

Hell. Now there are two blushing females at the table. I look over and Heather's mouth is completely gaping open and practically on the floor.

The waitress manages to walk away while I turn to Heather and take her mouth, kissing the hell out of her. I growl in response and sign the bill when the waitress comes back with it. We get up and head to the door, with my hand on her little ass, letting her know that I am ready for her.

CHAPTER
Nineteen
unfathomable

Heather

I CAN'T BREATHE.

We're in a hotel room just off of Times Square. It's a boutique hotel. The rooms are lavish and unique.

He's there again.

Licking and savoring and penetrating and sucking. He's enjoying this just as much as I am, and it's only making me want him more.

My back arches off of the white down comforter as I come again. He's working me hard and fast. I think he wants to be inside of me just as bad as I want him there.

"NOAH!" I shout out, but I can't hear myself: my ears are ringing and all my senses are fixated on what he's doing down there with his tongue.

"Fuck, you are so damn sexy when you come," he says, his mouth muffled by my sex.

"I've never been so libidinous and so thoroughly satisfied in my life," I say softly.

"Just lie back and savor this, baby. You taste so sweet. Every spot I kiss on your body tastes like raspberries or pineapples, and I can't get enough."

He starts running his tongue around my pink, swollen clit again and thunderbolts run through my veins, making my body convulse into another orgasm. He's got me so worked up and sensitive, I'm not sure if I can come again after this.

He's so cocky and playful as he easily slides a finger and then a second into me. "You're ready for me, ballerina."

He kneels up and moves me farther up the bed.

I'm limp. I'm exhausted. But I want him. I love how he feels inside of me; I love how he makes me feel when he's inside of me.

He's teasing my entrance with the head of his thick, monstrous cock. "Noah...please!" I cry out of desperation, my body trembling with need. Need of another orgasm? No, there's no way. He's wrung me out and still wants more. My body has a hankering for his, and I'm not going to fight it.

He's always so placid. He's never been overtaken with passion and emotion when it comes to sex, whereas I'm a complete mess. I'm literally shaking and he's so...in check. Perpetually.

I'm inching my hips forward, trying to get any relief. He enjoys teasing me like this, pushing me to my limits. Then swiftly he's stretching me. His ample cock fills me entirely—I wouldn't be able to stretch a millimeter more. "YES! Oh...Fuck!"

"Mmm," he croons against my skin as he kisses up my neck. "I like that dirty mouth of yours."

He's grinding his hips against mine achingly slowly and it's torment. His sizeable hand cups my ass possessively. I can only moan. I have no words. The way he works my body is out of this world, pushing me closer and closer.

"Fuck, you're still so tight, but we got this, baby." He's moving in and out, filling me slowly each time.

"Noah...I need it hard!" I manage to say loud enough for him to hear me.

He stops moving as I look up at him through lust-filled eyes. He's braced above me, an unnamed expression on his face. "What?"

he asks.

I can tell something has changed.

He wants this.

He's wanted to let go with me, but he's been holding back. How can that even be possible?

"Fuck me. I want you. I want you so hard and deep."

His ocean green eyes glow and I can tell he's going to give me exactly what I'm asking for. "Are you sure? You'll let me know if it's too much?"

Why is he so perfect? What man asks that before he goes balls deep into a girl? "I'll let you know. Please?"

"Okay, get up. You're going to need to hold onto the bed."

Uh oh! I slide off of the bed and brace my hands at the end of the bed. He simply pulls my ass back against him and runs his hand all the way up my spine. I glance back at him and he's taking in every single freaking inch of my naked body. I feel so vulnerable, but safe too.

My knees are quivering as he pushes back into me slowly, making sure I can get accustomed to him in this new position. The new angle is stretching me even more. The big tanned hand of his that was running up my spine is now gathering my hair. I feel him wrap it around his fist before he lightly tugs.

I think I'm going to explode.

His pace starts out smooth and slow, but I can tell he's waiting for some sign from me, telling him I'm okay before he goes strong. He's penetrating me to the fullest extent; I feel the veins on his thick shaft pulse. As he starts to pick up speed he uses his other hand to rub my ass cheeks playfully.

It all happens at once. He starts pounding my sex, and I can't take it. His hand swats my ass as his other hand tugs on my hair.

I whimper as he brings his hand down on my ass cheek again. He then soothes the sting by rubbing the spot where he hit. My skin is moist from perspiration and I'm not the one doing all of the work. I push my ass back against him hard and he grunts loudly.

"I love this little ass," he says through his teeth, as he slaps my other ass cheek, and then soothes it like he did the other.

"Your cock is so deep inside of me. Noah! Yes!"

"Damn right! This pussy is mine. You are so wet for me, Heather."

He makes me feel like a porn star and I'm panting, wanting more. He makes me feel so comfortable and confident. His hand that was on my ass moves around to the front of my body to rub my clit, while his colossal cock slams into me ruthlessly. This is hot, sensual, and intense; I don't want it to stop. I don't want to come yet.

"Oh yeah, yeah, yeah, yeah, yeah! Right there!"

"Come for me, baby," he commands and my body willingly obliges. I come so hard that my sex pushes his thick, magnificent cock out of me. He replaces it immediately and pumps into me a few more times.

I'm coating his cock with my slick wetness as he's slamming into me. He stills and I feel him. His hot spurts of come shooting into the depths of my wet sex. He hasn't even pulled out of me yet, but I can feel his come oozing out of me and sliding down the inside of my thigh.

We stay like that for a while until we are both able to catch our breath. Without warning he slides out of me and sits down on the edge of the bed with a brash grin on his face. I take a few minutes to compose myself before sitting down next to him.

His arm automatically snakes around my waist, pulling me down with him onto the bed, where I lay in his arms wallowing in a sated bliss. Unconsciously, I move my hands into his damp hair and smile sleepily.

THIRTY MINUTES LATER, he moves his large delectable body farther up the bed. He pulls me on top of him and I think he's about to pass out, but he surprises me when he rubs his cock against my sex. Again?

I move my hand back, and I feel like I can barely get my hand around him. He easily slides into my wetness this time. Once he's completely buried inside of me I sit up and place my hands on his chest. Starting to rock my body, I'm fucking him like a swing set as I smile down at him. I ride him hard and fast.

"You like that, baby? You like it that fast?"

"Yes…" I hiss out desperately.

A fleeting moment passes when I think that we might lead to something, but I quickly change my thought direction to his cock and how he feels inside of me. His hands grip my waist, holding me still as he pummels my pussy. I can feel his heavy balls hitting me every time he slams up into me. He's hitting every sensitive spot in me all at once.

"I'm going to come!"

"Yes! Come for me like you've never come for anyone else."

I'm lost in my own orgasm as it hits me.

I come so hard and hastily that I lose myself to this man.

I've never felt anything like this.

My body is at such a physical high that I'm almost numb.

"Holy fuck! That's it, baby!" He grunts louder than I've heard him grunt before.

"NOAH!" I'm still coming. I feel wet, so wet and so sated. I think he comes; I think I feel him lose his load deep inside of me, but I'm unsure. I feel high from my orgasm. The next thing I comprehend is him pulling me down to his chest, kissing my neck, my cheeks and then my lips.

"I've never seen anyone do that before," he whispers into my ear.

Anyone do what? I try to think, but then I really feel us. We're both wet. More than I've ever felt before during any sexual activity. "That was so intense. I want you to do that to me again," I say sleepily.

"I will, ballerina, but not right now. Let's get you cleaned up."

"I'm fine," I argue.

"Let's go shower. Then you can sleep." I don't understand why he wants to shower right now when I'm so content, so infatuated with this man.

He eases out of me and holds onto my ass as he sits up. I manage to blink my eyes open and take in the wet bed underneath us. He's got liquid of some sort on his sexy abs. I look into his eyes and freeze.

"What...what happened? Was that me?" I'm panicking and my breathing is becoming fast and deep.

"Shh, baby. It was. You finally let go with me, baby; it was the sexiest thing I've ever seen."

"How? Noah, I can't...I've never done that."

"You did. I'd like to make you do it again. I've never seen a woman lose herself so entirely before."

I am so mortified. I quickly cover my face with my hands.

"Hey..." he says, as he moves my hands from my face. "You are so gorgeous, baby. How did that feel?"

"I...are you sure? You're covered in it."

"I'm sure. Relax and tell me how it felt?" His fingers move a long strand of hair behind my ear and I know I'm turning red.

"I've never felt anything like that before."

"Good. I'm glad I have something that no other man has ever experienced with my girl."

Oh my! He's rather possessive and so skillful.

"I want you to do it to me again, but not now. I'm so tired."

He's holding up my body weight as he moves off of the bed and carries me to the bath.

"You have my word, my beautiful baby."

For the next hour he runs his hands over me slowly with the soap, washing me as I lean my body against him, trying my hardest not to fall asleep.

Once the hour passes we get out and he dries me off. I just stand there. I've got nothing left in me. I can dance two shows back to back, but this man does me in. He picks me up again, and I don't complain because I don't think I could walk back to the bed if I wanted to. I'm not entirely sure how he's still awake. He stops walking and I open my eyes just enough to see what's going on. He's set me down on the armchair while he calls down to the front desk to ask to have our linens changed.

I can tell he's smiling by the sound of his voice before he hangs up. I feel his lips on the top of my head a second later, whispering, "my girl."

I smile and nod.

"Yours," I tell him softly.

The next thing I know he's laying me down on the bed. I'm naked, I think, and I curl up onto my side, as he moves the clean comforter over me.

"Goodnight, my little ballerina."

I moan softly, feeling cold without his arms around me. "Where are you going?"

I force my eyes open enough to see him pull off his towel before lying down next to me and getting under the covers.

"Nowhere, baby. I'm right here."

His strong arms surround me as he pulls me on top of him, and that's the last thing I remember before the sleepy blackness becomes me.

CHAPTER
Twenty
sweet tooth

Noah

I TAKE IN A deep breath when I wake up from a deep sleep. Heather's hair is all over my face and tangled in my scruff. I have one eye open, squinting while the other is still closed. Why the fuck did I not close the damn curtains last night? There's more light in this room than there is pink in her wardrobe, and that's saying something.

I lift my head and look over at my sleeping beauty. She's the definition of perfection. Made just for me. She's still fast asleep. Turning my head, I look at the alarm clock. Holy fuck, she's been sleeping for almost ten hours. She's lifeless to the world and hasn't moved in what seems like days. Is she dead?

Was I too rough and she was too afraid to tell me? I scrub my hand down my face and across my stubble.

Christ. I can't fuck this up. I don't think I took it too far last night.

I believe I thoroughly wore her out yesterday. I've never wanted anything so much in my damn life before her. I'm not sharing her, and I'm not letting go. This beautiful woman solely belongs to me.

If there is one thing that I am thankful to Mae for, it's Heather. The only reason I met my girl was because of Mae's obsession with the ballet. Fuck, I feel like that's the only thing I really know about Mae. I don't know who she really is. She's been hiding behind some motherly façade for years. Shit. I don't want to think about this with my girl in my arms.

I move her hair to the side and tilt her face up, whispering, "Ballerina?"

Her nose twitches and her eyelashes flicker a tiny movement. Well, at least I know she's alive. I chuckle to myself. Better take it easy on the girl, Ryan, or she'll never ask for it again.

She moves a little more, oddly enough, squirming on top of me. She's cold. Fuck, her hands are freezing. I make sure the comforter is around us and adjust the pillow under my head before surrounding her in my warmth. She nuzzles my chest automatically, finding her preferred spot.

She's beautiful when she's awake or asleep. I'm the luckiest motherfucker in Manhattan today: my girl is warm and comfortable, my apartment and shit are being moved up next week, and I'm always going to be close to her. I can't do long distance, not with her.

She starts to fidget in her sleep and I have to choke back a laugh. The sounds she's making are fucking hysterical and adorable all at once. Is that a moan? Or a whimper? It almost sounded like a swear word. Does she talk in her sleep? I'm determined to find out.

"What was that, ballerina?" I ask softly. I want to know if she'll answer me in her sleep. Her body stills and she whimpers as if she's crying. Maybe she's having a bad dream? I'm not entirely sure.

"What's wrong, baby girl?" I ask and she nuzzles against me then breathes in quickly.

"Noah..." She moans in a long, drawn-out breath.

"I'm here. Are you okay? Are you sore?"

"Yes, but it feels good," she mumbles. I can't tell if she's awake or not.

"It does? How come?" I ask, as I try to run a hand through her knotted hair.

"Because my boyfriend is amazing at this thing called sex."

I can feel her smiling against my chest and I know she is finally awake. I've been waiting hours to kiss her. I tilt her chin up and take her mouth with mine.

"How did you sleep, beautiful baby?" I ask as our lips are still grazing each other's.

She hums softly and blinks those gorgeous fucking eyes. "I think I was in a coma, but I had a nightmare."

I frown. "Do you have them often?" She doesn't answer me for the longest time. I tilt her chin up. "Do you?" I ask again.

She nods her head but doesn't say the words.

"About what, baby?" I need to know what plagues her so I can fix it. She tenses in my arms and I can tell it's something bad.

"Him," she says in almost a whisper. My fingers clench automatically and my protective side surges forward. I sit up and look at her.

"Heather? Did he ever hurt you?"

She shakes her head. "He just likes digging his fingers into my body when we're on stage. And he tried to force me to sleep with him when we were seeing each other. That's all. He was just really rough. I also have dreams about my parents, and the day they died. It's like I was in the plane with them…"

She stops talking and all I can do is tighten my arms around her little frame. "I'm here, baby."

"I know," she says softly.

In an attempt to change the subject I say, "Would you like to come apartment hunting with me today, beautiful? I need my girl's opinion if she's going to be staying the night."

She nods slowly. "I'd be happy to help." I hear a soft sigh come from her lips as she smiles contently with my arms locked around her.

"Good. We'll get breakfast and head out. We're not in a rush so take your time getting ready. I like seeing you naked anyway." I smirk when she smacks my chest.

"Baby!"

I still. It's the first time she's called me that. Fuck, it feels good. I have goose bumps in my soul. This girl is more than perfect for me. I'm not sure I can live up to the guy she needs to be with. I can't be certain that I'm made for her. I feel as if she needs someone better suited.

But I'm slowly but surely breaking down her walls, brick by brick. She hasn't realized it yet, but fucking help me when she does. Something tells me this little ballerina can be a handful when she wants to be. Either way, she's going to belong to me.

AFTER CHECKING OUT of the hotel and grabbing a cab back to Heather's apartment, I start to strip down, leaving my clothes in a pile at her front door, awaiting her reaction.

Her eyes scan my body as I stand in her entry foyer, stark-ass naked.

"What are you doing?"

I shrug and wink at her. "Free-balling it."

"Why?" she asks as her eyes focus in on my cock.

"Because you rather enjoy it when I'm naked. Are you hungry? I can make us breakfast."

"Yum! I love that you can cook."

I laugh and kiss her neck before swatting her ass. "Go freshen up if you'd like, and come down when you're ready, baby. I'll be waiting."

"You come down when you're ready," she says cheekily, and I know she doesn't mean downstairs.

"I'll do it when you have all of your enthusiastic energy back. Deal?"

"Deal!" she yells back at me as she heads upstairs.

Seconds later I hear her yell, "Waiiit!" before she comes hauling ass down the stairs.

"Where in the hell did all that energy come from?" I ask and stand in front of her. She's out of breath and leaning against a pantry door, her hair wild.

"I...uh...I'll make us something to eat. You go shower first."

I grin slowly. She's clearly hiding something. I didn't go to law school and not learn when people are lying.

"What are you hiding, Heather?"

She squeals and stands firm in front of the pantry. "Nothing," she insists.

"I call bullshit, baby."

"Uhmm. Go shower!" She all but yells.

"Not until you let me into that pantry." I walk toward her and snake my arms around her little waist, but she stands firmly against the door, unbudging.

She's looking around the room for inspiration.

"Ballerina? You can move or I'll move you."

She still refuses to budge. Now I'm more than intrigued. Smirking, I easily lift her and toss her over my shoulder. Reaching for the handle, she screams and squirms wildly.

"Noah. Wait!"

I laugh and open the door swiftly. "What in the hell are you hiding from m—Holy..."

She's smacking my ass, trying to get down as I take in the biggest collection of candy I've ever seen outside of a grocery store. She has an entire shelf stocked full and solely dedicated to different types of chocolates. Above the chocolate shelf are huge six-pound bags of what I can only assume are Gummy Bears and Swedish Fish. The next shelf up, she's got every flavor of Sour Straws. My eyes move down all of the shelves to the bottom one where there are two thirty-six-count boxes of Gushers. Hell, I thought they discontinued those. I'm getting a cavity just looking at this candy stash.

"Now things are starting to make sense. Now I know why you taste so fucking sweet all of the time, you little candy hoarder."

"What happened? I blacked out." Her voice is full of sweet guilt.

I set her down on her feet while I stare into the pantry with an open mouth. "Where's all your damn food?" I turn and look down at her and she's biting on her cheek again.

"Uhm, in the fridge?"

"Oh yeah? Are you sure that's not filled with ice cream and popsicles?" I ask, trying not to laugh as she hugs my arm. I swear her eyes go wide and she dashes to the fridge, standing in front of it. "You have got to be kidding me."

She's looking up at me with the cutest fucking expression. "I have a sweet tooth..." She explains as if it's no big deal.

"A sweet tooth is one huge fucking understatement for what you've got, baby." I pick her up and set her aside before I open the fridge and freezer. There are KitKat's in the fridge and gallons of ice cream and popsicles fill the freezer. Ah, and one packet of bacon.

Well fuck, I can't break her heart now, or her apartment will be overcome with different flavors of gelato and ice cream. It's a damn good thing I don't plan on it.

"NOAH! I'm going to bite you."

I growl seductively. "Bite all you want, ballerina...before your teeth fall out."

Before I know it, she grabs my hand and turns it palm up, biting down hard on the meaty part of my hand, opposite my thumb.

"Ah, fuck!" I yell, yanking my hand back. She stands up on her toes and grasps my face with one hand, kissing me fiercely. I return it, taking her mouth, kissing her just as hard.

The next thing I know she's taking off, running up the stairs to her bedroom. I take off after her and bolt up the stairs, catching the door right before she's about to close it.

"You said bite, so I did!" she shouts as she tries to close the door with great difficulty.

"Oh yeah? Maybe I'll go and toss all the sugary treats out if you don't let me in."

"You would not."

"Watch me." I let go of the door and run back down the two flights of stairs, but before I can even open the pantry door she jumps on my back and covers my eyes. "NO! DON'T TOUCH THE CANDY!"

I laugh and get her off my back and pin her against the wall, both of her hands trapped in one of mine above her head. Her breasts are heaving. Her stunning jade green eyes are locked with mine as I press my body against hers. "I think I'm going to keep you and your sweet tooth," I say as I move one arm around her waist. We're both naked and I'm having a hard time concentrating on anything besides her body right now.

She tilts her head up and swipes my lower lip with her tongue. "Oh yeah? I'm hard to tame, Mister Ryan."

"You're one hell of a feisty ballerina, but I wouldn't tame you. I...you're too fucking adorable when you're attempting to be pissed off at me." Hell, I know she can feel how hard she makes me. How much I need her. She's killing me.

"It's not an attempt, handsome."

I groan when she sucks my lip into her mouth and lets go.

"I can be mean as a snake when you mess with my candy."

She wiggles out of my grip and walks back up to her bedroom. I'm standing there, staring after her, watching her naked body retreat. And fuck if I'm not fully hard again. I'm not sure if it's her body or her sexy-as-hell attitude. But I want it. All of it.

I CAN HEAR the shower running now, so I retreat back to the kitchen, deciding to remain naked. I know she doesn't mind seeing all of me. A few minutes later there's a knock on her front door. Assuming that it's FedEx or something, I stride across the room to the door and swing it open. Intense blue eyes meet mine. This blonde-haired woman standing before me has Heather's facial features and small frame. My eyes widen in shock.

"Surpri...Hello!" the woman says, obviously expecting to see Heather at the door.

Shit. I move behind the door quickly. "Can I help you?" I ask, and she walks in with her mouth gaping open.

"Who are you and why are you in my sister's apartment?" I think she suddenly realizes or remembers something because her eyes light up and she claps excitedly.

"You're Heather's Greek god!" she squeals a little too loudly. My girl and her sister obviously share the same bubbly enthusiasm.

"Greek god, huh?" I ask cockily.

"Yes! Now get some clothes on before my man, Brannon, gets up here. Nice ass by the way. Where is that sex-fiend sister of mine?"

"She just got into the shower."

When she turns around, I haul ass—naked ass—to the L-shaped sectional couch and grab Heather's pink blanket. I now know that it's one of her favorite things. I quickly fold the blanket and wrap it around my waist as I would a bath towel.

I turn and her sister is watching me until the apartment door opens again. A tall male walks in and eyes me suspiciously.

"I'm going to go out on a limb here and guess that you're Brannon?"

He laughs and sets a bag down at his feet. "Yeah, man, but who the fuck are you?"

I can tell that this guy is extremely protective of both Heather and her sister. I hold my hand out. "Noah Ryan, and Heather's boyfriend."

"BOYFRIEND?" her sister squeals, and I've noticed that the shower has turned off.

Brannon takes my hand and shakes it while I laugh at her sister, whose name I'm having a difficult time remembering from the conversation I had with Heather. Hell, she was naked at the time. How the hell was I supposed to remember a name while her tits were in my face?

"Sorry, guys, but would you mind if I got dressed? I'll let Heather know she's got company." Hell, what a first impression.

They both nod and I'm about halfway up the two flights of stairs when Heather appears at the top.

Her eyes catch mine and she moans softly. "Why'd you cover up? I was hoping you were going to join me in the shower and fuck me senseless again." She pouts cutely and I suck in a sharp breath.

"Heather Adalyn Lane! Since when do you curse? And have bucketloads of sex without telling me?" her sister yells up at her. Heather's face pales and she looks down, finding her sister and Brannon staring up at her.

I'm at a loss for words. So I just watch her and gauge her reaction to the scene in front of her. Me, naked with her blanket around my waist, while her sister and Brannon are behind me. She squeals just like her sister did earlier and covers her mouth with both hands.

"Dani!"

Right, Dani. That's her name.

"Sister!" Dani replies, and runs past me up the stairs before squealing and colliding with Heather in a hug, as if it's been years since they last saw each other. I turn back and look at Brannon. He answers my question before I'm able to ask it.

"Yeah, man, they are always like this." He laughs and shakes his head.

I laugh too and head up the stairs, noticing a spark of excitement I haven't seen in Heather yet. She's obviously very close with her sister from what I can tell. I'm enjoying the little glimpses of the girl she hides from me. Piece by piece, I'm breaking my way through. I can't help but laugh at the two of them as I squeeze by them in the hallway. They're still hugging each other, and bouncing up and down. I walk into Heather's room and shut the door, free to drop the pink blanket and hop in the shower. I figure I'll give them time to catch up.

CHAPTER
Twenty-One
ardor

Heather

"**Y**OU HAVE TO tell me about that Greek god, who I walked in on, catching him completely naked!" Dani squeals as she squeezes me harder.

"You did what?"

"Yup, you heard me. Naked, and I could smell the sex on him, you fiend."

I turn beet red. Oh my God, she saw him. And his...gahhh! A surge of jealousy quickly rushes through me for the tiniest moment. I know she's my sister and she's in love with Brannon but I can't help it. "You saw him?"

"Oh sister, no. He covered up too fast then moved behind the door. I just got a look at his fine ass." She looks back at Brannon. "Sorry, baby."

"You're good, babe. Has anyone eaten? I'm starving." Brannon complains as he swishes his sandy blonde hair to the side. He reminds me of a movie actor, but I'm not sure which one. I've never been able to place him. He's from California so naturally he has tanned skin.

I gasp and shove her. "Dani!" Covering my face in embarrassment, I talk through my hands. "Brannon, I'm so sorry you have to put up with her." Dropping my hands, I look at her and lower my voice. "Dani...I haven't told him much about me. So you keep your big mouth shut. Got it?"

"What do you mean you haven't told him much about you? Like your disgusting candy addiction, which I'm going to go raid right now."

She runs down the stairs and almost knocks Brannon over in the process. "Hell, babes, cool your tits." He turns to me. "She's been dying to see you ever since I surprised her with the tickets yesterday," Brannon says while he watches her.

He's so madly in love with my sister and I envy their relationship. I'm glad she's found her Prince Charming, but I want mine too—especially now that Noah is in my life. Could he be my Prince Charming? I walk down the stairs after her and wrap my arms around Brannon's waist and hug him hard. "You're so sweet to her. Thank you for the surprise. I missed you both."

"No problem. You're like my little sister anyway, and I'm going to have a talk with your boyfriend. No one fucks with my Lane girls."

"Heather! Where are the Fruit Roll-Ups? Don't you dare hide them from me." Dani's voice echoes through my apartment's high ceilings.

I pull back and poke at his chest. It's hard but not as hard as Noah's. "You be nice to him, Brannon Mitchell Henley." Letting go, I run into my kitchen, hollering the whole way. "Don't you dare touch them, Danielle!"

"Fuck, using my full name on me now too, huh? You must be serious about this guy, sassy toes," he says as he follows me down the stairs to my sister.

"Heather! Share with me." Dani pouts and bumps me with her hips, trying to scoot me away from my candy closet.

I don't hear him approach, but I feel him. My body comes alive with an electrical storm whenever he's near. I look back to the foot of the stairs and he's smiling at me. My body fills with lust and wild wanting when his eyes lock on mine, my heart thudding audibly, when a shrill cry from Dani breaks the air.

"Ha! I found them." She turns around and almost falls over herself. She's staring at my Greek god.

Noah strides across the room in those low hip-riding jeans that hug his ass and a black V-neck. I think this is my favorite outfit on him. Especially when he's barefoot. He's next to me a second later, sliding his arms around my waist. I breathe him in. I can't help it: he smells so good. This beautiful, unique Greek god has got my body in knots, and he's the only one that can work those knots out of me. He hasn't said anything to me since my sister showed up, and I'm suddenly nervous as Brannon eyes my man. I think he feels my body stiffen because he tilts my chin up and takes my lips.

I've never kissed or been kissed by anyone in front of my sister or Brannon, but right now I don't care. My body molds into his as I kiss him back. My sex aches as he sends thunderous shivers through me. I'm getting lost when suddenly I hear Dani somewhere in the background. "Whoa, Momma."

Noah smiles against our kiss and moves his hand down to my ass when we move away from each other. I glance up at my sister just in time for her to smack Brannon's chest hard.

"Babe! Why don't you kiss me like that?" she demands.

Noah's laugh reverberates through his chest and I smile up at him. His hand squeezes my ass, telling me he wants me.

"Danielle, cool it. I kiss you a thousand and one different ways, and you love each and every damn one of them," Brannon says, and Noah's laughing again. I can't help but giggle at my sister. "Now let sassy toes enjoy her Greek god."

I hide my face in Noah's chest for they've just let my nickname slip. Their surprise visit is going to be the death of me. "You two are excruciating," I groan into his chest.

"Oh little sister. You're so cute. I love you," Dani says too innocently.

"Can we go and eat now, please? I'm fucking ravenous."

Brannon is about to start begging for food soon.

"Are you ready to go, beautiful?" Noah asks and I melt. His deep, raspy voice is my favorite sound. He runs his finger over my forehead, smoothing my hair behind my ear, as I look up at him and nod. Letting go of me, he grabs his socks and shoes, putting them on while I find my coat.

Dani claps her hands. "This is going to be a double date. Where are we going to eat?"

A double date? I shake my head. Dani, I'm going to kill you.

"Fine by me," Noah answers her. "You pick."

Can he be any sweeter? I grab my purse and keys, and lock up while everyone waits in the hall. As we wait for the elevator, I tug on Noah's hand and whisper to him, "Is this okay? I know you wanted to look for an apartment today."

"Relax for me, baby. It's fine. Just as long as you're okay with my staying another night. The last thing I want to do is annoy the fuck out of you." He kisses me sweetly just as the elevator arrives.

I beam up at him, taking the initiative and lacing my fingers with his for the first time. So very girlfriendish. "I don't mind. It's not as if you'll be able to move in tomorrow anyway...and I like having you at my place. It's much more fun."

He looks down at our hands and I think he knows that it's the first time I've really initiated anything too. He squeezes gently. The doorman gets us a cab immediately, and Noah gets in first. I decide to put on my big-girl panties and scoot to the middle seat so I can be closer to him, rather than an entire seat apart, which feels like miles. Dani slides in after me and Brannon takes the front passenger seat.

"*So*, Heather," Noah says playfully, "do you kiss on the second date?"

I can't help but giggle—he's always so fun and playful. My sister looks at us sideways and smiles. I shrug and answer him. "That depends."

"Depends on what?" he asks smoothly, as he leans into me. I know Dani is watching us, but I can't help it. He makes me feel so comfortable. The cab heads toward Central Park.

"Depends on if I think he's cute or not. I'll let you know." I'm not sure if it's because my sister is here or because I'm feeling more comfortable around him but I'm letting my guard down a little bit. What man doesn't like a playful girl?

"Well, I'm screwed. Cute is not how I would describe myself," he says, as we pull up to a restaurant by Union Square.

Brannon pays the fare and he and Dani get out of the taxi. Alone with Noah for a moment, I tilt my chin up and take his earlobe into my mouth. Suck gently. Whisper, "It's a good thing I think you're sexy, Noah. You'll get that kiss tonight."

His growl fills the car and I squirm. "Baby, I was made to kiss you. Everywhere."

Suddenly my door opens and Dani pokes her head in. "Jeez, you two. You haven't had enough of each other yet? Come on, we're starving."

"Sorry…" We get out and he pulls me close. I wrap my arm around his torso while his arm is around my shoulders, keeping me warm as we walk into the restaurant where we are quickly seated and given menus. A few minutes later, we all place a drink order and then brunch.

"Are you going to eat my shrimp this time, ballerina?"

"Yes," I answer. "Are you eating my bacon?" I look up just in time to see both Dani and Brannon staring with looks of surprise on their faces.

"Possibly…" He smiles and rests his hand on my knee, before taking a sip of his Bloody Mary.

"So…Noah, tell us how you two met?" Dani asks. She's too curious about him. I don't blame her though. He could make any woman squirm in her panties.

Oh my God! I forgot to put *panties* on.

Heaven help me if he finds out. He'll think it was on purpose. It wasn't—I just lose my mind when I'm around him, which I need to stop doing. I need to keep my head in this and not get in too deep. I take a much-needed drink from my Mimosa and nervously run my finger up and down the champagne flute's stem.

"We met on Christmas Eve actually. I went to see The Nutcracker with…" He pauses and I realize it's his mother. I mean, kidnapper.

That woman. Oh Noah, I know it hurts. He's being so strong about this, but I can see it's killing him inside. Moving my hand down I place it on top of his, lacing our fingers together in an attempt to reassure him.

"And he saw me on stage. Our eyes met and I lost myself in him. I think he eye-F'ed me on stage actually. In front of everyone. Afterward, he came to my rescue when Nik was being a colossal jerk!"

Dani scoffs and rolls her eyes. "I hate Nik. I told Heather he was bad for her. What a creep."

Looking down at our fingers, I fidget and start aimlessly playing with his. "Yeah, I guess I didn't listen, huh?"

"That guy's a motherfucking prick," Noah says suddenly then takes a drink. He's so tense—dammit, Dani. I know she didn't mean to bring up something so horrible, but he was in such a playful mood.

"Oh yes, he is. I'm glad you agree, Noah." Dani is all smiles.

"Baby?" I say softly and he looks at me, feigning a smile that's not his. I run my hand into his hair and pull him down to kiss me. I want to be the slight calm in his storm. He's brooding, and I want it to stop. I want my confident, cocky, sensual boyfriend. When his lips find mine, he kisses me hard and fast, taking my lips like he needs them to breathe. I think he does on some level; I know I can calm him down, just as he does me.

Brannon orders another round of drinks for the table as I slide Noah's hand up my thigh.

I can feel his tension: it's still there in his chest and in his kiss. So I slide his hand farther. And thank God, it's working. I feel his thumb brush along my inner thigh. He's rubbing where my panty line should be. My tights usually make it easy for him to feel everything. He pauses and pulls back from our kiss. He doesn't say anything; he just stares at me, questioning. I've never used sex as a weapon before, but I'll do just about anything to keep my Greek god from being upset.

Brannon coughs. "Should we, uh, find another booth?"

Noah smiles his genuine smile—not one that doesn't belong to him. "No, man, we're good. What do you do for a living, Brannon?"

Brannon dives into conversation while Noah pulls his Galaxy out of his pocket, typing something quickly then putting it away. My purse vibrates and I reach into it to grab my phone.

"I run my own construction company. I don't get dirty with the boys: I do more of the architectural work. It comes as a package deal that way. My company benefits tremendously."

I'm not paying attention to them as I click on his message. **Baby, are you wearing panties?**

How the hell did he know?

I quickly type out a reply and hit send. **No :) enjoy your brunch.**

I watch him check his phone again and smile. **You're so beautiful today, and you belong to me.**

I reply: **Yours.**

"Sounds like it could be fun. What about you, Dani? Do you dance too?" Noah asks.

She starts laughing and almost spits out her Mimosa. "Oh no. Heather is the graceful one. I've always been the klutz of the family. I'm a public relations manager for a few different actors and actresses in LA. Well, I manage the entire firm that works with the stars."

"Well, shit, that's one hell of a job. Do you work for anyone worth mentioning?"

"They all are, but I'd rather not drop names to my sister's boyfriend. What about you, Noah, what do you do?"

"Well, I just moved up to New York two weeks ago…"

Dani stares me down. Oh crap. I forgot to tell her.

"…And I've been studying for the bar exam."

I feel like her questions might head toward a dangerous road so I send her a text. **Dani, no more questions. I'll explain later.**

I hit send and watch her fumble for her phone while Noah and Brannon start talking about sports. Her eyes flicker up and meet mine and I can tell she's not happy. She hates it when I hide things from her. But I know she understands because she puts her phone away and changes the subject.

"Oh Heather? What color are your nails today?" Dani asks.

Frick. Noah's attention is swayed from baseball teams to Dani. "I think it's called Hawaiian Charm."

Noah lifts my hand to inspect my nails. "Weren't they covered in glitter yesterday?"

I pull my hand back to my lap. "Yes," I say, giving Dani a death glare. *Don't you do it, Dani.* By the look on her face, I can tell she doesn't give a crap about what I want. A slow, evil smile spreads across her face.

"Heather hasn't shown you her nail polish collection?"

God, I'm going to kill her. I kick her under the table and stare. She just makes a face at me.

"Nail polish collection? Fuck, it can't be anything like her candy closet."

Yep. I'm going to kill her.

"It can be, and it is. You should ask her to show you when you get back tonight. I believe the number of bottles she has is in the hundreds now. She even has sheets of paper with the color description, name, and a little sample of each color—for every single nail polish bottle she has."

I could cut out her tongue right now. Why don't we just tell all of Heather's secrets? My face is radiating heat, I'm sure.

He reaches for my hand and squeezes when the waitress finally brings our meal out.

"I'll have to take your word for it, Dani. But hell, I do know my girl's fingers and toes are colorful when I suck on them."

I'm. Going. To. Die. I'm being hit from all sides. Is this embarrass-the-crap-out-of-Heather day? I take in a deep breath and shake my head. "Okay, guys. New subject."

Noah's lips are on mine before I can utter another word. Mmm, he tastes good. I breathe in his cologne and relax. This calming effect we have on each other is starting to come in handy.

"Do you want a shrimp?" he asks when our lips part, forking one up from his side order.

I nod and open my mouth. He's staring at my lips when I close down over the fork. This feels right. Us. I suddenly remember we're not alone.

"Dani? How long are you guys staying in town?" I ask.

I watch him through my peripheral vision as he takes a bite of his omelet, but completely ignores his shrimp and grits.

"Uhm, I think for the week? Is that right, babe?" she asks Brannon, who nods with his mouth full of food.

I giggle and kiss Noah's cheek then notice that he hasn't eaten any of his side order. "Did you get the shrimp and grits so I could steal your shrimp?"

He just winks and I melt. That has got to be the sweetest, sexiest thing anyone has ever done for me. It's such a small act, but it speaks volumes.

"Thank you," I say as I fork up a shrimp from his plate and eat it.

"You're most welcome, ballerina."

I enjoy the rest of the meal out with my three favorite people, making small talk, trying different Mimosas and Bellinis.

I'm grateful for each of them.

My sister.

My what I can only guess will be my future brother-in-law.

And my Greek god.

CHAPTER
Twenty-Two
greek god

Noah

SHE'S BEEN MINE for four weeks now. Dani and Brannon just left to head back to LA. They stayed a little over a week and helped me find an apartment—available immediately, which I've learned is almost an impossible task in NYC—as well as move in. I don't live far from my ballerina. I couldn't stand it if I did. My loft is small and simple, but it's more than enough for me.

Heather and I can't manage to be apart for one night, even if we're not strewn naked all over each other. I relish the feeling of her in my arms. She keeps me grounded and sane, especially with all this shit going on.

Joel has yet to contact me regarding my birth parents, so I make a mental note to call him soon.

Coen is currently on a flight to New York City. I might not have friends in high places, but the few friends I have always have stuck by my side.

Currently Heather is rehearsing for a showcase that her ballet company is putting on for some local charity in the beginning of February, so I'm going through a few things by myself as I unpack the last box. I realize this box must have come from Mae's house because I don't recognize its contents.

The box is filled with documentation from the diner as well as bill invoices. I turn the box upside down, dumping its contents out to make sure there's nothing that belongs to me in it before I send it back with Coen. A large white binder makes a thud on my hardwood floor. I've never seen it before and it wouldn't surprise me if it too is filled with old paper bills.

I reach for it anyway and open it. The first page is blank so I flip to the next. It's not as much of a binder as it is a photo album—the old ones with the transparent plastic that you peel off of the sticky backing and place the pictures on it. I pause on the next page. It's a newspaper clipping with a picture of a distraught-looking woman surrounded by microphones. Frowning, I read over the article.

What the hell?

It's an article about a missing newborn.

I flip to the next page and then the next, each of them containing the same newborn baby's name, Amanda. The article states that the baby had been found in a New York City dumpster after being discarded by her kidnapper. I think I'm going to be sick.

I flip to the next page expecting another article on Amanda, but instead there's a name and year written in large black handwriting— Mae's handwriting: "Amy — 1982."

I turn the old, dusty page. There's another newspaper clipping of a young couple, obviously hurting. The article reads very similar to the first article on Amanda's mother. Newborn kidnapped from New York City Hospital. No traces. No leads. Just fear.

I flip through the next page, and the next, and the next until I get to a picture of a dumpster on a newspaper clipping. The title reads, "Kidnapper Leaves Newborn To Die."

My hands are shaking as I skim through the paragraphs of this article. *Found in a New York City dumpster. Two days old. Starving, but alive. Police have noticed a trend forming from the last newborn kidnapping eleven months prior to Amy's.*

The next page is blank, with only a name and date written on it: "Laura — 1983." I flip through, not wanting to see faces this time. I know it's going to be the same as Amanda's and Amy's stories. I stop when I reach another blank page with black writing, "Megan — 1983."

I flip through at least four more names, each sticking in my head: "Elizabeth — 1983," "Sarah — 1984," "Rachel — 1984," and "Mary — 1984."

That's what? Seven? Each of the names are followed by multiple newspaper cut-outs of their families, efforts to rescue them, fake ransom notes, and the words "serial kidnapper" everywhere.

Fuck.

I'm halfway through the white binder, and I can't take this shit anymore, but I will myself to turn one last page…fucking willing it to be blank…for there to be no more names. I flip the page.

"Noah — 1985."

I can't bring myself to turn to the next page. Instead I get up and pour myself two fingers of bourbon. I swallow the liquid and it burns all the way down. I then grab a beer and pop it open.

I lose count of how many beers and fingers of bourbon I've had. All I know is the room is spinning and I'm pissed as fuck.

"Disgusting bitch!" I yell as I toss the fucking binder across the room. It hits the wall and falls to the floor. I know I need to turn this shit over to the FBI, but I can't bring myself to turn that damn page. One fucking page and I'll know who I am. Who my parents are and where I belong.

Time passes and I'm not sure what's going on anymore. I'm slumped against the fridge, drinking a beer when there's a knock on the door.

"It's fucking open," I try and yell out, but I know my words are slurring together. Please be my girl. I want my girl.

"Dude, are you fucking wasted without me?" Coen appears around the corner and I swear there are three of him, even when I shut one eye to try and focus.

"Nah. Where's my girl?" I'm trying to get my phone out of my pocket, unsuccessfully.

"Shit, man, you're seriously gone. What's going on? Did the FBI give you more information? Did you watch the news?"

I shake my head lazily and point to the binder on the floor, "That motherfucking thing. I'm in it."

Finally I get my phone out and unlocked, slowly typing out a message. I'm not sure how I spelled everything right, but I did. At least I think I did.

Baby. I need you. My place.

"Who are you texting, man? Give me your phone. You know what happens when you drunk-text. Noah, you said you wouldn't get this drunk again."

"Man, fuck you. I don't know who I am. Where's Heather?"

"Heather? You're still seeing her? Damn, she must be treating you well. Come on, buddy, let's get you off the floor."

I feel strong arms around me as I'm dragged across the room to the couch. Hell, I can't even feel my legs.

"She belongs to me—don't you fucking touch her!" I spit out at Coen.

"Chill, man. I'm happy for you; you truly deserve her."

I groan, my body deciding to fight the alcohol. Hell, the only spinning I want to feel is from her. I want her to set my world right. She's my axis. She's my girl. She's not here. Where is she?

I look down at my phone and frown when I don't get a message back. "Did you talk to her? Did you tell her I had a fucking problem? DID YOU?"

"Dude, you need to calm down. I haven't even spoken to her. Here, drink some water."

He hands me a tall glass full of water, but my vision blurs and the glass cracks under the pressure of my hand. It shatters, but I hardly feel it as I form a fist around whatever is left of it.

"Coen? Did they sentence that lying bitch? Did they? Is she finally locked up?" There's red on my hands and on the couch. Heather helped me pick out this couch.

"I'm not sure what's going on, man. Without your birth parents coming forward, they don't have much evidence to go on for your kidnapping."

"I sure as hell have evidence. Hand me that damn binder."

"You're going to get blood on it. Listen, we'll talk it over when you're sober." He takes the beer from my other hand and fury overcomes me.

My phone suddenly vibrates and I reach for it…see a text from Heather.

I'm leaving practice. Is everything OK? Did Coen make it there?

She's the only thing that's keeping me from losing it. Hell, I could punch the fuck out of someone right now, just like I used to in college. One motherfucker ticks me off when I've been drinking and the entire bar will know about it.

"Dude, you have to quit drinking. Especially if she's going to show up. The last thing you want is for her to upset you while you're feeling like this."

"Shut up, dickweed."

"All right, man. Are you going to at least let me get those shards of glass out of your palm?

"Don't lay a hand on me."

"You got it, man. I'll wait for you to pass the hell out."

Coen sits down on the other side of the room, keeping his distance from me. He learned the hard way. Don't mess with me or touch me. I'm not afraid to deck someone. He had a black eye for two weeks our junior year.

My mind betrays me and goes back to the binder. Her fucking sick, psycho bullshit. I text Heather again.

Get here.

Heather

HIS TEXTS ARE worrying the crap out of me. My taxi finally makes it through gridlock traffic and pulls up to his apartment building. I get out and pull my coat tighter around me as I walk inside and ride up the elevator to Noah's floor, hating that I didn't change and am still in my tights with just a sweatshirt hanging off one shoulder. I was hoping to make a different impression when I met Coen again, but Noah's messages were making me nervous. Finally reaching his floor, I'm about to use my key when I notice it isn't locked. Walking inside, I call out as I take off my coat. "Noah?"

"Get the fucking door. My girl is here," I hear him yell out and moments later Coen is standing in front of me.

"Coen? Hi. Is he okay?"

Something inside me is screaming warnings. Something is wrong. Very wrong. The look on Coen's face is a mixture of regret and warning even though he smiles.

"Hey Heather. Uh..." He's running his hand through his hair and avoiding my question. "He's had a few drinks."

"What's a few?" I ask.

"I'm not sure. He was like this when I got here. He keeps asking for you though. I'm hoping you'll calm him down before he hurts himself further."

"Hurts himself? Further?"

I look up as Noah stumbles into the doorway, leaning against the doorframe. "You hitting on my girl, asshole?" He's bleeding, but I can't tell where he's bleeding from.

My eyebrows knit together in confusion. "Noah? What happened?" I push past Coen and over to Noah. I've never seen him like this before. There's something different. It's not him—not my Noah. I reach down and grab his hand and turn it palm up. Why is he just standing here bleeding?

I look from Noah then over to Coen. "What's going on?"

"Careful. Anger, alcohol, and Noah don't mesh well together. He doesn't let people handle him when he's drunk."

"Fuck you!" Noah yells out to Coen, then looks down at his big hand in both of mine. "Don't tell her what to do. I fucking missed you, little ballerina."

"Why is he mad?" I look up at Noah. "Why are you mad? And

why are neither of you concerned about your hand?"

"I'll show you…" Noah says before almost falling on his butt.

"Baby…be careful!" I wrap my arm around his torso and let him drunkenly lead the way. "You'll let me clean your hand up after you show me, right?"

"Yeah, but it doesn't hurt."

He's beyond drunk. He's not even walking in a straight line. We get to the living room and he plops down onto the couch as he grabs his beer. He's completely forgotten that he was about to show me something. I stand there looking at him. Coen follows and sits down on the couch next to him with a beer in his hand. I really freaking wish someone would start talking. "Uhm…hello?"

He looks up at me, and smiles like a drunken fool, my drunken Greek god. "See that binder over there?" he says, pointing to the wall. "Bring that over here. I'll show you."

I walk over and pick up the binder that's on the floor and walk back, starting to wonder if I even want to know. I sit down between Noah and Coen, and set the binder on my lap.

Noah reaches over and opens it. The first page is blank but then he turns it and there's a name and year on it. "Flip through it, until you get to me—1985," he slurs then leans his head back on the couch.

"What the hell is this? A scrapbook?" Coen asks.

I silently flip through the pages. With each turn, my stomach plummets. Oh my God. Did she do this to all these babies? My heart is in my throat and I'm afraid of what I'll find. I don't want to see anymore. Finally, I get to the page with Noah's name and birth year. I look over at Coen and shake my head. I have to get up before I burst into tears. I feel so much pain for this grown man sitting next to me. He has to be massively hurting inside.

I slide the binder off my lap and put it on Coen's. Getting up quickly, I make my way to the kitchen and grab a beer for myself. I think Noah has passed out and for a moment I'm relieved. I don't want him to see me like this. He doesn't need me to be upset right now. Opening my beer, I lean against the marble island with my back to the guys.

Coen walks into the kitchen with the binder. It's still on Noah's page when he sits it down next to me on the counter top.

"Do you think he's gone farther than we have?"

I shrug because I've got no words. I hear Noah groan on the couch as I take another sip.

"He's really torn up about this shit." Coen leans against the counter beside me. "I can't imagine going through what he's going through right now. I'm glad he has you though, and I'm glad he's out of Arizona. The media and news crews are still parked outside his old apartment and her house."

I wipe a tear away with the back of my hand.

"I can't believe that even happened. Is that why he's drunk? I've never seen him like this. I don't know what to do to help him." I push off from the counter and busy myself with wetting a washcloth to clean his hand with.

"I'm assuming the binder is what caused him to drink. He must have just found it. I don't recall him talking about it before. I've seen him like this more times than I can count when someone pissed him off at the bar when he was completely wasted in college."

I hear the couch move and look up. Noah is getting up and he looks so unbelievably mad. "Are you trying to get with my girl?"

Coen takes a few steps back and shakes his head frantically. "Dude, you know I wouldn't do that. Calm down for me, buddy."

I'm in shock. The look on his face is murderous. I take a step forward, making sure my voice is soft. "Baby? Come here."

He stumbles forward as I move toward him. I don't care what Coen said about touching him. I want to comfort him, so I do. I press my body to his and hug him. His arms move weakly around me. His voice is soft and full of emotion when he says, "I need you."

My heart breaks wide open for him and I look up into his sad, half-closed eyes and nod. "I'm here, baby." Moving my body, I lead him over to the sink. "Coen, will you grab that stool so he can sit while I get his hand cleaned up, please?"

Coen moves quickly and brings the stool over. I help my Greek god sit down and cup his face. He looks so lost in this moment. I brush my lips against his softly. "I'm not going anywhere." I think he understands me because he nods.

"Coen, would you mind running across the street to get him something to eat?"

"Yeah, no problem. I'll be right back."

I run the water, making sure it's not too hot or too cold before I move his hand under it. It's then I realize there are small shards of glass embedded in his hand.

Talking softly to both him and myself while I run his hand under the water, I murmur, "Baby, what did you do to yourself?"

Hearing the front door close, I know that we're alone. I get the pieces out of his hand without great difficulty, glancing up at him every now and then to make sure he isn't in any pain. And to be quite honest, I don't know if he feels anything at the moment. After getting the last piece out, I clean his hand with a mild soap and dry it lightly. Applying a few bandages before moving between his legs, I wrap my arms around his neck and hug him to me. "Once you eat, we can go to bed, okay?"

He's been watching me clean his hand the entire time and now he's peering into my soul with those drunken ocean green eyes. "Yeah. Are you going to stay?" His hand somehow finds my ass. I try not to giggle because even in this drunken, pissed-off, self-loathing state he's in, he still wants me.

I smile softly and lean in, biting down on his shoulder, letting him know in my own special way that I want him too. "I would never leave you alone like this."

He growls. "Will you be naked in my bed tonight?"

How the crap is he thinking about me being naked now? "Noah…"

"Mmm, what?" He nuzzles my neck, and he doesn't smell like himself. He smells like beer and rubbing alcohol.

"You should probably just sleep tonight. You're not going to feel well tomorrow, I'm afraid."

"But you'll still be naked, right?" His hand squeezes my ass and I squeal, not expecting it.

"Only if you behave, baby. And one more thing: Coen isn't hitting on me. He's being a good friend."

He growls into my neck and I know he's still too drunk to think rationally. Hearing the front door open and close, I push against Noah's rock-hard chest, forcing him to sit up. "Time to eat, handsome."

"You?" he queries with a smirk on his face as Coen walks in and puts the bag of food down on the counter.

"I got, like, six burgers and fries. I didn't know how much he would eat and if you were hungry? Unless you're a vegetarian?"

What the frick? Why does everyone assume I'm a vegetarian? Pointing at Noah, I answer his question, "No. Food," and then turn to Coen. "No, I'm not a vegetarian. And thank you for running to get that." I turn and grab a few bottled waters for us while the guys start to eat.

I hand Noah a bottle of water as he's chewing lazily. He's taken one bite of the burger. His eyes are closed and he's propped himself up on his elbow on the countertop, so I try and coax him to eat some more. I kiss his cheek and whisper in his ear, "If you eat that burger and fries, I'll sleep in the nude tonight."

I know that what I've said registers with him because he groans and opens his eyes, taking a few more bites of his burger. I laugh softly at his eager attempt and run my fingers through his hair. "Don't choke on it, baby." I look down and smile when I see him eating crinkle fries. He's so stinking wasted that he doesn't even realize what he's eating. I'll be sure and remind him of it tomorrow.

He finishes his fries and pushes them aside, making a face. Once he takes the last bite of his burger, he looks up at me. "Bed?"

I smile. He's got the sweetest, most hopeful expression on his face. "Yes, bed. Go on and I'll be right in." Watching him get up and walk slowly down the hall without another word, I breathe a sigh of relief, knowing the storm has passed. For now.

"I've never seen him so composed when he's agitated and drunk," Coen says from the other side of the island. "I'm glad he's got you, Heather. Do you mind if I crash on the couch?"

"Of course not. Let me grab you some blankets and pillows." I go down to the hall closet in search of them.

Just as I find them, Coen reaches up from behind me to grab the bedding. "I got this. Go to him."

"Oh. Thank you, Coen, for watching over him back in college and now. You're two for two."

He winks at me. "Anytime. Night, Heather." He turns and walks back to the living room and I head into the bedroom.

After shutting the door, I turn to see Noah's large, muscular body sprawled on top of his bed, his shirt halfway off. "Oh baby…"

I walk over. He's completely out, which I expected. What I didn't expect was his massive erection. Son of a…even in his sleep? Reaching over his body, I pull his other arm out of his tee-shirt and get him undressed. I'm practically out of breath when I finally get his jeans off. I'm not even going to attempt to remove his boxer briefs. Pulling my sweatshirt over my head and taking my bra off, I stand there topless while I put my hair into a messy bun. I pad around to turn out his bedside lamp before I take off my tights and panties. Crawling onto the bed, I curl up into his side.

He exhales loudly and wraps me in his arms, holding me tightly against him. He's asleep, but he manages to mumble, "My girl."

CHAPTER
Twenty-Three
imperative proof

Noah

JOEL IS ON HIS way back to New York City after a trip to New Jersey for some FBI business. This binder is exactly what Joel needs to help prove Mae's guilt. I can't stand that I'm handing her over to the feds, but she stole my life. There will always be a place in my heart for Mae—the woman brought me up—but the hatred and anger quickly overpower that feeling.

Heather has been mostly quiet throughout today. She hasn't even mentioned what happened last night. Hell...I'm not even too sure what happened.

The one thing that's still bugging the shit out of me is what's on the page after my name. I tell myself that I have every right to know who my parents are, and now I've found them. I flip through the heavy card stock paper of the binder to my name. I inhale as I turn the page and prepare to literally meet my makers.

It's blank.

I fucking loathe that woman for what she's done to me. She's kept everything from me. I look up from the blank page and find Heather on the floor in the living room with a dustpan, sweeping up glass. I look down at my hand and clench it into a fist, welcoming the pain.

Suddenly, Coen is at my side and claps me on the back. "Hey man, feel like shit today?" He chuckles and pulls out the chair beside me and sits down at the table. I rub my hand down my face.

"That's an understatement." Exhaling loudly, I look over at him and lower my voice. "Did I...I didn't make her cry last night, did I?" He looks over at Heather who is currently trying to clean the blood off the couch cushion.

"Who, her?" He nods in her direction. "Nah, man. That one is tough as nails. Keep a hold of her."

I feign a smile. "Thank God. I don't plan on losing her." I get up and grab some ibuprofen from the cabinet. "Little ballerina? Did you want to get breakfast?"

She looks up from the floor. "Huh? Oh. Of course. You feel up to it?"

I frown for a split second because she seems distracted and lost in thought. "I do. I'd like to treat my girlfriend and my best friend. You two go get dressed. I'll clean up this mess," I say as I walk over to Heather and kiss her lips.

"I'm almost finished. Just give me a minute." She turns away before I can argue. There's something wrong and I'm going to find out what it is.

"Coen, we'll be right back," I say before scooping Heather up into my arms and carrying her to my bedroom, and to the shower. I turn on the water and step in with her in my arms, both of us fully dressed.

She shrieks loudly and tries to squirm out of my grip. "What are you doing?"

"Oh no you don't, ballerina." My arms tighten around her and I hold her under the cool spray, pressing my lips hard to hers... kissing the breath out of her. She stops squirming as her hands move into my hair.

I feel her body relax against mine even with the cold water

beating down on us. "Talk to me, ballerina," I say sensitively as I kiss her neck.

Her soft moans fill the shower. "About what?"

I nip at the slender column of her neck. "What's bothering you, baby?"

"I just…I don't understand how you're so put together with everything that you're going through right now. Well, except for last night."

I run my tongue up her neck to the shell of her ear as she speaks. Her body shudders. "Are you mad at me?" I ask and instantly regret it. I don't want to know.

"Mad at you? Why would I be mad at you?" she says, as she circles her arms around my neck.

I'm relieved. Fuck, I'm relieved. I set her down on her feet then press her against the shower wall. "Because of last night."

"Because you were drunk?" Her clothes are plastered onto her figure.

"My behavior last night was probably less than acceptable. I'm sorry if I said or did anything to upset you or piss you off. I, uh, I have always been an angry drunk when people piss me off. If I was like that to you, I won't ever forgive myself. You deserve more."

She's looking at me with those gorgeous green eyes. "You weren't like that to me, Noah. I was so worried about you though. I've never seen that side of you."

"I'll be okay, baby. I've got you, and that's a fuck ton more than what I've ever had before. You're my girl, right?"

Her smile lights me up from the inside. "I haven't stopped being your girl since the first time you asked."

My chest is about to explode. She's so damn perfect, so understanding. I want to keep her forever. I lean down and kiss her temple.

"You are one hell of a girlfriend, baby."

She blushes as I pull my wet shirt off of her body, sliding my hands up her wet, silky skin.

She shivers from my touch and pulls my shirt off of me. I'm taken by surprise when she grabs the back of my neck and forcefully pulls me down. She's in a frenzy. Her hands are everywhere. Holy shit. What's gotten into her? Slipping my tongue into her mouth, I taste raspberries.

"Noah...I need you."

Holy shit. She's gotten my pants undone and they lay in a damp mess at my ankles with my boxer briefs.

"Baby, I haven't been inside of you for more than twenty-four hours; it's going to take me hours to get you warmed up again," I say, as her hands move over my skin, and then cup my balls. I'm hard as marble.

"No. I can't wait. Please don't make me."

She's begging me for it and fuck if it isn't the hottest damn thing she's done. "Baby, we have Coen waiting on us. Can you wait until after breakfast? We'll just go to the place across the street and then you're all mine. Joel is going to come and pick up the binder from the restaurant too. After that I plan on making you come like a freight train until your gorgeous body can't handle another second of it."

She's whimpering in frustration and lets go of my balls. Thankfully, because I was about to take her regardless of what I said. I shut the water off and kiss her forehead. "Just wait, ballerina."

She growls cutely and then pouts. My ballerina is damn sexy.

"Noah..." she says, drawing my name out. "You swear you'll be inside of me all night?"

I laugh and wrap her in a white towel, "You have my word, baby."

She gets out of the shower without another word. We're learning as we go, this thing between us. But I'm in too deep to back out now. Hell, I don't want to. I watch her as she dresses. She doesn't know it—she's never noticed. But it's something I do. When she doesn't think anyone is looking...I can see her. One day she'll relax and be herself around me.

She's running my comb through her hair while I finish drying off and move over to the toilet to relieve myself. All the damn alcohol I drank last night is still not out of my system. She comes walking back in with her head down, probably eyeing her toenail polish when she finally looks up.

"Noah, I..." She gasps then makes the funniest squeaking sound and covers her eyes. "Oh my God!" She turns around and stomps her foot. "Are you peeing?"

I look down at myself then back up at her. "Uh, I believe that's what this is called."

She shrieks and runs out of the room quickly. I can hear her mumbling something as she runs out and it cracks me the hell up.

"Girls pee too!" I yell out after her.

"Yes, but not in front of their boyfriends!" I hear her reply before I finish up and wash my hands then wrap my towel around my waist. Walking out to the living room I hear Heather yell at Coen.

"I can't believe you guys! You're so super gross!" She's standing there in her towel as I walk up. Coen has his hands up in defense.

"Whoa, little lady. What in hell did I do? Why am I gross?" He's looking from her to me and all I can do is laugh.

"Get your naked little ass back into my bedroom. Coen might be my friend, but he's still a hornball."

She narrows her eyes at me before tightening her towel and stomping past us. She's cute as hell when she's pissed. I like it. I've never seen that side of her. But shit, something tells me she can be a little tornado when she's really mad. I look over at Coen when she disappears around the corner and he's got his head cocked to the side, staring at where her ass just was. I scowl and shove him, only partially joking. "Watch yourself, dick. She's mine."

He steps back and puts his hands up, "You got it, man. Don't pee in front of her though. I asked her if she saw a fucking spider." He busts out laughing.

I laugh and turn to walk down the hall to my bedroom. "She's never called it a spider before."

I'VE GOT MY coffee and Heather's still brooding next to me. Her bottom lip is sticking out in a pout when our breakfast is brought to us. I notice she doesn't have bacon on her plate so I give her two of my four strips. "Eat up, baby, you're going to need your energy."

She looks up at me and silently puts them back on my plate. She's fucking pissed and I'm loving every minute of it. It's another side of her that I haven't seen before and I'm relishing it. Bring it on, ballerina. I can't help but smirk as I sip my coffee while Coen talks to me about someone who wants to buy my truck. Out of the corner of my eye, I see Heather reach over and take one of the pieces of bacon off my plate. That's right, sassy toes, act like you're mad all you want. I'm figuring you out.

The waitress walks past and I get her attention, asking her for a side order of bacon. She nods and walks off. I look up just in time to see a man in a dark suit walk through the doorway.

"Coen, is that Joel?"

Coen turns his head and waves to the man. "Yeah."

He makes his way over to our table and we all exchange handshakes. "It's good to meet you, Joel."

"Same here, Noah. Would you mind if I joined you for some coffee?"

"No problem, man. Go for it."

Joel orders coffee when the waitress brings the extra side of bacon. I set it between myself and Heather before turning back to Joel. "Have you gotten any more updates?"

"Unfortunately not. The court is waiting on your piece of evidence."

"That makes sense." I hand him the binder that Heather takes out of her huge purse. I don't know why she doesn't just carry a backpack around. He takes it and randomly flips through it then nods.

"This is exactly what they need. Thank you, Noah."

"Nah, man, thank you. You've really been a lot of help."

I look down at my plate to grab a piece of bacon, but the three I had left on my plate are gone, as are the extra four pieces we got. Damn, my woman is a bacon whore.

"Would you like a copy of this binder before I turn it in as evidence?" Joel asks, as he stirs the creamer into his coffee.

"No. I don't plan on keeping anything of hers."

"I'm not going to argue with you about that again," he says, remembering how pissed I was about it on the phone a few weeks ago.

Coen must notice my unease so he pipes in, "So how've you been, you dipshit? I haven't seen you in a while. How's that blonde girl you were fucking?"

I'm thankful for the change in subject. Turning to Heather, and keeping my voice low, I ask, "So...are you going to stay mad at me all day?"

She's got the last piece of bacon in her hand and she's looking out the window, ignoring me, chewing slowly. Smiling, because she's cute as fuck like this, I lean down and take a bite of her bacon before she can pull it away.

She turns toward me and gapes. "Don't eat my bacon."

"Should I eat something else?" I tease as I nuzzle her neck. I smile against her skin when she huffs. I could eat her alive. "I'm not going to lie...you're fucking adorable when you're pissy."

She nudges me with her elbow and I pull away, looking down at her. "Don't make me beg, ballerina."

"What would you beg for?" she asks softly, while Joel and Coen talk about some woman sitting in the booth behind us, daring each other to ask her for her number.

Tilting her chin up, I run my thumb along her lower lip. "I'll beg for anything when it comes to you."

"Will you now?" she asks then feeds me the rest of the piece of bacon she's holding.

I nod and chew. "Anything. Name it."

"Surprise me," she says softly as her hand moves to my cock. I harden immediately.

I put my hand on top of hers and squeeze. Leaning down, I bury my nose in her hair, inhaling deeply. "I'm begging you...to stay mad at me all day because it fucking turns me on."

That gets a giggle out of her and I smile. "You smell so damn good, ballerina. I can't wait to get you home alone."

"Hey you two lovebirds, did you want to go out with us tonight? We're hoping to pick up some easy ass," Coen says.

I look down at Heather questioningly. "Up to you, ballerina."

"Can I think about it? You owe me something first."

I wink down at my girl and nod.

"No problem, little lady," Coen says as he and Joel get up, putting a fifty-dollar bill on the table. We'll catch you two later. We're going to tour New York City for a few hours.

"All right guys, thanks." I get up to shake Joel's hand before they leave. "Coen? You got a key, man? I'll probably be at Heather's."

"Nah, I don't."

I take my keys out of my pocket, removing my key from the ring and handing it to him, glad Heather has the extra one to my place.

He takes it and nods. "Later, you two." They walk out and I hold out my hand to help Heather up. "You ready to go back to my place?"

"I thought we were going to mine? My bed has more bounce to it."

I laugh and pull her to me. "Your place it is."

CHAPTER
Twenty-Four
ravaging her

Noah

WE'VE BEEN AT it for hours. I'm not entirely sure what the time is either, but all I know is her pussy is wet, warm, and snug. I can't get enough of her warmth engulfing my cock. We're two individuals trying to work the other up before we both succumb to passion, which we've accomplished multiple times tonight. I'm so entirely consumed with her. When her phone vibrates on the nightstand, it's the furthest thought in my mind. I want nothing but to make her happy, and to feel satisfied each time I fill her.

We've been coming together tonight and it's hotter than the surface of the sun in her bedroom. She knows exactly when to slow down the tempo to allow me to focus on all of the sensations she gives me, as I've learned to do for her.

Our bodies are hot and tangled under the sheets when she bites my shoulder, silently asking for another round. I growl and move quickly so I'm hovering over her lean, naked body. I run my fingers down to her pussy, down the only strip of hair on her and to her clitoris.

She looks up at me as I enter her again. She's so ready for me, ready to explode on me. I have to pause to gain control of my impending orgasm. Her petite hands move down the ridges of my body. She wants to touch me everywhere. Her hands wander up to my jaw and she pulls me closer to her so I can kiss her intimately. Every kiss of ours is full of such immense passion and need. Sure, I've kissed women before, but not like I've kissed my girl.

The spark and lust that I feel in every single kiss with her just makes me want another. It makes me want to bury myself in her, and not leave. She's bewitched me, and I'm not going anywhere. No other woman has made me forget who I am. No other woman has made me want to forget who I am and be the man she needs me to be.

Our lips are locked together as she rocks her hips slightly, imploring me to progress. I comply and tilt my hips in a slow, rocking motion. My hands are braced above her head as I watch us move together. Her body lifts off of the mattress as I hit her deeply. She whimpers in delight with her eyes shut. She's savoring every single movement.

We're no longer fucking.

We're making love. She's mine and I'm going to treat her right. I'm going to take care of her.

Though calm, we're both yet so riled up as I rotate my hips, just how she likes it. Every single time we've been in a frantic frenzy trying to rip each other's clothes off, wanting nothing more than to get lost in each other as fast as we can, as many times as we can, but this time is different.

We're both taking it slow and relishing every inch, every tight muscular motion we make against each other. Her eyes open slowly as she blinks up at me.

"You feel so amazing that I don't want it to end."

Smirking, I say, "We can go as long as you want or need to."

"You're one of a kind, Noah."

"Just for you, ballerina."

She hums her approval then squeezes my biceps. "You belong

to me. Completely."

"As you do to me. Don't forget that."

Her nipples end in hard peaks and her skin is drenched in sweat from all of our action. She pushes her body up to mine. She wants me closer, so I still…then slowly pull out of her before lying down on my side and moving her in front of me. I push into her again while I'm spooning her, her back to my front as my hands roam around to cup her remarkable tits.

"Is this what you wanted? My hands on you?"

"How did you know?" she answers breathlessly.

"I've been paying close attention to my baby's needs."

She leans back against me as I move inside of her. Her walls enclose my shaft, squeezing me. Licking the shell of her ear, I whisper, "Come with me, baby. Let me feel that pussy pulse."

The moan that escapes her lips is almost my undoing. Her entire body stiffens in my arms, and then she shakes and quivers as waves hit her repeatedly. I join her. My balls seize up and I explode into her, her quivering pussy swallowing what I give her.

She's breathing heavily when her body goes limp in my arms, but I can still feel her pulsing down the length of my shaft.

"You are so beautiful, Heather."

She sighs contently in my arms as I kiss the back of her head. I move while inside of her, pulling her on top of me. She leans up for a kiss and I give it to her before she rests her head back down on my chest and shuts her eyes.

"My showcase is tomorrow. You should…" she yawns lazily "…invite Coen and Joel."

"Will do, ballerina." I reach over to the nightstand and find my phone, quickly sending a group text to the guys.

Hey fuckers. Heather's charity showcase is tomorrow and is being held to raise awareness of anorexia. Proceeds will go to the foundation called KMB for Answers. 7 p.m. David H. Koch Theatre.

Moments later my phone buzzes while I'm half asleep. Two messages—the first is from Joel.

I'll be there.

And another from Coen.

Count me in. There better be some gorgeous women at this place.

Joel replies to Coen.

Calm your boner, asshole. I'm sitting right next to you.

Coen shoots back.

Enjoy the redhead on your lap and shut up.

I laugh and type another message.

Manwhores. Have a good evening.

I put my phone on silent then shut my eyes, falling into a deep sleep with my girl safe on top of me.

CHAPTER
Twenty-Five
for answers

Heather
February 11th.

THE THEATRE IS jam-packed for the charity showcase. I'm standing at the edge of the curtain that's hiding all of the performers from the audience's view. After a few minutes of searching I find Noah at last. He's looking directly at me and winks from the fifth row on the orchestra level. My Greek god is fitted out in a specially tailored tux with a dusty pink button down shirt. It fits him perfectly and shows off all of his yummy muscles. He had to pin me down and stop me from ripping the crap out of the tux when he was finally dressed. I always want him. I've never wanted a man so much in my life.

He's the epitome of all men. And all mine.

I'm falling hard for this man. Crap. I can't even think about that right now. Taking a deep breath to steady my thinking, I turn around and almost run right into Nik. Ugh. I step around him and the three girls who are falling over themselves to get his attention. I'm looking all over the place for Dillen; she's here somewhere.

"Heather Lane. You stop in your tracks right this second!" I hear Dillen yell out and I turn to see her in her full costume.

"Dillen!"

Dillen Ascher and I have danced together for seven years, and apart from Dani, I call her my best friend. She's about my height, but she has gorgeous mahogany curls with freckles all over her nose. I call her my twin because we finish each other's sentences and say the same things at the same time. We're like an old married couple: we bicker over the most trivial things.

She's been dancing for the Royal Ballet in London, which has been my ultimate career goal. I've wanted to dance in the Royal Opera House for as long as I can remember. My mother, Ayla, always said that if I kept on my toes, I could do anything. I've done exactly that, literally and figuratively.

She runs up to me and we collide in a hug. "Eeeek!" I screech. "I miss you! When did you get back into town?"

"Heather, I've missed you so, so much! I'm so sorry I haven't called you. I've been so incredibly busy in London. That and the time difference sucks."

She's squeezing the life out of me. I hope she's not smearing her makeup on my white costume. "Ohh...that's okay, sweetie. We've got to go out soon—I've got so much to tell you."

"So let's go out tonight. I need a drunken night out on the town with my bestie. GIRLS NIGHT!" She yells it a little too loudly and gets a 'shh!' from a ballet mistress.

I clap excitedly. "YES!" The lights flicker and we let go of each other's hands. "Okay, meet me in my dressing room after the show. I want you to meet someone."

"Someone?" she whispers excitedly while walking away from me. "He'd better have a friend."

I laugh quietly and take my place, hoping that Noah will be okay with my having to dance with Nik once again.

I'm the opening act in front of all of these people. Please, please don't let me fall. The stage goes dark as the curtains open and music starts. Showtime.

Giselle has been one of my favorite dances. In the ballet world, it's a favorite amongst many. I'm playing a young, beautiful peasant girl being wooed by Nik's character. I've been focused for the first five minutes of my solo, but now...now Nik has taken the stage with me. Even though I can't see him, I can feel his storm—Noah's—as he watches me dance with Nik. Nik is truly an amazing dancer, but his personality kills everything he has going for him. I've been playing my part to the tee, but Nik seems to be adding extra touches here and there. They're not part of the choreography and it's throwing me off. I can't take any more. I try to think of my Noah—it's his hands on me, he's the one wooing me, but it's not working. Nik has such a negative vibe, and Noah is nothing but positive. I know that Noah can sense my unease, even from where he sits. I can't hide anything from him, even if I tried. I'm really giving thought to quitting this ballet company and looking for another—anything to get away from Nik.

I'm waiting for the orchestra to finish their piece so I can go backstage. I love this particular charity and this is all for a great cause, but I wish I had declined taking the lead role for this.

When my dance ends there is a deafening round of applause that fills the theatre. Looking out at the audience, I see they are actually getting up out of their seats.

A standing ovation? For us?

Nik signals to me and steps back. The spotlight falls directly on me and I swear the applause gets louder. A standing ovation... for me? I swallow hard and move offstage as I'm supposed to. The audience isn't supposed to applaud until the very end.

Holy crap! I'm standing against a wall backstage with a bottle of water, catching my breath. What just happened? I've never received a standing ovation before. I'm lost in thought when suddenly Nik steps in front of me.

"Impressive, Heather."

I glance up and force a smile. "Thanks, you too," I say, faking all of my enthusiasm toward this jerk.

He leans against the wall beside me and grins. Emphasizing his accent, he adds, "You and I make a great team."

I shake my head and toss the empty water bottle in the trash. "I think that's the last time, Nik."

"Last time? Lanie, what are you talking about?" He grabs my wrist and forces me to face him.

"Would you stop calling me that?"

His grin sickens me. "You used to love my nickname for you."

"That time has passed," I respond and am relieved to hear Dillen's shrill voice before I see her.

"My bestie!" She rounds the corner and swallows me in a hug.

Thankfully Nik backs off and she pulls me down the hall to my dressing room. "Heather! Holy hell, you amazing little shit! How did that feel? Was it amazing? Hell, I had goose bumps when they stood for you." She fires off the words rapidly as we descend the dark hall.

I can't help but giggle with her. She's always been a huge supporter of mine. We get into my dressing room and she shuts the door. "Listen, I heard my mistress talking to one of the Royal Ballet's other mistresses and they were talking about you. I think you're a shoo-in. You could come live with me in London."

My jaw drops. "WHAT? Me? Why would they want me?"

She scoffs. "Are you kidding me? Do you have any idea how many studios are going to offer you a contract after that performance?" She sits down on the pink chair and smiles up at me. "You've gotten better than me. Your jumps are higher, and you're so much more graceful. What gives?"

I smile shyly. "I've been stretching a lot more."

"Stretching, huh? Why don't I believe you?" She sticks out her tongue at me and I toss my blush brush at her.

"Okay, fine. I'm seeing someone…" I stick out my tongue back at her.

"What? Give me all the damn details, you little shit." She jumps up and pulls my hand so I'm sitting down next to her.

I'm finally getting to gush about my man and I let it all spill as quickly as it can spew out of my mouth.

"He's the yummiest, sexiest Greek god. All muscle. He's going to be an attorney. He's constantly studying for his bar exam, and the sex...is un-freaking-believable. I can't get enough. He makes me come so many times each night that I forget my name. I forget how to count. Oh my..." I cover my face because I'm so embarrassed. "Don't judge me, Dill."

"I'm not judging. I'm so interested. What's his name?"

I smile and uncover my face. "His name is Noah."

"Mmm, Noah." She moans loudly

I laugh. "I know, right?"

She throws her arms around me and hugs me tightly. "You lucky shit."

We're giggling like two schoolgirls when the door opens and in walks my Greek god.

"Well, good evening, ladies." Noah's deep voice breaks up our giggles. My heart crashes against my rib cage when I hear his voice. I can't help the way he makes me feel.

"Hi. Is the show over?"

His laugh fills the small dressing room. "No, baby, it's intermission. I wanted to come back here and congratulate you. Now get your little ass in my hands."

Dillen is staring. Yes, blatantly staring at my man in his tux.

I get up and walk over to him and wrap my arms around his neck before kissing him passionately, my entire body on fire for him. His hands move down my white costume to my ass. He picks me up and I wrap my legs around him as he holds me.

"Shit! You two are scorching!" Dillen says while dramatically fanning her flushed face.

I giggle against his lips. "Hush. It's been, like, a whole hour since I've seen him."

"An hour? Shit. Should I see myself out? Hi, Noah, I'm Dillen. Your little ass's best friend."

He smiles and sets me down. "Hello, Dillen, it's great to meet you," he says. His eyes are watching my bestie squirm in her tights.

"I've heard you've stretched the hell out of Heather. Where do I get a man like you, huh?"

He barks out a laugh and I cover my mouth. She's just like

Dani. "Dillen!" I all but shriek.

"Oh come on. He has to have some friends. Maybe not as gorgeous in a tux, but close?"

Noah's arms snake around me from behind and he rests his chin on the top of my head. "I've got two in the audience. So you've got a fifty-fifty chance."

I love his hands on me like this. I move my hands to his arms and hold him to me. Wait...love?

No. Don't even go there, Heather. "Baby, don't throw her in the lion's den."

"If she's asking for it..." He chuckles and laces his fingers with mine "Are we celebrating your performance tonight, ballerina?"

"Wait. Ballerina? I am officially jealous."

I giggle shyly and tilt my head back, kissing under his jaw. "If everyone wants to go out, I'll go."

"Deal!" Dillen squeals and smacks my butt before she walks out of my dressing room. "I have my dance coming up, so you better clap for me, bitch!"

"Good luck. I'll be watching," I call out after her.

"What do you say you come and sit on my lap for the rest of the night?"

I turn in his arms, looking up at him. "I wish I could, baby, but I'm supposed to stay backstage just in case I'm needed. But I'll make you a deal..." Taking his earlobe into my mouth, and twirling my tongue around it, I say, "After the show, I'll be on your lap all night long."

He groans and squeezes my ass. "That, I'll take. Even when we go out, or you'll owe me." He cups my face and takes my mouth slowly, painfully slowly, showing me just how much he cares. He speaks against my lips softly, "You were unbelievable on stage."

I relish the way he tastes. Smells. Feels. I want him. "Really? Thank you. I was really surprised." I don't want him to stop kissing me.

"Yes, and I don't think I was the only one who thought so. My girl got one hell of an applause. I better head back to my seat. Text me so I can find you afterward?" he questions as he steps back through the doorway. My body moves toward him when I'm not thinking about it and he seems to notice. "You going to take me up on that offer?"

The cocky bastard. He knows what he's doing. "No. Later, we have a deal remember? I'll find you afterward; just make sure there are no pillars this time."

He smiles and winks. Oh crap, I want to jump his bones. I blow him a kiss and turn back to my mirror to reapply my lipstick.

He laughs before walking away, mumbling something incoherent.

After a few minutes I head back upstairs and wait with the rest of the dancers. Watching Dillen perform, I admire how graceful she is and envy her. My thoughts drift to what she said..."They were talking about you."

Everyone backstage is quiet and appreciating the art that is being performed on the stage when someone calls out my name. "Heather Lane? I'm looking for Miss Heather Lane," a shorter, blonde dancer says.

"Yes, that's me." I raise my hand up so she can see me. She makes her way over to me, and smiles shyly.

"It's nice to meet you, Heather. My name is Jules. I dance for the Royal Ballet and I've been asked by our director to come find you. He'd like to have a few words with you now, if you wouldn't mind," she says in a textbook English accent.

I'm completely caught off-guard; my eyes are wide with surprise. "Oh. Okay."

She turns and I follow her quietly. My stomach has lurched up to my throat. She leads me to a quiet white hallway that is lined with dressing rooms. She knocks on the door numbered 1491.

"You were brilliant on stage, Heather. I cannot believe I got to watch from the wings." She throws her arms around me and hugs me. Uhhh...what the heck is going on? This total stranger is hugging me.

"Thank y-you," I stutter and she giggles just as the door opens.

"Heather Lane?" A tall, dark-haired gentleman asks. I can tell he's a dancer by the way he holds himself. He's English as well.

"Yes, that's me. I'm afraid I don't quite know who you are..."
I'm so freaking self-conscious.

He smiles and signals toward a chair. "Please have a seat." I step through the doorway and take the seat he is gesturing to.

"Heather, it's a pleasure to meet you. I'm Oliver Norwich. I hold the title of director at the Royal Ballet. I've asked you back here because I am interested in offering you a position at my company. We've been watching you for some time now, and we are incredibly impressed. I have an offer letter for you on the side table."

I look to my left and see the letter. My eyes barely glance over the details before I look back up at him. "I'm sorry, I...don't know what to say. I'm stunned."

He beams down at me. "That's not a problem. Please feel free to take the letter with you and read it over. However, I expect an answer in three days. By Valentine's Day to be precise."

"Three days? You want me to join you in London?" My hands are trembling as I pick up the offer letter.

"No, that's when I would like to have an answer. I ask that you seriously consider it. My personal mobile number and email are on the letter. Please feel free to call me at any time."

I'm numb. I have no idea what to do right now. I manage to say, "Yes, of course. I'll let you know."

How in the hell is it already Valentine's Day? I hadn't even realized.

Focus Heather.

"Brilliant. Head out to the pub tonight. Have a splendid time while celebrating your success."

I smile and stand on unstable legs. "Thank you, Mr. Norwich."

"You're welcome, Heather. I'd love to have you be a part of the company." He opens the door and leads me out, back to the stage. We part ways and I go to my dressing room. I can't believe Dillen was right.

I sit down in my pink chair and stare at my reflection in front of me. My God. This is a dream come true for me. Mom would be so proud. I burst into tears when she invades my mind.

"Oh Momma..." Grabbing tissues from the dresser, I blow my

nose and dab at my eyes. Crap! Don't mess up your makeup, Heather.

My phone goes off in my purse and I fish it out. It's Noah.

Hi, my beautiful girl, where are you?

Hi, handsome. I'm in my dressing room.

We're waiting out in the lobby. Take your time, ballerina. Just know I can't wait to have my hands on you.

I'm changing now, baby. I'll be out soon. I can't wait either.

That's my girl.

He melts my insides. He's so sweet and charming. I just wish my momma could have met him.

The thought makes me start crying again and I have to force myself to calm the F down.

I give myself to the count of ten to relax. One. Two. Three. Deep breaths, Heather. Four. Five. Six. You have an amazing boyfriend and now an offer letter. Seven. Eight. Nine. Ten. I get up and fix my makeup before changing into a dress I thought Noah would love when I bought it. It's a long-sleeve, black lace dress with an open back. It's barely appropriate as the hem sits right beneath my butt. The dress is form fitting, hugging me in all of the right places. Noah seems to love my lace panties, so I'm hoping he'll love this outfit. I slip my feet into my red Yves St. Laurent's and glance at myself in the mirror. The makeup is hiding the tears I shed for my mother. On your toes, Heather.

Straightening my back, I grab my clutch and place everything else into my dusty pink gym bag. Walking out into the lobby, I stop to sign a few autographs with my neon pink marker for a group of little girls who are waiting patiently.

My body comes alive and I know he's close. I feel his large warm hand run down my open-backed dress along my spine. It's obvious that I'm not wearing a bra. I turn around, straight into his arms. "Damn, ballerina. Are you trying to get me hard in front of all of these people?" His eyes roam up and down my body as he smirks deviously.

I smile. "Maybe."

He looks into my eyes and I see his smile falter for a split second. He recovers quickly and he searches my face for something.

Then he cups my face and kisses me so softly, telling me he cares and knows that something is wrong.

I pull back and smile, saying softly, "Ready to go out?"

"Damn right I am." He takes my hand and leads me over to where Joel and Coen are standing.

"There she is!" Coen gives me a brief hug. I can't help but smile shyly. "That was the best ballet I've ever seen."

Aww, he's being so sweet.

"You douche. That's the only ballet you've ever seen." Joel laughs and crosses his arms. He always looks like an FBI agent, every time I see him.

"Thank you, Coen. Oh, I almost forgot. My friend Dillen will be going out with us tonight. Is that okay?"

Coen makes a face. "Another dude? Fuck. This is turning into a sausage fest." I look over at Noah and we smile at each other knowingly.

Within minutes I hear Dillen's melodic voice ring through the lobby. "Hey, you future prima ballerina. Let's go."

I turn to look. She's still got her hair up in a bun just like me and she's wearing a skintight red dress that cuts diagonally across her chest. It's super cute and I'm making a mental note to buy myself one. I love how it has only one sleeve and its length is almost as short as mine.

I beam when she reaches us. "Oh shut up. I'm far from reaching prima." Turning back to the guys, I note Coen's mouth is hanging wide open. "Coen...Joel...this is my best friend, Dillen." She steps forward and holds out her hand, palm down. She's never been afraid to demand what she wants.

"Well hello, gentlemen. Which one of you is taking me dancing?"

Both Coen and Joel step forward. Noah chuckles and says, "You fucking hornballs. Get your shit together."

I can't help but laugh with him. Both of these guys are drooling over Dillen.

"Oh it's okay," Dillen says, "I can take both of them." She takes their ties in her hands and spins around, walking toward the door as they follow her out. They high-five each other while she pulls them after her.

I look up at Noah as we walk out after them. "They have no idea what they've gotten themselves into."

"The fuckers will soon find out. As long as they know you're mine though, I don't mind what happens." We run my duffel out to my Buick before we all pile into a cab. He pulls me onto his lap and wraps his arms around my waist.

Relaxing against his chest, I'm quiet, watching the city out the window. I'm needing a drink...quickly. For an entire evening, I don't want to think about the decision I have to make. I just want this night. With him. My Noah. Turning my head, I whisper, "Can I wear your coat? I'm a little cold."

He quickly takes his arms out of his coat and drapes it over me, pulling me against his chest again. "Is that better, baby?" He's placing small kisses on any part of me he can.

I nod. "Yes, thank you." I want to touch him as much as he wants to touch me. Turning my head, I brush my lips against his neck, breathing in his cologne.

"You're welcome, beautiful." I hear him say as his chest reverberates.

I close my eyes for what feels like two minutes, but then I hear Noah's soft, raspy voice again. "Ballerina? Would you rather go home? You're exhausted."

All the sounds around me are muted. I'm focused on him alone. My eyes flicker open. "No, baby, I want to be out with you."

"I want to be with you too. I don't mind going home with you though." Running his hand to the back of my head, his thumb and index finger rub my earlobe.

I lean my head into his touch. "Take me out, please?"

He nods and presses his lips to mine. I moan softly then look to the side, expecting to see Coen, Joel, and Dillen, but it's just us. Even the driver is standing outside. "Where is everyone?" "I sent them inside about twenty minutes ago. I didn't want to wake you."

"Oh. I'm so sorry." Sitting up, I pinch my cheeks to wake up. "I can't believe I fell asleep." I scoot off of his lap and move to open the door.

"Heather?"

My hand freezes on the handle. He hardly ever calls me Heather. He knows something is wrong, knows me too well already. How did that even happen? I've been so careful, so reserved. Hardly any emotion. Right? Turning my head to face him, I say, "Yes?"

"Tell me the truth..." He stares at me and I'm about to blurt it out but he speaks again. "Did he hurt you? Did he put his hands on you backstage?"

"No, it was nothing." That's not what I was expecting. I smile and continue to open the door. "Come on, let's go have some fun."

He follows me out of the cab and pays before I hand him his jacket back.

"You look beautiful, baby." He takes my hand and leads me inside to where Dillen has both of the men enchanted as she leans against the bar. All three of them are smiling like idiots.

"Hey fuckers." Noah calls out. "Baby, what do you want to drink?"

"Something strong," I reply, holding his hand.

He places his credit card on the bar and asks for two shots of Fireball Whiskey. He pulls me next to Dillen, and stands in front of me, essentially caging me in.

"Bestie!" Dillen squeals and throws her arms around me, regardless of Noah's protective, strong arms being in the way.

I hug her back as best as I can. "Hi, gorgeous. Please behave yourself with these two." I point toward Coen and Joel.

"Oh don't ruin my fun. I won't scare Noah off, I promise."

"I'm not worried about him." I giggle and let her go.

"Good, or I'd kick his ass."

Noah hands me a shot and holds his up. "To my beautiful girlfriend."

"To Heather!" Everyone chimes in and slams their shots on the bar before throwing them back. Noah's lips find mine and I swear the music is turned up. I can feel it pounding in my body. It may not be the right kind of pounding, but for now it'll have to do. Coen orders another round of shots and pulls Dillen's butt into his crotch. What a little manwhore.

Her eyes light up and she hollers loudly. I'm all smiles. Everyone is having a great time. Everything is perfect. I feel Noah snake his arm around my waist and pull me into him. I love having his hands on me. He's kissing my neck and I tilt my head, giving him more access.

I've got goose bumps.

His lips are eager and I can tell he's smiling. "You're so sexy, Heather."

Joel groans and mumbles something about finding his own girl. "Coen, you better get your dick sucked tonight," he says and punches Coen's arm as he walks to a girl in the middle of the dance floor.

"Shit, you can move, Dillen!" Coen pipes in with his hands on Dillen's hips as she grinds her behind into him, blatantly ignoring Joel.

"I've had a lot of practice, so you better be ready for me," Dillen whispers, a bit too loudly.

Circling my arms around Noah's neck, I murmur, "Dance with me? I want all of these girls to be jealous that you're mine. Too many are staring at you in this tux."

"Do you want me to take it off?"

I unbutton a few buttons on his dusty pink shirt and lick his chest. "No way."

I can feel how hard he is between us. I purposely push my body against him more than it is.

"You're mine later." He bites my neck, his teeth sinking down into my skin. I can't help the moan that escapes my lips. I feel Dillen and Coen's eyes on us, but I don't care. I'm soaked and my skin is alight.

I growl and press against him harder. "Don't tease me."

"Tease you? You love when I tease you, baby," he whispers and moves his hands to cup my ass cheeks.

A girl nudges her way to the bar next to us and orders a Long Island Iced Tea then looks over at us as Noah is kissing my neck. She bites her lip and smiles oddly at me.

Noah looks up and turns my chin, kissing me hard and fast,

demanding I give him my full attention.

"Noah? Noah Ryan?" the girl next to us asks curiously.

His kiss slows and his hand is riding up my rib cage while he turns his head. He slowly pulls away from my lips when he sees this girl. What the fuck?

"It's me!" she croons while Noah looks at her, trying to place her. "Alexis Keeley!" she says, pushing her breasts up, showcasing them for my man.

His eyes widen and his smile falls. "Holy shit. How have you been, girl?" He doesn't let go of me.

My jealousy level has just gone through the roof.

Noah

WHAT THE FUCK is Alexis doing in New York City? How the hell is she at the same club as us? Of all the clubs in the city, she comes to this one?

I can feel Heather's body tighten as Alexis moves closer to us.

"I have been amazing." She steps close, too close and lays her hand on my chest, grazing my pec with her fingernails. "I live in London now actually." I think she recognizes Heather because she covers her mouth.

"Oh! You're Heather Lane. I've heard about the offer and I saw you perform. You're pretty good."

Offer? What offer?

"Yes, uhm, hi. It's nice to meet you," Heather replies politely as she's running her fingers through the back of my hair. Damn, she feels so good on me but her body is still tense.

"I'm sorry, how do you two know each other?" Heather asks.

"Noah and I used to date back in college. I believe it was our junior year, so, like, what? Five years ago? I see you haven't lost your touch with the ladies, Noah."

Touch with the ladies? What the hell is she talking about? I can tell she's making Heather uncomfortable.

I laugh the comment off and try to deflect the conversation onto her. From personal experience, I know she loves to talk about herself.

"Are you still dancing?"

Her smile broadens. "Of course I am—that's why I'm here. And since I'm here, how about you buy me a drink or take me out after this party? We can reminisce about old times."

And with that, Heather stops touching me. She turns to the bartender and orders something. It's too loud in here and I can't hear. I watch her take a shot of tequila. I need to fix this quickly.

"Listen, it's good to see you, but I'm out with my girl. We can catch up some other time, but enjoy your evening," I say courteously, before turning around, and when she tries to hug me, I press my front against Heather's back and kiss her neck.

"I'm sorry, baby…"

Coen leans in, tearing his hands off of Dillen. "Mother of all fucks. Was that Alexis?"

I can only nod. I hate when my girl is upset. "Yeah," I finally say, shaking my head so he knows to drop the subject. He nods and turns his attention back to Dillen who is now dancing with another girl as well as Joel. I can see where this is headed—not on my fucking bed they don't.

Heather seems to relax when my hands are on her and I feel her body lean back against mine. She's just ordered another drink. "Am I going to have to carry you out of here tonight?"

She pushes her ass into my crotch and I'm hard as stone. "We'll have to wait and see, mister. Can we go dance now?" she asks as she spins on her toes to face me.

I order two more shots before leaning closer and kissing down her neck, my arm around her waist, pulling her tight against me. "Relax, baby…you're so tense," I say against her neck.

"I'm sorry, it's just…I'm insanely jealous right now. Your ex-girlfriend just pawed you and thrust herself against you, and I had to just stand here and watch...”

“I know, but you belong to me, and I to you. Please trust me when I say that there is no one else I’d rather be with. You’re my only girl, ballerina.”

She looks up at me with the most unreadable expression behind her eyes, “Are you really going to meet up with her sometime?”

I recognize that look: her protective wall is up. I grin slowly and run my hand up her back. “Hell no. That was me trying not to be a total dick.”

A sexy smile forms on her face and she hands me a shot. I want to do nothing but hold her and please her.

She licks those lips to entice me and takes her shot. I quickly follow then take her to the dance floor. She’s giggling and cutely drunk as she dances in my arms. She moves fluidly as her hands move into the air forming graceful patterns. The way her beautiful figure moves to the beat makes me almost lose my mind. I run my hand down her spine. She’s slick with perspiration from the heat sparked off by the large crowd gathered in this meager space.

My hands are on her hips as she shakes her ass. Hell, she dances just as well as she fucks. I can’t wait to get this lace off of her. Dillen and Coen join us on the dance floor and start noisily grinding against each other. Holy shit. I know he’s getting his dick wet tonight!

Joel comes up and sandwiches Dillen in between him and Coen. They’re all so damned drunk, there’s no telling what’ll go down tonight. All I know is I’m going down on my girl tonight.

Heather starts kissing me desperately. I wrap her in my arms and kiss her just as desperately in return. She’s high on me and drunk on tequila.

“Noah?”

“Yes, baby?” I ask against her lips.

“Take me to your bed?” She’s so damned excited.

I slide my hand down to her ass and squeeze. “I thought you’d never ask.”

She squeals excitedly and leans over to Dillen. I can see her lips moving, but I have no idea what she’s saying. The music is too damn loud.

They giggle and talk to each other for an agonizing minute. My eyes are on Heather's ass. Fuck, that dress is so short. I may not be able to wait until we get home. She finally leans back.

"Those three are going to stay here while you ravage me!"

That's it. I scoop her up and toss her over my shoulder, ensuring her ass is covered. I walk to the bar and close out my tab before striding out of the club right past Alexis while sassy toes smacks my ass drunkenly.

I have all of about five minutes of restraint before I have to be inside her. There are cabs lined up outside and I quickly choose one, getting her inside before sliding in next to her. I give the driver my address. Before I know it, she's straddling me, kissing my neck while unbuttoning my shirt the rest of the way.

"You are going to get us in trouble, ballerina. Put my jacket on—it's damn cold and I don't want the driver checking out what belongs to me." She quickly slides her hands into my tux jacket and then she's back down on me, biting and kissing.

She's different: in a frenzy and possessive. She's not listening to a word I say. Her hands get the last button undone and they start to run all over my chest. She's making these noises that make my cock lurch in my slacks.

Her lips are now moving across my chest, over my nipples as she fumbles with my belt. I don't want to tell her to stop. I never want to tell her to stop, so I let her do what she wants. I don't give a fuck about the driver. I'll tip him well.

I think my ballerina might enjoy having an audience. She pulls my cock out and strokes me twice before moving her hand down between her legs. She gets up and hovers over the top of me, holding her panties to the side. Holy shit! This can't happen here. She's blitzed out of her mind and not thinking right. I grab her hips. "Whoa, whoa. Heather? Baby...hang on, we're almost home."

She pushes down on me, hard. I grunt because she's tighter than ever. I haven't warmed her up since before the charity showcase. She's still ready for me though and I'm inside of her, deep inside of her as she rocks her hips. Fucking shit. What's gotten into her? My hands clench her hips in an attempt to still her.

"Noah, please!" she begs as she tries to move her hips in my grasp.

Screw it. I take her lips and loosen my grip so she can move as much as she wants. She's feisty and bites down on my lower lip. The moans coming out of her are insanely erotic.

The cab driver is talking on the phone in another language and he's got some sort of techno music blaring. I'm thankful for the noise; I don't want anyone hearing my ballerina come but me.

She throws her head back and sighs. Fuck, she's so snug. I'm going to come inside of her if she doesn't stop soon. She's riding me so fast as I hold her steady.

"I'm going...to...YES!"

Her warm little cunt tightens its hold on my shaft as she comes. Her body is a quivering delight in my arms. My heads falls back to the headrest. Groaning loudly, I hold off my own orgasm. Damn, are we there yet?

She stills and looks at me with twinkling eyes. "What a rush!"

"Holy shit, baby. Are you into exhibitionism?"

She laughs and throws her head back. "Baby, I don't think I have a fetish. Wait...did you come? I didn't feel you...Did you fake it?"

Chuckling, I kiss her throat and shake my head. "I will when we get into my bed...or on the sofa...kitchen table...wherever I decide to take you."

"How about all of those places?" she asks as I lift her off of me and put my achingly hard cock away. The taxi comes to a stop just in time.

I zip back up and loosely put my belt back on. Tossing a fifty up front to the driver, I open the door; Heather stumbles out and squeals from the cold.

Getting out, I swoop her up into my arms, carrying her upstairs to my apartment. "My sexy girl. Let's get you naked." I set her down and turn so I can get her a tall glass of ice-cold water. When I turn back around she's naked, leaning against the counter top.

I smirk and take off my shirt, standing in just my slacks. "You're ready again?"

"I'm always ready for you."

She gets onto the kitchen counter. I'm going to eat her out until she can't take it anymore. As I stride toward her, she leans forward, pushing her breasts together. This definitely is a different Heather. Either something's up with her or she's just entirely too drunk. I lean down and take a nipple into my mouth while palming her other breast.

Her moans make my cock twitch. I bite her nipple then move to the other to do the same thing before licking down her surfboard flat stomach to her pussy. My teeth find the inside of her thigh, biting down hard as she churns in my arms.

"You like that?"

"Yes…" Her voice is almost too raspy, not hers, as I kiss her little cunt.

"You're so ready for me, but I want to taste you. Over and over again." Pulling her ass to the edge of the counter, I dive my tongue into her soaking wet pussy, licking her softly as I enjoy her sweet taste. Her hands move into my hair and pull as I make her come hard, again and again. "Fuck, you taste good."

"NOAH! I need you inside of me," she protests when I swirl my tongue around her pink clit. I'm going to drive her crazy, sucking on her lips, biting occasionally.

"PLEASE!" she yells and crushes my head onto her cunt.

I groan loudly. Not fucking happening, ballerina. Her feet are resting on my shoulders. Her toes start to curl and I know she's close. My tongue is relentless against her as she squirms and comes hard. I can feel her core tightening as she lets her coiled body explode.

Relaxing her gorgeous body, she pants my name. Swiping my tongue between her folds once more before standing up, I look down at her as I undo my slacks and drop them.

A cute growl pierces my ears as I take my heavy cock out. I want her against the wall. I want to see her face when I fill her this time. Picking her up without warning, I crush my mouth to hers as we crash into the wall.

She screams as I part her legs, sinking the head of my cock into her folds. I love it when she loses her mind. My hands dig into her thighs when I thrust up into her. Her pussy is still so fucking tight—I'm about to lose my shit as well. "You like it when I fuck you hard, don't you?" Grunting with every thrust, her breaths are coming out in a rush. Her sharp nails dig into my back.

"Yes. Harder...HARDER!" she yells out as I pound her. She better come soon or I'll lose it without her. As if on cue her body tightens and explodes with energy. Visible waves are crashing into her repeatedly. I slam my cock into her over and over again while she comes, pressing her back against the wall harder.

I have total control over her, over us. She loves when I take over and fuck her like it's the last time I'll ever be inside of her. My balls firm up and I come, hot spurts of semen filling her tight, spasming cunt.

I've got her hands pinned against the wall. She fucking loves that too. I had to take them when she dug into my skin. I have no doubt that I will wake up with scratches covering my back.

She looks up at me, and smiles sweetly, as though this sexy, erotic little devil just vanished and she's my angel again.

"Noah Ryan, you are so amazing at this."

"You better believe it, baby." My lips find hers in my embrace as I let go of her wrists, allowing her to latch onto me.

Groaning against her skin, I add, "Making you come is going to be my new full-time job."

We're like this for minutes, kissing each other slowly against the wall in my kitchen. She's as light as a feather but something heavy is weighing on me, something lost in the back of my mind. I can't pull it to the front, but it's there somewhere. She hums into my mouth and I love it. I love that sound—she makes it after we've fucked each other thoroughly.

She wiggles her ass so I ease her down onto her feet.

"The way you make me feel, little ballerina, is like the ocean to my sand. You mold me and form me however you want; I'm in it for the ride."

CHAPTER
Twenty-Six
a valentine's offer

Heather
February 13th.

I HAVE TO GIVE the Royal Ballet my answer soon. I have to tell Noah today—I can't keep this from him. I think he knows something is up from the way I have been acting. He's been himself, but he's quiet.

We're back at my place after spending two nights at his loft. The hours passed slowly as we lay naked on his bed, talking about the most mundane yet important things: his favorite childhood memory, what his childhood might have been like, and if he'd even want to meet his birth parents. He said he's sure he wants to, but said he couldn't do it alone. I'd go with him if he asked me, of course. He's my man and I'm going to be there for him just as he has been here for me this past month and a half.

Tomorrow is Valentine's Day. It's going to be one of the few times that I'll actually have a Valentine. I have no idea what he's planning, but he's been getting random phone calls and leaving the room to take them.

I'm not sure how I'm going to break this to him, or how he's even going to react. He's a pretty calm individual, with that one exception. Since then he's been my same ole Noah: sweet, sexy, cocky, irresistible…and just all-around perfect.

I'm currently sitting cross-legged on the couch surfing the web for Noah's Valentine's gift. I'm getting cranky because I have no clue what to get him and no clue what he's got up his sleeve. Every time he walks by me, I have to close my MacBook and wait for him to go away. I've got so much on my mind—I'm so frustrated, I may just swear out loud.

"Hey baby?" Noah calls out from the kitchen. "We're going out tomorrow night. Wear something sexy for me?"

I don't know what's come over me, but before I can stop myself, I reply in a low, grumbly voice, "Don't I always wear something sexy for you?" I'm still searching the Internet with my chin in my hand, not having any luck.

He walks back to the living room and sits down next to me. I slam my MacBook closed and look up at him.

"Baby, talk to me? What's bothering you?"

I sigh heavily and lay my head against the back of the couch, chewing on the inside of my cheek. "Nothing. I'm fine."

He moves the laptop off of my lap and onto the pink coffee table before lifting me onto his lap. "Don't give me that, ballerina. Tell me what's going on."

Crossing my arms over my chest. "I'm cranky."

"Why? What happened to make my girl cranky? Do you want me to beat someone's ass in?" he asks, as he kisses the shell of my ear and down to my collarbone.

I mumble my reply, "No. I haven't had any gummy bears in, like, five days. And it pisses me off. And I can't find your gift."

I can tell he's trying not to laugh. "Ballerina, don't worry about a gift. I just want you, and as for your gummy bears…I can make a run to the grocery store if you'd like. I don't mind, but I know there's more to this than a gift and gummy bears."

"But I am worried about your gift."

He smiles down at me and kisses me slowly, holding me to him. I feel my body melt into his and I know he does, too.

"What's really bothering you? Tell me, baby, please."

I shut my eyes and lay my head against his chest. He's so good for me: he always knows exactly what I need.

"I got an offer at the showcase," I say softly.

"What kind of offer?" he implores.

I start playing with his fingers absentmindedly, watching his chest rise and fall slowly...evenly. "The director of the London Ballet wants me to dance for them."

I don't know if I'm seeing things or not but I swear his breathing just stopped.

"London? As in London, England?"

His heart is beating faster, more intense than it was.

"Yes. They want my answer tomorrow."

He's quiet and so am I. I don't know what to say and I can tell he's thinking, contemplating. When he finally speaks, his voice is thick...raspier. "Were you going to tell me?"

Was I? Of course I was...but I didn't. This internal battle is killing me slowly. "I was, and I should have earlier. I'm sorry. I've been struggling with it so much." I quickly dash the stupid tears that fall away.

He lifts me off of his lap with great ease and sets me on the cushion beside him. He doesn't speak for the longest time and I swear I'm about to sob uncontrollably. He has never pushed me away from him. Never. I'm trembling inside. I can't even describe the way I feel right now.

Crushed? No.

Devastated. Yes.

Finally, he moves. He gets up from the couch and leaves the room. I have no idea where he's gone, but he doesn't want to be in the same room as me. And I can't even blame him. I think he went to my bedroom so I move off of the couch and drag myself to my room.

"Noah?" I ask, tears threatening to overtake me.

"Are you considering it?" he asks, as he stares out my tall windows.

I stare down at my feet. I can't even answer him. He takes my silence as confirmation and I hear him again. "Why?"

"Noah...it's been my dream for as long as I can remember. My mother...she told me I had nothing stopping me. I just had to stay on my toes." Choking on my words, I grip the sleeves of Noah's favorite sweater. "I can't just say no..."

His voice is cold and it stuns me. "So it's a yes then?"

He won't even turn around and look at me. I walk closer to him. "I haven't decided yet."

I want him to look at me. I want him to hold me like he was, but I understand why he's pulling away from me. His "mother" and now me. All the women he has ever trusted. She and I...hurt him. His breathing is uneven. I swear I can feel the heat radiating off of his body—a new storm is brewing.

"Baby?" I reach out and touch his arm. He's tense and vibrating with an unnamed emotion.

"I..." He pauses to look down at me. "I can leave you alone to decide. I know you have a lot to think about."

His jaw is tense and rigid, his chest rising and falling rapidly with each breath he takes. I can't tell what he's going to do...I can't tell if he's mad or upset or what? Both? My Noah...

"I don't want you to leave..."

"...not yet," he adds onto my sentence.

I can't help the tears that fall once he says that. I don't even know who's staring back at me. Those eyes...aren't his. His body radiates so much heat but he's so cold. I never wanted this to happen...to get this close. I wasn't supposed to care about anyone else. This was just sex. Just a New Year's Eve fling. But I went and got too close to the storm. Now I'm being ripped apart. The tears are steadily falling down my cheeks. I haven't cried in front of anyone since my parents' funeral. He walks up to me and wipes my tears away with the pads of his thumbs then kisses me tenderly before leaving the room and then my apartment.

February 14th – Valentine's Day

I HAVEN'T SPOKEN to him since he left last night. I don't even know if he went home. I spent the rest of my night crying and searching for a gift for him. I found it. I paid extra to have it delivered to me today. It's the most perfect thing I could give him.

After a long soak in the tub, I get out and pick up my phone. There's one text from my man.

Be mine?

I didn't think I had any left in me, but the tears start to fall steadily down my face again. I type out my reply through blurry eyes.

Of course I will.

I sit on my bed in only a towel, internally begging him to respond. My phone vibrates.

Can you be ready in twenty minutes? I'm coming to get you.

My heart is pounding in my chest to the point where it actually hurts. I'm going to bruise my own body parts from being so riled up. I look at my reflection and cringe. My eyes are red and swollen and there are dark circles from my lack of sleep last night. I haven't slept without him since he came to New York. I can't sleep unless I'm in my spot, on his chest. I take a steadying breath to keep from sobbing again and I reply.

Yes, I can be ready.

Standing up to get ready, I'm unsure now about how I should dress. He said he wanted sexy, but that was before. Before last night.

I'll see you soon, my ballerina.

His text makes me want to laugh and cry at the same time. He's been through so much, yet he's such an incredibly positive person. I drop my towel and run to my closet, tossing clothes out as I look

236 • J. Epps & S. Brümmer

for the perfect outfit.

I find my little flared black skirt and bite the inside of my cheek. This is going to be cold! I dig through my drawer of leggings, stockings, and pantyhose until I come across ones covered in little black hearts. I get a matching set of bra and panties, lace of course. I find my knitted navy blue sweater, black knitted scarf and my black leather jacket. I get dressed quickly then slip my feet into my Christian Louboutin Belle Boots.

By the time I finish my makeup, there's a knock on my door. My heart leaps because I know it's him. This feels like our first date again. God, that seems so long ago, yet it has only been seven weeks.

SEVEN.

And I'm completely addicted to this man. How? How did I let this happen? I make my way down the stairs and try to swallow my heart before opening the door.

I pull the too-heavy door open and drink him in: his blue denim shirt, a charcoal polka dot tie that I bought him, a gray shawl cardigan with the middle two buttons done up, his favorite navy bomber jacket and gray dress pants with a brown leather belt. He looks edible.

But above all else, I notice two things: his cologne—my favorite scent—and his eyes. They're back; they're his again. My Noah. I'm so beyond nervous. I smile shyly. "Hi. Happy Valentine's Day."

"Happy Valentine's Day, baby." His body is against mine before I know it and his hand is moving to the back of my head. His lips find mine an instant later. His kiss isn't forceful: it's needy. He needs me just as much as I need him. As we kiss, his other hand moves to the small of my back.

"Are you going to get cold?" he whispers against my lips.

I'm completely caught off-guard. After last night, I never expected him to talk to me again, let alone touch me like this. My eyes flutter closed with his lips touching mine. "I don't care."

"I'll keep you warm, I swear." He smiles against my lips. "Now let me spoil my beautiful girlfriend."

I nod in approval and we leave with our fingers laced together.

Surprisingly he doesn't lead me to my car, but we ride down in the elevator instead. Walking out of the building, we head toward a man in a suit and driver's hat standing next to a pink limousine.

I gasp and stop dead in my tracks. "It's pink!"

I'm practically jumping up and down in excitement over this ridiculously loud paint job. We walk over and the driver opens the door for us. I try to climb in as gracefully as I can with a skirt on, trying my best not to flash the whole world.

I can hear Noah laughing when he gets in behind me. I sit down and he joins me, picking up two glasses of champagne, and handing me one.

"To us, baby. To my valentine."

I think I'm blushing. I decide to kiss him instead of sipping my champagne first. "To us."

His lips linger on mine and I'm about to pull away when his hand glides up my neck and softly cups the back of my head, keeping me firmly planted. His lips move against mine slowly and I feel his tongue graze the seam of my lips. In a natural reaction to him, I part them, as if his mouth is commanding mine to open for him. I find myself moving closer; my chest is lightly brushing his as our kiss continues to be soft yet sensual. His thumb is caressing my jawline while his tongue expertly strokes mine. I can't help the small whimper that escapes me. I'm so wet now, just from his slow, passionate kiss.

I smile against his soft lips. "Where are you taking me, Greek god?"

"Just wait and see, baby. This night is all about us."

I love it when he calls me baby. I love his pet names for me. Wait…love?

Yes…I can admit it. I love it. The limo comes to a stop and I can barely see out of the windows.

He takes my hand and helps me out, making sure I don't flash anyone. We walk into the China Grill and we're taken to a table for two.

"I hope you don't mind but I've ordered for us already. I didn't want to wait as we have another stop to make."

The waitress comes over and takes our drink orders. Given the atmosphere I decide on ordering a bottle of warmed sake. I sit back in my chair and take in the impressive décor.

"Noah, this is too much."

He reaches for my hand and grins mischievously at me. "You're worth it, Heather. All of it."

The waitress comes back, but Noah doesn't move his hand from mine. She places our drinks down and quickly returns with spicy edamame and fried dumplings. We thank her before she leaves the table.

I scrunch up my nose at Noah, "Dumplings?"

"Consider it your valentine's gift to me…by eating a dumpling." He winks and leans forward, picking up a dumpling with his chopsticks gracefully, and holding it up to my mouth.

"Open up," he says with a little too much enthusiasm.

I can't hide my smile, nor can I deny him this. It is after all, Valentine's Day. Narrowing my eyes at him playfully, I take the dumpling into my mouth. His eyes lock onto mine and I know he truly wants me to like it. He wants us to have something else in common…even if it is just a dumpling.

I chew slowly, tasting the flavors that explode in my mouth. Surprisingly…I like it. Really like it. He's waiting for my critique so I finally swallow and ease his pain. "Okay, you were right. Those are delicious," I concede.

The smirk that glides across his face shows his sultry, cocky, egotistical victory. "Damn right they are."

I giggle as another dish is brought to the table. Our waitress informs us that everything is served family style and Noah ordered Szechuan beef with udon noodles.

I can't help but smile. He's thought of everything. I want to keep that smile that he's wearing. He hasn't mentioned yesterday; it's like it never happened. He's back to his warm, affectionate self… times ten. "Noah, this is amazing. Thank you."

"You're welcome; I hope you enjoy it."

"I will." I bring my fork to my mouth and look up. I'm about to say something but he's staring. "What?" I ask shyly.

"You're just so damn gorgeous. I can't help but think of that dirty mouth elsewhere."

I wither in my seat—I love it when he's cocky. Taking a bite, I moan softly because frankly it's the best Szechuan beef I have ever tasted.

"That good, huh?" he asks teasingly.

I nod and dab at my lips with my napkin. "Yes."

He takes a bite and groans. I almost spit out the sake. "Are you making fun of me, Noah Ryan?"

"I would never…" he says, right before taking another bite.

He's super-playful tonight and I'm swooning over it. He unexpectedly gets up and scoots his chair over so he's to the right of me instead of opposite me. His cologne surrounds me and I take a deep breath.

"Hi," I say, moving my hand to his thigh, taking a sip of my sake, my thumb absentmindedly grazes his thigh. I'm anxious to give him his gift, so instead of waiting, I reach for my clutch and take out the small box, setting it on the table in front of him. "Happy Valentine's Day."

"You got me something? You didn't have to do that." He excitedly reaches for the box and opens it, revealing two silver cufflinks with numbers engraved in each one. "Wow, thank you baby. What do the numbers mean?"

I'm almost nervous to tell him. "It's...uhm. It's silly. It's the longitude and latitude coordinates for my place." I shrug, hoping he doesn't hate it.

He looks up at me with shock on his face. "You'll always be with me that way. Baby, this is the best gift I've ever gotten. Thank you."

"You really like it?" I'm relieved. I've never bought a man a gift before, other than my dad.

"I do, baby, thank you." He leans forward and kisses me then signs the check the waitress brought us after we finished eating. "Are you ready to head to our next spot? And will you hold onto these so I don't lose them? Please?"

"I'm ready." Taking the box, I put it back in my clutch. I'm about to stand up when he extends his hand to help me up. It's such a sweet act, and it's so like him to do that. My heart fractures inside my chest. He deserves so much. He deserves to be happy. He's such an amazing, caring, compassionate person. I don't know if I can ever give him what he deserves. I take his hand and he helps me up then laces our fingers together before we walk out. "Where are we going next?"

"To my place," he says nonchalantly.

"Okay."

He helps me back into the limo when we get outside. His hands on my hips ignite something inside me and I want to be as close to him as possible. When he slides in next to me, I scoot over to him, our thighs touching. He looks down at me and I can barely see his expression in the dark. He's got the interior accent lights on low. It's very romantic and I can feel our spark. It's still there. He puts his warm hand on my thigh and I get chills. I think I shiver.

"Are you cold?" he asks me.

I shake my head. "I'm okay."

My voice is soft. I look down at his hand as he caresses one of the hearts on my tights with his thumb. He's lost in thought, staring out of the window when I look back up at him. I'm afraid to ask what he's thinking.

I have only a few hours to get back to Mr. Norwich with my answer. I've cried so many tears over this whole situation. I just don't know what to do. I don't want to think about it. Not tonight. Not until I have to.

Noah leans over and kisses my neck so tenderly. "Do you want to change into one of my shirts and sweatpants later to get more comfortable?"

I nod and look up at him. Suddenly it hits me without warning. I don't know why but that question made me so emotional that I start to tear up. I wanted to dress sexy for him on Valentine's Day. But I brought my stupid clutch and forgot to pack something cute to wear. I'm a freaking mess on the verge of a meltdown.

"Baby?" He tilts my chin up and presses his lips to mine. "What's wrong?"

I'm trying to hold back the tears that threaten to fall. I'm sure my voice gives me away. "You're just so sweet, Noah."

"You're my girl, Heather. You deserve to be treated like the queen you are." He lifts me onto his lap and wraps his arms around my waist. I feel insanely safe with him; I've never felt so safe before with anyone. And that's all it takes. The tears flow freely and I can't stop them.

"Ballerina…I'm here," he says softly as I rest my cheek against his shoulder. He runs his thumb over my cheek to brush the tears away.

This is the second time I've cried in front of him. There goes my F'ing makeup. I'm trying to just concentrate on my breathing. No need to hyperventilate tonight and completely ruin his Valentine's Day. He's running his hand up and down my back as the limousine comes to a stop. He doesn't say anything but he lifts me and carries me out and thanks the driver before dismissing him.

When we get into his apartment, he sets me down on my feet and kisses my tear-dampened lips. On the kitchen counter sits a bunch of printed-word paper roses, which are set in a pink vase.

I smile up at him and lean over the bunch of roses. I try to amuse him by picking up and smelling one. Oh! They smell like him, like his cologne. I look up at him before returning the rose to its vase. "Baby, they're beautiful. Thank you."

"You're welcome, ballerina. This way, you will be able to hold onto them.

I think I'm over my cry-fest. Pulling myself together, I kiss him slowly. "I'm sorry."

"You have nothing to apologize for. Come on, I want to show you something." He laces our fingers together and leads me into his living room.

As soon as I enter the room I freeze. There are hundreds if not thousands of fairy lights.

They're somehow suspended from his vaulted ceiling. All the furniture has been moved and in its place…a tent, with the opening facing his floor-to-ceiling windows that overlook the city. My mouth is agape. I have no words. My breathing is coming fast and my heart

242 • J. Epps & S. Brümmer

is fluttering like a hummingbird's wings.

"What do you think? It's not overkill, is it?" he asks, as he pulls me toward the tent made from white sheets. There are pillows and blankets inside. He must have bought pillows just for this.

"I..."

I can't even finish my thought. The tears are back. I throw my arms around his neck and bury my face in his chest.

"You remembered my perfect date?" What in the hell is wrong with me? *Pull it together, Heather.*

"Of course I did. It's too cold outside, so I made you your own stars."

I can't let go of him so I jump and wrap my legs around his waist and latch onto him like a little monkey. "Baby, it's the most beautiful thing I've ever seen." I start placing kisses all over his face. I'm so excited. So overjoyed. It's my fantasy date.

He chuckles and wraps me in his rock-hard yet silky arms. "I'm so glad you like it. Fuck, I was concerned you'd hate it."

"Are you kidding me?" I almost shriek. Pulling back to look at him, I see he looks so happy. There's a twinkle in his eyes again. Ugh, I love that smile on him. "I love it, Noah."

"I..." He pauses and looks at me. "I'm glad you like it. Let's get you into something comfortable before we get in."

I smile brightly and nod. I'm like a little kid about to go camping. But without the bugs.

He puts me down and pats my ass. "There are clothes on my bed for you...go ahead..."

I squeal and take off to his bedroom. Lying on his bed, folded neatly, is a pair of black sweats that swallow me but they're my favorite. And a plain white tee-shirt. As I take my clothes off, I realize that Noah never wears prints on his shirts, only solids. I know it's a weird thing to recall but I do. I leave on my lace bra and panties, figuring they're the only things sexy I brought with me.

I walk back to the living room to Noah holding up two large steaming white mugs with marshmallows on top. "You made me hot chocolate?" He has thought of everything.

He nods eagerly and holds out a mug. He's stripped down to his undershirt and boxers, and there are now two tents in the room. I take the mug and blow on it before taking a sip. Oh yum! He made this with milk. The only way anyone will ever get me to have milk is in my ice cream, milkshakes, and hot chocolate. "Mmm, Noah, this is so good."

"I'm glad. Your stars are waiting for you, ballerina," he says, gesturing to the tent entrance.

I smile and walk over to the entrance and carefully get in without spilling my hot chocolate. Suddenly, the overhead lights go out and all that's on are the twinkling fairy lights. I'm beyond thrilled.

He gets into the tent with me and sits down behind me so I can lean against him while we both stare out the window. Large white snowflakes start to fall and I giggle. "It's snowing!"

I'm grinning like an idiot. I've got everything I could ever want right here. My stars…my Noah…his smell…lying on his chest…hot chocolate. It's the perfect date. He's perfect.

"Now that I didn't plan for." His chest moves with his deep, raspy laugh.

I smile and giggle with him. "Are you sure? You've thought of everything else."

"Just for my beautiful girl. Happy Valentine's Day, my valentine."

I turn my head and kiss him gently. "Happy Valentine's Day, my Noah."

He groans and takes my mug, putting it aside and then his. His hand cups my face and he starts kissing me passionately. Slowly, sweet, tender, and magical. I place my hand in his hair and tug as his hand moves down my throat. He's holding my throat in one hand as he applies the tiniest bit of pressure. His fingers slowly move up until they are holding my jaw and throat rooted in place. I don't even have the words. What he's doing to me…the way he's holding me captive…I'm loving this side of him.

My back is still against his chest and my head is angled in just the right way for this kiss. The temperature in this tent has jumped at least ten degrees. I want him to touch me. I need him to touch me. I can feel him growing harder underneath me and I know for a fact that he can get even harder. Without breaking our kiss, I boldly take his hand and force it down my body. He lets me move his hand over my breasts and down my stomach as his fingers dig into my skin on the way down. Our kiss becomes a little more heated and I hear a slight rumble in the back of his throat. I love that I can get him worked up. I slip our joined hands beneath my sweats and we graze my sex over my lace panties. He's nipping at my lips with his teeth every so often but when I slip our fingers under my panties and through my wet folds, he full-on bites me.

Although our fingers are still laced, he pushes his middle finger up into me. I'm beyond wet and ready for him. I gasp against his lips when he pushes up against my most sensitive spot. I rock my hips in response to his finger and he groans into my mouth. "Baby..."

He moves swiftly and before I know it I'm on my back underneath him. I'm scrambling to get his boxers off as he pulls his sweatpants off of me, but leaves my panties on. I finally get his boxers off, then his shirt. He's kissing up my stomach and pushing his shirt off, grumbling, "Why the hell did I even put clothes out for you?"

I'm breathing fast and hard, running my fingers through his hair. "I don't know..." I move my arms out of the shirt and toss it somewhere. He's moving slowly now. Tasting me, savoring every single thing about me.

It takes him an hour to get me ready to accommodate his size, but once I'm ready, he takes my bra off. His lips press against mine as I pant. He hasn't let me come yet. He wants me to feel him when I'm ready and aching.

"Noah...baby, I..."

I can't take anymore. I'm quivering with need. I've been begging him for the past hour to let me come. If I don't soon, I'm going to combust.

He ever so gently pushes into me, slowly but surely. He's so hard and I've never felt him like this before. Both of us are so raw and aching. His thrusts remain constant and slow as I circle my arms around his neck.

He won't go any faster than this. My kisses are fast and needy while he continues to slow me down with deliberate, passionate strokes of his tongue. He's brought me to the edge a million times but never lets me fall.

"How does that feel, baby?" His lips move against mine as he speaks. His warm breath mixes with mine as my body stiffens. Is he going to let me feel this? Is he going to let me soar?

I whimper softly against his lips. "Don't stop. It feels so good."

The way he thrusts his hips drives me crazy. He does it so well. Unlike anyone before. I feel powerful knowing that I took him first. Before anyone else could. Me. Nobody can take that away from me.

He's breathing through his teeth when he grunts and pushes in deeper than ever. I fall.

Hard and fast.

I've lost myself hundreds of times to this man, but this feels different.

It's so raw, and filled with passion.

I gasp out, unable to catch my breath.

He comes gloriously inside of me, filling the limited space he has left.

My body is shaking under his and I'm still coming. And so is he. He thrusts again and I feel every single pulse as he empties himself into me. He's pulling back and I look up at him as my breathing evens out. He's staring into my eyes. He's not saying anything but I can tell he wants to. My voice is soft when I speak.

"Noah? What's wrong?"

"I couldn't ask for a more gorgeous, compassionate, and addictive girlfriend."

He smiles and slowly pulls out of me. He takes his time cleaning us both up. He gets up and out of the tent to put his now-used shirt into the washer. When he comes back, he's carrying a small navy-blue giftbag with the word Swarovski written on it. His sexy, naked body moves down next to mine. He lays his head on my lap and hands me the bag when I sit up.

"You butthead! You didn't need to get me anything. You already gave me the most perfect date," I say, as I eagerly open the bag.

"Yes I did, ballerina. I'll always treat you the way you are

246 • J. Epps & S. Brümmer

supposed to be treated."

He's looking up at me from my lap, watching as I open the little box and pull out a pair of Puzzle Greige pierced earrings. They are so perfect and simple, with long stems leading down to the crystal. The fairy lights catch the crystals, making them sparkle even more.

"Noah, they're beautiful." Taking them out of their box, I put them in my ears. "How do they look?" I ask, holding my hair back and up off my neck so he can see.

"They look even more beautiful on you than I could have imagined. Are you sure you like them? The only jewelry I've ever bought was a brooch or two for Mae..." He trails off as he traces patterns on my inner thigh. I don't want to lose him to the horrid thought of her. I lean forward and kiss him passionately.

Running my fingers through his hair gently—I know he enjoys it when I do that—I say, "Thank you for everything tonight. I've loved every minute of it."

He hums his appreciation and nuzzles my naked sex. "You're welcome, baby."

His eyes grow heavy as I play with his hair and before I know it, he's asleep. His muscular chest rises and falls with each shallow breath he takes.

I ease myself back onto the pillows and watch him sleep, continuously running my fingers through his dark hair. He looks so peaceful, his lips parted slightly. God, the way his dark lashes fall in contrast to his skin tone. I've never taken the time to take in just how good looking this man really is.

But it's more than that. His personality and caring demeanor throw him into a category all his own. It's just not possible that he exists. I think back to Christmas Eve, all the way up to now, everything that he's done for me, said to me, and made me feel. He's amazing...and he's given himself to me in every way. Physically and emotionally. What I've feared would happen has happened, without my even realizing it.

I'm scared of what comes next. How is it possible to feel this way about a man in seven weeks?

I'm not sure where he wants this to go, but I'm not sure I can take it any further. I don't know if I can deny my dance career for a man...but this man? Both are once-in-a-lifetime and I've stumbled across both of them at the same time, at the wrong time.

I muster up my courage and make sure he's asleep before I move and replace a pillow under his head. There's one last thing I have to do today.

I kiss his soft lips gently before moving out of the tent. I can't help but be distracted by the thousands of glittery lights above me. God, he put so much time and effort into this night. He deserves so much better than me. I make my way over to my clutch and take out his cufflinks and my iPhone. I compose an email to Mr. Norwich:

To: **Oliver Norwich**
From: **Heather Adalyn Lane**
Subject: **The Royal Ballet Offer**

Dear Mr. Norwich,

I apologize for the last-minute decision, but I accept your offer to join the Royal Ballet.

Best,
Heather A. Lane

I drop my phone back into my clutch because it suddenly weighs a thousand and one pounds.

CHAPTER
Twenty-Seven
heart throb

Heather

I SMELL BACON. I sigh and blink my eyes open slowly. I'm alone in the tent. Suddenly, I'm nauseous. The reality of what I have to do hits me and I double over with pain. Please don't let this break me…us. I ease my way out of the tent and pull on his sweats and tee. Finding him in the kitchen cooking, I see he looks happy. Beyond happy. Why?

"There she is. Good morning, ballerina."

"Hi, uhm, can we talk, please?" I ask nervously.

He turns off the gas stovetop and walks over, taking my hand, and leading me to his relocated couch. "Is everything okay?"

He's playing with my fingers, touching me in an attempt to calm me down. He figured out a few days after we'd been dating that a simple touch of his can turn my day around, but I can't let this happen now. He leans in and he's about to kiss me. I want nothing but those lips all over me right now. I want to feel that calming effect he has on me, but I pull back instead.

"Noah, I can't."

I'm undeniably terrified of being in love with him. I have to get up off of the couch and walk into his bedroom, picking up and folding my outfit from yesterday, pretending this isn't affecting me. He follows me in, but doesn't say a word.

"I've decided to accept the position and I will be joining the Royal Ballet. It's an internationally recognized ballet company, which is based in the Royal Opera House in Covent Garden, London. It'll be too hard to continue whatever this is from that far away." My heart breaks into a million pieces when I say the words out loud.

Silence fills the room and I wait for him to say something.

"But...you're mine," he replies softly. I hear the anguish in his voice and it cuts through me like a knife. I'm on the verge of tears and I know if I turn around and face him, I'll crumble to the floor at his feet into a pile of nothing. Choking back the tears that threaten me, I try to speak.

"Noah..."

I feel the bed dip as I fold my shirt. "Whatever this is? You can't even put a name on what we have, Heather?"

He gets up just as quickly as he sat down and starts pacing the room. "We're over? That was you breaking up with me? Over what? London? The fucking ballet?"

I turn to look at him with a tear-stained face. He's exactly right. I drink him in while I still can. He's so handsome with those dark, broad shoulders. "It's my life, Noah."

"Right. Of course it is. Just your life." He moves quickly to the closet and when he emerges, he's wearing a loose-fitting shirt with a long-sleeve *Under Armour* shirt underneath it, with sweatpants and his running sneakers.

"That's not fair!"

"Fair? You want to know what's not fucking fair?" He's gritting his teeth and his eyes are rimmed in red. "Finding out your entire damn life was a huge lie, and then chasing a woman across the fucking country because she's the only thing that makes you feel alive, the only thing that fucking matters anymore—and she runs. She runs so fucking far away that I have no chance of catching her again. That's what's not fucking fair!" he shouts.

Silent tears are streaming down my face as he stands in front of me, waiting for me to say something.

"Nothing? Fuck!" He runs both of his hands through his gorgeous dark hair that's gotten too long. "I can't believe you're calling this over before you've even spoken to me. You know I'd give my fucking life for you to stay, but I don't think anyone would trade my damaged heart for a grain of sand now."

"I don't want to hurt you. Please!"

He shakes his head as he swallows hard and walks out of the bedroom. Before I can force my legs to move, I hear the apartment door slam shut. He's gone.

I just left him. My Greek god.

I crumple onto the floor, my breaths ragged and shaky.

CHAPTER
Twenty-Eight
cessation

Noah

I FEEL EMPTY.

Maybe if my heart stopped, it wouldn't fucking ache like this. I'm sick to my stomach as I round the corner to my apartment building. I've been running in the snow for three hours.

Every time I try to forget her, I see her gorgeous face. I see her smiling under the lights in the tent last night. The lights that took me hours to hang. Everything I did yesterday, every fucking detail was for her. I knew she was struggling with the decision, but never did it once cross my mind that she'd choose a foreign country over me.

I feel betrayed.

I feel like death.

The soul-crushing feeling only intensifies as I run up the nine flights of stairs to my apartment, torturing myself physically to try and stop this pain.

I'm uncertain how to process these emotions that are taking swings at me every chance they get.

Opening my apartment door, I stride through every room, and every room comes up empty. I want to—no, need to—tell her how I feel about her. She needs to know. But she's gone.

I ram my fist into the metal frame of the door, hearing a pop, but not giving a fuck. I've been welcoming the physical pain since I stepped outside into the freezing cold snow for a run. I have nothing left. No ballerina, no mother, no family. If someone wanted me alone, he or she has succeeded.

I want to fucking lash out at everything; I want to hurt anything and everything. I want someone else to feel this obnoxious pain. I make my way back to the kitchen and grab a beer. That's when I see the bacon. I toss the pan and bacon into the trash receptacle.

Screw the ballet. I won't ever go see another shitty attempt at a ballet again, I swear to myself childishly. Because she's the only one that makes it worth it anymore...

I march indignantly into the living room. Fuck me. The tent and the motherfucking stars are still up. I can't look at this shit, let alone clean it up. I need to get out of here. I can still smell her perfume; I can feel our magnetic pull being sliced in half. She's part of someone else's magnetic field now. Not mine.

I decide to take a cold shower before getting dressed and heading over to Joel's place. He called me earlier when Heather was still asleep, informing me that he had something to talk to me about. I pound on his door a little too hard when I arrive. "Open the door, Joel."

He opens it and takes in my mood. "Shit. Girl problems?"

Fuck, is it that fucking obvious? "You don't want to know," I state as I stride past him and into his living room, taking a seat in the brown leather recliner. "What did you need to talk to me about?"

Joel grabs a binder full of papers and hands it to me. "This is essentially from Mae Ryan. To sum it up, everything has been under your name, even that diner she loved, and it has been for years. All of the funds from those accounts are under your name."

"Wait, what?"

He simply shrugs and answers, "It's all yours, everything."

I just stare at him.

"Seriously, dude? Do you not watch the news? She was convicted yesterday during her trial. She's serving a sentence of three years, but will be eligible for parole depending on behavior."

My eyebrows shoot up. "Why the fuck did you not tell me?"

"I thought you'd be keeping up with the trial—it's my bad, man."

"Nah, you're good. I apologize. I'm not in a good place right now. Heather has decided to move to London. Shit, is Coen still in the city?"

"Well shit, I thought the two of you had something good going. The best way to get over her is to get on top of someone else, dude. Coen? He didn't tell you? Shit, you've been in the dark...he's decided to move up here. He said Phoenix is dry as hell compared to NYC."

I laugh and shake my head. "He's not talking about the weather or the booze, is he? Oh shit, what happened the other night with Dillen?"

He flicks me off. "Coen got that nice piece of ass. They fucked up to the minute he got onto the plane back to Phoenix."

"I don't doubt that. The man has game. All right, I better get going. Thanks for the folder of shit."

I get up and shake Joel's hand. "No word on my birth parents yet?"

"No. I've been searching day and night. If I knew where the kidnapping took place, it'd be easier. I'll be in contact."

"Thanks, man." I open the door. "I'll see you around."

I leave his apartment and find myself wondering what the hell is next.

I'VE BEEN STARING at my phone for the last hour, wanting to call her. Or her to call me. Or text...or anything. I don't even know when she's leaving. Hell, it could be tomorrow. Christ, how long is that flight? Wait...she doesn't fly. How in the hell does she have a passport if she doesn't fly? A ray of hope shoots through me. If I can have her by default then so fucking be it.

I decide to stop being a pussy and send her a text.

Can we talk please?

I'm sitting at a restaurant bar, waiting, and willing my damn phone to go off, but it doesn't and now I know it won't. It's been hours since she broke my fucking heart, since everything in my world faded to gray —a dark, colorless hole of nothing, with no more pink glitter.

I continue to drink. I know this isn't going to end well so I might as well be oblivious to the pain. I try sending her another text.

I'm sorry I walked out. Don't go.

I won't let the light on my phone go off as I wait for a response. I try again.

Ballerina, please. Fuck, this hurts!

I don't understand what went wrong. I thought things were great between us. I thought she was happy. I never pushed her. Never forced her to reveal anything about herself. I let her do it on her own. What else could I have done?

Unless...shit, I can't think like that...but how can I not? Was I just a good fuck to her? Someone who did everything I could to make her happy, to make her stay? I hope she enjoyed the ride on my cock while it lasted.

I feel used and broken. Nothing, not even alcohol, can halt this physical ache.

My thoughts are quickly interrupted when a thick Russian accent invades the room, "Well, look who we have here…"

I turn my head to the side and look into pernicious eyes.

"Ah." he says before ordering a vodka, neat. "You must have just found out about the London offer."

I swing around stormily and stare the motherfucker down. "Excuse me?" I manage to say in my not-so-sober-state.

"Yeah, I know about it. Don't worry: I'll be taking good care of her."

Rage surges through me and I almost pass out from the sheer force of it. My vision blurs and I know it isn't from the liquor. "You'll what?"

"I don't believe I stuttered, you stupid fuck!"

My body moves on its own accord and I stand up, towering over him. I know what's coming and I don't care. I'm not holding back. That old, familiar feeling creeps through my veins…that feeling I get when some douche finally crosses the line and I lose my shit. And quite frankly, this prick deserves everything he's about to get. "You're making a big fucking mistake."

"What the fuck are you going to do, huh? Punch me in front of a crowded restaurant?"

"Damn right I am."

I stop thinking for a second before my body reacts. My fist meets his face with profound force. His body buckles back and into the bar stool behind him. He lunges toward me, but I hold the fucking scrawny asshole away at arm's length before laying another punch into his abdomen. He bends over, hugging himself, and I grab his vodka off of the bar before downing it. "Fucking dick."

I pay my tab and leave, deciding that I'll punish myself more and walk home. As soon as I make it home, I regret it. I regret that I let her lead me on, not my recent erratic behavior. The thoughts that are running through my head are ones I'd rather not think about. She's leaving me for Nik? She's been lying to me about this ballet shit? Why wouldn't she just come out and say it?

Remnants of our last night together are everywhere. I don't want to look at it. I don't want to smell her.

I don't want to pick it up either.

Instead, I grab a bottle of liquor from the cabinet and go to my room, slamming the door behind me because it fucking feels good to do it.

Ensuring that all my blinds are closed and the lights are off before I sit down on the bed, I take a swig straight from the bottle. My face is wet with emotion over my girl.

No longer mine.

I belong nowhere now, and with no one. The two women I trusted with every fiber of my being are both gone.

CHAPTER
Twenty-Nine
on my toes

Heather

I'VE BEEN SINGLE for a week now, and it's been the longest week of my life. He keeps texting me, asking to talk and begging me not to leave, but if I talk to him, I know I won't follow through with my lifelong dream. Everything I've given up for my dance career would be for nothing if I didn't jump at this opportunity.

My plane boards in fifteen minutes, and I'm trying not to get sick. My stomach is in knots. I can't believe I'm about to get on this plane. I quickly type a text to Dillen and Dani.

Hi, I'm about to board. I'll try to get Wi-Fi on the plane so you two can calm my nerves.

I think I'm going crazy. The first flight I've been on since I was a child has to be an overseas flight?

Dillen replies first.

I have your flight number and I'll be at the airport to pick you up in the morning. I love you and you're going to be okay. I can't wait to squeeze the shit out of you!

Then Dani chimes in.

Sister, I thought Noah was going with you?

They call for first class to board and I do, finding my seat. It's a new plane, so I have my own little space. It's like diagonal seating. I check my phone once I'm settled and after I've taken a sleeping pill.

Crap. I should have known she would think that. The attendant asks us to shut our cellular devices off so I send a simple text.

No, he isn't. I have to go. I can't explain. I love you guys. Xoxo

THE PLANE JOLTS and I feel an awful falling sensation. My eyes fly open as I struggle to breathe in. My heart is racing. My chest is pounding. I feel so incredibly lightheaded and faint—I think I'm going to pass out or die right here. Right now.

The gentleman sitting across the aisle looks at me then reaches over, placing his hand on my forearm. "Calm down there, miss. It's nothing but a tad of turbulence."

I feel like yelling back at him that's it's much harder than he realizes, but I'm frozen as my body shakes uncontrollably. He reaches up and presses the button to call the attendant. She walks over and kneels down next to me. I can't even turn to look at her. I'm so scared. We're falling out of the sky, aren't we? I find myself internally asking her.

"I think she's having a panic attack. Could you please bring over a glass of cold water and two bottles of white wine?" the elder English gentleman asks.

"Oh sweetheart, it's okay." She tries to soothe me, but it's not working. I still can't breathe. I'm hyperventilating as I try to fill my lungs with a sufficient amount of air.

"I'll be right back." She gets up and hurries away to the front of the plane. A second later, she is back.

I need to escape, but I can't see much. I've got visional snow and I'm experiencing severe derealization. My hands are shaking so drastically the attendant holds up the straw to my lips. I can't feel anything anymore as I watch my blurry finger twitch. This sense of impending doom won't leave me.

I try to drink from the straw, but I'm too anxious. My chest is wet with sweat, and my cheeks are wet with tears. I feel a strong hand rubbing my back as I lean forward. My mind automatically goes to Noah, but I stop shaking when I realize it's not him, when I realize he won't ever want to touch me again.

I need him. He's the only one that can make this stop.

"You're going to need to drink more than that, sweetie," the hostess says. I manage to take in a big gulp and straighten up, wiping my eyes. I feel like I can finally catch my breath. So I shut out all of the people watching me and focus on my memories of his face. His strong jaw, his tanned skin, and those ocean green eyes I drowned in daily.

"How...how long was I like that?" I ask the attendant softly.

"Barely a minute, sweetie. Did you want to stand up and stretch your legs?"

"No, please no. I won't be able to. Just...how much longer until we land?"

"We have about five hours to go. Are you going to be okay? I have some sleeping tablets; would you like those?"

"Uhm, no. Thank you. I have some in my purse." I lean forward and pick up my navy Longchamp shoulder tote. "I'm sorry, what's your name?" I ask, as I dig through my travel-sized makeup bags.

"My name is Marlene. Can I get you anything else? I'll be sure to wait on you for the rest of the flight if you're comfortable with me. You don't fly often, do you?"

"I'd appreciate that, Marlene, and no...I don't." She hands me the glass of water so I can take my pill, "Thank you." My hands are still shaking, but I'm able to take the sleeping pill without spilling water all over myself. She takes the glass once I've had enough. I place my purse down and lay back, covering up with my pink blanket, forcing my eyes shut.

I'M WOKEN FROM a heavy sleep and a dream about Noah. It was more of a memory than a dream. I got to relive the first time he kissed me, the first time he touched me possessively. The first time he kissed me down there.

"Ma'am? We've landed and everyone else has deplaned."

"Noah?" I ask sleepily, trying to open my eyes, blinking when a shape of a woman comes to me, and I slowly realize where I am. Exactly 3,459 miles away from him and everything I know.

"Thank you for everything, Marlene."

"It's no problem, ma'am. Enjoy your stay," she says cheerfully.

I sigh melodramatically and get up slowly, picking up my tote and carrying it off the plane. I'm glad I checked in all of my luggage. I walk up the ramp, following the signs leading me to baggage claim. Heathrow Airport has a huge sign announcing international arrivals that I walk past before I'm tackled from behind.

"YOU'RE HERE!" Dillen yells into my ear as she hugs me from behind.

I sag with relief and turn to hug her, holding onto her. My legs almost feel like Jell-o. "Dillen, that was horrifying!"

"You made it. I'm so crazy proud of you!" She holds me out at arm's length to check that I'm still in one piece. "Did you eat? Do you want to shower?"

Shaking my head, I say, "I haven't had an appetite. But I would like to shower."

"All right, let's get your bags and we'll head to my place. I actually just moved to a two-bedroom apartment so you're in luck, little shit."

I try to smile. I truly am happy to see her but I'm just dead inside. "I really appreciate your letting me stay with you. I know it's sudden."

"Hush. Let's go."

We walk to baggage claim with our arms linked together and easily find my Louis Vuitton luggage and haul them out to her cute Fiat. Somehow we get them to fit and we head to her apartment. She's trying to explain London to me during the drive, but I'm too tired to pay much attention. I remember her saying that her apartment is the tallest building in central London. The apartment building is called Strata.

The building is beautiful and there are little hints of pink everywhere.

"How long will it take me to get used to the time change?" I ask, as I get out of her petite car and stretch.

"It usually takes me three days to get used it, but being your first time, it could take up to a week. Let's get you showered and fed." We walk into her apartment and she stops me, grabbing my arm before I walk into the guest bedroom, "Are you okay, little shit?"

I feign a smile. "I'm okay. It's just been a long week. And then the flight."

She wraps her arms around me and hugs me tightly; it's just what I need.

Pulling back and smiling, she says, "We are getting drunk tonight, little shit."

"I'm not sure I can stay awake for that long." I giggle as she walks away and I shut the door to get ready for the day.

AFTER I SHOWER and get dressed, I walk out into Dillen's gray and blue modern living room. She's sitting on the sofa, in her ballet tights, reading a book.

I'm nervous: I'm on edge and I can't seem to calm myself down. There's only one person who can calm me, and I'm positive I'll never see him again. "Okay, I officially hate being the new girl," I say as I sit down next to her and curl my feet up under me.

"I believe you bypass being the new girl when everyone already knows your name." She tosses a pillow at me and laughs.

"So. Everyone will be looking and judging. Ugh. It's like high school all over again."

"Heather! Don't be a sourpuss. You are the first person they have recruited in forever. Everyone will be drooling over you, trust me. And if it's any consolation, I've heard the young male dance teachers and choreographers literally arguing over who gets to have you." She pauses to think for a second. "Okay, I can't be certain if they were talking about taking you, or having you in their classes and dance groups..."

"Oh jeez." I have no desire to think about another man. Or ever be with one.

"Okay, let's go, grab your duffel." She hops up and grabs her black duffel and car keys.

We're walking down the stairs when she speaks again. "It's a good thing you're taken because these Englishmen would devour you."

My heart fractures a little more. Oh God, I can't talk about this now. I'll be a sobbing mess. "Oh stop it," is all I can think of to say. I climb into the passenger side, which is the opposite of what I'm used to. It's so weird: I feel like I'm in a different world.

We arrive at the Royal Ballet House in a measly ten minutes. After she parks, we walk in together and I swear there is a welcoming committee at the door.

I'm so overwhelmed that I can't even think. I'm meeting everyone at once. There are ballerinas everywhere but suddenly my heart slams into my chest when I come face to face with someone familiar.

She makes a beeline for me and smiles eerily as I take in her overly tight blonde bun, which mimics a poorly done facelift... "Well, well, well, if it isn't Noah Ryan's girlfriend. Is he here with you? I'm Alexis, by the way. You might remember me from the bar when you were too drunk to hold yourself up..."

I'm so stunned that I'm nailed to the spot. I can't even believe what I'm seeing. She's a ballerina? In this company? I'm about to speak and let her know that I had only just begun to drink that night when my attention is pulled in another direction.

The commanding voice of the mistress breaks through the crowd. "Okay, ladies, break it up. Let Miss Lane breathe," she says in a beautiful British accent as she walks up to me. I'm immediately comforted by her calm demeanor and welcoming smile. "Welcome, darling, I'm Cora Silsbury. We're delighted that you've joined us. Welcome to the Royal Ballet."

"Thank you. This is all so incredible."

She smiles sweetly at me. "I'm glad to hear that. Now, let me take you on a tour and we'll get to our private session. It'll be just the two of us for a while."

I quickly blow Dillen a kiss before following Mistress Silsbury around the dance house.

This place is amazing. The First Position studio was beautiful and modern but the Royal Ballet house is absolutely stunning. I would love to be able to share this with my mother; she would be so proud.

Cora leads me into a large studio and closes the door. "I understand that you just flew in, Heather, so this won't be a long practice. I would just like to see a piece of the performance from the charity showcase. I was unfortunately ill and unable to fly to New York for the occasion."

"Oh of course. If I could just stretch out first?"

"Of course you can, darling. I'll get your locker combination and keys for you. Feel free to plug in any device in the corner for some music. I'll be back."

With that, she turns and walks out of the studio and for the first time in forever, I'm alone. I've made sure to always be around someone since I broke his heart—I just can't stand the pain by myself. He's not texting me anymore either and I know, deep down, that I've lost the only man I've ever had such immense feelings for.

"OKAY. THE PIZZA is ordered," Dillen sings, as she comes back in the living room and plops down on the couch excitedly. "Eekk! I'm so excited you're here. I've never had a roommate before."

I'm sitting cross-legged on the couch facing her. "I'm happy I get to be your first."

"So..." she croons, "is lover boy going to be visiting any time soon and do I need earplugs?"

I knew this was coming, but I know I won't be able to talk about it without tears present. I shake my head and look down. "No. I... uhm...we broke up."

"What? Oh Heather. I thought that he might have been your one. I'm so sorry." She reaches for my hand and squeezes.

I shake my head as the tears fall. "It's all my fault, Dillen. He's so perfect. I just ruined everything. I left him for this."

She looks shocked, but she moves closer to me and hugs me tightly. "Oh little shit, it's going to be okay. Was he not interested in a long-distance relationship?"

I sniffle and cry harder. "I never asked him. I...I'm afraid to get too close. I think I was falling in love with him."

She pulls back a little and grabs some tissues, handing them to me. "I think you already were in love with him. I've never seen you so happy before. Oh me and my big mouth! I'm sorry."

She's right. I think I already was. I was just too stupid to latch onto it and embrace it. "I'm so ridiculous, Dillen. He needed me and I left him."

"Needed you? Sweetie, you weren't his only lifeline. Don't be so hard on yourself," she says firmly.

I gasp and pull back, my eyes wide. "But I was! His mother... she..." Shaking my head quickly, I add, "He doesn't have anyone. He's all alone."

"Alone? It's not your fault he moved up to New York City. Plus, Coen is moving up to the city too. So he's not alone."

She hands me the tissue box and gets up. Walking to the kitchen, she grabs a bottle of chilled white wine and two wine glasses before she joins me on the couch again.

I blow my nose loudly. "Coen's moving?"

She pours me a glass and hands it to me. "He is. I think he's going to stay with Joel until he finds a place. Heather, he is so sexy in bed."

I'm finally able to smile as I dab at my eyes. "So you two hit it off, huh?"

"I'm not sure what is going on, but I think I might have a schoolgirl crush on his sexy ass."

"He's sweet." I'm feeling better, knowing he'll be there for Noah.

"He's an asshole too. But I think it's kind of sexy. He calls me every night to get a little kinky and freaky on Skype."

I laugh and cover my face. "No details, please!"

"He's so nice and big," She growls with her teeth showing.

"Oh you kinky butt," I say as I shove her with my foot.

Suddenly I find myself thinking that there's no way he is as big as Noah.

Dillen jumps up when there's a knock on the door. She pays for the pizza then brings it to the couch. "Dig in, little shit. And tell me how your first day went."

I'm about to take a bite when I start to feel emotional again. Noah and I had pizza on our first date. I'm a wreck. "It went well. I love Mistress Silsbury; she's so sweet."

Dillen moans and smiles. "This is my favorite pizza place. It's called Princi. Take notes. I'm glad you like her; she's great."

"Got it." I take a sip of wine. "Okay, so...Alexis. Is she always that rude and abrasive?" I ask and take a bite.

"Alexis. She's the bitch of the company. She thinks everyone loves her when really everyone despises her ass. I think she's from Arizona? I'm not sure though, but she sleeps around like she makes money off of it. Slut."

"Yeah, I guess she and Noah dated." I look down at my toes and fidget. I don't want to even think about Noah and her together— she's so not his type.

Dillen makes a face like she smelled something horrid. "You have got to be kidding me?"

I shake my head. "I know. He never talked about it with me."

"That's disgusting. You made him get tested before you two did anything, right?"

I chew on my cheek. "Well...no. But there was a reason."

"Heather Lane! Did I not teach you better than that?"

"You did, but..."

"I'm sorry," she interrupts me, "I shouldn't be scraping at a semi-healed wound. I think it's time to be happy again. I'm going to make you laugh until your nonexistent belly hurts and then some more." She quickly cleans up the living room while I sip my wine.

I don't have the heart to tell her that it's a waste of time. I feel like I've made the worst mistake of my life.

When she comes back, she refills my glass almost to the brim. "I'm here for you, little shit."

"Thank you. I'll be okay; I just need something to take my mind off of him."

"Another handsome fuck?" she proposes and I roll my eyes at her and shake my head no.

"I'd just like to go to bed. It's been a long day."

"Stay out here with me, instead of lying in there alone and being all depressed." She pouts cutely and I smile and shake my head.

"You're ridiculous, Dillen."

"You know me, little shit. All right, fine. Go get your ass to bed and take one of those sleeping pills you took on the plane." She downs her wine and looks at me, "I'm going to hit the hay too. I mean...Skype Coen." She blushes beet red and hugs herself.

"I'm going, I'm going." I lean over and hug her. "I love you."

She squeezes me a bit too tightly, but I don't mind. She dances down to her bedroom and blows me a kiss from her doorway before shutting the door.

Getting up and taking the last sip of my wine, I make my way to the guest room and sit on the edge of the bed. I'm trying to do anything to get my mind off of the sadness I constantly feel, so I turn on my iPad and start shopping, which usually makes me feel better. I start to peruse Nieman Marcus' shoe department when my email signals a new addition to my inbox. Without thinking of it, I close my browser and open my email. It's from everyone at First

Position. It's mostly just the girls saying they miss me and hope I'm adjusting well to the time change. I actually laugh when they warn me that I might pick up an accent while I'm here. I scroll down and look at the attached photo. It's a picture of everyone at the company. My smile falls when I glance over Nik's face. I'm about to close the email when my eyes shoot back to Nik's picture. "Holy..." His nose is swollen and he has a brutal black eye.

My eyes move down to the cast around his wrist. What happened? A very large part of me has a feeling that Noah had something to do with Nik's injuries. If he did...I can only imagine what Nik did to provoke him. He wouldn't do such a thing though, would he? Even if he did...it would have been because of me. I glance down at my mom's wedding band. Sighing loudly, I whisper to the room, "Did I make a mistake, Momma?"

CHAPTER
Thirty
dearest scheming

Noah

I HAVEN'T LEFT the confines of my apartment for the last week and a half. Facing the real world is stressing me out to the point of hibernation. My Galaxy buzzes with an incoming call. I reach for it, wanting to see Heather's name and picture flash across the screen, but it's Joel.

"Hey man."

"Noah, I'm glad you picked up. Listen, I'm coming over because the two of us need to talk. I'd rather not discuss this over the phone."

"I'll see you shortly then." I hang up without bothering to say goodbye.

I get into the shower and freshen up before changing into sweats. I pull on my ASU sweater, but quickly take it off and toss it across the room. It smells like her. I need to get my shit together. I can't live like a lonely motherfucker for the rest of my life. I force myself to stand tall and breathe in deeply when the doorman calls to let me know Joel is here. A few minutes later the doorbell rings, and I make my way over and swing the door open. What in all hell can be so important that he can't tell me over the phone?

"What's up, man?" Joel greets me before striding past me and into my apartment.

"Can I get you a beer?"

"Uhh...yeah, man. You'll need one too."

"I've had my fair share," I say, before grabbing two beers and walking out onto the balcony, looking out at the city as I take a seat.

Moments later, Joel joins me and sits in the other seat. He's quiet as he drinks his beer, contemplating what he has to say before uttering the words aloud.

"Okay. So what's the news?" I'm irritable and I'm sure it shows.

"To break it to you easily...I found them." He looks over at me, gesturing for me to drink, so I do.

"I found your parents."

I'm not entirely sure what to say.

My world has been turned upside down and inside out since Christmas Eve. Now, everything has just stopped. What in the fuck? Why? Why did he have to find them now, when she's gone? My mind is running over hundreds of questions but I can only stare at my beer. Just my damn luck.

Fuck it. I don't give a shit anymore. Taking a long drink, I sit back in my chair. "Don't tell me. I don't want to know anything about them."

"Dude, don't say shit like that. You can't just ignore this."

"I won't. You obviously know my birth name. Please get me a new birth certificate. Once you've gotten that birth certificate, I want you to file a name change for me. To me. To Noah Bradley Ryan. That's who I am; it's who I've been my entire life. I won't change that. It's my one constant."

He watches me as I speak and nods. "I can do that for you. I'll have their contact details ready for you whenever you decide to talk to them. "

I nod. "Have you been in contact with them?"

"No, I haven't said a word to them. I think they deserve to hear from me only when you are ready. You've been put through the wringer man, and now you've been left out to dry."

I know he's talking about her and it pisses me the fuck off. I don't give a shit if she tore what I had left of myself into miniscule pieces. No one will ever speak badly of her in my presence, even if she's back with that douche.

"Don't talk shit about her, man. She doesn't deserve it. She followed her lifelong dream that I got in the way of. Just a pawn in one hell of a chess game."

"I'm sorry. Look, there'll be others. Trust me. Are you into redheads? I've got this girl's number who would be great for you…" He stands up and downs his beer.

I just shake my head no. He nods and sets his empty bottle down. "I'll let you know when I finish getting your birth certificate and name changed." He starts to walk back toward the door but stops and turns back to me. "Don't you want to know your birth name?"

"If I know all of it, my ass will willingly go look up who I am and who my parents are. Give me my first name. I'll deal with this in stages."

He nods and smiles a little. "Jorden."

I laugh once and shake my head. Take a drink. "Nope. That doesn't work for me."

He laughs with me. "Thanks for the cold brew. I'll be in touch."

"Later." I stay seated while he shows himself out. There's no damned point in getting up.

A FEW HOURS after Joel leaves, my apartment is clean and I'm on my way out the door for the first time. There's a package on my doorstep and I assume it's my protein-shake powder for after a workout. I put the box inside and walk downstairs, stopping at my mailbox. It's overflowing with random flyers and advertisements.

There's one letter in the box addressed to me without a return address on it.

Sliding my finger under the edge and ripping open the top of the envelope, I pull out a letter and my eyes scan the unfamiliar, elegant, handwriting. As soon as I start to read, my heart slams against my rib cage and I sit down slowly on a nearby step. It's from her. I can't focus long enough to read it from beginning to end. My eyes keep picking out random words. "I'm sorry...not me...lead you on." Finally I go back to the beginning and read.

> *Noah,*
>
> *I hope you're doing well. I know I owe you an apology and much, much more. I'm sorry for leaving the way I did. I'm sure you don't want to see this, but I think of you daily. You can't meet someone like you and just forget that special person. I know you must hate me for what I did and I don't blame you. I don't deserve you and I won't forget you. I couldn't answer your calls or texts because if I did, I wouldn't have been able to leave. I know you'll find someone who'll treat you the way you deserve. It's just not me.*
>
> *I feel like I owe you an explanation as well. I did not intend on getting close to you. I assumed, in the beginning, that what went on was just a fling. But you pulled me in and turned my life around. I don't regret anything—please don't think that. I just haven't allowed myself to get close to anyone since my parents died. I'm sorry. I just want you to know that I enjoyed every minute we spent together. I wouldn't change a thing. I just pray I didn't lead you on. I'll miss you terribly. Good luck in everything you do.*
>
> *XOXO Heather*

I have to read the letter a few more times before I am able to wrap my head around exactly what she is saying. I realize the point of the letter was to apologize for leaving me, but I don't understand why she'd go out of her way to write me a letter like this if it were that easy for her to leave.

In the back of my mind, I find myself wondering if she's left- or right-handed. That's something I should have found out in the beginning. Did we start this relationship off the wrong way? Did she need something more and I just didn't give it to her?

I doubt I'll ever find out if I just sit here on my ass and not do anything about it. I look at the letter in my hands again and grab my phone from my pocket. I search for a number and when I find it, I hit dial. It rings a few too many times and I don't think anyone is going to answer, until I hear a voice on the other end.

"Hello?" She sounds winded.

"Dani? Dani Lane? This is Noah. Do you have a couple of minutes to talk?"

"Noah? Sure! Give me one second. Brannon and I are running around naked."

Oh fuck me, that is too much information. I squeeze my eyes shut and run a hand over my face while I wait for her to come back from whatever the hell she is doing.

"Okay, I'm back. What's up? Can you not get hold of Heather? She said she was getting an English number today."

Shit. I guess Heather hasn't even told her sister? Well, this should be a fun conversation. "Uh, Dani, your sister left me. She hasn't spoken to me since the day after Valentine's."

There's a brief period of silence before she says anything. "Oh. Noah, I'm so sorry. I had no idea. She tends not to share things with me that she's still struggling with. I think she's too proud to be emotionally unstable."

"Too proud? I thought you two were really close?"

"We are, but she likes to keep to herself, especially if she feels like she is going to be judged for something. Then she just doesn't tell me until it's over with and all of her feelings toward whatever it is—or was—are resolved."

I frown as I listen to her. "I didn't know that about her. I don't even know if she's left- or right-handed. Fuck, I should have treated her better. Maybe we wouldn't be fucking up each other's lives if I made her want to stay with me. I tried, Dani. I tried so damn hard." There's emotion in my voice so I refrain from speaking another word.

"She's left-handed," Dani says softly. "And I don't think you were bad for each other. I haven't seen my sister that comfortable around anyone before. Maybe she got scared…I'm not sure."

Scared? I scared her off? Just my fucking luck. "Thank you. Dani, I have a favor to ask."

"Of course, what's the favor?" Her voice is soft and I think there's pity behind it. Fuck, I hate for anyone to feel pity for me but at this point, I'll do anything to get her back.

"I don't know where she's staying, what her new number is, where the ballet school is located, or anything. I'm going to get her back. I didn't chase after her when she left me. That solely is the biggest mistake I have made…the worst decision of my life. But talking to you now and reading a letter she just sent…I know she's still mine. I've chased her to New York, and I'll chase her all around the globe before I give up."

"Awww, Noah! That is so amazing. Yes, I'll help you." I can hear her clapping excitedly on the other end and I have to smirk. She's just like Heather in so many ways. Fuck, I miss her.

"Great, thanks. Let me get inside so I can get a pen and paper. I need to write this shit down." I get up and haul ass up the stairs, taking two steps at once before I get to my apartment and unlock the door. I scramble for paper and pen before Dani changes her mind about helping me.

I pull out a piece of paper from under a week's worth of mail and flip it over. I'm about to take pen to page, but the words, "You'll always be mine,' in Heather's handwriting stop me.

My heart is aching in my throat when I answer her little written plea out loud. "Always, baby."

"What was that?" Dani's voice breaks up my thoughts of her.

"Uh, nothing." I grab another sheet of paper, deciding not to ruin this one. "Okay, I'm good: go ahead."

She gives me her new address and promises to call me with her new number when Heather gives it to her.

"I owe you one. Thank you!"

"It's not a problem. You seem to know what my sister needs

more than she knows what she wants. She deserves you, Noah. You make her happy. So thank you. I won't let her know you're sneaking around."

"I just hope I still have a chance. I have to make a few more phone calls. I'll let you know when I leave. Thank you, again," I say as I open my laptop and search diligently for a flight. Thank fuck that Mae had all of those assets in my name; it's enough to hold me over for a year.

"Bye, Noah. Good luck!"

"Bye." I hang up and call Joel.

I have a huge favor to ask him, and right now I'd pay any amount of money to get this right. I let her slip through my fingers once and now I'm going to fight for her like no one has ever fought for her before.

She's all I have left to fight for.

She's all I want.

All I need.

My ballerina.

Joel answers on the fifth ring. "Hey man, did I forget something at your place?"

"Hi. No. Listen, I need a passport and I need it fast. I just booked a flight to London a week from today. I don't give a fuck what name it's in. Just get it to me."

"London, huh? I'll see what I can do. I just got off the phone with your attorney. He has your birth certificate and is overnighting it to me as we speak."

"That's great. Thank you. I'll pay whatever it is I need to pay. I just need to get to London. Yesterday."

"I'll have it done. You'll see me when I have the passport in hand."

"Thanks, man. I appreciate it."

We hang up and I start pacing the inside of my apartment before sitting back down after a while at my laptop and pulling up Heather's address on maps online. She's right in central London and I'm ready to be there. I'm ready to show her that I'm worthy enough for her, and that she doesn't have to send me an apology letter. I just want her. I accept the person she is and I don't plan on changing any of it. I just care enough to fight for something—someone— I want.

She's someone I never saw myself with, but now I can't see myself without her. I want more out of this damn life I've been living. I'm on the hunt for who I am, and I can't find that without her. She's become my wall: she stabilizes me when I need her and right now I'm walking on a tightrope, trying my damnedest to balance, but I know I can't keep that balance for too much longer. I need her there to lean on.

I've never been afraid to lose what I need to lose in order to better myself, but this, this life without her is not going to better me. I'm going to invest in the person I trust the most, the person I need to be with the most.

I'll make her mine again, and I'm not letting go.

I can and I will.

No excuses.

I'm fucking coming for you, ballerina.

CHAPTER
Thirty-One
impassioned

Heather

WE ARE WHO we choose to be and Alexis is the worst possible person I know.

I'm disciplined. I'm strong. Ballet is who I am, and I don't have a backup plan.

I've been part of the Royal Ballet for just over two weeks now and I can't stand her. She's always pointing out the tiniest of mistakes I make, making my life a living hell. She reminds me of Noah daily, now that she knows we're no longer together.

"Heather, we're all supposed to wear pink pointe shoes today, not those ugly things you have on!" she calls out when I walk into the ballet house.

"Oh? Are you sure you're not just jealous of my custom pointe shoes?" I say over my shoulder as I walk past her. All ballerinas know that pointe shoes are the real high heels. They are beyond compare.

"Bitch. No wonder Noah dumped your skinny ass!"

I choose to ignore her as I walk into the studio on my own and turn the music on to start practicing my routine. It's a Saturday and only the extremely dedicated dancers are in the ballet house today, which makes me wonder why she's here.

It takes me thirty minutes to warm up before I start running through my routine. My choreography, ironically, is about not waiting for the storm to pass, but instead to embrace it and dance in the rain. My mind is set in my choreography as I repeat my inner monologue.

Long neck.

Shoulder back.

Elbows up.

Arms out.

Ribs in.

Stomach in.

Butt tucked.

Stretch thighs.

Point toes.

Relevé.

Thumbs in.

Reach. Breathe. Extend.

Square hips.

Energy and smile!

I'm so lost in my dance that I don't notice the door open and a second body walks into the room until she speaks. "Don't sickle," she yells out and I almost fall out of my fouetté en tournant.

I turn in the direction the voice is coming from, only to find Alexis. "What are you doing in here? You know this is a private room."

"I wanted to talk to you. Or are you too high-ranked to say a word to me?"

"What would I have to say to you, Alexis? You're rude and ignorant. I don't need you in this studio. Please feel free to show yourself out." I start counting and begin to dance again.

"Don't be a bitch, Heather."

I stop and walk over to my music, turning it off and staring at her. "Excuse me?"

She crosses her arms and smirks.

I swear I want to smack it right off her face.

"What do you want?" I ask with every bit of irritation in my voice.

"I want to know why you were dumb enough to leave that sex god."

I'm taken aback by her question. I'm sick of her crap, so I stop being nice. "Wow, is that any of your business?"

"Kind of, since we're both his exes now."

I'm not even going there with her. "Still. I don't know what you want from me?"

"I want to talk about him. Surely you want to brag about his size...he's incredibly hung!"

I roll my eyes and walk back over to my music. "I'm not talking about this with you. Have a nice day," I say dismissively.

"So you don't care that we both fucked the same guy?" She's standing with her hands on her hips, waiting for me to react.

I think I just threw up in my mouth. I almost trip and fall. What? I thought he...but he said..."What did you say?"

"I'm almost positive you heard me. I enjoyed my time with him. Did you? Or could you not handle him?"

I turn around and face her. "I'm..."

I stop, shaking my head in confusion before trying again. "You slept with him?" I seriously think I'm going to pass out. He lied to me? Why would he? Suddenly it hits me. He lied to get me in bed.

"Uh, duh. Who the hell wouldn't sleep with that fine piece of ass?"

I'm literally going to be sick. "I see. Uhm, how long were you together?"

"It was five years ago but I think we were together for about two months."

"Well, good for you. Are we done here?"

"Oh no, sweetie. It's obvious that you didn't put out and that's why he left you. What a shame. It's a good thing I went through my old phone to get his number because he's been sending me some rather inappropriate pictures."

Jealousy surges through me. I've never wanted to harm someone before but at this moment..."I'm happy for you. Are you done trying to provoke me?"

"Provoke you? No, I'm just making small talk." Her phone goes off and she looks at it. "Well, speak of the devil himself! Bye-bye now."

I look down at her phone and then at her retreating back as she walks away. As soon as the door closes I fall to my knees, unable to hold it in anymore. I can't believe I fell for it. I can't believe I let him trick me. The floodgates break and I sob uncontrollably into my hands.

I never expected him to be that kind of a guy. I'm so, so stupid! I should have known. He seemed so sincere. What a lying jerk! Wiping my eyes, I get up and change out of my pointe shoes and put on my flats, deciding that was the last time I cry over him. "What a fucking asshole!" I'm so beyond angry, maybe even more upset with myself. I should have never sent him that letter, I think, shoving my things into my bag angrily.

Anger.

That's all I'm feeling right now. I grab my phone and send a text to Dillen: **We're going out tonight. I'm getting drunk! And do not tell me no.**

I look at my contacts list and have the sudden urge to send him a message. I feel so betrayed.

I want him to hurt as much as I'm hurting right now. I storm out of the room and into the main hall. Alexis is smiling at her phone while she finishes reading a text out loud to her friends. "Aw! He called me his ballerina. I'm so going to suck his dick."

My heart just stopped. I don't think anything could hurt me worse than that. He's calling her ballerina? That was my name.

 I hate her. I fucking hate her.

Dillen sends a reply.

I love it when you're feisty. Me, you, Jack, and José! YES!

I just got out of the shower. Meet out front; I'll drive by the

drop-off area. I hope you don't mind if I'm wet ;)

Only she would say that.

I don't mind. I just need to drink and forget. I have to come home and change.

On my way.

A few minutes later Dillen pulls up with Am I Wrong by Nico & Vinz blasting in her speakers.

I open the door and get in. "Dillen, I fucking hate her! Today couldn't have gone any worse."

"Whoa. Uh-oh. Who are we talking about?" she asks, as she takes in my foul mood.

"Who do you think?"

"Okay, I should have guessed. What happened? Spill it all."

Dillen drives back to her apartment as I fill her in on my eventful, nails-against-a-chalkboard day. It takes the entire drive and when I finally stop to breathe again, we are in her apartment and she's pouring me a large glass of wine.

"Thanks," I mumble as I take the glass by its stem.

Dillen is just staring at me. "I really don't know what to say, Heather. He didn't seem like a lying piece of shit. But anything is possible nowadays."

I swallow the glass of wine then set it down on the counter. "Can we just go out, please?"

"Of course we can! Go get into the sexy little gold number we bought for you on Thursday."

I smile for the first time in what feels like forever. Feeling loose from the wine, I go into my room to get ready. When I finally emerge from my room, Dillen is lounging on the couch flipping through a celebrity gossip magazine dressed in a nude canvas-like dress with a cheetah print clutch and black stilettos. There's a triangular piece of sheer fabric running down her cleavage. All together, she looks gorgeous.

"Super cute, Dill. Are you ready?"

She looks up at me and smiles brightly. "Heather, you are a sight for sore eyes, you little shit. I love how shiny that dress is. Turn around. I want more!"

I laugh. "Shut up. You've already seen me in it when I bought it."

"But not the entire outfit. Those black stockings make the dress, and those heels. Oh little shit, you are going to get some D tonight."

I point at her. "No. No way. I am not going there. I just want to dance, get drunk and forget about my problems."

"That I can help with. Let's go." She jumps up and grabs my hand, pulling me out of the apartment. We take the long elevator ride down thirty-five floors until we are in the lobby where she asks for a cab to be called. I have to keep from thinking about the last time I went out. It only reminds me of him.

We get in a cab soon after we step outside and we are whisked away to Club KOKO.

"You're going to love this place. It looks like an old dance theatre."

"I can't wait!"

Once we arrive, we walk into the club, holding hands as we make our way through the crowd. Crap, this was such a bad idea. Everywhere I turn I either feel or see a pair of eyes on me. I just want to get drunk. Is that too much to ask? Dillen finds the bar and orders us three shots each. One of each man: Jack, José, and Captain Morgan.

"Woohoo! Here's to being single." I raise one of my shots and hold it up to Dillen's.

"Here's to living with my best friend…in London." We both giggle and take our three shots.

I scrunch my nose and squeeze my eyes shut. "Holy hell!"

"Shit!" She breathes in deeply and makes a face. "That burns."

I giggle and order us each three more.

We take them and Dillen does this little dance when she finishes the shots. "Let's go dance. As if we don't do that enough."

"Yes!" I grab her hand and we head out to the middle of the dance floor. We start to move to the music as the alcohol takes over our bodies, warming them in ways no man in this club can.

I'm not sure how many hours pass of us drinking and dancing, but I'm struggling to dance with my heels on. We're thankfully standing next to a barrier dividing the dance floor from a walkway. I'm using it to help me stay up straight as I sway with Dillen to the music.

I'm having so much fun and without fail, I'm starting to feel emotional. Slurring my words, I scream over the music, "I love my best friend!"

Dillen's arms flail around me as she squeezes me to her. "I love you too, little shit. Are you having fun?"

With a goofy grin on my face, I answer her. "I'm having the best time. Let's get one more drink."

"Okay, one more." She takes my hand and we drunkenly walk to the bar where she flaunts her breasts to get the bartender's attention in the crowd. "Two more!"

I pout, trying for cute. "I want some of those…" Looking down at my own pair with disgust, I gasp with an idea and look up. "Ohmigod! I'm going to get a boob job!"

She laughs too loudly and looks at my boobs. "I like yours. They don't bounce around like water balloons when you are dancing."

I sigh dramatically. "But that's what I want." My fuzzy brain starts running overtime. "What if that's what Noah wanted? Big boobs."

She takes our shots and hands me one. "I like your boobs, so you should too. I think Noah liked your boobs too."

I wave my hand in dismissal and take my shot. I don't even feel it go down anymore. Dillen takes the glass and puts it down on the bar before struggling to get into her clutch. The music is booming and I can feel each and every vibration move through my body. Dillen pulls her phone out and holds it up to her ear, mouthing "Coen" to me as she grabs my hand and leads me toward the exit sign hanging atop a large double door. We go out onto the smoking patio where the music can't be heard as loudly and I can hear my heart in my ears.

When she mouths Coen's name, I instantly get mad again. How dare he be friends with Noah after what he did? Even though it's never a good idea to drunk-text, I do it anyway. Trying to text him… well, thank goodness for autocorrect.

I just hope you know that I know you lie.

I sit down next to Dillen on an outdoor couch and cross my legs while I wait for Noah to text me back. Moments later, my phone vibrates.

Hold up. What did I lie about?

I angrily type out my reply, my fingers hitting the screen a little too hard.

Don't continue to lie! I found out that I wasn't the only one you slept with. I can't believe I fell for your shit.

What? Who the hell said that? THAT is a lie. I never lied to you, Heather. I have to go. I'll talk to you later.

Excuse me? He's dismissing me? Uh-uh. No, no, no!

Don't bother! Have fun with your next conquest.

I don't get a text back from him and it makes me furious. Oh the nerve!

"Dillen, I want to go home," I say as I pout with my arms folded. She looks at me, nods, and tells Coen she'll call him back. Disconnecting the call, she helps me stand and we make our way to the bar to pay for our tab. We stop at the bathroom on the way out because I have no idea how long the cab ride is going to be. After pushing through hordes of people, we finally exit the club and to the sidewalk where Dillen flags down a cab driver. I've never wanted to be so alone before.

"Dillen?" I ask as we ride to her place. She's drunkenly leaning against me. Or I'm leaning against her. I'm not sure, but either way we are helping each other stay upright.

"Mmm?"

"It'll stop hurting, right?"

"The alcohol or Noah?" she slurs.

I whisper in her ear, "Don't say his name. He's probably sexting Alexis."

"Troll!" she cries out as the cab comes to a stop. "Don't think that." She pulls out £30 and we get out, helping each other through the lobby and to the elevator.

I take off my heels and look at my phone, frowning and getting mad again. "Why? Stupid jerk!" I show her my phone. "See! No reply. Wanna know why? Cause he's onto his next girl."

"Was he not upset when you left him, little shit?"

The elevator pings and we exit, going to the apartment door. She struggles to unlock it but finally, after what feels like an eternity, it opens.

"Lies. All lies. Crap, I have to pee."

"Go pee," she says, and the door shuts behind us and she locks it. "I'm going to pass out on the kitchen floor. The tile is going to be cold and I am so hot." She takes off her dress before lying down on the kitchen floor in just her matching underwear.

I laugh as I step over her and head to the bathroom but I get sidetracked when I pass her pantry. Opening it, I find some cookies.

"I want some." She giggles and stretches her arm out.

I walk over with the package and lie down on the floor next to her. We giggle and eat our cookies and I completely forget about having to pee. I've also forgotten about how mad I am. The alcohol finally takes a toll on us and our eyes grow heavy as we laugh on the floor. "I love you, Dill."

"I love you, little shit," she squeals and nudges my foot. "Take me to bed…" she whines.

I laugh and try to sit up. "What? I can't carry you." But I try anyway. We laugh hysterically when we fall repeatedly all over each other, finally making it to her room where we both crash on her bed and fall asleep.

CHAPTER
Thirty-Two
prized pursuit

Noah

THE PLANE WAS literally rolling down the runway when I got Heather's text. I've never been so fucking frantic to type out a text before. I have no idea what she's talking about. I've never once lied to her. I want nothing more than to get on the plane's Wi-Fi and email her to tell her I'm coming and that I wasn't being an ass. There are no other girls, and I doubt there ever will be with the way she makes me feel. Once the plane reaches 10,000 feet, the flight attendant announces that we are allowed to use our laptops and other approved electronic devices. Meanwhile, I'm having an internal battle with myself. I can't tell her because she'll run.

It took Joel to the last minute to get my new ID and passport. The passport is not under Noah Ryan; it's under Jorden Somer. As much as I hate seeing that name next to my passport picture, it's better than losing my ballerina. I haven't asked Joel for my parents' names, and I won't until I'm ready.

I'm anxious as all hell on this plane, and I'm going to be until

I see her and make her mine again. Dani helped me with the hotel arrangements. All of the hotels in her area were fully booked, but apparently Brannon has some hookups in London and I now have a suite in the hotel across the street from Dillen's apartment.

I cave in and pay for the plane's Wi-Fi when I get out my tablet. Instead of emailing her, I type in "Jorden Somer, 1985 kidnapping" into Google search. The first article title that comes up reads "Jorden Somer—Taken After Birth."

I exit out and set the tablet in the empty seat next to me. I can't read that shit. These were the articles that were supposed to be clipped out and added into that white binder of Mae's with the others. I can't and won't read them. They'll tell me more about my life and parents than I want to know right now.

Hours pass before I am able to pick up the tablet. I decide to type out an email in preparation of sending it to Heather in case she pushes me away, in case she wants nothing to do with me.

> To: **Heather Lane**
> From: **Noah Ryan**
> Subject: **My Thoughts**
>
> *My little ballerina,*
>
> *I've been lost without you these past few weeks. I can't begin to describe the physical ache I have inside of me all of the time…*

I finish typing out the email and I save it to my draft folder, in preparation for the rejection of a lifetime.

Christ, this flight takes forever. I can just imagine how Heather handled it on her own. The thought of her afraid and upset makes me sick to my stomach.

To think that she faced her fear of flying alone just to get away from me also makes me sick. Wait…was she alone, or was he flying with her? Jesus, am I making a mistake by going after her?

She went to great lengths to get away from me.

The flight attendant walks through the cabin offering beverages when I'm scrolling through my tablet's gallery—picture after picture of my ballerina. The flight attendant asks me if I'd like a drink and I request something stiff. Her eyes catch the photo on my screen: it's the first picture of Heather I ever saved.

"Now she was a handful on the plane," the flight attendant says.

"Excuse me?" I ask, as she passes me a miniature bottle of vodka.

"She was on a flight to Heathrow International a few weeks back. Poor thing had a panic attack."

"Wait...you were on the plane with her?"

"Yes, sir. She flew in first class. She was so darling and so upset. I wouldn't be able to forget a sweet thing like her."

"Yeah, me either. Was she alone?" I ask the question under my breath but she seems to hear me.

"She was. Are you a relative of hers?" she asks as she hands me a small bag of pretzels. Fuck, I can breathe again.

"No, I'm actually her ex. She chose London over me and now I'm going after her."

"Really?" She seems surprised. "That was over two weeks ago, I'm sure. You're a bit late, if you don't mind my being so blunt."

"Yeah, I know. I had a few hiccups in the road that I had to get through before I could come get her."

I empty the two bottles of vodka over ice and hand the empties to her.

"Well, let her know that Marlene said hello and that I hope she's doing well...and I hope it's not too late for you."

Taking a deep breath in, I nod. "Will do, thank you."

She smiles and pushes the beverage cart forward, farther down the aisle, and she takes another drink order.

WE'VE LANDED AFTER the longest flight of my life. I'm tired. But there's one thing keeping me going. I have a feeling that after her texts, this won't be easy. My thoughts on her being a little tornado were correct.

She's mad. She thinks I've lied.

I've never been forceful with her—I've yet to push her. But I'm done being passive. She's going to listen to me whether she wants to or not.

After making my way through border control and customs, I grab my bag from the turnstile at baggage claim before getting into a cab, and giving the driver my hotel address.

The ride isn't too long, but my mind is racing anyway. I'm on edge, not only from what I have to do, but also because this damn driver is worse than a New York cabbie. Not to mention, it's fucking with my head that he's sitting on the opposite side of the car and we're driving on the left.

Thankfully, we arrive at my hotel without being killed in the process. I pay and get out. Instead of going inside like any normal person, I stop and turn around to face the building that holds Heather. I want to go now. I'm anxious as all hell. I force myself to go check in and find my room. It's too big, much bigger than I'll ever need, especially if she rejects me. I decide to shower before walking over to Heather's apartment building.

The time change is killing me. It's six in the morning in New York, but eleven in the morning here. I'm looking forward to laying my head down and passing the hell out. I should have slept on the flight, but I was too anxious.

After showering and getting dressed in pants and a V-neck with a sweater on, I head out, my hair still wet. I'm ready to see my girl.

I get by the doorman by walking next to a resident as if we're together. I don't want to announce my arrival and give Heather a chance to run. As I walk up to her apartment door, I can't fight the depth of emotion I feel for this woman. Knocking impatiently, I need her to answer the damn door. I knock again, but still no one answers.

Where in the hell is she?

A part of me wants to call.

But the caveman in me wants to bust down her door, throw her over my shoulder, and take her home.

Where she belongs. Not here.

I run my hands through my hair and decide to take another chance. I have to get into that ballet house. I have to find her.

CHAPTER
Thirty-Three
verdict

Heather

IFEEL LIKE MAJOR crap. Whose idea was it to drink all that liquor last night? I'm totally blaming Dill for this one. Alexis has done her best to annoy the frick out of me today. She really knows how to get under my skin. But since I'm being paid to be here, I try to let it roll off my back. I really don't know what Noah ever saw or sees in her. She's loud, abrasive, blonde...

"Ladies, let's take our fifteen-minute break and start from the beginning when we return," Mistress Nadine, the group dance instructor, calls out.

I'm so tired. I have yet to sleep well since I left the States. Well...Valentine's Day to be exact. I got too used to sleeping on top of him. Dillen walks up to me with a bright smile on her face. I grimace and grab my towel and water bottle. "How are you so chipper today?"

"I live on caffeine, little shit. You need to get with it. Even I can tell you're not right on your feet today. Let's go get some water," she says as she links arms with me and we walk out of the studio.

"When's tea time? I need a freaking nap," I ask while I wait for her to refill her bottle.

"You need more than a nap. You need to sleep for a week straight." She moves her bottle and drinks from it, downing more than half of it.

Filling my bottle up, I'm about to take a sip when my stomach does a little flip because I see Alexis on her phone again and she's smiling. Okay, I need to get over this situation, like, now. My stomach isn't feeling all that great and this cold water is making it worse. I turn my back to her and face Dillen. "How much longer? I really want to go home and sleep for, like, two days."

"We have thirty minutes left and then we stretch as a class. Mistress Nadine likes to do everything together. Even party." She giggles as we head back into the studio.

"What? I can't see her drinking. She's so polished." Sitting down, I start to stretch.

She nods excitedly and makes a blow-job motion. "She's the little ho of teachers!"

I cover my mouth before my gasp fills the room then fall on my back, laughing.

Dillen dies laughing at my reaction and the entire room is staring at us. "Oh little shit, God I love you."

Mistress Nadine flits back into the room and claps a few times to get everyone's attention. "Okay ladies, let's finish up, and we'll end for the day."

I jump up and Dillen smacks my butt. "Hey! Watch it."

We get into formation and the music begins.

The next fifteen minutes are intense and I'm beyond ready when she says it's time for our stretches. We're all tired from today's practice and I'm glad it's almost over. She has us lie on our backs and get into a grand plié, having our partners lean against the barre and stand on our inner thighs, right above our knees. I hate this stretch. It works, but it's not comfortable.

Dillen is having the time of her life stretching me like this. "Just wait until it's your turn, Dill."

She laughs and throws her head back. She has the biggest smile on her face when she looks back down at me, but her eye catches something and her smile falls. She's staring and I grunt as she bears her full weight on my legs.

"Ah! Holy crap, Dill. Ease up."

I'm squeezing my inner thighs to help me stretch.

Looking up at her, I focus on my breathing.

"Uh...Heather?"

She steps off of me cautiously before holding her hand out to help me up. Her gaze is still fixed; she won't even look down at me. I hear a shrill cry and watch as Alexis bolts off of her partner and toward the door. "Noah!" she exclaims.

I'm still lying on my back when I look up and behind me. I can't believe what I'm seeing. A whole barrage of emotions hits me: anger, hurt, lust, betrayal, jealousy. I see Alexis run to him and lock her arms around his neck. I think I'm seeing things. The smile that was once on my face is gone.

I have to look away because I think I'm going to be sick. He's come here to see her obviously. They've been in contact. I'm looking up at Dillen...and for once she's speechless.

"Heather..." Dillen says as she again holds her hand out to me. I take it, scrambling to get up as Mistress Nadine calls it a day.

"Dill, I have to get out of here, now."

I look back at him and our eyes lock as he pushes Alexis off of his body. He has a look of shock on his face, and I'm not sure if it's toward me, or her. The air buzzes with electrifying energy— it's so strong that it's almost palpable. I feel it enter my body like a drug. The magnetic pull between the two of us seems to have intensified since Valentine's Day. It's making me hot, too hot. And damp between my legs.

He takes a step toward me. I can't move. Dillen is tugging at my arm, but I almost fight her. He strides across the room coming at me, looking confident and cocky. Alexis tries to grab his hand but he shakes her off. I let Dillen drag me in her direction, out of his pull zone.

She yanks me out the back door and into the empty hallway.

"What the hell is he doing here?" she yells out and hands me her car keys. "Go. I'll get our shit and meet you at the apartment."

Taking her keys, I roll my eyes. "He's not here for me."

"Oh bullshit, Heather. He just tossed crazy-bitch off of him," she says as the door opens and he's there. His steps don't slow as he stalks toward me. I can smell him and oh my…the things he does to me.

I'm suddenly out of breath. His mere presence takes it right out of me. I back up as many steps as I can before my back hits the wall.

"Stop running from me, please." His deep, raspy voice penetrates me. He reaches down and takes my hand, forcefully lacing his fingers with mine and tugging as he steps back.

I let him pull me, leading us to the end of the hallway, into a cramped, diminutive room. I know I should panic, but I can't. The simple act of him lacing his fingers with mine lets me know he's not going to do anything stupid. He's not Nik.

It's a dominant move. He's never shown this side of himself before. I like it, but I'm still so angry. I tug against his hand. "What are you doing?"

I can almost see his heart pounding in his chest. "Just...talk to me. Please."

Looking up at him, seeing his strained expression, I wonder what it is. "What?"

He's still holding my hand, and I don't think he's going to let go anytime soon. "I know it's taken me too long to come and get you, and there are no excuses, but I'm not letting you walk away from me. Not again. I'll fight for what's mine."

I try yanking at his hand again, anger flashing across my face. "I'm not yours!"

He pulls on my hand hard enough to send my body crashing into his. He snakes his other hand around my waist to hold me flush against him. "I'm not leaving until you are. Why are you so mad at me?" he pleads.

His body touching mine is messing with my head. He's so warm and I can feel his heart beating. I can't stay like this. I won't be able to think. My sex aches at his nearness. I squeeze my eyes shut to clear my head. I look back up at him. "You lied to me!"

"Lied to you about what exactly?" His face is stern, demanding.

My jaw is clenched stubbornly. "You lied and said you were a virgin just to get me to sleep with you. And I know you slept with her." I say the word her as an expletive.

"What the fuck are you talking about? I was a fucking virgin when I slept with you—you are the one and only woman I have ever made love to. You! Who the hell said I wasn't a virgin, huh? Was it Alexis?" He's holding me tighter, ensuring I can't run.

"Yes." I'm so mad I could cry. "She obviously knew things about you," I spit out, narrowing my eyes as I lower my voice. "Private things."

"Private things? Like what? That I have a massive cock? I messed around with her. It was years ago, back when I was studying for my undergrad. She means absolutely nothing to me. I didn't even know she would be here."

"Yeah, I'm sure you didn't." I turn my head, unable to keep eye contact any longer. Just thinking about him in bed with her makes me want to vomit.

"Are you fucking believing her word over mine? Some little cunt spouts lies and you're going to believe it?" He stiffens and moves his hand down to my ass, squeezing too tightly before lifting his hand and smacking the same ass cheek—hard. Oh God, it stings.

"Noah!"

His chest is rising and falling quickly. His jaw is clenched. Did he just smack my ass?

"Stop this shit, or I'll do it again," he hisses through his teeth.

I'm stunned. "Stop what?" I hiss back at him, reaching around and moving his hand off of me.

"Stop believing these lies. I have never lied to you. Why the hell would I chase you across the country and now halfway around the world, if that were a lie? If you were just one hell of a good fuck?"

I'm biting the inside of my cheek as he leans in and grips the back of my neck with one hand, angling me so his tongue flutters at the shell of my ear. My stomach constricts and I almost dissolve into his arms. I haven't felt him in weeks and his tongue is sending my body into overdrive. I don't mean to allow it, but a gasp escapes me.

His darkened mood lifts a little when he whispers, "I want this relationship to work, and for it to mean more to you than any other relationship has ever meant. I'll do anything to get you back, to have you be my ballerina again."

His lips move along my jaw and he kisses me before I'm able to think about everything he just said. I'm a ball of shaking nerves. I can't think. I can't respond. My fingers grip the front of his shirt on their own accord.

He loosens our laced fingers then binds me in his arms. He waits for me to move before bringing his lips against mine. It's now that I realize what a mess I am. My entire body is damp with perspiration and I'm in my black leotard with a black wraparound skirt. His chest expands as he speaks against my lips when I refuse to move. "Let me in, baby."

I shake my head and pull back. "Let me go, Noah."

He tries to swallow as he looks down to the ground. "Why?"

I instantly feel horrible. I just need a few seconds to think about everything. I can't with his lips on mine. Thank God he's holding me because my legs are feeble.

I struggle to pull myself together when he looks up at me. "Why are you here? For her? Your new ballerina?" I ask.

He closes his eyes briefly then looks up. His nostrils flare and his jaw clenches while he inhales deeply. His voice is constricted when he responds.

"No. I'm here to win you back. I'm here for you, and only you—my only ballerina. I can guarantee you that I'm not leaving this country without you."

"I..." Not knowing what to say to him, I stammer. I can't fall in love with him. It can't happen. He's still lying. He was texting her.

"You what? I need you to talk to me." His warm, smooth hand moves to the back of my neck, gently running the pad of his thumb over my searing skin.

My eyes flutter closed. His touch calms me and he knows it. "You've been texting her."

He pulls me close and breathes me in. "Who have I been texting? Your sister?"

I shake my head. His closeness is killing me. I want him. I need him. Even if just for one more night. "Her. I saw you text her."

"Alexis? I don't even have her number. How would I text her? Why would I even want to text her?" he says quickly.

I look down at my toes because I know now that I believed every lie she's fed me. How could I have been so stupid?

Because I wanted any reason to push him away, any reason I could find. "I need some time."

He nods slowly and kisses my temple. It feels like he's the one who broke up with me, the one who broke my heart, and he's asking me to come back...but it's not. I did that to him and he's strong enough and so willing to take me back.

I don't deserve him. I know I don't.

He swallows his emotions before releasing me. His eyes water, but he stands firm and nods again. "You have my number."

It's official: I've never felt so bad about myself. I've made this man upset more times than I can count. I nod my assent and look away. "I'll text you later. I need to go shower."

He stands there watching me as I walk away from him and back into the hallway to Dillen, where she's holding back a throng of ballerinas, all trying to eavesdrop. "Let's go."

She hands me my bag as I walk briskly past Alexis. She heads to where Noah and I were standing and I don't even care. I have to get out of here, go somewhere to clear my thoughts.

We're walking quickly down the empty corridors and out to the parking lot to Dillen's car when she finally asks, "Well? What happened?"

I fill her in on everything as she drives to her place. What he said, what he looked like, how he smelled. "I can't believe he's even here, Dill," I say, as I get out of the car when she parks. "I've got so much to think about and I don't know where to begin."

"Take your time, little shit; everything is going to be okay. Hell, I wish Coen or some man would chase me like he chases you."

I grimace when my stomach flips again, thinking about what

she just said. "It is kind of sweet, huh?" I say, smiling softly, as we walk into the apartment.

"Kind of? Heather, he is head over heels for you."

Biting the inside of my cheek, I change the subject—I need to sit and think. "Okay, I'm going to shower."

"Okay, I'm going to nap then go online shopping. Feel free to join."

I laugh and head to my room. "The nap or shopping?" I call out over my shoulder.

"Both!" she yells out and goes into her room.

I head into the bathroom. As the hot water hits me, I think about his lips on mine, the smell of his cologne, and the sound of his voice.

I missed him. So badly. I have to admit to myself that I didn't want him to stop touching me. When he promised me that he wasn't leaving the country without me, I wanted to just give in. He's so freaking passionate about what he wants. And right now, he desires me. I'm beyond afraid to fall in love with him. But if he knows that, maybe this could work. Maybe we could just see each other like this. Maybe I made an irrational decision and should have asked his opinion beforehand.

After my long shower, I'm getting ready for bed when my phone vibrates on the nightstand. I pick it up and open my inbox to a new email from Noah.

To: **Heather Lane**
From: **Noah Ryan**
Subject: **My Thoughts**

My little ballerina,

I've been lost without you these past few weeks. I can't begin to describe the constant physical ache I have inside of me. A part of who I am has left me, but I'm going to fight to get that part back. I admit, I should have fought for it much sooner. And I should have fought much harder to keep it, but life has a way of taking the things we cherish and setting fire to them then laughing when we are made to watch that treasured item burn in front of us. I've lost you, and life is determined not to let me forget. There's a constant burning ember that won't be extinguished, no matter how hard I try to stomp it out.

Heather, to me, you are the most cherished thing that has ever been mine. I can't begin to explain how empty I feel. Before you, I lost everything, and then you slid right on in like you knew you belonged in my life, like you knew you could numb the pain of the knife in my back. You did exactly that. If you're reading this then you've let me go again, and you have my word that I'll watch that ember burn for the rest of my life. That ember is the only visible light in my life, and as much as you push me away from you, know that what I feel for you won't fade. I'm no good with goodbyes—I just walk away. I did that to you and I regret it immensely, but this time I hope I stood firm when you chased me away. I hope, more than anything, that I was strong enough to say goodbye and be the one to watch you walk away because I'll at least know where you're going.

I wrote this on the agonizing flight to London earlier today. I haven't slept, I can't eat, and I feel like I can't breathe without you. I wanted you to know that I cared, and just how much.

Goodnight, gorgeous.

You'll always be mine.

Noah Ryan.

I'm sitting on my bed with tears streaming steadily down my face. I can't hurt him any more. I scroll over to my favorites and hit dial.

"Heather?" I hear him answer, his voice thick with emotion.

"Hey. Did I wake you?"

"No, I just went to a chip shop for dinner. I'm headed over to the London Eye right now to see London from the sky at night."

I can hear people buzzing around in the background and I'm so jealous of all the women who get to lay their eyes on him.

"Oh okay. Well, I won't keep you. I just got your email and I..."

I turn my head away from the phone so he doesn't hear me sniffle. "Do you want to meet up tomorrow?"

"Tomorrow?" He speaks again before I can reply. "Would you... have you been to the London Eye yet? If not, I'd like to take you."

"No, I haven't. Do you want me to meet you?"

"I'm not going to push you, but I'd really enjoy it if you'd join me."

His voice is low and raspy. It sounds so sexy. I love his voice. And I want to smell him again. "Okay, I'll meet you there after I get dressed." The line is quiet for a few seconds, "Noah?" I prod.

"Yeah, I'm here. I...uh...I can't wait to see you. I'll wait outside the ticket office."

"Okay. Bye." I hang up and take a deep breath. Crap. What do I wear?

CHAPTER
Thirty-Four
the storm

Noah

I WAS GOING TO ask for a general admission ticket to the London Eye, but instead I've just purchased something called "Cupid's Capsule." It's a private capsule for two with a bottle of Pommery Brut Royal Champagne, and Hotel Chocolat Pink Champagne Truffles. The price includes a personal London Eye host, but I asked that no one else be in the capsule with us.

I'm nervous as hell now, as I wait for her on the steps of the ticket office. I'm glad that I changed before I went out to dinner because it's gotten colder.

I find myself checking the crowd of people…looking over every brunette's face to see if it's her…constantly checking the watch that Mae got me, the one thing I've held onto from the woman. I don't see her at first but the wind howls and I get a trace of her perfume. Her perfume stands out to me like nothing I've ever scented before. I turn around to find her walking up the steps behind me.

She's looking up at me through those long, dark lashes as she gets to the top step.

"Hey." Damn, she looks gorgeous. She always does.

"Hi," she replies in a soft, sexy voice. I'm seconds away from taking her lips but I stop myself.

"You look beautiful, Heather." I offer my hand out to her and she takes it. She laces her fingers through mine as we walk up to a separate set of gates, rather than the general admissions line. "I hope you don't mind, but I bought us an hour of rotation. I thought it'd be a good and private place to talk."

She looks up at me as the wind blows her hair. "That's fine. We do need to talk."

A strand catches in her deep red lipstick. A distant memory comes forth of when I first touched her at the movie theater. Her lips have never been so luscious. I move my hand up to her face and move the strand away before brushing her cheek with my thumb while we wait for the next capsule to become available.

"The capsule will not stop; you are to step on while it moves," the woman says, as we start walking toward an empty capsule. Heather's grip tightens on my hand and we step into the capsule. They shut the door and I lead her to the other side.

"We're in here alone?"

I nod, suddenly worried I made a mistake. "Is that okay?" I ask, hoping to God she's okay with it since we're stuck in here for an hour.

"It's perfect," she says as she eyes the champagne and truffles.

"Those came with the package. Would you like a glass?"

"I probably shouldn't, but I feel like I need it right now," she says.

Well fuck. Is this going to be an hour of my heart being ripped from my chest? I let go of her hand reluctantly and move to pour her a glass.

I watch her as I fill each glass. She's staring out at the darkening sky, but she's lost in thought instead of taking in the view. Walking over, I hand her a glass. "Are you okay?" I'm cautious as fuck. I decide that treading lightly is the only way to go.

"Oh thanks. Yes, I'm fine. How long are you going to be in

London?"

"I'll be here for as long as I need to be in order to win you back. All I have are my studies, and I can do that anywhere that's quiet."

She looks up at me and is about to speak but closes her mouth and walks over to the bench in the middle of the capsule. I decide to give her space. Turning around to face her, I lean up against an iron beam. The sky is darkening quickly and a rumble of thunder echoes through the clouded London sky.

"Marlene from British Airways told me to say hi. Coincidentally, I had the same flight attendant as you." I'm trying to break the ice, and start a conversation, instead of us just staring at each other.

There's a look of surprise on her face. "Oh!" she says, a brief smile appearing before she covers her face. "Oh my God, that flight was horrible. I was a mess."

I chuckle and smile. "Yeah, she told me you didn't have a good flight. She then proceeded to inform me how late I was to chase you, and that I don't have a chance."

She looks up at me and frowns. "Well, that was rude. She doesn't..." But then she stops talking.

"What?" I step closer and crouch down in front of her. "She doesn't what?" I ask.

"She doesn't know what she's talking about."

"I think she was halfway right about how late I am. I'm sorry I couldn't come sooner, but I couldn't get a passport or ID until the day I left. I've lost you to him, haven't I?" She's not pushing me away from her as I rest my hand on her knee.

"Him? Noah, there's no one else. There hasn't been."

I can't find the right words to say in this moment. I know that this is my only chance of winning her back, and I'm going to succeed.

"How did you?"

"How did I what? How'd I get a passport?" I ask her for confirmation and she nods.

"Joel figured out who I am and where I was kidnapped from. My passport and ID are both under the name of Jorden Somer. The person I was supposed to be."

Her expression is blank. "Your name is Jorden?"

"Yeah. That's all I know though. I can't bring myself to go further. I'm scared as hell about what I'm going to find."

She places her hand on mine. And scrunches her nose, shaking her head slightly. "You don't look like a Jorden." And with that, she smiles. The one that I've missed. The one that drives me crazy.

I chuckle and sit next to her as we crest the top of the Eye. "Yeah, I don't think so either. Joel is in the process of having my name changed to Noah Ryan."

There's a flash of lightning that lights up the now dark and brooding sky. Heather jumps and takes my hand. "I like you as Noah. I don't see you as anyone else."

I can't help what happens next. I'm attracted to her like no other. I wrap my arm around her waist and pull her onto my lap. She doesn't fight me on it. My natural instinct is to protect her, and keep her out of harm's way.

"You do?" I ask gruffly. She licks her lips and rests her head on my shoulder as we head down the Eye. Another roar of thunder shakes the capsule and my arms automatically tighten around her.

"Yes," she replies softly and I can feel her breath against my neck. Right now would not be a good time to get an erection.

"Would you mind if I kissed you right now?" My hand is moving into the back of her hair as she glances up at me.

She shakes her head—thank fuck. I angle my head and lean in slowly, my eyes focused solely on her lips. She meets me halfway, and my lips are on hers, tasting her as I've wanted to for the past few weeks.

Damn, she tastes like no other. She inhales, and I slip my tongue in just past her lips as she circles her arms around my neck. I move my hand down through her long strands of hair to the small of her back. She moans softly as her body goes limp to my touch.

"Come back to me, baby," I whisper, speaking against her lips.

She nods and I swear I almost lose it. My fingers clench and I accidentally pull too hard. I have to remind myself to keep calm. My tongue slips farther into her mouth and my chest feels like it's going to shatter.

She tightens her arms around my neck as our kiss becomes

deeper—needy and heated. Fuck, my heart is pounding so hard, it's about to rip my chest clean open.

She's mine.

I stop kissing her to whisper, "My little ballerina."

"Yours," she mutters and buries her face in my shoulder, biting while she's at it.

Oh Christ. I know what she wants. I want it too. I slip my hand under her shirt and caress her flat stomach with my thumb. Hell, I've missed her. Her body jolts under my touch just like she used to.

We've just crested the top of the Eye again when the sky lights up in an electric blue. Electricity crackles through the air and a loud, deafening roar of thunder follows immediately afterward.

"Damn!"

"Is it safe to be up here right now?" she asks as we both look out onto the city of London as another bolt of lightning strikes behind Big Ben.

"I don't believe it is. I'm sure they're starting to take people off."

We watch as another lightning bolt hits, and something explodes underneath it, sparking pink, orange, green, and blues hues.

"Holy shit."

The sparks die down and sections of the city start blacking out, one after another until the London Eye jerks and we're left suspended in the dark.

"Noah…"

She gasps and her grip tightens on me. She hates heights. But I love that she's holding onto me. Doing anything I can to distract her, I lean down and nuzzle her throat, kissing gently then darting my tongue out to taste her. "It's okay, baby. I've got you." Licking up her neck, I feel her body relax.

"Please don't let go of me."

"I don't plan on it, ballerina. As long as I'm breathing, I'm not letting go." My lips move down to her collarbone as a few more lightning strikes light up the sky and a heavy pelting of rain hits the capsule, causing it to sway.

She's starting to breathe heavier and I'm getting hard from it.

At this point, I don't think I can stop touching her even if she tried to pry my hands off of her body.

"Noah? This storm is really scaring me."

"I'm sorry—I should have checked the weather forecast before we came up here. I was just so excited to see you."

Moving her slender hands up my chest—the way she used to—she says, "It's okay. So was I."

I pull back and look at her. "Ballerina, if you don't stop touching me soon, I'm going to make love to you right here."

"Do you want me to stop?" Her voice is highly erotic, as her hands frantically work at unbuttoning my shirt.

"I've never wanted you to stop before. I won't ever ask that of you." I kiss her temple then swiftly remove my arms from my jacket and lay it on the bench behind her. "Lie down for me, baby."

She moves off my lap and lies down on my jacket. I'm harder than I've ever been.

"Noah?" she questions, and I look down at her. She's crooking her finger for me to come to her.

I move to hover over her. Her fingers find my shirt again and undo the last two buttons before pulling it open. She gets it off of me and bundles it up, placing it underneath her head. I feel exposed as fuck, but I know no one can see us, not with the heavy sheet of rain hitting the capsule and we're cloaked by the darkness of the citywide blackout.

She leans up and sucks on my lower lip, making me groan. "Don't warm me up, please. I can't take it. I just want you now," she begs.

"Hell, baby, I can't do that to you. It's been weeks since you've had me."

I run my hands down her body and under her shirt to cup her breasts. She pulls my head down to kiss the life out of me and I'm sure her deep red lipstick will be all over my jaw when we're done.

Her nails claw up my chest and fuck, it feels good. I'm seconds from losing my shit. "Baby, calm down."

Shaking her head in refusal, she nips at my jaw. "I want you too bad."

I hurriedly undo her snug jeans and pull them down as another bolt of lightning strikes, too close this time. I grab her lace panties and pull hard so the lace disintegrates.

She spreads her legs and reaches down to touch herself. I'm mesmerized. She's writhing underneath me and I just stare—it's the hottest thing I've seen.

"It's my turn to touch my girl. I'll do this, if that's what you need—I won't warm you up." I slide my fingers down to her pussy as my tongue dips into her mouth.

When I hear her moan, I slide another finger in. "That's right, baby. Let me hear you."

I push my fingers up into her sweetly wet and tender spot as she reaches for my pants, pushing them off of me. She's soaking wet and ready for me—I don't think I'll need to warm her up too much. Helpless moans are leaving her throat as she finally grasps my cock with one of her fists.

"Noah, please! I need to feel you push into me…and fill me… so deep."

Fuck, she's so aroused and I'm about to take her in a place where anyone can see—the capsule above us, beside us, and whoever else is watching the cameras if the lights go on. I rock my fingers inside of her as her little cunt clenches around my fingers.

I pull out my fingers and grab her thighs, pulling her forcefully to me. Her tight, little ass slides against the bench. I kneel up and grab my hard cock.

"Spread them open, baby." I lean down with one arm and brace myself over her. Stroking my cock while I watch her.

She does what I ask as I push the head of my thick cock inside of her dripping wet pussy.

Holy hell, I'm not sure I can do this. I lean down and take her mouth. "How deep do you want me to go?" I ask her as I rock my hips painfully slow.

"I want to feel every inch of you."

I don't want to hurt her, but I want nothing more than to give her what she wants. I take her mouth as I slowly push another inch into her. She's slowly, but surely accommodating my size. Edging my dick in farther, I groan with every inch. Heather's lithe body is squirming underneath me as soon as I fill her completely.

"Are you okay?"

"I'm so much more than okay. Please…make love to me…fuck me! Anything!"

I pause and look down at her, our eyes searching each other's. "Say that again?" I ask, as I start to pull my length out of her.

"Make love to me or fuck me. I just want you."

I stop moving and run a thumb over her cheek before tracing her lips. "I'm in love with you, Heather Lane."

She's looking up at me with her mouth open. Fuck, fuck, fuck! Did I just screw this up? She suddenly pulls me down and runs her fingers through my hair. Speaking softly against my lips, she whispers, "I love you, Noah."

I can breathe.

This beautiful woman loves me. I'm completely reassured and I know that she won't run again.

We're taking our time and I'm paying attention to every move her body makes. Those three words seem to have massively intensified this moment. I'm captivated by her, the total package. The mysterious and magnetic allure is stronger now than it's ever been. It might be the electricity fluctuating in the air from the storm, or it's us.

The smile on her face makes me feel incredible that I can make her so undeniably happy. She makes me feel accepted and appreciated, and loved like never before. She thinks I'm worthy of the love she has for me, and it feels unbelievable.

I feel like lightning struck my body because I'm hot. I feel like I've been dipped in lighter fluid and set on fire with her ember. Our lips find each other's in a passionate embrace—our tongues can't move fast enough as I push into her again. Her body bows to me with each time I fill her as much as she can take. My balls are slapping heavily against her gorgeous ass.

"Baby!" she shrieks.

Shit, I love it when she calls me that. I can't get deep enough. I'm going to lose control—I can't help it. Her body is begging me and I need it.

My thrusts become harder and deeper, but I keep my steady speed. Leaning down, I bite her neck, growling harshly.

She gasps and her back arches. "That's it, beautiful. Come for me. I love you. Damn, I love you." Thrusting deep as I grip her thigh, I push my tongue into her mouth and taste her again.

She stiffens as my veins run up and down the walls of her pussy. She tightens around me and I grit my teeth, trying to avoid my orgasm as it continues to build. I have all the time in the world for her and I need to convey that to her.

"Noah, I'm so close!"

"Then give it to me, baby. I want to feel it roll through you like never before."

I'm touching, teasing, and pulling on her body in any way I can. I know what my touch does to her because her touch does it to me too. I know the ways her body reacts. I dart my tongue out against her neck before I sink my teeth into her hard.

Her entire body stills then explodes in radiant pleasure. Her words are barely coherent when she yells out, "Oh yes! NOAH!"

She sounds amazing when she comes. Groaning against her skin, her pussy quivers around my cock. I want her to say it again. I bite her again and thrust up harder. Her wetness drenches my cock. "Tell me, Heather."

Thunder shakes the capsule. "I...I love you."

Her words rock my world more than the thunder does this capsule. She's still squeezing my cock as I thrust in and out of her, stilling when my balls draw up and I spill into her. Jets of hot come spurt over and over again as I lose myself to my beautiful girl. Her hands pull me down. Our lips lock in a fierce grip as she squeezes me, ensuring to drain everything I have pent up.

Her body shakes fiercely and I hold her little frame to mine. Our breathing matches, both racing to catch our breath. I'm licking the perspiration from her neck—I love her taste. She's mine forever and I bet my fucking life I won't be letting go.

"That was unbelievable," she pants.

"I didn't hurt you, did I? You were so wet and ready for me

though. Did you miss me, ballerina?"

"Not one bit; I only missed that overfull feeling I got from you." She giggles as I kiss her neck and move a hand down her body as I slide out of her soaking wet pussy. I cup her cunt and push my finger inside of her then proceed to pull it out of her and circle her pink clit before I hold my finger up to her lips so she can taste us.

Dammit, she knows how to get me worked up in a hurry. Her tongue slips out and licks up my finger before sucking on it. She moans when she tastes us. I crush my mouth to hers fast and hard, squeezing her breasts. "I love you, baby." I've never told any woman that before and I can't help but continuously tell her. I need her to know.

"We taste so good together, handsome. And I love you too."

"Should we get you off your back and dressed? I can't have you catching a cold in this endless winter we seem to be living in." I move off of her and she sits up, stretching her legs out.

She's quiet. Not good. I reach for her top and hand it to her and then reach for my own, putting it on just as the Eye starts moving again.

"Well shit, they must have gotten the generator running or something. I have a hotel room if you'd like to join me? I'm rather enjoying having you all to myself."

"I'd like that a lot." She jumps up and pulls her jeans on without those panties I ripped to shreds. "What hotel are you staying in?"

"The one right across from your apartment building. Your sister helped me book it, as well as find you."

Her smile kills me. "You really went to a lot of trouble, Noah," she says as she runs her fingers through her sex hair.

"I'll go to any lengths or distance to get you back."

"I'm yours."

"Damn right you are." I pull on my shirt and she walks over to me, buttoning it up for me. I think she enjoys dressing me just as much as she enjoys undressing me. "Thank you, baby."

She puts on her jacket and I help her into my coat afterward, not wanting her to be cold once we're out of this glass capsule. Our fingers are laced together as the door slides open and we step out.

It's still storming, but so is our relationship.

Heather Lane is the reason I haven't slept in forty-eight hours. She's the reason I didn't change the name on my passport and ID. She's the only thing that's keeping me whole and together. She's been mine again for all of two hours, and I'm the happiest bastard on this planet.

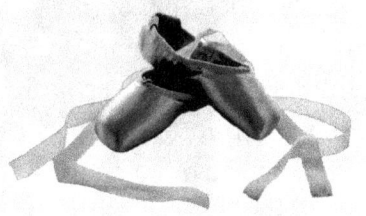

Epilogue

Heather

I'VE BEEN LYING awake for hours just watching this gorgeous man sleep. The Greek god is once again mine, and I'm beyond thrilled. I'm still in shock that he flew across the world for me, and that my scheming sister helped him to track me down. I can hear his heart beating regularly as I lie on top of him.

In my spot.

On my man.

I lean up and kiss his jaw, whispering, "Do you want to know what my favorite thing is?" He's dead asleep, so I'm sure he won't hear me, but I've got plenty of early mornings to tell him over and over again. "Waking up with you."

He's so tired and I don't want to wake him. I can't help but nuzzle him though…anywhere I can. His chest is rock hard but still so comfortable to lie on. I cannot believe that he said he loved me. What's even crazier…I said it back. I've been terrified to fall in love with him all along. But Dillen was right: I already was.

He breathes in deeply when I kiss his pectoral muscle and his arms tighten around my body. I decide that I'll wake him up with breakfast. I know he hasn't been sleeping—I can tell by the look in his eyes—but I hope he's at least eating. I move up and kiss his lips before quietly sliding out of his arms to get dressed. I head downstairs to the hotel restaurant to order us breakfast. I make sure to get an extra side of bacon for us to share.

They are taking their sweet time with my order and I decide to get some coffee as well for Noah. I know he likes it and I want him to relax. While I wait, I find myself thinking about last night. It was amazing. We reconnected in such a way that I doubt we could ever duplicate it. I made such a horrendous mistake by leaving him and I know I can't ever make it up to him. I feel horrible for the way I acted, but I'll do anything I can to make him happy.

I reach into my purse for my phone. There's a text from Dani.

Sister, did your yummy Greek god in a golden-sash toga come to your rescue?

My smile is huge while I reply: **You sneaky butthead! Yes, he did. And thank you for helping him.**

Her reply comes back almost instantly. **So you're back together? It worked? FINALLY! The world is whole again.**

I can't help but laugh: **Yes, we are. And...he told me he loves me.**

Oh you lucky lady! I love you the most though. I'm going back to bed. Night-night.

I look at my watch and see that it's still late there: **Night, sister. I love you too.**

Finally, they bring my order and I take it upstairs. I open the door as quietly as I can and walk inside. He's standing there in all of his naked glory, but he looks restless and his chest is tight. He's breathing heavily and I can see the veins on his arm popping out, leading down to his clenched, white-knuckled fists. He's too pale, but his eyes widen when he looks up and sees me at the door.

"Baby? What's wrong?" I'm sure he can hear the panic in my voice. He doesn't look good. I walk toward him cautiously, setting our breakfast down on the table.

"You're here?" he says panicked, as he strides toward me and lifts me up to his chest. His skin is damp. "Fuck...I thought you left me!" He buries his face in my hair and breathes in heavily.

"Oh baby...no." I run my hands up his chest and over his shoulders, in an attempt to calm him. God, what have I done to him? "I just went to get us breakfast. You were sleeping so well that I didn't want to wake you."

His grip on me is tighter than I've ever felt. I think he's shaking from the panic. Tears sting my eyes. I can't stand that I hurt him the first time, but this is killing me. I've wrecked him. He needs to know that I'm not going to run away from him. He's mine.

"Noah? Please talk to me?" I pull back to make him look at me, rubbing my thumb under his dark eyes gently.

"I'm good, ballerina. Hell, I need you. I love you, Heather."

Pointing my toes, I start nuzzling his neck, my whole body attuned to his, placing soft, gentle kisses, whispering sweet things to him. Soon, I feel his body relax significantly. "Come eat something. I got us bacon."

"Mmm, my girl and her bacon." He sets me on my feet and we sit down at the small dinette in the suite to eat.

"I have a favor to ask, ballerina."

I sit close to him and rest my hand on his thigh. I feed him a piece of bacon before biting from the same strip. "Anything, Noah. What do you need?"

He places his hand on mine and sighs heavily. "Would you mind meeting my parents with me?"

I accidentally drop my fork and it clatters loudly against my plate. Recovering, I look up at him. "I...yes, of course."

He gets up and kisses my cheek before pulling on a pair of those skintight boxer briefs. He comes back with his tablet and sits down, pulling my chair toward him.

"Can't get enough of me, can you?" I ask.

He laughs and shakes his head. "No, I can't, ballerina."

He pulls up his email on the tablet and there's one unread email from Joel. "Last night before you met me at the London Eye, I asked Joel to email me all the information he had regarding my parents."

I'm chewing on my lip—I can feel his tension. His finger hovers over the email. He's not moving. My poor Noah, he's so nervous. I'm here for him no matter what. He needs to know that. I lean my body into his and rub his rock-hard thigh with my hand. "Go on, baby; I'm here. You can do this."

He nods and taps the screen. The email opens and two names in boldface are the first thing we both see.

To: **Noah Ryan/Jorden Somer**
From: **Joel Aldrich**
Subject: **Birth Parents**

Noah,

I've attached all the documentation I have found on your parents. I'm more than willing to help you get in contact with them. Let me know when you're ready.

Father: Henry Somer

Mother: Ellery Somer

Henry and Ellery have been married for thirty-three years. They married in 1981, and Ellery gave birth to you in 1985 at Mount Sinai Hospital in New York City. They have since relocated to Southampton in Long Island, New York. They currently reside in Southampton with your grandmother, Hazel Somer.

Best of Luck!

Joel Aldrich.

He pulls up the search engine and types in "Henry Somer, Southampton" then hits enter. My heart is beating wildly, but for other reasons. Links pop up on the left-hand side of the page and picture after picture fill the right-hand side box. I immediately recognize his face. I inhale sharply and sit up straight.

Oh my God. I know him.

The End

Be on the lookout for book two:

A WINTER'S DATE

The Date Series

Stay in contact with Jess & Sasha (JSAuthors)

www.JSAuthors.com

Facebook: /JSAuthors

Twitter: @JSAuthors

Instagram: @JSAuthors

Please find and follow our Pinterest board, JSAuthors, to see small snippets of our inspirational photos for *It's A Date*.

Acknowledgements

We would each like to thank every single person who has encouraged us to pursue this book as well as the upcoming series.

Thank you to my friends and family, near and far. Oceans apart have had no effect on who you all helped make me today. Specifically, I would like to thank my father, Andrew, my mother, Vanessa, and my brother, Tynan. Without the love and support I receive from the three of you daily, this book would have never been possible. Thank you for always cheering me on to be my own person in everything I have done. I love you all!
-Sasha.

Thank you to my husband, Jason, for your undying love, support, and encouragement through this entire process. I love you.
-Jess.

Collectively, we thank the following people for their time they contributed to making this book what it is today:

To our beta readers, Kristina Bedolla, Ashley Scales, Andrew Brümmer, Jillian Crouson-Toth, Lauren Denni, and Tara Thomas. Thank you for taking the time out of your day to read over our manuscripts and devote countless numbers of hours to it.

To Aleatha Romig, for being the most amazing role model any aspiring author could ask for. Thank you for all of your help when answering our silly little questions. We absolutely adore you!

To Dani Naas, thank you for your friendship and continuous support.

To Lexi Brodie, thank you for helping us get our names and book out into the world.

To Lisa Aurello, the world's most remarkable editor. Thank you so much for all of your hard work, time, and effort!

To Judi Perkins, we cannot thank you enough for the most beautiful book cover! The knowledge and talent you bring to the table is simply amazing.

To Cassy Roop, thank you for your expertise in formatting, and for always sharing encouraging words.

To our two PA's, Dani Naas and Ashley Scales, we cannot thank you enough for all you have done for us. You are two of a kind, and we're so grateful for everything you do.

To all of the beautiful women at Concierge Literary Promotions (Keelie Chatfield, Judi Perkins, and Ruth Martin), we cannot begin to thank you for keeping us sane and at ease with all things PR. Your positivity is much needed.

The biggest thank you to my best friend: I couldn't have done this without you.

Lastly,

Thank YOU for reading It's A Date.

-JS

www.ingramcontent.com/pod-product-compliance
Lightning Source LLC
Chambersburg PA
CBHW072129250626
47159CB00007B/2621